STORIES OF PEOPLE & CIVILIZATION
THE ANCIENT NEAR EAST

FLAME TREE PUBLISHING
6 Melbray Mews, Fulham,
London SW6 3NS, United Kingdom
www.flametreepublishing.com

First published and copyright © 2024
Flame Tree Publishing Ltd

24 26 28 27 25
1 3 5 7 9 10 8 6 4 2

ISBN: 978-1-80417-615-3

All rights reserved. No part of this publication may be reproduced, stored in a retrieval system, or transmitted in any form or by any means, electronic, mechanical, photocopying, recording or otherwise, without the prior written permission of the publisher.

Cover and pattern art was created by Flame Tree Studio, with elements courtesy of Shutterstock.com/ Zvereva Yana. Additional interior decoration courtesy of Shutterstock.com/cupoftea.

Judith John (lists of Ancient Kings & Leaders) is a writer and editor specializing in literature and history. A former secondary school English Language and Literature teacher, she has subsequently worked as an editor on major educational projects, including *English A: Literature* for the Pearson International Baccalaureate series. Judith's major research interests include Romantic and Gothic literature, and Renaissance drama.

The text in this book is compiled and edited, with a new introduction. The text in chapters 'Mesopotamia' and 'Assyria' is from *The Historians' History Of The World* by Henry Smith Williams, Volume I (Press of J. J. Little & Co., New York, 1905). The text from 'Babylon' is from *Myths of Babylonia and Assyria* by Donald A. Mackenzie (The Gresham Publishing Company, London, 1915); 'The Persian Empire, Cyrus the Great, and The Fall of Babylon' is from *The Seven Great Monarchies – Book 5: Persia* by George Rawlinson (Oxford, 1862); and 'Phoenicia' is from *History of Phoenicia* by George Rawlinson (Longmans, Green, and Co., London, 1889).

A copy of the CIP data for this book is available
from the British Library.

Designed and created in the UK | Printed and bound in China

COLLECTOR'S EDITIONS

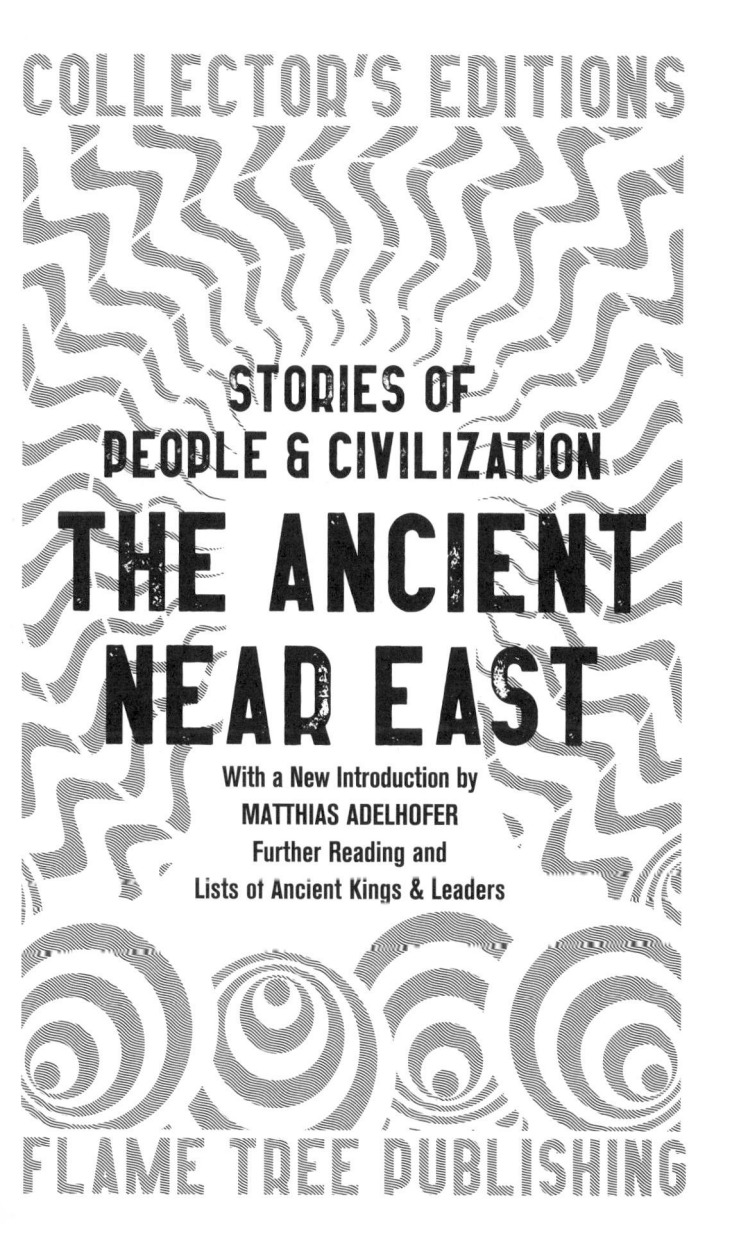

STORIES OF PEOPLE & CIVILIZATION
THE ANCIENT NEAR EAST

With a New Introduction by
MATTHIAS ADELHOFER
Further Reading and
Lists of Ancient Kings & Leaders

FLAME TREE PUBLISHING

CONTENTS

Series Foreword 12

Introduction to the Near East Ancient Origins.. 18
History and Cuneiform 21
Prehistory 23
    The Uruk Period (*c.* fourth millennium BCE)
    and the Invention of Writing 24
Early Bronze Age (*c.* third millennium BCE) 25
    The Early Dynastic Period (first half of the
    third millennium BCE) 25
    The Old Akkadian or Sargonic Period
    (twenty-fourth–twenty-third century BCE) 26
    The Third Dynasty of Ur
    (*c.* twenty-second–twentieth century BCE) 28
Middle Bronze Age (*c.* 2100–1550 BCE) 28
    The Isin-Larsa Period
    (*c.* first quarter of the second millennium) 29
    Old Assyrian Trade (*c.* twentieth–nineteenth century) ... 29

CONTENTS

    Samsi-Addu (*c.* nineteenth century)..29

    Old Babylonian Period
    (*c.* nineteenth–early sixteenth century) 30

Late Bronze Age (*c.* 1550–1200 BCE) 31

    Mittani 32

    The Kassite Dynasty..33

    The Hittite Empire..34

    Assyria..34

    Climate Change and the Sea People (from *c.* 1200 BCE)............35

Iron Age (*c.* first millennium BCE) 35

    The Neo-Assyrian Empire (*c.* tenth century–612 BCE) 36

    The Neo-Babylonian Empire (*c.* 612–539 BCE) 37

    The Achaemenid Empire (mid-sixth century–330 BCE)............38

    The Seleucid Dynasty (312 BCE–63 CE) 39

    The Parthian (around 240 BCE–224 CE)
    and Sassanid Empire (224–651 CE)... 40

    The End of Cuneiform Culture... 40

Further Reading 42

Mesopotamia **47**

The Beginnings of History 48

The Oldest King of Babylonia 54

The Rulers of Shirpurla 55

Kings of Kish and Gishban..66

The First Dynasty of Ur... 71

Kings of Agade... 74

The Kings of Ur 78

Accession of a South Arabian Dynasty 80

Babylon 83
Buildings, Laws and Customs of Babylon 83
- Architecture 87
- Society and Laws 89
- Betrothal, Marriage and Divorce 91
- Business and Land Laws 96
- Physicians 99
- The Origins of Art 104

The Golden Age of Babylonia 108
- King Sumu-la-ilu 109
- King Sin-muballit 110
- King Hammurabi 117
- Communication, Scribes and Deliveries 119
- King Samsu-iluna 124
- King Abeshu 126

Assyria 130
The Assyrian Empire 131
Land and People 135
Assyrian Capitals: Asshur and Nineveh 138
The Rise of Assyria 139
The First Great Assyrian Conqueror 150
The Reign and Cruelty of Asshurnazirpal 155
Shalmaneser II and His Successors 168
Tiglathpileser III (745–727 BCE) 177
Shalmaneser IV 185
Four Generations of Assyrian Greatness (722–626 BCE) ... 186
Sennacherib 200

CONTENTS

Esarhaddon and Asshurbanapal 223
Esarhaddon's Reign (681-668 BCE) 229
Asshurbanapal's Early Years (668-652 BCE) 241
The Brothers' War (652-648 BCE) 254
The Last Wars of Asshurbanapal (648-626 BCE) 261
The Decline and Fall of Assyria (626-609 BCE) 267

New Babylon 276
The Breakdown of the Empire 277
Renascence and Fall of Babylon 282
Contemporary Chronology 284
Nabopolassar and Nebuchadrezzar 286
The Followers of Nebuchadrezzar 292
The Reign of Nabonidus (556-538 BCE) 293

The Persian Empire 299
The Beginnings of the Empire 300
   Persian Politics 302
Cambyses and Cyrus the Great 303
   Lydia 306
The Great Advancement... 308
   Thales and Harpagus 313
Conquest in the Far East 315
The Final Fall of Babylon 319
The Legacy of Cyrus the Great 323

Phoenicia 328
Phoenicia, Before the Establishment of the

Hegemony of Tyre 331

Phoenicia Under the Hegemony of Tyre (1252-877 BCE) ... 339

Phoenicia During the Period of its
   Subjection to Assyria (877-635 BCE) 358

Phoenicia During its Struggles with Babylon
   and Egypt (about 635-527 BCE) 376

Ancient Kings & Leaders **393**

CONTENTS

THE ANCIENT NEAR EAST

STORIES OF PEOPLE & CIVILIZATION
THE ANCIENT NEAR EAST

SERIES FOREWORD

Stretching back to the oral traditions of thousands of years ago, tales of heroes and disaster, creation and conquest have been told by many different civilizations, in ways unique to their landscape and language. Their impact sits deep within our own culture even though the detail in the stories themselves are a loose mix of historical record, the latest archaeological evidence, transformed narrative and the unwitting distortions of generations of storytellers.

Today the language of mythology lives around us: our mood is jovial, our countenance is saturnine, we are narcissistic and our modern life is hermetically sealed from others. The nuances of the ancient world form part of our daily routines and help us navigate the information overload of our interconnected lives.

The nature of a myth is that its stories are already known by most of those who hear or read them. Every era brings a new emphasiz, but the fundamentals remain the same: a desire to understand and describe the events and relationships of the world. Many of the great stories are archetypes that help us find our own place, equipping us with tools for self-understanding, both individually and as part of a broader culture.

For Western societies it is Greek mythology that speaks to us most clearly. It greatly influenced the mythological heritage of the ancient Roman civilization and is the lens through which we still see the Celts, the Norse and many of the other great peoples and religions. The Greeks themselves inherited much from their neighbours, the Egyptians, an older culture that became weary with the mantle of civilization.

Of course, what we perceive now as mythology had its own origins in perceptions of the divine and the rituals of the sacred. The earliest civilizations, in the crucible of the Middle East, in the Sumer of the third millennium BCE, are the source to which many of the mythic archetypes can be traced. Over five thousand years ago, as humankind collected together in cities for the first time, developed writing and industrial scale agriculture, started to irrigate the rivers and attempted to control rather than be at the mercy of its environment, humanity began to write down its tentative explanations of natural events, of floods and plagues, of disease.

Early stories tell of gods or god-like animals who are crafty and use their wits to survive, and it is not unreasonable to suggest that these were the first rulers of the gathering peoples of the earth, later elevated to god-like status with the distance of time. Such tales became more political as cities vied with each other for supremacy, creating new gods, new hierarchies for their pantheons. The older gods took on primordial roles and became the preserve of creation and destruction, leaving the new gods to deal with more current, everyday affairs. Empires rose and fell, with Babylon assuming the mantle from Sumeria in the 1800s BCE, in turn to be swept away by the Assyrians of the 1200s BCE; then the Assyrians and the Egyptians were subjugated by the Greeks, the Greeks by the Romans and so on, leading to the spread and assimilation of common themes, ideas and stories throughout the world.

The survival of history is dependent on the telling of good tales, but each one must have the 'feeling' of truth, otherwise it will be ignored. Around the firesides, or embedded in a book or a computer, the myths and legends of the past are still the living materials of retold myth, not restricted to an exploration of historical origins. Now we have devices and global communications that give us unparalleled access to a diversity of traditions. We can find out about Indigenous American, Indian, Chinese and tribal African mythology in a way that was denied to our ancestors, we can find connections, plot the archaeology, religion and the mythologies of the world to build a comprehensive image of the human experience that is both humbling and fascinating.

The books in this series introduce the many cultures of ancient humankind to the modern reader. From the earliest migrations across the globe to settlements along rivers, from the landscapes of mountains to the vast Steppes, from woodlands to deserts, humanity has adapted to its environments, nurturing languages and observations and expressing itself through records, mythmaking stories and living traditions. There is still so much to explore, but this is a great place to start.

Jake Jackson
General Editor

STORIES OF PEOPLE & CIVILIZATION
THE ANCIENT NEAR EAST

THE ANCIENT NEAR EAST

INTRODUCTION
& FURTHER READING

INTRODUCTION TO THE NEAR EAST ANCIENT ORIGINS

u_4 ri-a u_4 sud-ra$_2$ ri-a
ĝi$_6$ ri-a ĝi$_6$ bad-ra$_2$ ri-a
mu ri-a mu sud-ra$_2$ ri-a

'In those days, in those remote days
In those nights, in those far-away nights
In those years, in those remote years'

With these lines start 'The Instructions of Šuruppak', a Sumerian poem of collected aphorisms about how to live a good and honest life. The numbers in subscript are used to specify the particular sign used in the original Sumerian text. For instance, there exist at least four different signs that are read 'u' but only the one with the meaning 'day'. The poem is told to the literary figure of Ziusudra who, according to the various accounts of the Mesopotamian flood myth, is the only person to attain eternal life and survive the deluge that had been sent by the great god Enlil to wipe away the noisy humans. The earliest version of 'The Instructions of Šuruppak' dates back to the Early Dynastic period of Sumer in the first half of the third millennium BCE. The poem's incipit rings true for any work on the history of the Ancient Near East whose beginnings – and end – lie several millennia in the past. It does doubly so for the present book which reproduces important works that had been written at a time when research into the Ancient Near East was still young but already mature enough to provide first historical syntheses. The classical and biblical sources, which were until then the only available sources of information on the vast region, could for the first time be critically contrasted with sufficient first-hand texts and archaeology; note just now the motif of the flood story. With good cause, Sumer, or Mesopotamia at large – a later Greek denomination for the lands between the rivers Tigris and Euphrates – has been called the 'cradle of civilization'. Writing was invented there for the first time in human history and cities reached an unprecedented level of complexity. Today, we are still influenced by the Ancient Near East in that the origins of astronomy lie there – an hour has 60 minutes and a minute 60 seconds because of the ancient use of a mixed sexagesimal (base 60) and decimal (base 10) system – and, of course, the art of beer brewing was cultivated there, to name but the most prominent pieces of cultural heritage.

As the eclectic selection of chapters to follow demonstrates, the Ancient Near East, as an area home to cultures and societies of varying influence on one another, is far from definite and static. It is rather a historical construct of the respective scientific disciplines (archaeology, anthropology, history, philology etc.) studying the myriad aspects of human life in this vast region. Located in the far west of this area, Egypt is most often treated as its own subject of study, although ties to Mesopotamia and most certainly the Levant always existed. One of the reasons for this is that Egypt's ancient heritage was (re)discovered and understood at a slightly earlier date in modern times than Mesopotamia through the discovery of the Rosetta Stone in 1799 CE in ancient Memphis. The trilingual inscriptions found especially at the Persian capital of Persepolis – written in Old Persian, Neo-Elamite and Neo-Babylonian (all using different kinds of cuneiform scripts) – ultimately enabled the decipherment of ancient Mesopotamian cuneiform writing in the nineteenth century.

Thus, barring Egypt, studies in the Ancient Near East may direct their gaze at Anatolia, the Arabian Peninsula (even shifting it across the Bāb al-Mandab into Ethiopia), the Levant, Greater Syria and Mesopotamia, that is the Fertile Crescent, all the way to the Iranian plateau, and even the Indus valley. Next to archaeology focusing on material culture, it is philology, the study of text and language, that grants us most insights into the Ancient Near East through the written texts detailing both the ancients' daily lives and their literary ambitions. So specific subdisciplines of Ancient Near Eastern studies are often defined along the lines of languages and the people associated with them. These languages include Hittite and Luwian spoken in parts of Anatolia; Ugaritic, Phoenician, Hebrew, Aramaic and Eblaite spoken in the Levant and Syria; Ancient South Arabian languages like Sabaean and Ḥimyaritic; Hurrian and Urartian spoken mostly in Northern Syria, Anatolia and Northeastern Mesopotamia; Akkadian (with the two main dialects of Assyrian and Babylonian) and Sumerian spoken mostly in Mesopotamia; as well as Elamite and Old Persian spoken mostly on the Iranian plateau.

INTRODUCTION & FURTHER READING

HISTORY AND CUNEIFORM

History had for a long time been defined by written records of past events and processes, too often neglecting the equally important material culture unearthed by archaeology. For the Ancient Near East, this makes the cuneiform writing system(s) the most important medium of transmission – next to Egyptian hieroglyphs. It is also the oldest writing system in the world. Having been invented in ancient Sumer, probably in the city of Uruk, in the middle of the fourth millennium BCE, cuneiform would be used for more than three and a half thousand years until the textual record peters out in the first few centuries CE.

Cuneiform, from Latin *cuneus* 'wedge', was written by pressing one tip of an angular stylus, most often made of reed, into wet clay. At different times and in various guises this method of writing would be used over the vast area that may be described as the Ancient Near East, with Mesopotamia as the nucleus of 'cuneiform culture'. Sumerian is the first (identifiable) language put to writing, its speakers having lived in the relative south of modern-day Iraq or southern Mesopotamia, where resources like stone and wood are sparse but clay abounds. Sumerian is categorized as an isolated language because no related languages are known to us, although (questionable) efforts to connect the agglutinative language to Turkic or Finno-Ugric languages continue to this day.

In the third millennium BCE, speakers of Elamite beyond the Zagros Mountains, and then speakers of Semitic languages in the cities of Ebla and (a bit later) of Akkad adapted the Sumerian script to the purposes of their respective languages. The great analytic effort of the Akkadians to adapt the Sumerian script to their needs especially influenced the world for some two and a half thousand years. Roughly from the second millennium onwards, modern scholars largely distinguish two dialects/languages of the Akkadian language family, Babylonian and Assyrian. The Babylonian language and script gained strong cultural influence over virtually the entire Ancient Near East. In the Late Bronze Age, it provided a common medium of written communication, a *scriptura franca* so to speak, between Elam in the east, Assyria and Babylonia further west, Mittani in the centre, Egypt in the south-west, the Hittite empire in the north-west and many smaller polities in between.

All these may be reasons why Mesopotamia is often at the heart of Ancient Near Eastern studies and why the largest part of the present book deals with its history, as will this introduction. Equally important, however, is the simple fact that texts in Babylonian, Assyrian and to a smaller degree Sumerian were not only among the earliest to be rediscovered in modern times, but have been so in the greatest abundance. Probably no other ancient civilization comes close to the hundreds of thousands of Mesopotamian texts that survived the millennia 'imbedded in tenacious earth', as William Kennet Loftus, who was the first Western explorer to collect cuneiform tablets from ancient Uruk, puts it. The largest repository of Mesopotamian cuneiform texts, the Cuneiform Digital Library Initiative, counts over 360,000 catalogue entries.

INTRODUCTION & FURTHER READING

PREHISTORY

The tremendous written record notwithstanding, we must not forget that writing is not the only source of knowledge about past cultures; neither did writing suddenly spring into existence as the stroke of genius of a single overzealous temple administrator. It was administrative practices that were gradually refined until eventually a society saw the need for a new tool to deal with the complexities of procuring, processing and distributing resources.

There is, of course, little limit to how far back into the past one could look. At least cultures of the Pre-Pottery Neolithic period may play a part in telling the history of the Ancient Near East, when plants and animals were domesticated and the agricultural revolution occurred – although certainly not at a revolutionary pace, being, just like the invention of writing, a slow and gradual, albeit inexorable, process.

There is perhaps not a speck of land in the Near East where one might not stumble upon a stray shard of some clay object, be it bright red Early Bronze Age, red-gloss Roman, greenish-black Umayyad or even plain white modern. Thus, with good reason, pottery is the single most important material find for Near Eastern archaeology. Indeed, it is in the later stages of the Neolithic that techniques to fashion and fire clay spread. The late Neolithic Samarra and Halaf cultures with quite different social layouts are both worthwhile subjects of study. Lastly, in the Chalcolithic Obeid and Uruk periods, southern Mesopotamia was firmly settled, major cities were formed and writing was invented.

The Uruk Period (*c.* fourth millennium BCE) and the Invention of Writing

This period of the Ancient Near East is called after the city of Uruk in southern Mesopotamia. The city and its infrastructure grew in size and complexity incomparable to anything before or anywhere else in the world. Society became more stratified, with high temple officials at the top. State-sponsored labour became more sophisticated. A large-scale textile industry developed. Pottery was being mass-produced on the potter's wheel. A widespread trade and administrative network spanned the Ancient Near East, from Anatolia to Iran. Sites like Habuba Kabira on the Middle Euphrates (in modern-day Syria) shared much of the material culture and architecture with Uruk. The city plan of Habuba Kabira shows strong urban planning, so it seems there were also new cities popping up, most likely in service of the Uruk network. This was also the backdrop to the invention of writing, sometime in the early second half of the fourth millennium.

Sealed clay tokens representing real-world items for the purpose of counting and verification in administrative procedures, as well as cylinder seals, are usually seen as conceptual precursors of writing. The earliest texts are chiefly concerned with accounting and are often little more than spreadsheets. Writing developed as a pictographic system, pictures represented real things and concepts and could, in theory, be read in any language – or rather, without language. Thus, it is a matter of definition at what precise point in history we start calling more and more standardized sequences of signs 'writing' that encodes a specific language.

INTRODUCTION & FURTHER READING

EARLY BRONZE AGE (C. THIRD MILLENNIUM BCE)

With writing eventually informing the modern historian of languages and political entities ancient people may have attributed themselves to, it becomes easier to provide a history of events that we are perhaps most familiar with for short historical sketches such as this one. Nevertheless, we must bear in mind that the textual record is distributed very unevenly, both in absolute numbers and in specimens of individual genres. While we have a plethora of texts for some periods, veritable gaps during or in between periods of the following chronological scheme still exist.

By the Early Bronze Age, cuneiform writing had begun to be used for more and more different reasons, not just for the traditional administrative documents, but also for sign lists, which play with the writing system, for example thinking about how to write 'six-legged sheep', and later royal inscriptions, among others. For these different texts with their particular styles and vocabulary, phonetic qualities of individual signs were isolated and abstracted, so that also explicit grammatical information, like case endings, could be written, not just whole words.

The chapter 'Mesopotamia' by Henry Smith Williams roughly covers this period.

The Early Dynastic Period
(first half of the third millennium BCE)

The lands of ancient Sumer were populated with a multitude of small states usually centred around a city, such as Uruk, Ur or Lagaš. The rulers of Lagaš left several texts commemorating conflicts over waterways, indispensable for the irrigation of fields, with neighbouring Umma. The most famous of these is the so-called Stele of Vultures, depicting the affair on both the mundane and the mythological planes.

A great archaeological discovery was made at Ur during the excavations directed by Leonard Woolley from 1922 to 1934. In the so-called Cemetery of Ur, several royal tombs provided insights into the beliefs and culture around the kings and queens of the city. The finds explained how dynastic kingship developed in this period and came to provide a lasting counterpart to the temple in the ruling of a (city-)state.

Late in that period, the Syrian city of Ebla became immortalized due to its people's adaptation of Sumerian cuneiform for their own Semitic language; again for administrative, archival purposes.

All in all, we still understand quite little about the Early Dynastic Period. Until today, much of our knowledge has been based on the so-called Sumerian King List, a much later literary composition. The list starts with kingdoms from before the flood whose rulers lived for thousands of years, and its latest edition ends with the dynasty of Isin in the early second millennium.

The Old Akkadian or Sargonic Period
(twenty-fourth to twenty-third century BCE)

The kingdom centred on Akkad formed the first territorial state and is sometimes called the first empire in history.

INTRODUCTION & FURTHER READING

Most of the Sumerian city-states were conquered and administered by governors under the king of Akkad, which was one of the new ways of organizing a large state. Enheduanna, daughter of the first Akkadian king, was made chief priestess at Ur, also one of the main political figures of that state. Today she is celebrated as the first named poet, thanks to several religious literary texts attributed to her as author or narrator.

According to legend, her father Sargon (Akkadian Šarru(m)-kīn) was once cupbearer to the king of Kiš, Ur-Zababa, before attaining a throne for himself. He then conquered Mesopotamia and even ventured as far as the Levant in the west and Elamite territories in the east. Under his rule, the Akkadian language was made the kingdom's official language. As in Ebla, the Akkadians achieved a grand philological feat in analysing their own language – belonging to the Semitic language family and very different from Sumerian – and adapting cuneiform script to it. By this time, cuneiform script had become more syllabic rather than purely logographic, and the Akkadian scribes reinforced this process. Perhaps the greatest legacy of Akkad was cementing the cuneiform script as a flexible mix of logographic and syllabic writing, in whichever proportion cultural taste dictated.

Sargon's grandson and fourth king of Akkad, Narām-Suen, needed to reconsolidate the empire, with contemporary records talking about a multitude of rebellions during his reign. He became infamous in Mesopotamian memory both as one of the great kings of Akkad and as a cruel and supercilious ruler who had himself deified.

The Third Dynasty of Ur (c. twenty-second–twentieth century BCE)

After the Akkadian 'empire' fell to the invading Gutians from the Zagros Mountains, according to later stories, many Sumerian city-states split off.

Gudea, king of Lagaš, is well known due to his many inscriptions on stelae and statues commemorating various religious and governmental activities. These texts were programmatically different from the image of the Akkadian kings as conquerors. They were also chiefly written in Sumerian, initiating what we call the 'Sumerian Renaissance', the last flickers of Sumerian as a living language.

Ur-Namma, and his son and successor Šulgi, managed to reunite the Sumerian city-states with Ur as the new empire's capital. Their state was characterized by a highly sophisticated administration that involved a complex system of taxation and redistribution, minute records of products and workers, and standardizations of weights and measures. It is estimated that some 100,000 records survive today.

MIDDLE BRONZE AGE (C. 2100–1550 BCE)

The model of kingship created in the Third Dynasty of Ur was emulated by later generations. Texts of that time, such as royal letters and inscriptions, became part of the scribal curriculum. Larger territorial states sprang up more frequently in this age.

The Isin-Larsa Period (*c.* first quarter of the second millennium)

Akkadian had started to become the dominant language in Mesopotamia, probably from the Akkadian period on. In the two territorial states succeeding the Ur-III-empire, centred around Isin and Larsa respectively, Sumerian continued to be used as the main administrative language. Scholars still debate when exactly Sumerian as a spoken language died out. Sumerian would, however, retain immense cultural importance (akin to Latin in post-Classical Europe, or Classical Arabic in the Islamic world) and continue to be written throughout Mesopotamian history.

Old Assyrian Trade (*c.* twentieth–nineteenth century BCE)

In the early second millennium, Assur was an independent city-state conducting long-distance trade with Anatolian kingdoms. Virtually everyone, Assyrian men and women alike, could read and to an extent write, since writing was greatly simplified for their mercantile needs. With the older archaeological levels of Assur not yet reached, almost everything we know comes from the Anatolian city of Kaneš (modern Kültepe in central Turkey), the centre of Assyrian trade. The city holds great cultural value also in later Hittite texts, under the name Neša.

Samsi-Addu (*c.* nineteenth century BCE)

After the heyday of this international trade, Samsi-Addu managed to conquer much of northern Mesopotamia, including Assur and Mari, an important city and state on the Middle Euphrates with abundant royal archives for the modern historian. Samsi-Addu descended from a varied group of people known as Amorites, whose (Semitic) language is known mostly through personal names and a few loanwords in Akkadian texts. Many kings of the coming age would be of Amorite descent, among them probably the most famous of any Mesopotamian king, Ḫammurapi of Babylon – often, and especially in earlier literature, written Ḫammurabi, interpreting the name as a combination of an Amorite word ʿAmmu 'grandfather/(paternal) uncle' and a Babylonian one rabi 'big' as opposed to Amorite rāpiʾ 'healer'.

Old Babylonian Period
(c. nineteenth–early sixteenth century BCE)

In the third millennium BCE, Babylon was a minor settlement, barely ever mentioned in texts. Ḫammurapi changed this situation for ever, greatly expanding the kingdom's territories to eventually encompass all Mesopotamia from the Persian Gulf to well beyond Mari and Assur in the north. His most enduring and famous act was the fashioning of a diorite stela stylizing him as a king of justice, the 'Code of Hammurapi', often called the oldest law language in history. Well in tradition with earlier such inscriptions, like the code of Ur-Namma or the code of Lipit-Eštar (a king of the Isin dynasty), it is neither the oldest law code, nor is the inscription a law code in the strict sense. Contemporary laws make no mention of the inscription, and judgements usually impose hefty fines rather than adhering to the lex talionis, or 'eye for an eye' punishment, that is so prevalent in the royal law codes.

Another Old Babylonian king important to modern historiography is Ammi-ṣaduqa, four generations after Ḫammurapi. During his reign, astronomical tablets recording movements of the planet Venus over a period of 21 years were fashioned. These observations can be used to align the relative historical chronology with absolute dates through astronomical calculations. Since the recorded interval repeats every eight years, different dating schemes have been proposed: a High, Middle, Low and Ultra-Low Chronology. Ḫammurapi's reign can thus be dated to 1848–06, 1792–50, 1728–1686, or 1696–54 BCE. This is why only approximate dating has been given until now, although recent research makes a modified version of the Middle Chronology more and more likely – as, of course, is so often the case with the 'Golden Mean'.

The chapter on 'Babylon' by Donald A. Mackenzie deals with this period.

LATE BRONZE AGE (C. 1550–1200 BCE)

This age is characterized by a number of growing and waning territorial states and international diplomacy. Egypt expanded into Syria where it found its equal in the kingdom of Mittani. Eventually Assyria broke from Mittani's dominion and developed into another great power in the region. In Anatolia, the Hittite state continually grew in power. In the south, the Kassite dynasty stabilized Babylonia. Further west, the Elamite kingdom remained strong under changing dynasties. Besides military encounters, the power relations were constantly renegotiated through letters (with Middle Babylonian as *lingua franca*), gifts and royal marriages. The most famous letter archive – after which the main period of international correspondence in the second half of the fourteenth century is called – was discovered at the site of Tell el-Amarna in Upper Egypt, hence the 'Amarna correspondence'. Thanks to these diplomatic relations, we can follow the fate of many smaller states as well, such as Kizzuwatna in Cilicia, Alashiya in Cyprus and many more in Syria and the Levant, like Karkemiš and Emar in Northern Syria, or Phoenician Byblos. One notable city-state in the Levant was Ugarit, where an alphabetic cuneiform script was developed to write the Semitic language of Ugaritic. We typically know quite little about the beginnings and ends of most of these states and empires. The period ended in political and ecological chaos.

Mittani

Unfortunately, very little evidence from the heartland of Mittani has so far been recovered. Most of what we know comes from vassal kingdoms east and west of Mittani proper. Especially rich are the archives at Nuzi, a city in the kingdom of Arraphe, neighbouring the Assyrian kingdom.

Besides Babylonian for administrative purposes and spoken west-Semitic varieties, an agglutinative language called Hurrian was the main language of Mittani. Hurrian had great cultural importance beyond its native speakers as especially liturgical texts became very popular, for instance, in the Hittite lands.

INTRODUCTION & FURTHER READING

The kingdom is known for its military success, usually attributed to its novel use of horse-drawn war chariots.

King Šauštatar (around 1430 BCE) perhaps conquered the most territory in the history of Mittani, vassalizing Kizzuwatna in the west and Assyria and Arrapḫe in the east.

Mittani's strength started to decline when Tušratta was killed by the armies of the Hittite king Šuppiluliuma I.

From the fourteenth century BCE on, Mittani was slowly conquered by its former vassal Assyria.

The Kassite Dynasty

Structural problems in the Old Babylonian kingdom led to numerous rebellions, especially in the south where the so-called Sealand dynasty would establish itself. The Hittite king Muršili I dealt the finishing blow by sacking Babylon before returning home.

The power vacuum was filled by the Kassites, who were already famed as mercenary groups in the Old Babylonian period and had become a part of the military elite. What little we know about the Kassite language comes from personal names. Under this dynasty, Babylonia was relatively stable. The region gained a Babylonian identity with Marduk, city-god of Babylon, now firmly at the top of the pantheon replacing Enlil of Nippur – dealing a lasting cultural trauma to that city. Many of the classical Sumerian and Babylonian compositions were canonized and even created in this period (and under the following Isin II dynasty), such as the astrological omen series 'Enūma Anu Enlil', 'Ludlul bēl nēmeqi' which has similar themes to the biblical book of Job, and probably the creation myth 'Enūma eliš'.

The Hittite Empire

Hattušili I and his son Muršili I were the first to try to expand Hittite influence beyond the Taurus mountains in order to control the trade routes coming from Syria. Since they could not achieve organized control, however, Mittani fulfilled this role instead.

Towards the end of the fifteenth century BCE, Tutḫaliya I subjugated Kizzuwatna, which gained him international recognition and spread Hurrian heritage into Hittite territories.

Šuppiluliuma I, having risen to power perhaps after a *coup d'état* in the middle of the fourteenth century BCE, enjoyed great military success against Mittani, eventually making the Hittites the greatest adversaries to Egypt in the Levant.

Until the twelfth century BCE, the Hittite empire remained a great power in frequent contact with Egypt and Kassite Babylonia; not without hiccups, of course, such as an epidemic in the late fourteenth century BCE that devastated the people, the economy and the legitimacy of the king.

Assyria

With the weakening of Mittani after its defeat by Šuppiluliuma I, the Assyrian king Aššur-uballiṭ I seized the opportunity, subdued neighbouring Arrapḫe, and established himself in the international correspondence with Egypt and the other great powers.

Close cultural ties to the south did not hamper the occasional military conflict with Babylonia. Most of the kingdom of Mittani eventually succumbed to Assyrian dominance.

Climate Change and the Sea People (from c. 1200 BCE)

The end of this age appeared especially dire in Hittite reports, which describe famines due to droughts and cities ablaze, be it from environmental catastrophe or armed conflict, before the empire's complete collapse. None of the other states of the Near East remained unscathed, however. Egypt fell into disunity, Assyria contracted, Babylonia could not resist Elamite incursions. The Mediterranean regions saw great movement of people, and frequent violent raids by the so-called Sea People.

An abrupt climate change, causing average temperatures to drop by more than two degrees Celsius, certainly contributed to the upheavals of this time. This event, and a similar climate change at the end of the Early Bronze Age that had led to wide desertification in Greater Syria, could perhaps serve as a mirror for the human-made climate change of today.

IRON AGE (C. FIRST MILLENNIUM BCE)

Once the dust settled, much historical focus shifted to Assyria, which imposed its imperial ambitions on the entire Ancient Near East, founding the first empire in the truest sense of the word. In the Levant, the kingdom of Israel flourished, and the names of Assyrian (and Babylonian) kings would be remembered there, still informing our transcriptions of their names today. For instance – biblically speaking – the most famous Babylonian king Nebuchadnezzar II was called Nabû-kudurru-uşur in Neo-Babylonian.

From around the eighth century well into the first century BCE, the longest lasting empirical experiment of human history was conducted by the joint effort of priestly scholars throughout Mesopotamia, the so-called Astronomical Diaries. This virtually unbroken chain of cuneiform texts recording celestial, terrestrial, economic and political observations attempted to make sense of the world and its causalities.

Aramaic had suffused much of the Ancient Near East and was slowly replacing the Akkadian varieties of Neo-Assyrian and Neo-Babylonian as the dominant spoken language in Mesopotamia.

The Levant has been treated rather peripherally in Ancient Near Eastern history in this introduction. However, the final chapter by George Rawlinson focuses on Phoenician history from the Late Bronze Age to the rise of Persia.

The Neo-Assyrian Empire
(*c.* tenth century–612 BCE)

Assurnaşirpal (883–59 BCE) began greatly expanding Assyrian territory. However, it is not until Tiglat-pileser III (744–27 BCE) that political and administrative innovations were made that would transform the Assyrian state into an empire proper. Internally, governing power became more centralized and a standing army was established, among other reforms. Most important was a reorientation in Assyrian foreign policy. Rather than seeking to control trade routes through vassal states, as was the mode of operations in the Late Bronze

INTRODUCTION & FURTHER READING

Age, Assyrian ambitions were set on conquering territory and establishing provinces controlled by governors directly appointed by the Assyrian king.

In this period, people who the Assyrians called 'Arabs' appear for the first time in the historical record.

Most (in)famous in Assyrian history is the Sargonid dynasty, the final four great kings under whom the empire would stretch across the entire Fertile Crescent, from Elam to Egypt: Sargon II (721–05), Sanherib (704–681), Assarhaddon (680–69), Assurbanipal (668–31).

From this time, a great collection of cuneiform tablets was discovered in different palace areas at the capital city of Nineveh. In its inventory was the standard rendition of the 'Epic of Gilgamesh' as we know it today. As a catch-all term, this tablet collection is usually called the 'Library of Assurbanipal', although it was neither a single, true library nor did it belong solely to Assurbanipal.

Babylonia, having always been an area of conflict and cause for civil war in the Assyrian empire, ultimately made an alliance with the Medes who were equally waging war against Assyria, and together they put an end to the empire, destroying Nineveh and dividing up the remainder of the realm.

The chapter 'Assyria' by Henry Smith Williams goes into detail about the political history of this period.

The Neo-Babylonian Empire (*c.* 612–539 BCE)

Nabopolassar (626–05 BCE) saw to completely replacing the Assyrian empire with his own and managed to seize most of the former Assyrian territories during his reign.

It was the task of his successor Nebuchadnezzar II (604–562 BCE) to stabilize the empire, especially the Babylonian homeland, which was discordant as ever. The south was historically at odds with Babylon's dominion, already in the Late Bronze Age. Nebuchadnezzar II restructured temple organization and replaced the old elite families of cities like Uruk with ones from Babylon itself who were loyal to the crown.

The last Babylonian king, Nabonidus (555–39 BCE), sponsored great building projects throughout the empire just as Nebuchadnezzar had done before him, but alienated parts of Babylonia's high society. Stemming from Harran in northern Syria, Nabonidus was fond of promoting the cult of Sîn over Marduk, much to the ire of the Babylonian priestly elites. Moreover, he spent many years abroad in the oasis town of Tayma on the Arabian Peninsula. In his absence, he neglected important cultic duties, like participating in the New Year's festival, which again alienated Babylonian elites.

The chapter 'New Babylon' by Henry Smith Williams covers the political history of the Neo-Babylonian empire.

The Achaemenid Empire (mid-sixth century–330 BCE)

Cyrus the Great (559–30 BCE) built on the great cultural heritage of the Medes and Elam and took the Assyrian empire as a model for his own. With the local elites alienated from Nabonidus, Babylonia did not put up much resistance against Cyrus's march into the Near East. The penultimate chapter by

George Rawlinson covers in great detail Cyrus the Great and the rise of the Persian empire.

Darius the Great (521–486 BCE) consolidated the empire, then stretching from the Indus Valley to Anatolia and Egypt. He reformed the taxation system and organized the empire into satrapies (provinces ruled by governors). Moreover, he initiated building projects in Persepolis and Susa, and left behind many of the trilingual inscriptions that enabled modern decipherment of the cuneiform scripts, most famously the Behistun Inscription.

Two successive revolts in Babylonia, as well as in Egypt, strained Persian cultural tolerance towards its subjects, and Xerxes (485–65 BCE) completely reshuffled the upper echelons of Babylonian society. In Uruk, for instance, the main Ziggurat was destroyed, and the main cult shifted from the goddess Inanna to An, who was nominally the founding deity of the Sumero-Babylonian pantheon but had no significance for the cult since the third millennium BCE.

Written sources became less abundant after a switch to Aramaic as the main administrative language during this period, the records being written on more perishable materials than clay.

During its existence, the Achaemenid Empire enjoyed relative prosperity without the major internal, structural crises the Assyrian and Babylonian empires suffered towards their ends. That is why its swift demise at the hands of Alexander the Great puzzles historians to this day.

The Seleucid Dynasty (312 BCE–63 CE)

With the administrative structures still intact and Alexander having adopted Persian cultural syncretism, Seleukos I established his Hellenistic dynasty (next to Ptolemaios I in Egypt) as rulers of the former Persian territories with relative ease.

Berossos, a priest in Babylon, provided the dynasty with ideological support with a historical work about Babylonia in Greek, entitled *Babyloniaka*. The *Babyloniaka* influenced later historians like Flavius Josephus and is still of great worth to the modern historian despite its fragmentary state, unlike the unreliable works of Herodotus.

With Hellenism on the rise, and the empire facing old and new sociocultural challenges, this late age in Mesopotamian history deserves more attention than modern historiography has given it.

The Parthian (around 240 BCE–224 CE) and Sassanid Empire (224–651 CE)

In the second century BCE, the Arsacid dynasty conquered first western Iran and then Mesopotamia from the Seleucid empire, founding the Parthian empire.

Cuneiform continued to be used as a script only in some temple contexts until the first few decades of Sassanid rule.

The End of Cuneiform Culture

In the course of the first millennium BCE, Aramaic replaced Akkadian as the dominant spoken language in Mesopotamia. In its death throes, cuneiform, still writing in Babylonian and Sumerian, was only used by a few learned priests for liturgical purposes. The last Astronomical Diary dates to 61/60 BCE. With the last cuneiform tablet fashioned sometime in the late third century CE, this written culture that had taken the world by storm more than three millennia earlier faded into oblivion.

FURTHER READING

Akkermans, P.M. & Schwartz, G.M. *The Archaeology of Syria: from Complex Hunter-Gatherers to Early Urban Societies (c. 16,000–300 BC)* (Cambridge University Press, Cambridge, UK, New York, 2003)

Alster, B. *Wisdom of Ancient Sumer* (CDL Press, Bethesda, 2005)

Bauer, J., Englund, R.K. & Krebernik, M. *Mesopotamien: Späturuk-Zeit und Frühdynastische Zeit* (Universitätsverlag; Vandenhoeck & Ruprecht, Freiburg, Göttingen, 1998)

Beaulieu, P. A. A History of Babylon, 2200 BC–AD 75 (John Wiley & Sons Ltd, Hoboken, NJ, 2018)

Briant, P. From Cyrus to Alexander. *A History of the Persian Empire* (Eisenbrauns, Winona Lake, 2002)

Brinkman, J.A. A Political History of Post-Kassite Babylonia, 1158–722 BC (Pontificium Institutum Biblicum, Rome, 1968)

Charpin, D. *Reading and Writing in Babylon* (Harvard University Press, Cambridge, Mass, 2010)

Charpin, D. *Hammurabi of Babylon* (I.B. Tauris, London - New York, 2012)

Charpin, D., Edzard, D.O. & Stol, M. *Mesopotamien: Die altbabylonische Zeit* (Academic Press; Vandenhoeck & Ruprecht, Fribourg, Göttingen, 2004)

Daniels, P.T. 'The Decipherment of Ancient Near Eastern Scripts', in *Civilizations of the Ancient Near East*, Volume I, edited by J.M. Sasson (Carles Scribner's Sons, New York, 1995), Vol. 1, pp. 81–93

Dassow, E. von. *State and Society in the Late Bronze Age: Alalah Under the Mittani Empire* (CDL Press, Bethesda, 2008)

Fischer, P.M. & Bürge, T. (eds.). *'Sea Peoples' Up-to-Date: New Research on Transformations in the Eastern Mediterranean in the 13th–11th Centuries* BCE (VÖAW, Vienna, 2017)

Foster, B.R. *The Age of Agade: Inventing Empire in Ancient Mesopotamia* (Routledge/Taylor & Francis Group, London, New York, NY, 2016)

Foster, B.R. & Foster, K.P. *Civilizations of Ancient Iraq* (Princeton University Press, Princeton, N.J., 2009)

Frahm, E. (ed.). *A Companion to Assyria* (John Wiley & Sons, Hoboken, N.J., 2017)

Frahm, E. *Assyria: The Rise and Fall of the World's First Empire* (Bloomsbury Publishing, London, Dublin, Oxford, New York, New Delhi, Sydney, 2023)

Jursa, M. (ed.). *Aspects of the Economic History of Babylonia in the First Millennium* BC: *Economic Geography, Economic Mentalities, Agriculture, the Use of Money and the Problem of Economic Growth* (Ugarit-Verlag, Münster, 2010)

Lanfranchi, G.B., Roaf, M. & Rollinger, R. (eds.). *Continuity of Empire (?): Assyria, Media, Persia* (S.a.r.g.o.n. Editrice e Libreria, Padova, 2003)

Larsen, M.T. *Ancient Kanesh: A Merchant Colony in Bronze Age Anatolia* (Cambridge University Press, Cambridge, 2015)

Liverani, M. *Assyria: The Imperial Mission* (Eisenbrauns, Winona Lake, Indiana, 2022)

Martino, S. de (ed.). *Handbook Hittite Empire: Power Structures* (De Gruyter Oldenbourg, Berlin, Boston, 2022)

Niehr, H., Xella, P., Kühn, D. & Minunno, G. (eds.). *Encyclopaedic Dictionary of Phoenician Culture: Religion – Deities and Mythical Characters* (Peeters, Leuven, Bristol, 2021)

Nissen, H.J. *The Early History of the Ancient Near East, 9000–2000 BC* (University of Chicago Press, Chicago, 1988)

Podany, A.H. *Weavers, Scribes, and Kings: A New History of the Ancient Near East* (Oxford University Press, New York, NY, 2022)

Radner, K. *Ancient Assyria: A Very Short Introduction* (Oxford University Press, Oxford, United Kingdom, 2015)

Radner, K. & Robson, E. (eds.). *The Oxford Handbook of Cuneiform Culture* (Oxford University Press, Oxford, New York, 2011)

Sallaberger, W. & Westenholz, A. *Mesopotamien: Akkade-Zeit und Ur-III-Zeit* (Universitätsverlag; Vandenhoeck & Ruprecht, Freiburg, Göttingen, 1999)

Sasson, J.M. (ed.). *Civilizations of the Ancient Near East*, Volume I (Carles Scribner's Sons, New York, 1995)

Sherwin-White, S. & Kuhrt, A. *From Samarkand to Sardis. A New Approach to the Seleucid Empire* (Duckworth, London, 1993)

van de Mieroop, M. *Philosophy Before the Greeks: The Pursuit of Truth in Ancient Babylonia* (Princeton University Press, Princeton, Oxford, 2016)

Vanderhooft, D.S. *The Neo-Babylonian Empire and Babylon in the Latter Prophets* (Scholars Press, Atlanta, 1999)

Veenhof, K.R. & Eidem, J. *Mesopotamia: The Old Assyrian Period* (Academic Press; Vandenhoeck & Ruprecht, Fribourg, Göttingen, 2008)

Westbrook, R. & Beckman, G.M. (eds.). *A History of Ancient Near Eastern Law* (Brill, Leiden, Boston, 2003)

Xella, P., Zamora, J.Á. & Niehr, H. (eds.). *Encyclopaedic Dictionary of Phoenician Culture* (Peeters, Leuven, Paris, Bristol, 2018)

Matthias Adelhofer (Introduction) is trained in Akkadian and Sumerian philology as well as Ancient Near Eastern archaeology. Currently, he is studying letters exchanged in the course of Old Assyrian long-distance trade. From the materiality, general epistolographic practices, and form to the modes of rhetoric used in the texts, he is investigating the social norms and mentalities present in the correspondence. He has also studied Neo-Babylonian economic archives and the social networks of the persons featuring in them. He is especially interested in social and economic history, linguistics, and palaeography.

THE ANCIENT NEAR EAST

MESOPOTAMIA

In this chapter, Henry Smith Williams covers the early periods of Mesopotamia during the third and early second millennia BCE. Today we divide these into the Early Dynastic, Old Akkadian or Sargonic, Ur-III and Old Babylonian periods.

Smith Williams' understanding of the texts known at the time was good, and their presentation is nicely detailed. The conclusions drawn from the diverse texts, ranging from royal inscriptions to omen tablets much later than the periods under discussion are at times a bit too optimistic. As to explaining the circumstances around changing dynasties, his basis of evidence tends to be too meagre for his broad conclusions. Despite many uncertainties remaining, chronology has come a long way, and we can correct Smith Williams' dating by around 2,000 years.

Owing to the *zeitgeist*, the discourse may at times seem needlessly racialized. Overlooking the specific guise of the discourse, however, Smith Williams is correct in asserting that speakers of a Semitic language like Akkadian had lived in Mesopotamia already very early on. Attributing certain developments to a specific people is difficult or impossible. Sumer clearly was diverse from its very beginnings, and traces of Akkadian and other languages can be discerned already in the earliest texts. For the modern reader, some of the terminology may need elucidation:

Turanian was a term for the now obsolete reconstruction of a Uralo-Altaic language family, comprising Finno-Ugric, Turkic, Mongol and Tungusic languages. Here Turanian is used for Sumerian that had only recently been identified as agglutinative and so perhaps related. On top of that, Sumerian was even still being contested as a language rather than a secret code of Babylonian scribes.

Patesi is to be read 'ensi'. In the Early Dynastic Period, it is one of many titles for a ruler, which differed city-state by city-state. *Shirpurla* means Lagaš (modern Tell el-Hiba). The 'South Arabian Dynasty' is the Amorite dynasty of Babylon.

THE BEGINNINGS OF HISTORY

The Babylonians and Assyrians were two very important peoples of remote antiquity, inhabiting the region of the Tigris and Euphrates rivers in south-western Asia. The Greeks regarded these peoples as constituting one nation and called their country Mesopotamia, a name that could properly be applied to only a part of their territory. The Babylonians and Assyrians, themselves, on the other hand, regarded each other as alien peoples, though both belonged to the same Semitic stock. The Babylonians were the more ancient, and their territory lay to the south, where, many scholars believe, they had been preceded by a people of a different race.

MESOPOTAMIA

Though the seat of this early civilization is geographically small in extent, yet the peoples who entered into it were by no means homogeneous, nor was their history a continuous record of unbroken political succession. On the contrary, at least two different races of people were involved, – a Turanian stock in the early Babylonian history, a Semitic stock in all the later periods, – and at least three successive kingdoms or empires, not to speak of mere changes of dynasty. The earliest period known to us – that which left records at Nippur and Shirpurla, in old Babylonia – had its seat in the southern portion of the territory bordering on the sea; thence, seemingly, civilization spread northward. Assyriologists are not fully agreed as to the share which the non-Semitic race had in this early civilization. It has even been questioned whether these so-called Sumerians really existed at all. In any event the Semitic Babylonians acquired full control at a very early period.

The Assyrian kingdom – which came to be a veritable world-empire – had its seat at Calah and afterwards at Nineveh. It conquered and absorbed the old Babylonian kingdom, and then reached out for domination to the east and to the west, finally overrunning even Egypt.

The Bible accounts preserve records of some of its most famous kings, including Sennacherib. The Greek legends are chiefly concerned with a mythical Semiramis, the alleged founder of Nineveh, and with a seemingly mythical Sardanapalus, who perished after an inglorious reign, in the destruction of Nineveh, which came about suddenly and dramatically in the year 606 BCE – the Sardanapalus myth being, however, based on an actuality.

After the destruction of Nineveh, Babylon, the capital of Babylonia, resumed renewed importance as a world metropolis. Nebuchadrezzar, the most famous king of this period, besieged Jerusalem and carried the Israelites to his capital (the Babylonian capital). The classical accounts preserve reminiscences of the magnificence of Babylon in this period. The course of the New Babylonian empire, though brilliant, was brief, ending with the overthrow of Babylon by the Persians under Cyrus in the year 538 BCE. Babylon was not, like Nineveh, totally destroyed; but it never regained autonomy or anything approaching its former importance. It was one of the Persian capitals for two centuries, until in 331 BCE, with the downfall of the Persian empire, it passed into the hands of Alexander the Great, who, after his eastern conquests, chose it as the capital of his newly acquired empire. But Alexander died in his new capital almost immediately, and his death was the last great world-historic event that occurred in Mesopotamia. In the course of a few centuries thereafter, the whole region that for so many years had been the very heart of the world's civilization, became a barren wilderness, and Babylon itself, like Nineveh before it, was reduced to a mere earth-covered mound of ruins, the very location of which was practically forgotten.

Such a fate was tragic enough; yet after all it seems less cruel than the destiny of such nations as Egypt, and in later time, Greece, which live on in senescence long after all vestige of their power has departed. And in any event, Mesopotamia had had its full share of glory, for no other region of the globe, within historic times, with the possible

MESOPOTAMIA

exception of Egypt alone, has so long held rank as a centre of influence and civilization. If the earlier walls of the Temple of Bel (Baal) at Nippur really date from 6000 or 7000 years BCE as the records seem to prove, there was a continuous, powerful empire in Mesopotamia for at least five or six thousand years. The civilizations of Greece, of Rome, or of any modern state, seem mere mushroom growths in comparison.

In studying the history of Egypt we have caught occasional glimpses of this oldest Asiatic civilization of Babylonia and Assyria, and it is almost impossible to avoid drawing comparisons between these two countries, so closely related are the two peoples in the minds of all students. It is true that the ethnological types are quite different, and that the two peoples, during the greater part of their existence, did not mingle much with one another. Often they were at war, and it is traditional that for the most part the Egyptians repelled rather than invited any advances from their Asiatic neighbours. Nevertheless, their own interests dictated a commercial policy that led first and last to an extensive intermingling between all the contemporary civilizations of western Asiatic antiquity, and there are abundant evidences that the same influence extended also to the Nile Valley.

But even had this not been the case, – even had Egypt and Mesopotamia been shut off absolutely one from the other, – it would still be impossible...to disassociate the two, so many are the links of association between them. The fact that these two are the oldest civilizations...and the further fact that there has been a constant question in the minds of investigators as to which one of these ancient peoples can claim priority of development, form in themselves an indissoluble bond of union. Yet in some respects the story of the Babylonians and Assyrians is unique; because this well-nigh greatest of civilizations was blotted out absolutely almost before the oldest European civilization was under way. Egypt, indeed, declined in power at about the same period and permanently lost autonomy, but its pyramids and temples and numberless antiquities remain as obvious testimonials of its former greatness; whereas the monuments of Mesopotamia – the ruins of such wonderful cities as Nippur, Babylon, and Nineveh – were completely buried under the accumulating earth deposits of centuries, and almost absolutely lost to view. For more than two thousand years the names of these once famous cities were only reminiscences. No one knew accurately even their sites, and scarcely an antiquity of any description was known to be preserved that evidenced the sometime greatness of the Mesopotamian civilization.

During this long period a few reminiscences preserved in the writings of Berosus, Diodorus, Herodotus, and a few other classical writers, and in the text of Hebrew writings, gave all the clews that were obtainable, and apparently all that could ever be obtained regarding one of the most remarkable peoples of antiquity.

The entire destruction of the Mesopotamian civilization gave it peculiar interest. It should not be forgotten, however, that at least one other very important people of antiquity, namely the Hittites, met with a like fate. Probably there were still others whose names even are unknown to us. But the story of Mesopotamia stands quite by itself in the fact that it has been very largely restored to us through the efforts of modern explorers. We have seen that the decipherment of the hieroglyphics led to a much fuller understanding of Egyptian history than had previously been possible; yet, after all, these new revelations sufficed to fill in the outlines of an old story, rather than to create an altogether new one. But in the case of Babylonia and Assyria the modern investigators had virtually a blank canvas upon which to work in reconstructing the history. The Bible references and the classical myths gave but the most shadowy outlines. Yet traditions are all powerful for the transmission of knowledge in a vague form, and throughout all generations it had never been doubted that the reminiscences of Mesopotamian greatness had a firm foundation in fact, though few historians were visionary enough to dare hope that more tangible evidence would ever be forthcoming, and not even the most enthusiastic dreamer could have suspected that such records as the nineteenth century has restored to us had been preserved.

Even now, looking back from the standpoint of accomplishment, it seems almost incredible that the monuments of a great civilization – treasures of art, and voluminous literary records – should have been absolutely hidden from human view for a minimum period of more than two thousand years, and should then have been restored in almost their original condition. Yet such is the fact regarding the antiquities of Mesopotamia.

THE OLDEST KING OF BABYLONIA

c. 4500 BCE

The **oldest king of Babylonia** of whom we have any record is Enshagkushanna, whose date we have placed before 4500 BCE. He calls himself "lord of Kengi," the southern part of Babylonia. As to his nationality, whether he was a so-called "Sumerian" or a "Semite," we have no means of knowing. Besides "lord of Kengi," he seems to have had another title, viz. "king of..." The lacuna probably contained the names of the capital of the kingdom. He must have waged war against Kish in northern Babylonia, which city he terms "wicked of heart." He was the victor, and presented the spoil to "Enlil, king of the lands." Enlil – the later Bel – was the chief god in Nippur; Nippur accordingly was called En-lil-ki, the "city of Enlil." Hence Enlil of Nippur seems to have been the god who wielded the chief influence over the inhabitants of early Babylonia. From inscriptions of certain patesis of Shirpurla, as well as from those of Lugalzaggisi, we know that this temple was under the control of the king, who called himself accordingly *patesi-gal*, "the great patesi." But it also had its own "chief local administrator," the *dam-kar-gal*, who in his turn had several minor priests or patesis under him. The cult of this god seems to have been well arranged; the king, being the *summus episcopus*, had a host of other officers (priests) under him, who exercised the ordinary functions of the so-called priesthood of Bel. Few as the historical notices are, yet they enable us to get an insight into the condition of the land and of the people

MESOPOTAMIA

at this remote time. They show us that a struggle went on between the south (Kengi) and the north (Kish) which struggle lasted undoubtedly for several centuries.

Prominent cities at this time were the capital of Kengi, *i.e.* Shirpurla-Girsu, as we shall see later on; not Erech (Hilprecht), Nippur, and Kish.

It is necessary, however, before tracing the different steps in the development of Kish, to turn our attention to a kingdom called in the inscriptions "Shirpurla." The inscriptions of the rulers of this kingdom give us an impression of a power and might which presupposes centuries for its development. All that we know of its art and civilization tends in the same direction.

THE RULERS OF SHIRPURLA

c. 4500–4100 BCE

Shirpurla is the modern Tel-Loh (or Telloh) where De Sarzec found the inscriptions relating to the rulers of this dynasty. It is situated fifteen hours north of Mugheir, on the east side of the Shatt-el-Khai, and about twelve hours east of Warka. At this early time the city of Shirpurla seems to have included four component parts, viz. Girsu, Nina, Uruazagga, Erim. Thus it happened that one and the same king might call himself either "king of Shirpurla" or "king of Girsu." These suburbs were built by various rulers in honour of their favourite gods or goddesses. Whether Shirpurla is the right reading, or Sirgulla (Hommel), we do not know. According to Pinches, *Guide to the Kuyunjik Gallery*, p. 7, London, 1883, and *Babyl. Records*, iii, p. 24, Shirpurla may read Lagash, which reading is adopted throughout by Jensen in K. B. iii. We retain the old reading Shirpurla, because this writing occurs most frequently in the monuments.

The rulers of Shirpurla may conveniently be grouped under four divisions:

1. The dynasty of Urukagina – beginning with this ruler or his predecessor(s) and ending with Lugalshuggur and his successor(s).
2. The dynasty of Ur-Nina, ending with Lummadur.
3. The patesis between Lummadur and Ur-Ba'u.
4. Ur-Ba'u and his successors, ending with Gala-Lama.

To Urukagina, the oldest member of the first dynasty of Shirpurla, we have assigned the approximate date of 4500 BCE. His greatness consisted not so much in successful wars against the neighbouring cities, as in securing a peaceful administration for his country and city. As "king of Girsu-Shirpurla," he devoted his energy to the building of different storehouses, that should take up "the abundance of the countries," and erected temples for different gods – thus showing his devotion and piety. He built "for Nina the beloved canal, the canal Nina-ki-tum-a," and thus supplied his city with water. Bel of Nippur still exercises the highest influence. Ningirsu ("the lord of Girsu") is the chief city-god, under whose control the capital stands. He is the *Gud* or "hero" of Enlil. In somewhat later inscriptions, Ningirsu has the title *gud-lig-ga*, "the strong hero" of Enlil. Many other gods are mentioned in his inscriptions.

To this oldest dynasty of Shirpurla belongs also a certain En-gegal ("lord of abundance" or "very rich"). He, like Urukagina, calls himself "*lugal Pur-shir-la*," "king of Shirpurla." Besides this he bears the proud title "*lugal ki-gal-la*," "the great king," and terms himself *shib (dingir) Nin-gir-su*, "the priest of Ningirsu," a title similar to that of *patesi-gal*. From the title "the great king" we may venture to conclude that he, unlike his predecessor, must have carried his arms successfully against his enemies, who had previously succeeded in plundering Shirpurla; but fate decreed that his royal capital should be reduced to the seat of a patesi. Kish, having been defeated some time before by Enshagkushanna, seems to have acquired new strength. Its king, Mesilim, became lord paramount of Shirpurla, thus reducing its rulers to mere patesis. The name of only one of these earliest patesis is preserved to us, *i.e.* Lugal-shug-gur, who is mentioned in the inscription of Mesilim. The sovereignty of Kish over Shirpurla does not seem to have lasted very long. Shirpurla regained its former glory under a new dynasty, namely, that of Ur-Nina.

c. 4300–4200 BCE

With Ur-Nina begins a new dynasty, probably the mightiest of early Babylonia, the duration of its sovereignty extending from 4300 BCE to 4100 BCE. Looking at the art and the inscriptions of these kings, we cannot help thinking that in Shirpurla civilization must have been far advanced, so far advanced as to force upon us the conclusion that "several centuries have elapsed before men could reach this stage of civilization." The greater number of these art treasures are preserved in the Louvre; the inscriptions found on them have been published in *Découvertes en Chaldée* and in the *Revue d'Assyriologie*.

The first king of this dynasty was Ur-Nina (servant of Nina). The dynasty of Urukagina must have been reduced to mere nothingness by the kings of Kish, so that Ur-Nina found it easy to take possession of the throne. He must have been of an old family, for he mentions the name of his father and grandfather, who have the title neither of patesi nor of king. He, like his predecessor, seems to have been great in peace. He built temples and various storehouses. A passage in his inscriptions where he records the building of the "wall of Shirpurla" suggests that the old enemy, Kish, was still troublesome, so that he found it necessary to fortify his capital against the deadly enemies from the north.

The son of Ur-Nina, who succeeded him upon the throne of Shirpurla, was Akurgal. As yet no inscriptions of this monarch have been found. All that is known about him is gathered either from the inscriptions of his son (Eannatum) or from those of his father (Ur-Nina). In these inscriptions eight sons of Ur-Nina are mentioned. If we classify them according to their height, and take this as a basis for determining their age, we would get the following result:

UR-NINA
(1) Lid-da, (2) Mu-ri-kur-ta, (3) A-ni-kur-ra, (4) Lugal-shir, (5) A-kur-gal, (6) Nun-pad, (7) E-ud-bu, (8) Nina-ku-tur-a.

It is remarkable that the first-born, Lidda, is mentioned in only one inscription. Did he never succeed his father upon the throne of Shirpurla? Did Akurgal, his fifth son, in preference to all the others, inherit the royal sceptre, and thus become the immediate successor of Ur-Nina? Interesting as these questions are, we are yet, with the means on hand, unable to decide them. This much only we know, that both Eannatum and Enannatum I, call themselves "son of Akurgal." Another interesting fact is that Eannatum, in his "Stèle des Vautours," calls his father *lugal* ("king") of Shirpurla, while in his other inscriptions he only terms him "patesi of Shirpurla." Not very much can be concluded from this, because even Ur-Nina is styled by Eannatum "patesi of Shirpurla." The translation of this latter passage, is not yet certain. Ur-Nina's successor, however, – either Lidda or Akurgal, – may have lost the title "king" in consequence of an unsuccessful war. Eannatum, on the other hand, being more successful, resumes again for a short time the title "king" after his victory over Kish. This latter fact is very important. Eannatum expressly tells us that Innanna gave him the nam-lugal Kish-ki, "the kingship of Kish," while as ruler of Shirpurla he was only patesi. The state of affairs then was as follows:

Ur-Nina, a usurper, was able to constitute himself king of Shirpurla in consequence of the weakness of the patesis of Shirpurla who preceded him, they having been reduced by the kings of Kish to complete powerlessness. Ur-Nina's successors, however, were not able to retain the title of their father. Was it internal disharmony between the sons of Ur-Nina which caused this? They lost the title "king," and had to accept that of patesi. Undoubtedly they were forced to do this by one of the successors of Mesilim, *i.e.* by a king of Kish. Eannatum – a great hero – was able to overcome the old enemy Kish. He even was so fortunate as to add to his old title, "patesi of Shirpurla," that of "king" (sc. of "Kish") and by a stretch of this latter title he may have also called himself "king of Shirpurla." The successors of Eannatum called themselves, and are called without exception "patesis of Shirpurla."

c. 4200 BCE

After these preliminary remarks about the titles of the different members of the dynasty of Ur-Nina, we now turn our attention to Eannatum (*i.e.* "The house of heaven is stable"), the son of Akurgal himself. Whether he reigned contemporaneously with his brother Enannatum I or not, we cannot tell. The fact that the sons of Enannatum I succeeded upon the throne of Shirpurla makes it reasonable to suppose that Eannatum preceded Enannatum I. This latter ruler seems to have played only a minor rôle in early Babylonia history. Only two of his inscriptions have so far come down to us. Eannatum, his brother, on the contrary, is the greatest of the whole dynasty. The deeds of this monarch have been preserved to us on different monuments, among which the "Stèle des Vautours" is the most important. In order to obtain a full conception of his time we must compare this "Stèle" with the so-called "Cone" of Entemena. Those monuments in connection with the Galet A give us the following interesting piece of history:

The god of Shirpurla (Ningirsu) and the god of Gishban, at the instigation of Enlil (god of Nippur), agree to settle the boundaries between their respective territories (Cone i, 1-7). Mesilim, king of Kish, – a contemporary of Lugalshuggur, patesi of Shirpurla, – in the quality of lord paramount of Shirpurla, corroborates the result of this "settling of boundaries," and erects a statue on the junction of the two territories, to mark out the boundaries of the territory of Shirpurla on the one side and of Gishban on the other (Cone i, 8-12). Ush, however, a certain ambitious patesi of Gishban, is not satisfied with this decision. He takes away the statue which Mesilim had erected, and then invades Shirpurla, undoubtedly to extend his territory beyond the boundary previously fixed (13-21). A war between Shirpurla and Gishban ensues.

Mesilim, who feels dishonoured by this action of Ush, takes the side of Shirpurla and defeats Gishban (22-31). Gishban in course of time again becomes restless. It invades, under its patesi Gunammide, the territory of Shirpurla, and more specifically the Guedin, a district sacred to Ningirsu. "Gunammide, the patesi of Gishban, according to the command of his god...the Guedin, the beloved territory of Ningirsu he destroyed." Eannatum, after having fortified Shirpurla sufficiently ("the wall of Urnazagga he built"), and having led his armies victoriously against Elam and Gishgal, feels himself strong enough to deal a deadly (?) blow at Gishban. "Gishban he put under the yoke, twenty of its dead ones he buried." Having done this, he restores the sacred territory, the Guedin, to Ningirsu; concludes a treaty with Enakalli, (one of) the successor(s) of Gunammide; digs a canal "from the great river (*i.e.* the Euphrates?) to the Guedin," and makes the Gishbanites swear never to invade the sacred territory of Ningirsu again, nor to trespass this boundary.

"In the future time the territory of Ningirsu, when (the Gishbanites) should invade it again, the dyke and the canal, if they should trespass it, the statue, if they should take it away – at that time when they invade it, then the *sa-shush-gal* (*i.e.* Eannatum) of Utu, the powerful king by whom they have sworn, shall rise against Gishban."

"The Stèle des Vautours" has for its main object the commemoration of this treaty with Enakalli, patesi of Gishban, after the latter city had been defeated by Eannatum. But Eannatum was not satisfied with this; he imposes a heavy tribute upon Gishban, consisting of one karu of grain for Nina and one karu for Ningirsu, besides 144,000 (?) great karu. (Cone ii, 19 ff.) After having reduced Gishban to tranquillity, Eannatum also carries his victorious weapons against Erech (Warka) and Ur (the Ur of the Chaldeans), Ki-Utu (Larsa?) and Az (on the Persian Gulf) – the patesi of which latter city he kills – against Melimme and Arua. These latter cities were all in the neighbourhood of Shirpurla. Last of all he crushes and defeats Zuzu, king of Ukh. But even this does not exhaust the record of his victories. He becomes king of Kish – Kish, which for so long had itself been sovereign over Shirpurla. How this victory was accomplished is not evident from the inscriptions so far extant. Probably at some future time we may find an account of this war.

Eannatum was not only a hero in war, but also a wise administrator. He not only renewed three suburbs of his capital, one of which – Uruazagga – he even surrounded by a wall, but also improved the condition of Shirpurla itself by digging different canals, which he consecrated to his god Ningirsu: the Kishedin, which probably marked the boundary between the Guedin and Gishban, and which the Gishbanites had to swear never to cross; the Lummagirnuntashagazaggipadda along the territory of Ningirsu; and the Lummadimshar.

Urukagina, we have seen, was the first to build a canal, viz. one for Nina, which he called Nina-ki-tum-a. In the Cone of Entemena are also mentioned the canal Lummasirta, the Imdubba, and the Namnundakiggara. Here, then, we have the beginning of the most characteristic feature of Babylonia. Babylonia becomes the "land of canals," such as the psalmist had in mind when he wrote that touching psalm, "By the rivers of Babylon we sat down and wept." Further, Eannatum was not unmindful of his duty to the gods. He confesses that all that he is and that he has comes from his gods. Accordingly, he shows his gratitude by erecting sanctuaries for Enlil, Ninkharsag, Ningirsu, and Utu, and by restoring old buildings, which had been erected by his predecessors in honour of the gods, among which is to be found the Tirash.

In spite of the solemn promise of Gishban never to invade the territory of Shirpurla again, or to pass over the boundary canal, it very soon probably at the end of the reign of Eannatum, or better, at the beginning of that of Enannatum I – becomes rebellious as before. It invades the territory of Girsu, under the leadership of a certain Urlumma, patesi of Gishban, passes over the boundary canals which Eannatum had made, removes the steles erected on those canals in honour of Ningirsu, casts them into the fire, and even destroys the sanctuaries which Eannatum had built on one of these canals (*i.e.* the Namnundakigarra) in honour of Enlil, Ninkharsag, Ningirsu, and Utu, and lays waste the country. Enannatum promptly arises to chastise "those dogs" who had dared to break their solemn promise. Whether this battle was decisive or not, is not evident. It seems, however, that Enannatum I gained but a slight victory over Gishban.

For Entemena, the son of Enannatum, finds it necessary to renew the war with Gishban. "He puts Urlumma under the yoke," *i.e.* subdues him, forces him to return to his own country, and pursues him to the very midst of Gishban. This triumphant victory began with the decisive battle at the canal Lummasirta in the territory of Shirpurla. "Of his (*i.e.* Urlumma's) army sixty men on the side of the Lummasirta he left." On account of the severe loss Gishban fled. Entemena pursued after it, of which pursuit he records that "he left the bones of the soldiers (of Urlumma) in the field." Many of these soldiers of Gishban must have fallen, so many that Entemena was obliged "to bury their dead in five different places."

Arrived in Gishban, Entemena makes a certain priest of Innannaab-ki (or Nin-ab-ki), Ili by name, patesi of Gishban, probably after having deposed Urlumma. As a compensation for the new dignity thus conferred, Entemena commands Ili to build in the territory of Karkar – which latter had also become rebellious – boundary canals and some other buildings. The canal which Eannatum had built "from the great river (Euphrates?) to the Guedin" Entemena prolongs to the Tigris, and also repairs the other canals, which had been destroyed more or less by the Gishbanites, and dedicates them anew to Ningirsu and Nina.

Interesting also is the subscription of this Cone:

"When the men of Gishban the boundary canal of Ningirsu and the boundary canal of Nina – for the purpose of ravaging these territories – shall pass over, then may Enlil destroy the men of Gishban and the men of the mountains; may Ningirsu bring his curse over them; may he lift up his great power; may the soldiery of his (Entemena's) city be filled with bravery; may in the midst of the city be courage in their hearts."

With Lummadur, the son of Enannatum II, we arrive at the last representative of the house of Ur-Nina. Nothing but his name is known to us. From the absence of the title patesi behind his name, we may conclude that Enannatum II was the last patesi of the line of Ur-Nina, and that the old enemies, Kish and Gishban, have finally succeeded in overpowering Shirpurla.

It is hardly possible to look back upon this dynasty of Ur-Nina – which, as we have seen, dates from before 4000 BCE – without being impressed by the high civilization, cult, the many buildings and canals, military skill, and style of writing. Surely such a people as this could not have sprung into existence as a *deus ex machina*; it must have had its history – a history which presupposes a development of several centuries more. We would gladly follow up the history of the successors of Lummadur, but the lack of material prevents us from so doing. Passing, therefore, over an interval of about two hundred years in the history of Shirpurla, we turn now to the enemies of the "hero Ningirsu," *i.e.* Kish and Gishban (or, better, Gishukh).

KINGS OF KISH AND GISHBAN

c. 4200–4000 BCE

Various changes had befallen the land of Kish. When speaking of Enshagkushanna, we saw that Kish was defeated. It had, however, in course of time again increased in strength. Mesilim was able to establish himself as ruler over Shirpurla at the time of Lugalshuggur. His successors may have retained their glory for a considerable period. They were, however, not able to withstand the mighty weapons of Eannatum. This latter king not only shook off the old yoke which Kish had fastened upon Shirpurla, but even became "king of Kish." He must have reduced Kish to total impotence. Hence it came about that Kish was vanquished by another power, of which we shall hear shortly.

Just as Gishban, after its defeat by Eannatum, felt strong enough to disregard the solemn promise never to invade the territory of Shirpurla, so Kish, after its overthrow by Eannatum, seems to have rapidly regained its old power. For we find a certain En-ne-ugun, "king of Kish," who is also termed "king of the hordes of Gishban," desirous with the help of this latter city to extend the power of his capital. He was, however, defeated by a certain king of a certain country (the names cannot be read on account of the mutilated condition of the tablets). "His statue" – this unknown victorious king records, while relating his victory over En-ne-ugun – "his shining silver, the utensils, his property, he carried away, and presented them to Bel at Nippur."

MESOPOTAMIA

In course of time, however, and probably not very long after this defeat, Kish seems to have recovered from this blow. A certain Urzaguddu must have been very successful in his wars, for, in addition to his title "king of Kish," he calls himself also "king of ..." Unfortunately here again we have a gap, so that we cannot determine of what city he became king.

Very little is known of the next king of Kish, Lugaltarsi. At what time subsequent to Urzaguddu he lived we cannot tell. So much only is certain, that he reigned some time before Alusharshid, about 3850 BCE. His inscription – the only one so far known to us – is preserved in the British Museum in which he records the building of Bad-kisal in honour of Bel and Ishtar. We can now place Manishtusu and Alusharshid also among the kings of Kish. Both flourished somewhere about 3850 BCE, before Sargon I.

When reading the inscriptions of these kings, it is as if a new race were speaking to us, so widely different is the language used by these rulers from that of their predecessors, or of any other kings we have so far met with. We here find for the first time the so-called Semitic-Babylonian inscriptions. It is the same language which is also employed in the inscriptions of Sharganisharali and his successors, in that of Lasirab, king of Guti, and of Annubanini, king of Lalubu, all of whom were more or less contemporary with these kings of Kish. Scholars who believe that we must postulate two different races among the inhabitants of early Babylonia call the kings who wrote in this style "Semitic kings," while the others are referred to as the Sumerian population. As a result of this they read the names of these kings in a Semitic way. Manishtusu becomes Ma-an-is-tu-iro. Urumush becomes Alu-usharshid (*i.e.* "He – some deity – founded the city").

The inscription of Manishtusu, whom we place provisionally before Urumush, runs, "Manishtuirba, king of Kish, has presented (this) to Belit-Malkatu."

Of more importance, from the historical point of view as well as from the linguistic, is the next ruler who followed soon after the former. This ruler is Alusharshid. From his inscriptions – to be found in fifty-one fragments of vases, which have been excavated by the expedition of the University of Pennsylvania under Dr. Peters, and partly published by Hilprecht – we learn that he subdued Elam, on the eastern side of the Tigris, and the country of Bara'se (Para'se), from which lands he brought back these marble vases, and dedicated them to his gods at Nippur and Sippar.

For but a short period subsequent to Alusharshid does Kish seem to have enjoyed its old power. The might of Kish gave place to that of Agade, as we shall see shortly. Leaving, therefore, Kish for the present, we turn our attention to the other enemy of Old Shirpurla, viz. Gishban.

c. 4000 BCE

At about 4000 BCE, not long after the time of Eannatum, Gishban seems to have acquired new power and might. It directed its chief attention not so much towards Shirpurla as towards the south. Probably the rulers of Shirpurla had at this time been reduced to utter weakness by its old enemies

MESOPOTAMIA

(*i.e.* Kish and Gishban), of which enemies Gishban was destined to play the most important rôle in the development of ancient Babylonian history.

Lugalzaggisi, the son of Ukush, patesi of Gishban, we find at the head of the armies of Gishban, which he leads victoriously against the south. After Erech had opened its doors, the whole of Babylonia to the Persian Gulf fell an easy prey to the conquering hero. He, although originally only the son of a patesi, becomes king of Erech, nay, even king of the "whole world." "Enlil, king of the lands, has given to Lugulzaggisi the kingship of the world; *he* has made him to prosper before the world; *he* it was that had placed the lands under his sceptre – the lands 'from the rising of the sun even unto the going down of the same.' *He* it also was that gave him the tribute of those lands, which he made to dwell in peace, notwithstanding that they had been brought under a new régime." With these words Lugalzaggisi acknowledges, as the kings of Shirpurla did, that Enlil, and Enlil alone, had granted to him so unprecedented a dominion, extending from the lower sea of the Tigris and the Euphrates (*i.e.* the Persian Gulf) to the upper sea (*i.e.* the Mediterranean). Constituted thus "lord of the world," he now becomes its "summus episcopus." "In the sanctuaries of Kengi, as patesi of the lands, and in Erech, as high priest, they (the gods) established him."

To quote Hilprecht: "Babylonia, as a whole, had no fault to find with this new and powerful régime. The Sumerian civilization was directed into new channels from stagnation; the ancient cults between the lower Tigris and Euphrates began to revive and its temples to shine in new splendour." Thus, endowed with the highest temporal and spiritual power, he "makes Erech to abound in rejoicing." Nor does he forget the other representative cities of his domain: "Ur, like a steer, to the top of the heavens he raised." "Over Larsa, the beloved city of Shamash, he poured out waters of joy." His own native town and land receive chief attention: "Gishban, the beloved city of…to an unheard-of power he raised." He, as wise ruler and statesman, not only shows his good will and favour towards the larger and more influential cities, but also protects the weaker ones: "Ki-Innanna-ab he kept in an enclosure, like a sheep that is to be shorn."

Indeed, "Lugalzaggisi stands out from the dawn (?) of Babylonian history as a giant who deserves our full admiration for the work he accomplished."

Seeing that Semitisms occur in almost all the earliest inscriptions so far known to us, and that the rulers themselves may have been and probably were Semites – let us confess this – then the other question arises: At what time did the Semites come into the country, so as to induce the original inhabitants to employ expressions foreign to their own language? Where did they come from? To the last question, which has been repeatedly discussed by scholars, different answers have been given. Some make Africa the original home of the Semites; others Arabia; and Hilprecht, who last spoke of this problem, assigns for this purpose Kish, or better, Kharran some distance north of Babylonia. According to his theory, Lugalzaggisi, the great conqueror from Gishban (Kharran), was the first Semite to occupy any territory in Babylonia, and thus opened the way for the Semitic population. But Lugalzaggisi *does not antedate* Ur-Nina. Ur-Nina is a Semite, as we have seen, consequently Semites were in the country *before* Lugalzaggisi.

MESOPOTAMIA

Gishban is not Kharran, but the neighbouring state of Shirpurla; hence the Semites did not come from Kharran, but actually occupied already the whole country of Babylonia. Thus the two questions – when did the Semites invade Babylonia? and, whence did they come? – are still awaiting an answer. It is possible that some tablets may give us a key to this problem, but so far these tablets have not been found.

c. 6000–3800 BCE

But further, if the Semites at so early a time as 4500 BCE (Urukagina) had possession of Babylonia and had adopted the old language of the country, which language they interspersed with their own idiom, they must have been for a long time resident in the land. This would bring the immigration of the Semites back to at least 5000 BCE and earlier, when the Sumerian power began to decay. We must therefore push back the height of Sumerian influence to a yet more remote period.

Hence, whatever view we take in regard to the two peoples and their languages, we are led to the same general result: *Civilization and history must go back to at least 6000 BCE.*

THE FIRST DYNASTY OF UR

Of Ur – the biblical "Ur of the Chaldees" – we have already heard at the time of Eannatum. It was situated at the western side of the Euphrates, opposite the place where the Shatt-el-Khai flows into it. Up to the time of Lugalzaggisi it may not have been of very great importance. This latter ruler, however, "raised it like a steer to the top of the heaven," hence at no long period subsequent to Lugalzaggisi we meet two kings, father and son, ruling at Ur. It is not impossible that this dynasty may itself have brought about the overthrow of Lugalzaggisi, as to whose successors we have no information. Probably, also, it took possession of the more northern part of Babylonia (Nippur), for we find that both these kings present vases to Enlil, the "lord of the lands."

The names of these two monarchs forming the *first* dynasty of Ur are:

Lugalkigubnidudu, and his son (?); Lugalkisalsi.

Their dominion extended over Ur, Erech, and Nippur, probably also over Shirpurla, for the kings of the south could not have gained possession of Nippur without passing Shirpurla. This would explain why we know so very little about Shirpurla at this time. It is, however, remarkable that both these kings should call themselves first "kings of Erech," and then "kings of Ur"; while on the other hand, Lugalkigubnidudu expressly says that Enlil added (*tab*) the lordship (*nam-en*) to the kingship (*nam-lugal*), which lordship so added was Erech. We would expect that, if he were originally king of Ur, the title, "king of Ur," would come first. Here, then, we have an analogy to and a confirmation of the argument used in regard to Urzaguddu. The latter king had also two titles, viz. "king of Kish" and "king of ...," and it was argued that the latter title, "king of ...," was the original, *i.e.* Urzaguddu became later on "king of Kish." So here "king of Ur" was the original title; Lugalkigubnidudu subsequently became "king of Erech."

c. 4000–3800 BCE

How long this dynasty flourished, how many rulers were comprised in it, and when and by whom it was overthrown, we cannot tell. Probably, however, it was replaced by a mighty kingdom which arose in the north (that of Agade), destined to bear sway over "the four corners of the world."

Once more – before we leave southern Babylonia and pass over to the north – we have to direct our attention to Shirpurla. The traces which we possess of the life of Shirpurla and its patesis during this time (*i.e.* 4100-3800 BCE) are but fragmentary. Only one patesi is known to us from a tablet recently published by Thureau-Dangin, in the *Revue d'Assyriologie*. This patesi, Lugalanda by name, cannot have lived very long after Lummadur, for the writing of that tablet shows all the palæographic peculiarities of the inscriptions of Eannatum. Probably he belonged to those patesis over whom Lugalzaggisi or his successors may have ruled.

With the next two patesis, Lugalushumgal and his son (?) Ur-E, we arrive at the time of Sharganisharali [Sargon], 3800 BCE. A considerable gap in this period has still to be filled up. Let us hope that the future excavations, combined with the industry of the decipherer, will bring some light into this darkest of all periods in Old Babylonian history.

Mentioning only another patesi that belongs to this period, Ur-(dingir) Utu(?) – whose name is followed by patesi

KINGS OF AGADE

c. 3800 BCE

Agade, near the modern Abu-Habba, formed in olden times with Sippar a double city. It was situated near the Euphrates and north of Babylon. As early as 3800 BCE Semitic kings ruled in this city, extending their sceptres over the whole of Babylonia.

The first king, as far as our knowledge goes, was Sharganisharali, cited by us as Sargon I. He was the son of a certain Itti-Bel. This latter is neither called a king nor even a patesi. In this we may see a confirmation of the so-called "legend of Sargon," according to which this monarch was "of an inferior birth on his father's side," and so either a usurper or the founder of the dynasty of Agade. This legend – probably written in the eighth century BCE – purports to be a copy of an inscription written on a statue of this great king, and bears a certain similarity to the Biblical account of Moses. It reads: "Shargena, the powerful king, the king of Agade, am I. My mother was of noble family (?) (others: was poor), my father I did not know, whereas the brother of my father inhabited the mountains. My town was Azipiranu, which is situated on the bank of the Euphrates. My mother of noble family (?) (or, who was poor) conceived me and gave birth to me secretly. She put me into a basket of *shurru* (reeds?), and shut up the

MESOPOTAMIA

mouth (?) of it (?) with bitumen; she cast me into the river, which did not overwhelm (?) me. The river carried me away and brought me to Akki, the drawer of water. Akki, the drawer of water, took me up in...Akki, the drawer of water, reared me to boyhood. Akki, the drawer of water, made me a gardener. During my activity as gardener, Ishtar loved me. X + IV years I exercised dominion,...years I commanded the black-headed people (*i.e.* the Semites) and ruled them," etc. The rest of this legend tells us something about his campaign against Dur-ilu on the borders of Elam; it is, however, too fragmentary to be coherent.

In connection with this legend we would call the attention of the reader once more to the fact that not merely the identity of this Shargena with our Sharganisharali, his deeds and warlike expeditions recorded in the so-called "Tablet of Omens," with the date of his rule, have been doubted, but even his very existence. A series of new facts connected with the time of Naram-Sin and Sharganisharali have since come to light by the publication of a great number of contract-tablets written during the reign of these kings. These tablets are to be found in *Revue d'Assyriologie*, iv, No. iii. Hence it is now impossible to doubt the historicity of Sharganisharali, as was done by Niebuhr.

Down to the time of Hilprecht's publication of *Old Babylonian Inscriptions*, Part I, our knowledge of Sargon I was almost entirely drawn from the "legend" and the "Tablet of Omens". Hence it happened that the great deeds which were attributed to Sargon and Naram-Sin in the "Tablet of Omens" were said to be "purely legendary". Others thought that his deeds had been simply projected backwards; others again, not believing that Sargon I could have undertaken such expeditions and have become practically the "king of the four corners of the earth," invented another king Sargon.

Thanks to the excavations at Telloh and the industry of Thureau-Dangin, we are now in a position to prove that the statements of the "Tablet of Omens" are correct in almost every particular.

Let us hear what this "Tablet of Omens" has to say. Eleven of these "omens" are ascribed to Sargon and two to Naram-Sin. They generally begin with the phrase: "When the moon was in such and such position," then Sargon, etc.

The first omen records Sargon's expedition to and subjection of Elam.

The second tells how he marched to the land Akharri (*i.e.* the West-land), and subjected it, and that his army subjugated the *kibrati irbitta*, *i.e.* "the four corners of the world."

The third tells us that he brought sorrow upon Kish and Babylon, and built a city after the pattern (?) of Agade, and called it Ub-da-ki, *i.e.* "place (city) of the world."

The fourth records another expedition against the West and the taking possession of the four corners of the earth. So also the fifth omen.

The sixth omen is too fragmentary to yield any certain sense.

The seventh gives us a fuller account of the expedition against Akharri; he crosses the sea of the West and wages war against it for three years, takes it, erects there his statues, and transports the prisoners, whom he had taken, over land and sea.

The eighth describes the repairing of one of his palaces, which he calls "E-ki-a-am i-ni-lik," *i.e.* "the house": "so let us walk."

MESOPOTAMIA

In the next we hear of a campaign against a certain Kashtubilla of Kasalla, who had revolted. Sargon goes against him, conquers him and his army, and destroys the rebellious country.

The tenth probably is one of the most important. It reads: "Sargon, against whom under this omen the elders of the whole country had revolted, and in Agade had shut him up – Sargon went out, conquered them, and cast them down, subdued their army, and...."

The last omen tells us something about Sargon's campaign against the land Suri, how he overcame it, and took it, and how he destroyed its army.

The two omens relating to Naram-Sin record a campaign against Apirak (Omen i) and against Magan (Omen ii). In both expeditions Naram-Sin was so successful that he even took captive the kings of these countries, viz.: Resh-Ramman (Adad), king of Apirak, and N. N. king of Magan.

According to this "Tablet of Omens," then Sargon I subdued Elam, the "West-land," brought woe upon Babylon and Kish, conquered the country Kasalla, suppressed a revolt which had arisen against him while on his expeditions, and finally subdued the land Suri "in its totality."

c. 3750–2700 BCE

Sargon's son and successor, Naram-Sin, followed up the successes of his father by marching into Magan, whose king he took captive. He assumed the imperial title of "king of the four zones," and, like his father, was addressed as a "god." He is even called "the god of Agade" (Accad), reminding us of the divine honours claimed by the Pharaohs of Egypt, whose territory now adjoined that of Babylonia. A finely executed bas-relief, representing Naram-Sin, and bearing a striking resemblance to early Egyptian art in many of its features, has been found at Diarbekir. Babylonian art, however, had already attained a high degree of excellence; two seal cylinders of the time of Sargon are among the most beautiful specimens of the gem-cutter's art ever discovered. The empire was bound together by roads, along which there was a regular postal service, and clay seals, which took the place of stamps, are now in the Louvre bearing the names of Sargon and his son. A cadastral survey seems also to have been instituted, and one of the documents relating to it states that a certain Uru-Malik, whose name appears to indicate his Canaanitish origin, was governor of the land of the Amorites, as Syria and Palestine were called by the Babylonians. It is probable that the first collection of astronomical observations and terrestrial omens was made for a library established by Sargon.

Bingani-shar-ali was the son of Naram-Sin, but we do not yet know whether he followed his father on the throne. Another son was high priest of the city of Tutu, and in the name of his daughter, Lipus-Eaum, a priestess of Sin, some scholars have seen that of the Hebrew deity, Yahveh. The Babylonian god, Ea, however, is more likely to be meant.

THE KINGS OF UR

The fall of Sargon's empire seems to have been as sudden as its rise. The seat of supreme power in Babylonia was shifted southward to Erech, Isin, and Ur.

At least three dynasties appear to have reigned at Ur and claimed suzerainty over the other Babylonian states. One of these, under Gungunu, succeeded in transferring the capital of Babylonia from Isin to Ur. It is still uncertain whether Gungunu belonged to the second or third dynasty of Ur; if to the second, among his successors would have been Ur-Gur, a great builder, who built or restored the temples of the Moon-god at Ur, of the Sun-god at Larsa, of Ishtar at Erech, and of Bel at Nippur. His son and successor was Dungi II, one of whose vassals was Gudea the *patesi* or high priest of Lagash [Shirpurla]. Gudea was also a great builder, and the materials for his buildings and statues were brought from all parts of western Asia, cedar wood from the Amanus Mountains, quarried stones from Lebanon, copper from northern Arabia, gold and precious stones from the desert between Palestine and Egypt, dolerite from Magan (the Sinaitic peninsula), and timber from Dilmun in the Persian Gulf. Some of his statues, now in the Louvre, are carved out of Sinaitic dolerite, and on the lap of one of them is the plan of his palace, with the scale of measurement attached. Six of the statues bore special names, and offerings were made to them as to the statues of the gods. Gudea claims to have conquered Anshan in Elam, and was succeeded by his son, Ur-Ningirsu. His date may be provisionally fixed at 2700 BCE.

c. 2700–2340 BCE

The high priests of Lagash still owned allegiance to Ur, when the last dynasty of Ur was dominant in Babylonia. The dynasty was Semitic, not Sumerian, though one of its kings was Dungi II.

He was followed by Bur-Sin II, Gimil-Sin, and Ine-Sin, whose power extended to the Mediterranean, and of whose reigns we possess a large number of contemporaneous monuments in the shape of contracts and similar business documents, as well as chronological tables. After the fall of the dynasty, Babylonia passed under foreign influence.

ACCESSION OF A SOUTH ARABIAN DYNASTY

Sumu-abi ("Shem is my father"), from southern Arabia (or perhaps Canaan), made himself master of northern Babylonia, while Elamite invaders occupied the south. After a reign of fourteen years, Sumu-abi was succeeded by his son, Sumu-la-ilu, in the fifth year of whose reign the fortress of Babylon was built, and the city became for the first time a capital. Rival kings, Pungun-ila and Immeru, are mentioned in the contract tablets as reigning at the same time as Sumu-la-ilu (or Samu-la-ilu); and under Sin-muballit, the great-grandson of Sumu-la-ilu, the Elamites laid the whole of the country under tribute, and made Eri-Aku, or Arioch, called Rim-Sin by his Semitic subjects, king of Larsa. Eri-Aku was the son of Kudur-Mabuk, who was prince of Yamudbal [or E-mutbal], on the eastern border of Babylonia, and also "governor of Syria."

The Elamite supremacy was at last shaken off by the son and successor of Sin-muballit, Khammurabi, whose name is also written Ammurapi and Khammuram, and who was the Amraphel of Genesis xiv. 1. The Elamites, under their king, Kudur-Lagamar or Chedorlaomer, seem to have taken

Babylon and destroyed the temple of Bel-Merodach; but Khammurabi retrieved his fortunes, and in the thirtieth year of his reign (in 2340 BCE), he overthrew the Elamite forces in a decisive battle and drove them out of Babylonia. The next two years were occupied in adding Larsa and Yamudbal to his dominion, and in forming Babylonia into a single monarchy, the head of which was Babylon.

A great literary revival followed the recovery of Babylonian independence, and the rule of Babylon was obeyed as far as the shores of the Mediterranean.

BABYLON

In this chapter, Donald A. Mackenzie focuses on the Old Babylonian period, around the first half of the second millennium. From a modern point of view, the introductory part and architectural sketch of Babylon is somewhat hampered by an overreliance on Herodotus. If at all trustworthy, Herodotus would only have known of the Babylon of the late first millennium.

Mackenzie continues with Old Babylonian social history, including a long section on the role of women, as it can be gleaned from the Code of Ḫammurapi. Nevertheless, this must be read critically since the Code of Ḫammurapi provides a select and ideal picture of society for the purpose of legitimizing the king. In association with the 'law of an eye for an eye and a tooth for a tooth', in the next part he imagines the role of medical professions and practices. Again having little to do with the Old Babylonian period, Herodotus and Neo-Assyrian sources are mixed into this discussion somewhat too eagerly.

The final section of this chapter recounts the political history of this period with greater historical accuracy than the previous parts.

BUILDINGS, LAWS AND CUSTOMS OF BABYLON

The rise of Babylon inaugurated a new era in the history of Western Asia. Coincidentally the political power of the Sumerians came to an end. It had been paralysed by the Elamites, who, towards the close of the Dynasty of Isin, successfully overran the southern district and endeavoured to extend their sway over the whole valley. Two Elamite kings, Warad-Sin and his brother Rim-Sin, struggled with the rulers of Babylon for supremacy, and for a time it appeared as if the intruders from the east were to establish themselves permanently as a military aristocracy over Sumer and Akkad. But the Semites were strongly reinforced by new settlers of the same blended stock who swarmed from the land of the Amorites. Once again Arabia was pouring into Syria vast hordes of its surplus population, with the result that ethnic disturbances were constant and widespread. This migration is termed the Canaanitic or Amorite: it flowed into Mesopotamia and across Assyria, while it supplied the "driving power" which secured the ascendancy of the Hammurabi Dynasty at Babylon. Indeed, the ruling family which came into prominence there is believed to have been of Canaanitic origin.

Once Babylon became the metropolis it retained its pre-eminence until the end. Many political changes took place during its long and chequered history, but no rival city in the south ever attained to its splendour and greatness. Whether its throne was occupied by Amorite or Kassite, Assyrian or Chaldean, it was invariably found to be the most effective centre of administration for the lower Tigro-Euphrates valley. Some of the Kassite monarchs, however, showed a preference for Nippur.

Of its early history little is known. It was overshadowed in turn by Kish and Umma, Lagash and Erech, and may have been little better than a great village when Akkad rose into prominence. Sargon I, the royal gardener, appears to have interested himself in its development, for it was recorded that he cleared its trenches and strengthened its fortifications. The city occupied a strategic position, and probably assumed importance on that account as well as a trading and industrial centre. Considerable wealth had accumulated at Babylon when the Dynasty of Ur reached the zenith of its power. It is recorded that King Dungi plundered its famous "Temple of the High Head", E-sagila, which some identify with the Tower of Babel, so as to secure treasure for Ea's temple at Eridu, which he specially favoured. His vandalistic raid, like that of the Gutium, or men of Kutu, was remembered for long centuries afterwards, and the city god was invoked at the time to cut short his days.

No doubt, Hammurabi's Babylon closely resembled the later city so vividly described by Greek writers, although it was probably not of such great dimensions. According to Herodotus, it occupied an exact square on the broad plain, and had a circumference of sixty of our miles. "While such is its size," the historian wrote, "in magnificence there is no other city that approaches to it." Its walls were eighty-seven feet thick and three hundred and fifty feet high, and each side of the square was fifteen miles in length. The whole city was surrounded by a deep, broad canal or moat, and the river Euphrates ran through it.

"Here," continued Herodotus, "I may not omit to tell the use to which the mould dug out of the great moat was turned, nor the manner in which the wall was wrought. As fast as they dug the moat the soil which they got from the cutting was made into bricks, and when a sufficient number were completed they baked the bricks in kilns. Then they set to building, and began with bricking the borders of the moat, after which they proceeded to construct the wall itself, using throughout for their cement hot bitumen, and interposing a layer of wattled reeds at every thirtieth course of the bricks. On the top, along the edges of the wall, they constructed buildings of a single chamber facing one another, leaving between them room for a four-horse chariot to turn. In the circuit of the wall are a hundred gates, all of brass, with brazen lintels and side posts." These were the gates referred to by Isaiah when God called Cyrus:

> *I will loose the loins of kings, to open before him the two leaved gates; and the gates shall not be shut: I will go before thee, and make the crooked places straight; I will break in pieces the gates of brass, and cut in sunder the bars of iron.*

The outer wall was the main defence of the city, but there was also an inner wall less thick but not much inferior in strength. In addition, a fortress stood in each division of the city. The king's palace and the temple of Bel Merodach were surrounded by walls.

All the main streets were perfectly straight, and each crossed the city from gate to gate, a distance of fifteen miles, half of them being interrupted by the river, which had to be ferried. As there were twenty-five gates on each side of the outer wall, the great thoroughfares numbered fifty in all, and there were six hundred and seventy-six squares, each over two miles in circumference. From Herodotus we gather that the houses were three or four storeys high, suggesting that the tenement system was not unknown, and according to Q. Curtius, nearly half of the area occupied by the city was taken up by gardens within the squares.

Architecture

In Greek times Babylon was famous for the hanging or terraced gardens of the "new palace", which had been erected by Nebuchadnezzar II. These occupied a square which was more than a quarter of a mile in circumference. Great stone terraces, resting on arches, rose up like a giant stairway to a height of about three hundred and fifty feet, and the whole structure was strengthened by a surrounding wall over twenty feet in thickness. So deep were the layers of mould on each terrace that fruit trees were grown amidst the plants of luxuriant foliage and the brilliant Asian flowers. Water for irrigating the gardens was raised from the river by a mechanical contrivance to a great cistern situated on the highest terrace, and it was prevented from leaking out of the soil by layers of reeds and bitumen and sheets of lead. Spacious apartments, luxuriously furnished and decorated, were constructed in the spaces between the arches and were festooned by flowering creepers. A broad stairway ascended from terrace to terrace.

The old palace stood in a square nearly four miles in circumference, and was strongly protected by three walls, which were decorated by sculptures in low relief, representing battle scenes and scenes of the chase and royal ceremonies. Winged bulls with human heads guarded the main entrance.

Another architectural feature of the city was E-sagila, the temple of Bel Merodach, known to the Greeks as "Jupiter-Belus". The high wall which enclosed it had gates of solid brass. "In the middle of the precinct", wrote Herodotus, "there was a tower of solid masonry, a furlong in length and breadth, upon which was raised a second tower, and on that a third, and so on up to eight. The ascent to the top is on the outside, by a path which winds round all the towers. When one is about halfway up, one finds a resting-place and seats, where persons are wont to sit some time on their way to the summit. On the topmost tower there is a spacious temple, and inside the temple stands a couch of unusual size, richly adorned, with a golden table by its side. There is no statue of any kind set up in the place, nor is the chamber occupied of nights by anyone but a single native woman, who, as the Chaldaeans, the priests of this god, affirm, is chosen for himself by the deity out of all the women of the land."

A woman who was the "wife of Amon" also slept in that god's temple at Thebes in Egypt. A similar custom was observed in Lycia.

"Below, in the same precinct," continued Herodotus, "there is a second temple, in which is a sitting figure of Jupiter, all of gold. Before the figure stands a large golden table, and the throne whereon it sits, and the base on which the throne is placed, are likewise of pure gold.... Outside the temple are two altars, one of solid gold, on which it is only lawful to offer sucklings; the other, a common altar, but of great size, on which the full-grown animals are sacrificed. It is also on the great altar that the Chaldaeans burn the frankincense, which is offered to the amount of a thousand talents' weight, every year, at the festival of the god. In the time of Cyrus there was likewise in this temple a figure of a man, twelve cubits high, entirely of solid gold.... Besides the ornaments which I have mentioned, there are a large number of private offerings in this holy precinct."

The city wall and river gates were closed every night, and when Babylon was besieged the people were able to feed themselves. The gardens and small farms were irrigated by canals, and canals also controlled the flow of the River Euphrates. A great dam had been formed above the town to store the surplus water during inundation and increase the supply when the river sank to its lowest.

In Hammurabi's time the river was crossed by ferry boats, but long ere the Greeks visited the city a great bridge had been constructed. So completely did the fierce Sennacherib destroy the city that most of the existing ruins date from the period of Nebuchadnezzar II.

Society and Laws

Our knowledge of the social life of Babylon and the territory under its control is derived chiefly from the Hammurabi Code of laws, of which an almost complete copy was discovered at Susa, towards the end of 1901, by the De Morgan expedition. The laws were inscribed on a stele of black diorite 7 ft. 3 in. high, with a circumference at the base of 6 ft. 2 in. and at the top of 5 ft. 4 in. This important relic of an ancient law-abiding people had been broken in three pieces, but when these were joined together it was found that the text was not much impaired. On one side are twenty-eight columns and on the other sixteen. Originally there were in all nearly 4000 lines of inscriptions, but five columns, comprising about 300 lines, had been erased to give space, it is conjectured, for the name of the invader who carried the stele away, but unfortunately the record was never made.

On the upper part of the stele, which is now one of the treasures of the Louvre, Paris, King Hammurabi salutes, with his right hand reverently upraised, the sun god Shamash, seated on his throne, at the summit of E-sagila, by whom he is being presented with the stylus with which to inscribe the legal code. Both figures are heavily bearded, but have shaven lips and chins. The god wears a conical headdress and a flounced robe suspended from his left shoulder, while the king has assumed a round dome-shaped hat and a flowing garment which almost sweeps the ground.

It is gathered from the Code that there were three chief social grades – the aristocracy, which included landowners, high officials and administrators; the freemen, who might be wealthy merchants or small landholders; and the slaves. The fines imposed for a given offence upon wealthy men were much heavier than those imposed upon the poor. Lawsuits were heard in courts. Witnesses were required to tell the truth, "affirming before the god what they knew", and perjurers were severely dealt with; a man who gave false evidence in connection with a capital charge was put to death. A strict watch was also kept over the judges, and if one was found to have willingly convicted a prisoner on insufficient evidence he was fined and degraded.

Theft was regarded as a heinous crime, and was invariably punished by death. Thieves included those who made purchases from minors or slaves without the sanction of elders or trustees. Sometimes the accused was given the alternative of paying a fine, which might exceed by ten or even thirty-fold the value of the article or animal he had appropriated. It was imperative that lost property should be restored. If the owner of an article of which he had been wrongfully deprived found it in possession of a man who declared that he had purchased it from another, evidence was taken in court. When it happened that the seller was proved to have been the thief, the capital penalty was imposed. On the other hand, the alleged purchaser was dealt with in like manner if he failed to prove his case. Compensation for property stolen by a brigand was paid by the temple, and the heirs of a man slain by a brigand within the city had to be compensated by the local authority.

Betrothal, Marriage and Divorce

Of special interest are the laws which relate to the position of women. In this connection reference may first be made to the marriage-by-auction custom, which Herodotus described as follows: "Once a year in each village the maidens of age to marry were collected all together into one place, while the men stood round them in a circle. Then a herald called up the damsels one by one, and offered them for sale. He began with the most beautiful. When she was sold for no small sum of money, he offered for sale the one who came next to her in beauty. All of them were sold to be wives. The richest of the

Babylonians who wished to wed bid against each other for the loveliest maidens, while the humbler wife-seekers, who were indifferent about beauty, took the more homely damsels with marriage portions. For the custom was that when the herald had gone through the whole number of the beautiful damsels, he should then call up the ugliest – a cripple, if there chanced to be one – and offer her to the men, asking who would agree to take her with the smallest marriage portion. And the man who offered to take the smallest sum had her assigned to him. The marriage portions were furnished by the money paid for the beautiful damsels, and thus the fairer maidens portioned out the uglier. No one was allowed to give his daughter in marriage to the man of his choice, nor might anyone carry away the damsel whom he had purchased without finding bail really and truly to make her his wife; if, however, it turned out that they did not agree, the money might be paid back. All who liked might come, even from distant villages, and bid for the women."

This custom is mentioned by other writers, but it is impossible to ascertain at what period it became prevalent in Babylonia and by whom it was introduced. Herodotus understood that it obtained also in "the Illyrian tribe of the Eneti", which was reputed to have entered Italy with Antenor after the fall of Troy, and has been identified with the Venetians of later times. But the ethnic clue thus afforded is exceedingly vague. There is no direct reference to the custom in the Hammurabi Code, which reveals a curious blending of the principles of "Father right" and "Mother right". A girl was subject to her father's will; he could dispose of her as he thought best, and she always remained a member of his family; after marriage she was known as the daughter of so and so rather than the wife of so and so. But marriage brought her freedom and the rights of citizenship. The power vested in her father was never transferred to her husband.

A father had the right to select a suitable spouse for his daughter, and she could not marry without his consent. That this law did not prevent "love matches" is made evident by the fact that provision was made in the Code for the marriage of a free woman with a male slave, part of whose estate in the event of his wife's death could be claimed by his master.

When a betrothal was arranged, the father fixed the "bride price", which was paid over before the contract could be concluded, and he also provided a dowry. The amount of the "bride price" might, however, be refunded to the young couple to give them a start in life. If, during the interval between betrothal and marriage, the man "looked upon another woman", and said to his father-in-law, "I will not marry your daughter", he forfeited the "bride price" for breach of promise of marriage.

A girl might also obtain a limited degree of freedom by taking vows of celibacy and becoming one of the vestal virgins, or nuns, who were attached to the temple of the sun god. She did not, however, live a life of entire seclusion. If she received her due proportion of her father's estate, she could make business investments within certain limits. She was not, for instance, allowed to own a wine shop, and if she even entered one she was burned at the stake. Once she took these vows she had to observe them until the end of her days. If she married, as she might do to obtain the legal status of a married woman and enjoy the privileges of that position, she denied her husband conjugal rites, but provided him with a concubine who might bear him children, as Sarah did to Abraham. These nuns must not be confused with the unmoral women who were associated with the temples of Ishtar and other love goddesses of shady repute.

The freedom secured by a married woman had its legal limitations. If she became a widow, for instance, she could not remarry without the consent of a judge, to whom she was expected to show good cause for the step she proposed to take. Punishments for breaches of the marriage law were severe. Adultery was a capital crime; the guilty parties were bound together and thrown into the river. If it happened, however, that the wife of a prisoner went to reside with another man on account of poverty, she was acquitted and allowed to return to her husband after his release. In cases where no plea of poverty could be urged the erring women were drowned. The wife of a soldier who had been taken prisoner by an enemy was entitled to a third part of her husband's estate if her son was a minor, the remainder was held in trust. The husband could enter into possession of all his property again if he happened to return home.

Divorce was easily obtained. A husband might send his wife away either because she was childless or because he fell in love with another woman. Incompatibility of temperament was also recognized as sufficient reason for separation. A woman might hate her husband and wish to leave him. "If", the Code sets forth, "she is careful and is without blame, and is neglected by her husband who has deserted her", she can claim release from the marriage contract. But if she is found to have another lover, and is guilty of neglecting her duties, she is liable to be put to death.

A married woman possessed her own property. Indeed, the value of her marriage dowry was always vested in her. When, therefore, she divorced her husband, or was divorced by him, she was entitled to have her dowry refunded and to return to her father's house. Apparently she could claim maintenance from her father.

A woman could have only one husband, but a man could have more than one wife. He might marry a secondary wife, or concubine, because he was without offspring, but "the concubine", the Code lays down, "shall not rank with the wife". Another reason for second marriage recognized by law was a wife's state of health. In such circumstances a man could not divorce his sickly wife. He had to support her in his house as long as she lived.

Children were the heirs of their parents, but if a man during his lifetime gifted his property to his wife, and confirmed it on "a sealed tablet", the children could have no claim, and the widow was entitled to leave her estate to those of her children she preferred; but she could not will any portion of it to her brothers. In ordinary cases the children of a first marriage shared equally the estate of a father with those of a second marriage. If a slave bore children to her employer, their right to inheritance depended on whether or not the father had recognized them as his offspring during his lifetime. A father might legally disown his son if the young man was guilty of criminal practices.

The legal rights of a vestal virgin were set forth in detail. If she had received no dowry from her father when she took vows of celibacy, she could claim after his death one-third of the portion of a son. She could will her estate to anyone she favoured, but if she died intestate her brothers were her heirs. When, however, her estate consisted of fields or gardens allotted to her by her father, she could not disinherit her legal heirs. The fields or gardens might be worked during her lifetime by her brothers if they paid rent, or she might employ a manager on the "share system".

Vestal virgins and married women were protected against the slanderer. Any man who "pointed the finger" against them unjustifiably was charged with the offence before a judge, who could sentence him to have his forehead branded. It was not difficult, therefore, in ancient Babylonia to discover the men who made malicious and unfounded statements regarding an innocent woman. Assaults on women were punished according to the victim's rank; even slaves were protected.

Business and Land Laws

Women appear to have monopolized the drink traffic. At any rate, there is no reference to male wine sellers. A female publican had to conduct her business honestly, and was bound to accept a legal tender. If she refused corn and demanded silver, when the value of the silver by "grand weight" was below the price of corn, she was prosecuted and punished by being thrown into the water. Perhaps she was simply ducked. As much may be inferred from the fact that when she was found guilty of allowing rebels to meet in her house, she was put to death.

The land laws were strict and exacting. A tenant could be penalized for not cultivating his holding properly. The rent paid was a proportion of the crop, but the proportion could be fixed according to the average yield of a district, so that a careless or inefficient tenant had to bear the brunt of his neglect or want of skill. The punishment for allowing a field to lie fallow was to make a man hoe and sow it and then hand it over to his landlord, and this applied even to a man who leased unreclaimed land which he had contracted to cultivate. Damage done to fields by floods after the rent was paid was borne by the cultivator; but if it occurred before the corn was reaped the landlord's share was calculated in proportion to the amount of the yield which was recovered. Allowance was also made for poor harvests, when the shortage was not due to the neglect of the tenant, but to other causes, and no interest was paid for borrowed money even if the farm suffered from the depredations of the tempest god; the moneylender had to share risks with borrowers. Tenants who neglected their dykes, however, were not exempted from their legal liabilities, and their whole estates could be sold to reimburse their creditors.

The industrious were protected against the careless. Men who were negligent about controlling the water supply, and caused floods by opening irrigation ditches which damaged the crops of their neighbours, had to pay for the losses sustained, the damages being estimated according to the average yield of a district. A tenant who allowed his sheep to stray on to a neighbour's pasture had to pay a heavy fine in corn at the harvest season, much in excess of the value of the grass cropped by his sheep. Gardeners were similarly subject to strict laws.

All business contracts had to be conducted according to the provisions of the Code, and in every case it was necessary that a proper record should be made on clay tablets. As a rule a dishonest tenant or trader had to pay sixfold the value of the sum under dispute if the judge decided in court against his claim.

The law of an eye for an eye and a tooth for a tooth was strictly observed in Babylonia. A freeman who destroyed an eye of a freeman had one of his own destroyed; if he broke a bone, he had a bone broken. Fines were imposed, however, when a slave was injured. For striking a gentleman, a commoner received sixty lashes, and the son who smote his father had his hands cut off. A slave might have his ears cut off for assaulting his master's son.

Doctors must have found their profession an extremely risky one. No allowance was made for what is nowadays known as a "professional error". A doctor's hands were cut off if he opened a wound with a metal knife and his patient afterwards died, or if a man lost his eye as the result of an operation. A slave who died under a doctor's hands had to be replaced by a slave, and if a slave lost his eye, the doctor had to pay half the man's market value to the owner. Professional fees were fixed according to a patient's rank. Gentlemen had to pay five shekels of silver to a doctor who set a bone or restored diseased flesh, commoners three shekels, and masters for their slaves two shekels. There was also a scale of fees for treating domesticated animals, and it was not overgenerous. An unfortunate surgeon who undertook to treat an ox or ass suffering from a severe wound had to pay a quarter of its price to its owner if it happened to die. A shrewd farmer who was threatened with the loss of an animal must have been extremely anxious to engage the services of a surgeon.

Physicians

It is not surprising, after reviewing this part of the Hammurabi Code, to find Herodotus stating bluntly that the Babylonians had no physicians. "When a man is ill", he wrote, "they lay him in the public square, and the passers-by come up to him, and if they have ever had his disease themselves, or have known anyone who has suffered from it, they give him advice, recommending him to do whatever they found good in their own case, or in the case known to them; and no one is allowed to pass the sick man in silence without asking him what his ailment is." One might imagine that Hammurabi had legislated the medical profession out of existence, were it not that letters have been found in the Assyrian library of Ashur-banipal which indicate that skilled physicians were held in high repute. It is improbable, however, that they were numerous. The risks they ran in Babylonia may account for their ultimate disappearance in that country.

No doubt patients received some benefit from exposure in the streets in the sunlight and fresh air, and perhaps, too, from some of the old wives' remedies which were gratuitously prescribed by passers-by. In Egypt, where certain of the folk cures were recorded on papyri, quite effective treatment was occasionally given, although the "medicines" were exceedingly repugnant as a rule; ammonia, for instance, was taken with the organic substances found in farmyards. Elsewhere some wonderful instances of excellent folk cures have come to light, especially among isolated peoples, who have received them interwoven in their immemorial traditions. A medical man who has investigated this interesting subject in the Scottish Highlands has shown that "the simple observation of the people was the starting-point of our fuller knowledge, however complete we may esteem it to be". For dropsy and heart troubles, foxglove, broom tops, and juniper berries, which have reputations "as old as the hills", are "the most reliable medicines in our scientific armoury at the present time". These discoveries of the ancient folks have been "merely elaborated in later days". Ancient cures for indigestion are still in use. "Tar water, which was a remedy for chest troubles, especially for those of a consumptive nature, has endless imitations in our day"; it was also "the favourite remedy for skin diseases". No doubt the present inhabitants of Babylonia, who utilize bitumen as a germicide, are perpetuating an ancient folk custom.

This medical man who is being quoted adds: "The whole matter may be summed up, that we owe infinitely more to the simple nature study of our people in the great affair of health than we owe to all the later science."

Herodotus, commenting on the custom of patients taking a census of folk cures in the streets, said it was one of the wisest institutions of the Babylonian people. It is to be regretted that he did not enter into details regarding the remedies which were in greatest favour in his day. His data would have been useful for comparative purposes.

So far as can be gathered from the clay tablets, faith cures were not unknown, and there was a good deal of quackery. If surgery declined, as a result of the severe restrictions which hampered progress in an honourable profession, magic flourished like tropical fungi. Indeed, the worker of spells was held in high repute, and his operations were in most cases allowed free play. There are only two paragraphs in the Hammurabi Code which deal with magical practices. It is set forth that if one man cursed another and the curse could not be justified, the perpetrator of it must suffer the death penalty. Provision was also made for discovering whether a spell had been legally imposed or not. The victim was expected to plunge himself in a holy river. If the river carried him away it was held as proved that he deserved his punishment, and "the layer of the spell" was given possession of the victim's house. A man who could swim was deemed to be innocent; he claimed the residence of "the layer of the spell", who was promptly put to death. With this interesting glimpse of ancient superstition the famous Code opens, and then strikes a modern note by detailing the punishments for perjury and the unjust administration of law in the courts.

The poor sufferers who gathered at street corners in Babylon to make mute appeal for cures believed that they were possessed by evil spirits. Germs of disease were depicted by lively imaginations as invisible demons, who derived nourishment from the human body. When a patient was wasted with disease, growing thinner and weaker and more bloodless day by day, it was believed that a merciless vampire was sucking his veins and devouring his flesh. It had therefore to be expelled by performing a magical ceremony and repeating a magical formula. The demon was either driven or enticed away.

A magician had to decide in the first place what particular demon was working evil. He then compelled its attention and obedience by detailing its attributes and methods of attack, and perhaps by naming it. Thereafter he suggested how it should next act by releasing a raven, so that it might soar towards the clouds like that bird, or by offering up a sacrifice which it received for nourishment and as compensation. Another popular method was to fashion a waxen figure of the patient and prevail upon the disease demon to enter it. The figure was then carried away to be thrown in the river or burned in a fire.

Occasionally a quite effective cure was included in the ceremony. As much is suggested by the magical treatment of toothache. First of all the magician identified the toothache demon as "the worm". Then he recited its history, which is as follows:

> After Anu created the heavens, the heavens created the earth, the earth created the rivers, the rivers created the canals, the canals created the marshes, and last of all the marshes created "the worm".

This display of knowledge compelled the worm to listen, and no doubt the patient was able to indicate to what degree it gave evidence of its agitated mind. The magician continued:

> Came the worm and wept before Shamash,
> Before Ea came her tears:
> "What wilt thou give me for my food,
> What wilt thou give me to devour?"

One of the deities answered: "I will give thee dried bones and scented ... wood"; but the hungry worm protested:

"Nay, what are these dried bones of thine to me?
Let me drink among the teeth;
And set me on the gums
That I may devour the blood of the teeth,
And of their gums destroy their strength –
Then shall I hold the bolt of the door."

The magician provided food for "the worm", and the following is his recipe: "Mix beer, the plant sa-kil-bir, and oil together; put it on the tooth and repeat incantation." No doubt this mixture soothed the pain, and the sufferer must have smiled gladly when the magician finished his incantation by exclaiming:

"So must thou say this, O Worm!
May Ea smite thee with the might of his fist."

Headaches were no doubt much relieved when damp cloths were wrapped round a patient's head and scented wood was burned beside him, while the magician, in whom so much faith was reposed, droned out a mystical incantation. The curative water was drawn from the confluence of two streams and was sprinkled with much ceremony. In like manner the evil-eye curers, who still operate in isolated districts in these islands, draw water from under bridges "over which the dead and the living pass", and mutter charms and lustrate victims.

Headaches were much dreaded by the Babylonians. They were usually the first symptoms of fevers, and the demons who caused them were supposed to be bloodthirsty and exceedingly awesome. According to the charms, these invisible enemies of man were of the brood of Nergal. No house could be protected against them. They entered through keyholes and chinks of doors and windows; they crept like serpents and stank like mice; they had lolling tongues like hungry dogs.

Magicians baffled the demons by providing a charm. If a patient "touched iron" – meteoric iron, which was the "metal of heaven" – relief could be obtained. Or, perhaps, the sacred water would dispel the evil one; as the drops trickled from the patient's face, so would the fever spirit trickle away. When a pig was offered up in sacrifice as a substitute for a patient, the wicked spirit was commanded to depart and allow a kindly spirit to take its place – an indication that the Babylonians, like the Germanic peoples, believed that they were guarded by spirits who brought good luck.

The Origins of Art

The numerous incantations which were inscribed on clay tablets and treasured in libraries do not throw much light on the progress of medical knowledge, for the genuine folk cures were regarded as of secondary importance, and were not as a rule recorded. But these metrical compositions are of special interest, in so far as they indicate how poetry originated and achieved widespread popularity among ancient peoples. Like the religious dance, the earliest poems were used for magical purposes. They were composed in the first place by men and women who were supposed to be inspired in the literal sense; that is, possessed by spirits. Primitive man associated "spirit" with "breath", which was the "air of life", and identical with wind. The poetical magician drew in a "spirit", and thus received inspiration, as he stood on some sacred spot on the mountain summit, amidst forest solitudes, beside a whispering stream, or on the sounding shore. As Burns has sung:

> *The muse, nae poet ever fand her,*
> *Till by himsel' he learn'd to wander,*
> *Adown some trottin' burn's meander,*
> *An' no think lang:*
> *O sweet to stray, an' pensive ponder*
> *A heart-felt sang!*

Or, perhaps, the bard received inspiration by drinking magic water from the fountain called Hippocrene, or the skaldic mead which dripped from the moon.

The ancient poet did not sing for the mere love of singing: he knew nothing about "Art for Art's sake". His object in singing appears to have been intensely practical. The world was inhabited by countless hordes of spirits, which were believed to be ever exercising themselves to influence mankind. The spirits caused suffering; they slew victims; they brought misfortune; they were also the source of good or "luck". Man regarded spirits emotionally; he conjured them with emotion; he warded off their attacks with emotion; and his emotions were given rhythmical expression by means of metrical magical charms.

Poetic imagery had originally a magical significance; if the ocean was compared to a dragon, it was because it was supposed to be inhabited by a storm-causing dragon; the wind whispered because a spirit whispered in it. Love lyrics were charms to compel the love god to wound or possess a maiden's heart – to fill it, as an Indian charm sets forth, with "the yearning of the Apsaras (fairies)"; satires conjured up evil spirits to injure a victim; and heroic narratives chanted at graves were statements made to the god of battle, so that he might award the mighty dead by transporting him to the Valhal of Odin or Swarga of Indra.

Similarly, music had magical origin as an imitation of the voices of spirits – of the piping birds who were "Fates", of the wind high and low, of the thunder roll, of the bellowing sea. So the god Pan piped on his reed bird-like notes, Indra blew his thunder horn, Thor used his hammer like a drumstick, Neptune imitated on his "wreathed horn" the voice of the deep, the Celtic oak god Dagda twanged his windy wooden harp, and Angus, the Celtic god of spring and love, came through budding forest ways with a silvern harp which had strings of gold, echoing the tuneful birds, the purling streams, the whispering winds, and the rustling of scented fir and blossoming thorn.

Modern-day poets and singers, who voice their moods and cast the spell of their moods over readers and audiences, are the representatives of ancient magicians who believed that moods were caused by the spirits which possessed them – the rhythmical wind spirits, those harpers of the forest and songsters of the ocean.

The following quotations from Mr. R.C. Thompson's translations of Babylonian charms will serve to illustrate their poetic qualities:

BABYLON

Fever like frost hath come upon the land.

Fever hath blown upon the man as the wind blast,
It hath smitten the man and humbled his pride.

Headache lieth like the stars of heaven in
the desert and hath no praise;
Pain in the head and shivering like a scudding
cloud turn unto the form of man.

Headache whose course like the dread windstorm none knoweth.

Headache roareth over the desert, blowing like the wind,
Flashing like lightning, it is loosed above and below,
It cutteth off him, who feareth not his god, like a reed…
From amid mountains it hath descended upon the land.
Headache…a rushing hag-demon,
Granting no rest, nor giving kindly sleep…
Whose shape is as the whirlwind.
Its appearance is as the darkening heavens,
And its face as the deep shadow of the forest.

Sickness…breaking the fingers as a rope of wind
Flashing like a heavenly star, it cometh like the dew.

These early poets had no canons of Art, and there were no critics to disturb their meditations. Many singers had to sing and die ere a critic could find much to say. In ancient times, therefore, poets had their Golden Age – they were a law unto themselves. Even the "minors" were influential members of society.

THE GOLDEN AGE OF BABYLONIA

Sun worship came into prominence in its most fully developed form during the obscure period which followed the decline of the Dynasty of Isin. This was probably due to the changed political conditions which brought about the ascendancy for a time of Larsa, the seat of the Sumerian sun cult, and of Sippar, the seat of the Akkadian sun cult. Larsa was selected as the capital of the Elamite conquerors, while their rivals, the Amorites, appear to have first established their power at Sippar.

Babbar, the sun god of Sippar, whose Semitic name was Shamash, must have been credited with the early successes of the Amorites, who became domiciled under his care. And it was possibly on that account that the ruling family subsequently devoted so much attention to his worship in the Merodach's city of Babylon, where a sun temple was erected, and Shamash received devout recognition as an abstract deity of righteousness and law, who reflected the ideals of the most well organized and firmly governed communities.

The first Amoritic king was Sumu-abum, but little is known regarding him except that he reigned at Sippar. He was succeeded by Sumu-la-ilu, a deified monarch, who moved from Sippar to Babylon, the great wall of which he either repaired or entirely reconstructed in his fifth year. With these two monarchs began the brilliant Hammurabi, or First Dynasty of Babylonia, which endured for three centuries. Except Sumu-abum, who seems to stand alone, all its kings belonged to the same family, and son succeeded father in unbroken succession.

King Sumu-la-ilu

Sumu-la-ilu was evidently a great general and conqueror of the type of Thothmes III of Egypt. His empire, it is believed, included the rising city states of Assyria, and extended southward as far as ancient Lagash.

Of special interest on religious as well as political grounds was his association with Kish. That city had become the stronghold of a rival family of Amoritic kings, some of whom were powerful enough to assert their independence. They formed the Third Dynasty of Kish. The local god was Zamama, the Tammuz-like deity, who, like Nin-Girsu of Lagash, was subsequently identified with Merodach of Babylon. But prominence was also given to the moon god Nannar, to whom a temple had been erected, a fact which suggests that sun worship was not more pronounced among the Semites than the Arabians, and may not, indeed, have been of Semitic origin at all. Perhaps the lunar temple was a relic of the influential Dynasty of Ur.

Sumu-la-ilu attacked and captured Kish, but did not slay Bunutakhtunila, its king, who became his vassal. Under the overlordship of Sumu-la-ilu, the next ruler of Kish, whose name was Immerum, gave prominence to the public worship of Shamash. Politics and religion went evidently hand in hand.

Sumu-la-ilu strengthened the defences of Sippar, restored the wall and temple of Cuthah, and promoted the worship of Merodach and his consort Zerpanitum at Babylon. He was undoubtedly one of the forceful personalities of his dynasty. His son, Zabium, had a short but successful reign, and appears to have continued the policy of his father in consolidating the power of Babylon and securing the allegiance of subject cities. He enlarged Merodach's temple, E-sagila, restored the Kish temple of Zamama, and placed a golden image of himself in the temple of the sun god at Sippar. Apil-Sin, his son, surrounded Babylon with a new wall, erected a temple to Ishtar, and presented a throne of gold and silver to Shamash in that city, while he also strengthened Borsippa, renewed Nergal's temple at Cuthah, and dug canals.

King Sin-muballit

The next monarch was Sin-muballit, son of Apil-Sin and father of Hammurabi. He engaged himself in extending and strengthening the area controlled by Babylon by building city fortifications and improving the irrigation system. It is recorded that he honoured Shamash with the gift of a shrine and a golden altar adorned with jewels. Like Sumu-la-ilu, he was a great battle lord, and was specially concerned in challenging the supremacy of Elam in Sumeria and in the western land of the Amorites.

For a brief period a great conqueror, named Rim-Anum, had established an empire which extended from Kish to Larsa, but little is known regarding him. Then several kings flourished at Larsa who claimed to have ruled over Ur. The first monarch with an Elamite name who became connected with Larsa was Kudur-Mabug, son of Shimti-Shilkhak, the father of Warad-Sin and Rim-Sin.

It was from one of these Elamite monarchs that Sin-muballit captured Isin, and probably the Elamites were also the leaders of the army of Ur which he had routed before that event took place. He was not successful, however, in driving the Elamites from the land, and possibly he arranged with them a treaty of peace or perhaps of alliance.

Much controversy has been waged over the historical problems connected with this disturbed age. The records are exceedingly scanty, because the kings were not in the habit of commemorating battles which proved disastrous to them, and their fragmentary references to successes are not sufficient to indicate what permanent results accrued from their various campaigns. All we know for certain is that for a considerable period, extending perhaps over a century, a tremendous and disastrous struggle was waged at intervals, which desolated middle Babylonia. At least five great cities were destroyed by fire, as is testified by the evidence accumulated by excavators. These were Lagash, Umma, Shurruppak, Kisurra, and Adab. The ancient metropolis of Lagash, whose glory had been revived by Gudea and his kinsmen, fell soon after the rise of Larsa, and lay in ruins until the second century BCE, when, during the Seleucid Period, it was again occupied for a time. From its mound at Tello, and the buried ruins of the other cities, most of the relics of ancient Sumerian civilization have been recovered.

It was probably during one of the intervals of this stormy period that the rival kings in Babylonia joined forces against a common enemy and invaded the Western Land. Probably there was much unrest there. Great ethnic disturbances were in progress which were changing the political complexion of Western Asia. In addition to the outpourings of Arabian peoples into Palestine and Syria, which propelled other tribes to invade Mesopotamia, northern Babylonia, and Assyria, there was also much unrest all over the wide area to the north and west of Elam. Indeed, the Elamite migration into southern Babylonia may not have been unconnected with the southward drift of roving bands from Media and the Iranian plateau.

It is believed that these migrations were primarily due to changing climatic conditions, a prolonged "Dry Cycle" having caused a shortage of herbage, with the result that pastoral peoples were compelled to go farther and farther afield in quest of "fresh woods and pastures new". Innumerable currents and cross currents were set in motion once these race movements swept towards settled districts either to flood them with human waves, or surround them like islands in the midst of tempest-lashed seas, fretting the frontiers with restless fury, and ever groping for an inlet through which to flow with irresistible force.

The Elamite occupation of southern Babylonia appears to have propelled migrations of not inconsiderable numbers of its inhabitants. No doubt the various sections moved towards districts which were suitable for their habits of life. Agriculturists, for instance, must have shown preference for those areas which were capable of agricultural development, while pastoral folks sought grassy steppes and valleys, and seafarers the shores of alien seas.

Northern Babylonia and Assyria probably attracted the tillers of the soil. But the movements of seafarers must have followed a different route. It is possible that about this time the Phoenicians began to migrate towards the "Upper Sea". According to their own traditions their racial cradle was on the northern shore of the Persian Gulf. So far as we know, they first made their appearance on the Mediterranean coast about

2000 BCE, where they subsequently entered into competition as sea traders with the mariners of ancient Crete. Apparently the pastoral nomads pressed northward through Mesopotamia and towards Canaan. As much is suggested by the Biblical narrative which deals with the wanderings of Terah, Abraham, and Lot. Taking with them their "flocks and herds and tents", and accompanied by wives, and families, and servants, they migrated, it is stated, from the Sumerian city of Ur northwards to Haran "and dwelt there". After Terah's death the tribe wandered through Canaan and kept moving southward, unable, it would seem, to settle permanently in any particular district. At length "there was a famine in the land" – an interesting reference to the "Dry Cycle" – and the wanderers found it necessary to take refuge for a time in Egypt. There they appear to have prospered. Indeed, so greatly did their flocks and herds increase that when they returned to Canaan they found that "the land was not able to bear them", although the conditions had improved somewhat during the interval. "There was", as a result, "strife between the herdmen of Abram's cattle and the herdmen of Lot's cattle."

It is evident that the area which these pastoral flocks were allowed to occupy must have been strictly circumscribed, for more than once it is stated significantly that "the Canaanite and the Perizzite dwelled in the land". The two kinsmen found it necessary, therefore, to part company. Lot elected to go towards Sodom in the plain of Jordan, and Abraham then moved towards the plain of Mamre, the Amorite, in the Hebron district. With Mamre, and his brothers, Eshcol and Aner, the Hebrew patriarch formed a confederacy for mutual protection.

Other tribes which were in Palestine at this period included the Horites, the Rephaims, the Zuzims, the Zamzummims, and the Emims. These were probably representatives of the older stocks. Like the Amorites, the Hittites or "children of Heth" were evidently "late comers", and conquerors. When Abraham purchased the burial cave at Hebron, the landowner with whom he had to deal was one Ephron, son of Zohar, the Hittite. This illuminating statement agrees with what we know regarding Hittite expansion about 2000 BCE. The "Hatti" or "Khatti" had constituted military aristocracies throughout Syria and extended their influence by forming alliances. Many of their settlers were owners of estates, and traders who intermarried with the indigenous peoples and the Arabian invaders. As has been indicated (Chapter I), the large-nosed Armenoid section of the Hittite confederacy appear to have contributed to the racial blend known vaguely as the Semitic. Probably the particular group of Amorites with whom Abraham became associated had those pronounced Armenoid traits which can still be traced in representatives of the Hebrew people. Of special interest in this connection is Ezekiel's declaration regarding the ethnics of Jerusalem: "Thy birth and thy nativity", he said, "is of the land of Canaan; thy father was an Amorite, and thy mother an Hittite."

It was during Abraham's residence in Hebron that the Western Land was raided by a confederacy of Babylonian and Elamite battle lords. The Biblical narrative which deals with this episode is of particular interest and has long engaged the attention of European scholars:

"And it came to pass in the days of Amraphel (Hammurabi) king of Shinar (Sumer), Arioch (Eri-aku or Warad-Sin) king of

Ellasar (Larsa), Chedor-laomer (Kudur-Mabug) king of Elam, and Tidal (Tudhula) king of nations; that these made war with Bera king of Sodom, and with Birsha king of Gomorrah, Shinab king of Admah, and Shemeber king of Zeboiim, and the king of Bela, which is Zoar. All these joined together in the vale of Siddim, which is the salt sea. Twelve years they served Chedor-laomer, and in the thirteenth year they rebelled." Apparently the Elamites had conquered part of Syria after entering southern Babylonia.

Chedor-laomer and his allies routed the Rephaims, the Zuzims, the Emims, the Horites and others, and having sacked Sodom and Gomorrah, carried away Lot and "his goods". On hearing of this disaster, Abraham collected a force of three hundred and eighteen men, all of whom were no doubt accustomed to guerrilla warfare, and delivered a night attack on the tail of the victorious army which was withdrawing through the area afterwards allotted to the Hebrew tribe of Dan. The surprise was complete; Abraham "smote" the enemy and "pursued them unto Hobah, which is on the left hand of Damascus. And he brought back all the goods, and also brought again his brother Lot, and his goods, and the women also, and the people."

The identification of Hammurabi with Amraphel is now generally accepted. At first the guttural "h", which gives the English rendering "Khammurabi", presented a serious difficulty, but in time the form "Ammurapi" which appears on a tablet became known, and the conclusion was reached that the softer "h" sound was used and not the guttural. The "l" in the Biblical Amraphel has suggested "Ammurapi-ilu", "Hammurabi, the god", but it has been argued, on the other hand, that the change may have been due to western habitual phonetic conditions, or perhaps the slight alteration of an alphabetical sign. Chedor-laomer, identified with Kudur-Mabug, may have had several local names. One of his sons, either Warad-Sin or Rim-Sin, but probably the former, had his name Semitized as Eri-Aku, and this variant appears in inscriptions. "Tidal, king of nations", has not been identified. The suggestion that he was "King of the Gutium" remains in the realm of suggestion. Two late tablets have fragmentary inscriptions which read like legends with some historical basis. One mentions Kudur-lahmal (?Chedor-laomer) and the other gives the form "Kudur-lahgumal", and calls him "King of the land of Elam". Eri-Eaku (?Eri-aku) and Tudhula (?Tidal) are also mentioned. Attacks had been delivered on Babylon, and the city and its great temple E-sagila were flooded. It is asserted that the Elamites "exercised sovereignty in Babylon" for a period. These interesting tablets have been published by Professor Pinches.

The fact that the four leaders of the expedition to Canaan are all referred to as "kings" in the Biblical narrative need not present any difficulty. Princes and other subject rulers who governed under an overlord might be and, as a matter of fact, were referred to as kings. "I am a king, son of a king", an unidentified monarch recorded on one of the two tablets just referred to. Kudur-Mabug, King of Elam, during his lifetime called his son Warad-Sin (Eri-Aku = Arioch) "King of Larsa". It is of interest to note, too, in connection with the Biblical narrative regarding the invasion of Syria and Palestine, that he styled himself "overseer of the Amurru (Amorites)".

No traces have yet been found in Palestine of its conquest by the Elamites, nor have the excavators been able to substantiate the claim of Lugal-zaggizi of a previous age to have extended his empire to the shores of the Mediterranean. Any relics which these and other eastern conquerors may have left were possibly destroyed by the Egyptians and Hittites.

King Hammurabi

When Hammurabi came to the throne he had apparently to recognize the overlordship of the Elamite king or his royal son at Larsa. Although Sin-muballit had captured Isin, it was retaken, probably after the death of the Babylonian warlord, by Rim-Sin, who succeeded his brother Warad-Sin, and for a time held sway in Lagash, Nippur, and Erech, as well as Larsa.

It was not until the thirty-first year of his reign that Hammurabi achieved ascendancy over his powerful rival. Having repulsed an Elamite raid, which was probably intended to destroy the growing power of Babylon, he "smote down Rim-Sin", whose power he reduced almost to vanishing point. For about twenty years afterwards that subdued monarch lived in comparative obscurity; then he led a force of allies against Hammurabi's son and successor, Samsu-iluna, who defeated him and put him to death, capturing, in the course of his campaign, the revolting cities of Emutbalum, Erech, and Isin. So was the last smouldering ember of Elamite power stamped out in Babylonia.

Hammurabi, statesman and general, is one of the great personalities of the ancient world. No more celebrated monarch ever held sway in Western Asia. He was proud of his military achievements, but preferred to be remembered as a servant of the gods, a just ruler, a father of his people, and "the shepherd that gives peace". In the epilogue to his code of laws he refers to "the burden of royalty", and declares that he "cut off the enemy" and "lorded it over the conquered" so that his subjects might have security. Indeed, his anxiety for their welfare was the most pronounced feature of his character. "I carried all the people of Sumer and Akkad in my bosom", he declared in his epilogue. "By my protection, I guided in peace its brothers. By my wisdom I provided for them." He set up his stele, on which the legal code was inscribed, so "that the great should not oppress the weak" and "to counsel the widow and orphan", and "to succour the injured.... The king that is gentle, king of the city, exalted am I."

Hammurabi was no mere framer of laws but a practical administrator as well. He acted as supreme judge, and his subjects could appeal to him as the Romans could to Caesar. Nor was any case too trivial for his attention. The humblest man was assured that justice would be done if his grievance were laid before the king. Hammurabi was no respecter of persons, and treated alike all his subjects high and low. He punished corrupt judges, protected citizens against unjust governors, reviewed the transactions of moneylenders with determination to curb extortionate demands, and kept a watchful eye on the operations of tax gatherers.

There can be little doubt but that he won the hearts of his subjects, who enjoyed the blessings of just administration under a well-ordained political system. He must also have endeared himself to them as an exemplary exponent of religious tolerance. He respected the various deities in whom the various groups of people reposed their faith, restored despoiled temples, and re-endowed them with characteristic generosity. By so doing he not only afforded the pious full freedom and opportunity to perform their religious ordinances, but also promoted the material welfare of his subjects, for the temples were centres of culture and the priests were the teachers of the young. Excavators have discovered at Sippar traces of a school which dates from the Hammurabi Dynasty. Pupils learned to read and write, and received instruction in arithmetic and mensuration. They copied historical tablets, practised the art of composition, and studied geography.

Communication, Scribes and Deliveries

Although there were many professional scribes, a not inconsiderable proportion of the people of both sexes were able to write private and business letters. Sons wrote from a distance to their fathers when in need of money then as now, and with the same air of undeserved martyrdom and subdued but confident appeal. One son indited a long complaint regarding the quality of the food he was given in his lodgings. Lovers appealed to forgetful ladies, showing great concern regarding their health. "Inform me how it fares with thee," one wrote four thousand years ago. "I went up to Babylon so that I might meet thee, but did not, and was much depressed. Let me know why thou didst go away so that I may be made glad. And do come hither. Ever have care of thy health, remembering me." Even begging-letter writers were not unknown. An ancient representative of this class once wrote to his employer from prison. He expressed astonishment that he had been arrested, and, having protested his innocence, he made touching appeal for little luxuries which were denied to him, adding that the last consignment which had been forwarded had never reached him.

Letters were often sent by messengers who were named, but there also appears to have been some sort of postal system. Letter carriers, however, could not have performed their duties without the assistance of beasts of burden. Papyri were not used as in Egypt. Nor was ink required. Babylonian letters were shapely little bricks resembling cushions. The angular alphabetical characters, bristling with thorn-like projections, were impressed with a wedge-shaped stylus on tablets of soft clay which were afterwards carefully baked in an oven. Then the letters were placed in baked clay envelopes, sealed and addressed, or wrapped in pieces of sacking transfixed by seals. If the ancient people had a festive season which was regarded, like the European Yuletide or the Indian Durga fortnight, as an occasion suitable for the general exchange of expressions of goodwill, the Babylonian streets and highways must have been greatly congested by the postal traffic, while muscular postmen worked overtime distributing the contents of heavy and bulky letter sacks. Door to door deliveries would certainly have presented difficulties. Wood being dear, everyone could not afford doors, and some houses were entered by stairways leading to the flat and partly open roofs.

King Hammurabi had to deal daily with a voluminous correspondence. He received reports from governors in all parts of his realm, legal documents containing appeals, and private communications from relatives and others. He paid minute attention to details, and was probably one of the busiest men in Babylonia. Every day while at home, after worshipping Merodach at E-sagila, he dictated letters to his scribes, gave audiences to officials, heard legal appeals and issued interlocutors, and dealt with the reports regarding his private estates. He looks a typical man of affairs in sculptured representations – shrewd, resolute, and unassuming, feeling "the burden of royalty", but ever ready and well qualified to discharge his duties with thoroughness and insight. His grasp of detail was equalled only by his power to conceive of great enterprises which appealed to his imagination. It was a work of genius on his part to weld together that great empire of miscellaneous states extending from southern Babylonia to Assyria, and from the borders of Elam to the Mediterranean coast, by a universal legal Code which secured tranquillity and equal rights to all, promoted business, and set before his subjects the ideals of right thinking and right living.

Hammurabi recognized that conquest was of little avail unless followed by the establishment of a just and well-arranged political system, and the inauguration of practical measures to secure the domestic, industrial, and commercial welfare of the people as a whole. He engaged himself greatly, therefore, in developing the natural resources of each particular district. The network of irrigating canals was extended in the homeland so that agriculture might prosper: these canals also promoted trade, for they were utilized for travelling by boat and for the distribution of commodities.

As a result of his activities Babylon became not only the administrative, but also the commercial centre of his empire – the London of western Asia – and it enjoyed a spell of prosperity which was never surpassed in subsequent times. Yet it never lost its pre-eminent position despite the attempts of rival states, jealous of its glory and influence, to suspend its activities. It had been too firmly established during the Hammurabi Age, which was the Golden Age of Babylonia, as the heartlike distributor and controller of business life through a vast network of veins and arteries, to be displaced by any other Mesopotamian city to pleasure even a mighty monarch. For two thousand years, from the time of Hammurabi until the dawn of the Christian era, the city of Babylon remained amidst many political changes the metropolis of Western Asiatic commerce and culture, and none was more eloquent in its praises than the scholarly pilgrim from Greece who wondered at its magnificence and reverenced its antiquities.

Hammurabi's reign was as long as it was prosperous. There is no general agreement as to when he ascended the throne – some say in 2123 BCE, others hold that it was after 2000 BCE – but it is certain that he presided over the destinies of Babylon for the long period of forty-three years.

There are interesting references to the military successes of his reign in the prologue to the legal Code. It is related that when he "avenged Larsa", the seat of Rim-Sin, he restored there the temple of the sun god. Other temples were built up at various ancient centres, so that these cultural organizations might contribute to the welfare of the localities over which they held sway. At Nippur he thus honoured Enlil, at Eridu the god Ea, at Ur the god Sin, at Erech the god Anu and the goddess Nana (Ishtar), at Kish the god Zamama and the goddess Ma-ma, at Cuthah the god Nergal, at Lagash the god Nin-Girsu, while at Adab and Akkad, "celebrated for its wide squares", and other centres he carried out religious and public works. In Assyria he restored the colossus of Ashur, which had evidently been carried away by a conqueror, and he developed the canal system of Nineveh.

Apparently Lagash and Adab had not been completely deserted during his reign, although their ruins have not yielded evidence that they flourished after their fall during the very long struggle with the aggressive and plundering Elamites.

Hammurabi referred to himself in the Prologue as "a king who commanded obedience in all the four quarters". He was the sort of benevolent despot whom Carlyle on one occasion clamoured vainly for – not an Oriental despot in the commonly accepted sense of the term. As a German writer puts it, his despotism was a form of Patriarchal Absolutism. "When Marduk (Merodach)", as the great king recorded, "brought me to direct all people, and commissioned me to give judgment, I laid down justice and right in the provinces, I made all flesh to prosper." That was the keynote of his long life; he regarded himself as the earthly representative of the ruler of all – Merodach, "the lord god of right", who carried out the decrees of Anu, the sky god of Destiny.

King Samsu-iluna

The next king, Samsu-iluna, reigned nearly as long as his illustrious father, and similarly lived a strenuous and pious life. Soon after he came to the throne the forces of disorder were let loose, but, as has been stated, he crushed and slew his most formidable opponent, Rim-Sin, the Elamite king, who had gathered together an army of allies. During his reign a Kassite invasion was repulsed. The earliest Kassites, a people of uncertain racial affinities, began to settle in the land during Hammurabi's lifetime. Some writers connect them with the Hittites, and others with the Iranians, vaguely termed as Indo-European or Indo-Germanic folk. Ethnologists as a rule regard them as identical with the Cossaei, whom the Greeks found settled between Babylon and Media, east of the Tigris and north of Elam.

The Hittites came south as raiders about a century later. It is possible that the invading Kassites had overrun Elam and composed part of Rim-Sin's army. After settled conditions were secured many of them remained in Babylonia, where they engaged like their pioneers in agricultural pursuits. No doubt they were welcomed in that capacity, for owing to the continuous spread of culture and the development of commerce, rural labour had become scarce and dear.

Farmers had a long-standing complaint, "The harvest truly is plenteous, but the labourers are few". "Despite the existence of slaves, who were for the most part domestic servants, there was", writes Mr. Johns, "considerable demand for free labour in ancient Babylonia. This is clear from the large number of contracts relating to hire which have come down to us.... As a rule, the man was hired for the harvest and was free directly after. But there are many examples in which the term of service was different – one month, half a year, or a whole year.... Harvest labour was probably far dearer than any other, because of its importance, the skill and exertion demanded, and the fact that so many were seeking for it at once." When a farm worker was engaged he received a shekel for "earnest money" or arles, and was penalized for non-appearance or late arrival.

So great was the political upheaval caused by Rim-Sin and his allies and imitators in southern Babylonia, that it was not until the seventeenth year of his reign that Samsu-iluna had recaptured Erech and Ur and restored their walls. Among other cities which had to be chastised was ancient Akkad, where a rival monarch endeavoured to establish himself. Several years were afterwards spent in building new fortifications, setting up memorials in temples, and cutting and clearing canals. On more than one occasion during the latter part of his reign he had to deal with aggressive bands of Amorites.

The greatest danger to the empire, however, was threatened by a new kingdom which had been formed in Bit-Jakin, a part of Sealand which was afterwards controlled by the mysterious Chaldeans. Here may have collected evicted and rebel bands of Elamites and Sumerians and various "gentlemen of fortune" who were opposed to the Hammurabi regime. After the fall of Rim-Sin it became powerful under a king called Ilu-ma-ilu. Samsu-iluna conducted at least two campaigns against his rival, but without much success. Indeed, he was in the end compelled to retreat with considerable loss owing to the difficult character of that marshy country.

King Abeshu

Abeshu, the next Babylonian king, endeavoured to shatter the cause of the Sealanders, and made it possible for himself to strike at them by damming up the Tigris canal. He achieved a victory, but the wily Ilu-ma-ilu eluded him, and after a reign of sixty years was succeeded by his son, Kiannib. The Sealand Dynasty, of which little is known, lasted for over three and a half centuries, and certain of its later monarchs were able to extend their sway over part of Babylonia, but its power was strictly circumscribed so long as Hammurabi's descendants held sway.

During Abeshu's reign of twenty-eight years, of which but scanty records survive, he appears to have proved an able statesman and general. He founded a new city called Lukhaia, and appears to have repulsed a Kassite raid.

His son, Ammiditana, who succeeded him, apparently inherited a prosperous and well-organized empire, for during the first fifteen years of his reign he attended chiefly to the adornment of temples and other pious undertakings. He was a patron of the arts with archaeological leanings, and displayed traits which suggest that he inclined, like Sumu-la-ilu, to ancestor worship. Entemena, the pious patesi of Lagash, whose memory is associated with the famous silver vase decorated with the lion-headed eagle form of Nin-Girsu, had been raised to the dignity of a god, and Ammiditana caused his statue to be erected so that offerings might be made to it. He set up several images of himself also, and celebrated the centenary of the accession to the throne of his grandfather, Samsu-iluna, "the warrior lord", by unveiling his statue with much ceremony at Kish.

About the middle of his reign he put down a Sumerian rising, and towards its close had to capture a city which is believed to be Isin, but the reference is too obscure to indicate what political significance attached to this incident. His son, Ammizaduga, reigned for over twenty years quite peacefully so far as is known, and was succeeded by Samsuditana, whose rule extended over a quarter of a century. Like Ammiditana, these two monarchs set up images of themselves as well as of the gods, so that they might be worshipped, no doubt. They also promoted the interests of agriculture and commerce, and incidentally increased the revenue from taxation by paying much attention to the canals and extending the cultivatable areas.

But the days of the brilliant Hammurabi Dynasty were drawing to a close. It endured for about a century longer than the Twelfth Dynasty of Egypt, which came to an end, according to the Berlin calculations, in 1788 BCE. Apparently some of the Hammurabi and Amenemhet kings were contemporaries, but there is no evidence that they came into direct touch with one another. It was not until at about two centuries after Hammurabi's day that Egypt first invaded Syria, with which, however, it had for a long period previously conducted a brisk trade. Evidently the influence of the Hittites and their Amoritic allies predominated between Mesopotamia and the Delta frontier of Egypt, and it is significant to find in this connection that the "Khatti" or "Hatti" were referred to for the first time in Egypt during the Twelfth Dynasty, and in Babylonia during the Hammurabi Dynasty, sometime shortly before or after 2000 BCE. About 1800 BCE a Hittite raid resulted in the overthrow of the last king of the Hammurabi family at Babylon. The Hyksos invasion of Egypt took place after 1788 BCE.

BABYLON

ASSYRIA

In this chapter, Henry Smith Williams – author of a number of historical, medical and scientific textbooks – tells the political history of the Neo-Assyrian Empire, roughly covering the first half of the first millennium BCE.

As well as this he gives a short overview concerning the earlier Old Assyrian and Middle Assyrian periods in the second millennium to show the slow processes the Assyrian state underwent. Unfortunately, he has to lament the comparatively poor record on these earlier periods.

Although of course much more is known today, knowledge about the Neo-Assyrian period still greatly overshadows that of the earlier periods. This is not least due to the fact that these early archaeological levels have not yet been reached in Assur itself.

Starting with Assurnasirpal, Smith Williams can portray individual kings and their deeds in great detail. It bears no wonder that an overview of Neo-Assyrian history could follow the same pattern even nowadays. While we may be able to add many more nuances and details to both Neo-Assyrian political and social history, and the times of only telling history through the actions of great rulers has rightly passed, the baseline of Smith Williams' narrative holds true also today.

THE ASSYRIAN EMPIRE

The **Assyrian Empire** is in some respects unique in history. Despite the proverbial tendency of history to repeat itself, there has been no duplication of the tragic history of this wonderful body politic. It rose to be the most powerful of nations; it reached out and gained the widest empire that had hitherto been seen; its capital, Nineveh, was for a few centuries the metropolis of the world. But in the very fullness of its imperial flight it was struck down and utterly destroyed.

Other empires have been subjugated – Nineveh was annihilated. The very name "Assyrian" became only a long lost memory and a tradition. Late in the seventh century BCE, Nineveh was the boasted mistress of the world – two centuries later the mounds that covered her ruins were noted by the Greek historian Xenophon, who marched past them with the ill-fated Ten Thousand, merely as the relics of some ancient city of unknown name. So brief may be the highest fame! Yet the sequel is stranger still.

As we have seen, these forgotten mounds treasured secrets of history which they have since given up to the explorer. Moreover, our own generation and those to come will see Assyria restored thankfully to its rightful place in history. The details of its career are more fully known to us than those of almost any other nation of antiquity. There is a wealth of knowledge in this area. Such a phoenix-like regeneration is a fitting sequel to the fantastic career with its tragic dénouement, which is about to claim our attention.

c. 3000-1120 BCE

It must not be supposed that the Assyrian Empire came suddenly to the height of power just suggested. On the contrary, its rise was slow, and accomplished by intermittent impulses. Naturally enough, the growing nation has left us no such exhaustive records of its history during earlier days as have come to us from its time of might. Indeed, for some centuries after Assyria began to assume importance, we have but fragmentary records of its history. Only here and there a great monarch puts the stamp of his achievements upon an epoch so indelibly that time itself cannot wipe it out. Such names as Sargon II, Shalmaneser, and Tiglathpileser were remembered by posterity as the names of great heroes whose deeds various successors strove to emulate, and whose names were taken up, sometimes by usurpers of the throne, sometimes by legitimate descendants of royalty, and thus doubly perpetuated.

It is not till we are well within the last thousand years of the pre-Christian era, however, that the monarchs of Assyria come to be so well known to us as to seem like true historic personages in the same sense in which these terms would be applied to the Alexanders and Caesars of a later period. Such kings as Sargon II, Asshurnazirpal, Tiglathpileser III, Shalmaneser II and a little later, Sennacherib, Esarhaddon, and Asshurbanapal, left records so voluminous and so perfectly authenticated as to bring their authors into the clearest light of history. Nowhere else outside of Egypt have such full records been preserved of the deeds of ancient monarchs as in the case of these

Assyrian kings. Naturally enough, the record ceases before the destruction of Nineveh; there was no Assyrian scribe left to tell of that tragic event.

But now the scene shifts to Babylon; the kings of that principality take up the broken record, and for a few generations supply us with historical documents of the utmost importance. And where the Babylonian records end, the Persian chronicles begin. These are supplemented in due course by the reports of the Grecian historians, beginning with Herodotus, so that the historical sequence is practically unbroken....

It has already been pointed out that the earliest history of Assyria is no less obscure than that of early Babylonia. As nearly as the facts can now be restored to us, it would appear that for some centuries the people to the north of Babylonia were struggling for supremacy against the older civilization of the South. Gradually the northerners – the Assyrians, as they became known – gained in strength until, finally, about the beginning of the fourteenth century BCE, under Shalmaneser I, Asshur obtained a position at least equal to Babylonia. After the death of this monarch Assyria seems to have weakened for a time, and it is not until about 1100 BCE that another great monarch appeared to put the stamp of his personality upon the epoch. This new ruler was known as Tiglathpileser I. He has been called the first of the great Assyrian conquerors, though perhaps this estimate does scant justice to certain of his predecessors. In any event, he restored the influence of Assyria, subjugated Babylonia, and is said to have been the first Assyrian ruler to be crowned as "King of the

Four Corners of the Earth". It is believed that Nineveh was established as the capital of the empire in the reign of the son and successor of Tiglathpileser, who bore the unfamiliar name of Asshur-bel-kala.

c. 950–825 BCE

It is curious how largely the personality of an individual monarch dominates the history of an epoch among oriental nations. An illustration of this familiar fact is shown by antithesis in the scantiness of the records for about a century after the death of Tiglathpileser. Imperfect records reappear about 950 BCE, but it is not till about three-quarters of a century later that Assyria rises again to a time of might. Then, under Asshurnazirpal, one of the most enterprising and most cruel of conquerors, the stamp of Assyrian influence was put upon all surrounding nations. Shalmaneser II largely sustained the traditions of his father, and the power of Assyria was upheld, if not extended, by the next rulers, Tiglathpileser III and Shalmaneser IV.

How fully the deeds of these later Assyrian monarchs are known to us will appear in the succeeding pages. Monarchs of even greater celebrity were to come after; yet perhaps the reign of Asshurnazirpal (885-860 BCE) may not unjustly be regarded as the period when Assyria obtained its greatest power and its highest civilization. The bas-reliefs from the palace of Asshurnazirpal, which were exhumed by Layard and which are now exhibited in the British Museum, are in some respects the most perfect examples of Assyrian art that have been preserved.... The art of this time shows examples also of massive sculptures, such as the human-headed bulls and lions, in relative abundance. A curious feature of the later sculptures is that they usually present inscriptions written across pedestal and figure alike. Needless to say, these inscriptions record deeds of the great conqueror....

Even fuller records are preserved of Shalmaneser II. In particular, the black obelisk on which the deeds of this king are presented, both in graphic pictures and in extensive inscriptions, is one of the most famous of Assyrian antiquities....

LAND AND PEOPLE

The land of Assyria, in the more restricted sense of the term, lies for the most part on the left bank of the Tigris, and is bounded on the south by the Lower Zab. Hence, strictly speaking, it would not form part of Mesopotamia were it not that the capital importance of the Tigris to the country and the trend of its other rivers make it a kind of appendage to the alluvial plain, and that the mountain ranges of the north constitute a boundary which cuts it off from the rest of the world, and thus naturally assigns it to Mesopotamia. Consequently, as soon as the Assyrians gained their independence and started on a career of conquest, it was natural that they should first extend their borders in that direction.

Mesopotamia consists of a great low-lying plain divided by no physical barrier. It was natural, therefore, that the policy of all powerful rulers in that region should have had for its aim the political unification of all parts of the country, united as they were already by a common civilization and economic interdependence. The efforts of the Assyrians were likewise directed towards this end, though it was long before they obtained it. In the kingdom of Babylonia, which asserted its sway over the whole southern portion of the plain and its dependent provinces, they were at first confronted by an adversary strong enough to resist them, and all that fell to them for the time being was the northern half of Mesopotamia, the greater part of which remained under their dominion, and was merged into an Assyrian empire, just as the whole of Babylonia had been merged into a Babylonian empire....

The land of Assyria is very different from Mesopotamia proper. The nearness of the mountain ranges makes the climate cooler, and the soil is probably less productive than that of the lowlands along the river. Nor were the means of transport within its borders as good as in Mesopotamia proper, for the Tigris only constituted the frontier, and the swiftness of its current made it less well adapted for traffic than the Euphrates, which formed the most convenient natural line of communication in the plain of Mesopotamia.

In Babylonia we made the acquaintance of a country which had developed its own civilization, and one where the inhabitants held in proud and honourable remembrance the various stages of its economic and political development, – a sentiment reflected in the religious cults of the ancient cities, the centres of civilization. With Assyria it is otherwise. That country began to play its part in Mesopotamian history with the set purpose of appropriating what Babylonia had achieved. The Assyrians had no such gains, hallowed by the associations of thousands of years, to boast of in their own country. They were a tardy supplement to the Semitic immigration. They felt themselves an appendage to the Semitic population already settled in Mesopotamia, and consequently regarded its ancient cults as, in a measure, their own. The fact implies an unconscious confession that they had nothing analogous or equivalent to set against the old centres of Babylonian civilization, and, as a matter of fact, the chief towns of Assyria cannot for a moment be compared in importance with those of Babylonia. The most famous of the former owed their day of splendour to the rise of the Assyrian Empire or even, to some extent, to the fancy of individual kings; and when the Assyrian Empire passed from the stage of history these, its artificial creations, were abolished with it.

Babylonia rose again after every fresh blow, because her rise to the position she held had its root in a vital need of the peoples of anterior Asia; while soon after the fall of the Assyrian Empire the very names of the great cities of Assyria had passed from the memory of the dwellers in the land. The case is different with the cities of northern Mesopotamia, which belonged to the Assyrian Empire, but existed before its rise, and survived its fall. The only other exception among the large Assyrian cities is Arbela, which, being situated at the junction of the trade routes to northern Mesopotamia, Armenia, and Media, had probably been in existence before the time of the Assyrian Empire, and likewise retained its importance to a later period.

ASSYRIAN CAPITALS: ASSHUR AND NINEVEH

The oldest capital of Assyria was Asshur, situated on the right bank of the Tigris, on the site of the present Kalah Sherghat. It was originally the seat of rulers called patesis, who were probably subjects of the Babylonian monarchy. In the first half of the second millennium BCE these rulers extended their sway over the district which they styled "the land of the city of Asshur," and assumed the title of "king." Asshur was always held in honour as the ancient capital, but it lay so far to the south (being, in fact, almost beyond the borders of the country), that it soon became imperative for the "kings of Assyria" to transfer the centre of government to a more convenient place. Shalmaneser I (c. 1300 BCE) accordingly chose Calah for his residence. The natural result was the decline of the importance of Asshur, since its situation was not such as to assure it a leading position. In later times it subsisted mainly upon its old reputation, and enjoyed special privileges, which were confirmed even by Sargon. It was the seat of Asshur, the chief national divinity. The kings of Assyria, from Shalmaneser I to Sargon, held their court at Calah (Nimrud). Its consequence seems to have declined after the reign of Tiglathpileser I, for his son, Asshur-bel-kala, removed to Nineveh, which remained the royal residence till the reign of Asshurnazirpal. The latter rebuilt Calah and so improved it that it remained the capital until Sargon chose Dur-Sharrukin (Khorsabad), which in turn Nineveh replaced as capital.

Nineveh (Ninua), situated above Calah, on the left bank of the Tigris, and opposite the present town of Mosul ... was one of the oldest and most important cities of the province of Assyria, and was highly esteemed from the very earliest times of the Assyrian Empire as being the seat of a cult of an Ishtar known as "Ishtar of Ninua," to distinguish her from the Ishtar of Arbela.... It became the royal residence in the reign of Asshur-bel-kala, the son of Tiglathpileser (or even earlier), and remained so until the reign of Asshurnazirpal. But it really owed its fame as the capital and chief city of Assyria, which it represented in the eyes of other nations, to Sennacherib. He built an entirely new Nineveh, which was to show forth worthily the power and glory of the Assyrian Empire. His successors continued to reside there, and contributed to its splendour. Esarhaddon and Asshurbanapal built palaces there, and Nineveh formed the last bulwark of the Assyrian Empire....

THE RISE OF ASSYRIA

c. 1741-1300 BCE

The city of Asshur was originally a patesi-ship. The situation of Asshur seems to point to a close connection with Babylonia rather than with northern Mesopotamia, and for the present, at least, it seems most likely that we ought to regard it as a vassal state to Babylonia or the Kingdom of the Four Quarters of the World. Nor must we ignore the possibility that it may have formed part of the realm of the "Kishshati."

A record left by an Assyrian king enables us to determine one point of time, at least, when Asshur was still a dependency and ruled by a patesi. Tiglathpileser I built that part of the great temple of Asshur which was intended for the worship of the gods Anu and Ramman (Adad), and in the record he has left he observes that this temple was built by the patesi Shamshi-Adad, the son of Ishme-Dagan, patesi of Asshur, six hundred and forty-one years before the reign of his own great-grandfather Asshur-dan, sixty years earlier. Accordingly Asshur must have been ruled by patesis sixty plus six hundred and forty-one years before 1100, when Tiglathpileser was on the throne, and its exaltation to the rank of a kingdom must have taken place later than that. The names of two patesis of Asshur and those of their fathers are known to us from inscriptions of their own. One of them, Shamshi-Adad, and his father, Igur-Kapkapu, we may place before or after Shamshi, the son of Ishme-Dagan, with equal probability, while the form of the other two names, Irishum and his father Khallu, being simple and exhibiting nothing of the compound character of later Assyrian names, leads us to conjecture that they belong to an earlier period.

The names of these six patesis and their work in the building of the temple of Asshur represent our whole stock of knowledge concerning Asshur before it rose to be a royal city. The first king of Assyria of whom we know anything is Asshur-bel-nish-eshu, who is introduced to us by the Synchronistic History as a contemporary of the Kossaean king Karaindash of Babylon. As this monarch reigned some time about the first half of the fifteenth century BCE, there is an interval of over three hundred years between him and the patesi Shamshi-Adad, an interval of which we know nothing except that the rise of Asshur and the establishment of the kingdom of Assyria must fall within it.

Of the circumstances and conditions under which these events took place we know nothing in detail, but an explanation naturally suggests itself from the state of Babylonia. During this same period Babylonia had sunk to such a depth of decrepitude that her own strength was no longer adequate to secure her against hordes of invaders, and she could continue to exist only under the protection of the Kossaean kings and their armies. These disorders, which inevitably attend such a state of things, served, as they invariably do in the East, to promote the formation of new states under energetic and enterprising leaders, and to these circumstances the kingdom of Asshur probably owed its rise.

From the reign of Shalmaneser I (*circa* 1300) onwards the kings of Assyria bear the title of "Shar Kishshati" and even place it before that of "King of Asshur." "Shar Kishshati" means "King of the World," and the title is thus formed in the same fashion as the Babylonian "King of the Four Quarters of the World." And the Assyrian title, like the Babylonian, was not merely general in scope, but was bound up with the possession of a particular district and particular cities.

It is doubtful whether Assyria subdued the kingdom of the Kishshati from the outset, or gained possession of it at a later period. According to the scanty records at present open to us, the latter hypothesis seems the more probable. The first Assyrian king to bear the title of "Shar Kishshati" is Shalmaneser I (about 1300 BCE), and he gives it to his father, Adad-nirari I (or Ramman-nirari), although the latter does not assume it in his own inscription. Shalmaneser attaches so much weight to this title that on a couple of bricks, which date from his reign, he actually styles himself "King of Kishshati" alone, and omits the royal title of Assyria; and we therefore may conclude that the union of northern Mesopotamia and Assyria was the work of Adad-nirari and of Shalmaneser.

This would be at least one fixed point in the earliest history of Assyria from which to trace the development of the empire. Before Shalmaneser we have to do only with the little kingdom of Asshur, which was chiefly engaged in struggles with Babylonia and its eastern neighbours, and after his time with the united dominions of Assyria and northern Mesopotamia, the leading power of Mesopotamian civilization against the West and the attacks of barbarians on every side. The Synchronistic History is our principal guide to Assyrian history, as it was to the history of Babylonia before it came into touch with Assyria. We have but few inscriptions of the kings of this early stage of Assyria's existence, and only by the aid of the above-mentioned document can we more or less connectedly trace the course of history. Before the reign of Asshur-bel-nish-eshu, at which the chronicle now begins, we can be sure of nothing but a great blank.

c. 1450–1325 BCE

With Asshur-bel-nish-eshu, who reigned in the first half of the fifteenth century BCE, begins a line of kings with a certain degree of continuity. Of himself we only know what is told in the Synchronistic History, namely, that he concluded an alliance with Karaindash of Babylon by which they guaranteed one another in possession of their dominions. He was presently – though perhaps not immediately – succeeded by Puzur-Asshur [probably about 1420 BCE] of whom we are told the same thing. He entered into friendly alliance with Burna-buriash.

Of his supposed successor, Asshur-nadin-akhe, we know, from the letters of his son Asshur-uballit to Amenhotep IV, that he, like his Babylonian contemporary, held communication with the kings of Egypt. In an inscription of a later king mention is made of a building of his, the foundation of a palace at Asshur. For the rest, it is by no means impossible that he may have reigned before Puzur-Asshur, and that the latter, as well as Asshur-uballit, was his son.

We possess a letter written by Asshur-uballit to Amenhotep IV of Egypt. It gives an account of presents made to the king of Egypt – a war chariot yoked to two white horses, and a seal cylinder – makes excuse for the tardy return of Egyptian ambassadors on the plea that they had been stopped by the (nomadic) Sutu, and contains the usual importunate requests for richer presents in return. In Babylonia, Asshur-uballit succeeded in making way for Assyrian interference, and thus came a step nearer to the goal all kings of Assyria longed to reach, the suzerainty of Babylon. Apart from the attempt of Asshur-narara and Nabu-daian, which presumably came to nothing, the little kingdom of Assyria had been on friendly terms with Babylonia, and had made an alliance which probably contributed more to her own security than that of the other party. Internal troubles were the pretext which first rendered feasible his successful interference in Babylonian affairs.

The assassination of the Babylonian king by the malcontent Kossaeans, and the elevation of Nazibugash to the throne, gave Asshur-uballit an admirable pretext for restoring "order" in Babylonia and placing Kurigalzu, his other grandson, on the throne. Adad-nirari mentions another expedition of his against the Shubari. His successor, Bel-nirari I [about 1370 BCE], boasts in his inscription that he conquered the Kasshu (Kossaeans) and enlarged the borders of the land. This probably refers to a distinct campaign against the Kasshu, and not to the war with Kurigalzu II, in which he was likewise victorious. The latter enterprise also resulted in territorial expansion, which does not necessarily seem to have been made permanent.

c. 1325–1275 BCE

Pudi-ilu (about 1350 BCE), the son and successor of Bel-nirari, waged war, we are told by his son, Adad-nirari, against the otherwise unknown Turuki and Nigimkhi, who probably dwelt somewhere in the direction of Armenia, and extended the Assyrian frontier to the north (Gutium). Adad-nirari I (about 1325 BCE) has left an inscription which has been discovered at Kalah Shergat (Asshur). According to it, he, like his predecessors, waged most of his wars on the northeastern frontier of his kingdom, and endeavoured, by building cities, to revive the prosperity of the region occupied by the Shubari, Lulumi, Guti, and Kasshu of the northeast, which had been laid waste by previous wars. His inscription relates mainly to the buildings he erected in connection with the temple of Asshur. It is the first from Assyria with a definite date. It was indited in the limmu (*i.e.* the year of office) of Shulman-kharradu.

His son, Shalmaneser I (about 1300 BCE), was one of the mightiest Assyrian kings, and probably the first who raised

ASSYRIA

Asshur to a position equal, if not superior, to that of Babylonia. We do not know much about him from inscriptions left by himself, and are therefore obliged to depend on occasional statements of succeeding kings. He ruled over Mesopotamia westward to the Balikh at least, if not to the Euphrates, and assured to Assyria the possession of the northern tract between the Euphrates and Tigris, which was afterwards the provinces of Gumathene and Sophene. He founded colonies there, and planted them with Assyrian settlers to form a bulwark to Mesopotamia against the tribes of the north. Afterwards, when the power of Assyria was impaired, these colonies were in great straits, but they held their own, and were then reinforced by Asshurnazirpal, to whom they served as a welcome basis for the new Assyrian province of Tuskhan which he established there.

With the extension of the kingdom and the inclusion of northern Mesopotamia, the need of another capital than Asshur, which lay too far to the south, made itself felt. The city Shalmaneser chose for this purpose was Calah, which remained the capital down to the time of Sargon, except during the period of decline which followed upon the reign of Tiglathpileser I. His object in this change of residence was clearly to give expression to the altered state of things which had come about in Assyria and Mesopotamia. Assyria was not to be the privileged kingdom, but the two political organizations, Asshur and the Kingdom of the Kishshati, were to be equal members of the new empire, each retaining its own centre in Asshur and Kharran respectively, while the king founded his own capital for himself, to avoid giving the preference to either.

Shalmaneser's son, Tukulti-Ninib I (about 1275 BCE) [but probably somewhat earlier] was no less fortunate in his enterprises than his father. He was the first to achieve the object of every king in Assyria – dominion over Babylon. Adad-nirari III, in his list of his ancestors, styles him "King of Sumer and Accad," from which we may certainly conclude that he held the same sort of position toward the whole of Babylonia, and the kingdom of Babylon more particularly, as was afterward attained by Shalmaneser II – that is to say, he must have ruled over the several provinces of all Babylonia and exercised a kind of suzerainty over Babylon.

The rapid rise of Assyria seems to have been followed by equally rapid decline. For a hundred years we have hardly any information concerning it, and do not even know the names of the kings who reigned during that period. The lack of inscriptions, or, at any rate, of vaunting records in the reigns of later kings, seems in itself to indicate a time of humiliation, while the conditions which we find prevailing when our sources of information become more copious, show that soon after the reign of Tukulti-Ninib, and therefore probably before the end of the thirteenth century BCE, the power of Assyria must have been seriously curtailed and exposed to grievous shocks. Whence they arose we shall presently see.

There is scarcely a year in which additional information concerning this obscure period does not come to light. A recently deciphered fragment of the Babylonian Chronicle mentions an Assyrian king, Tukulti-Asshur-Bel, contemporaneous with Tukulti-Ninib, but of the relation of the two kings nothing is stated. Professor Winckler in *Altorientalische*

Forschungen, suggests that the former was the latter's son, and co-regent while he was engaged in ruling and reducing Babylon. Professor Rogers sums up the end of Tukulti-Ninib's life: "For seven years was this rule over Babylonia maintained. The Babylonians rebelled, drove out the Assyrian conquerors, and set up once more a Babylonian, Adad-shum-usur (about 1268–1239 BCE), over them. When Tukulti-Ninib returned to Assyria he found even his own people in rebellion under the leadership of his son. In the civil war that followed he lost his life, and the most brilliant reign in Assyrian history up to that time was closed."

c. 1275–1235 BCE

This rebellious son was not the above mentioned Tulkulti-Asshur-Bel, but Asshurnazirpal I. His reign continues the period of decline, and in it it is believed that Adad-shum-usur actually attacked Assyria. Next come two kings, Asshur-narara and Nabu-daian, whose reigns seem to have been contemporaneous (about 1250 BCE). A fragment of a clay tablet was found containing a letter from Adad-shum-usur to these two kings, in which he remonstrates on their folly in taking up arms against him, which shows that Babylon's power was still waxing.

We do not know how it came to pass that Assyria lost the ascendancy she had gained over Babylonia under Tukulti-Ninib, but it is certain that some fifty years later Bel-kudur-usur found himself relegated to Assyria proper, and was obliged to fight for the possession of his capital. [According to Professor Rogers, Meli-Shipak (about 1238 BCE) and Marduk-apal-iddin (about 1223–1211 BCE) were the Babylonian kings in this war. He places Adad-shum-iddin's death at 1269 BCE, and Adad-shum-usur's at 1238 BCE, basing these dates on some recent illuminative suggestions of Professor Hommel.] The Synchronistic History, which is incomplete at this point, states that Ninib-apal-esharra (who was probably the son of Bel-kudur-usur) was forced to retreat. The Babylonians appear to have pursued and besieged him in his own capital of Asshur, and there a battle was fought, in which, according to the apparent purport of the Synchronistic History, the Assyrians were beaten. But the victory, if victory it were, cannot have been decisive, for after the battle the Babylonians withdrew without making any further attempt to invade the remoter parts of the country. The defeat of the Assyrians must, therefore, have been more like a successful defence of their city. Slight as this clew is, it makes it evident that for a while Assyria had to fight for her life against Babylon, and that she held her own with difficulty. The development of this state of things must be sought in the great hiatus made by the reign of Bel-kudur-usur. The titles of the Babylonian kings of the period also go to prove that at this time Babylonia had actually repossessed herself of northern Mesopotamia.

Since we find Tiglathpileser in possession of much the same dominions as Tukulti-Ninib (though Sumer and Accad did not belong to him), the course of events during all the twelfth century, from Ninib-apal-esharra to Asshur-rish-ishi, is self-evident. The business in hand was the reconquest of what had been lost, and at it the succeeding rulers steadily and successfully laboured.

Of Ninib-apal-esharra, the Synchronistic History says nothing except that he successfully withstood the Babylonian attack, nor does Tiglathpileser mention any other deeds of his. The latter, however, expressly gives him the character of a capable commander, "who led the troops of Asshur aright," presumably with reference to his retreat after the death of Bel-kudur-usur and the repulse of the Babylonian king.

c. 1200–1116 BCE

His son and successor, Asshur-dan (about 1200 BCE), won some victories over Babylon and reconquered some parts beyond the Zab from Samana-shum-iddin (king of Babylonia). Tiglathpileser lays stress upon the fact that he lived to a great age (to about 1150 BCE). Of his son, Mutakkil-Nusku, no particulars are known. He probably carried on the work of his predecessors, for Assyria gradually regained all she had lost.

Then Asshur-rish-ishi (about 1140 BCE), the father of Tiglathpileser I, reports that he had reconquered the Lulumi and Kuti, whom Adad-nirari had formerly subjugated, and who had either fallen under the sway of Babylon or made themselves independent; and that he had repulsed the nomads, whom Adad-nirari had likewise driven back, and who had naturally taken advantage of Assyria's weakness to press forward again. His war with Nebuchadrezzar I, king of Babylon, seems to have been waged mainly for the possession of Mesopotamia, which the defeat of the nomads was also intended to secure. It is most probable that he gained his end, the evacuation of the kingdom of Kishshati, of which Nebuchadrezzar styles himself king in one of his inscriptions.

THE FIRST GREAT ASSYRIAN CONQUEROR

c. 1116–1050 BCE

Asshur-rish-ishi's son, Tiglathpileser I (Tu-kulti-apal-esharra, meaning "My help is the son of Esharra," *i.e.* the god Ninib), is the first of the great Assyrian conquerors. Directly after his accession to the throne he marched against the Mushke (Mushkaya) to conquer the districts previously taken by them. The Mushke (the Meshech of the Old Testament, and the Moschi of the Greeks) were defeated, as well as the people of Kummukh and the mountainous races of the Kharia and Qurkhi country stretching from the north of the Tigris to the Upper Zab. In the next campaign the same district was traversed, but the king then crossed the Lower Zab, and thence proceeded northward into the mountains. The whole mountainous district was then incorporated with the Assyrian kingdom, and Tiglathpileser was then able to proceed to the subjugation of the lands of western Armenia and Pontis, never before entered by the Assyrian rulers.

He crossed sixteen mountains, reached (what he calls the land of the Nairi) the upper Euphrates, which he crossed, and defeated in a great battle twenty-five kings [twenty-three according to others], who encountered him with their troops and war chariots. The enemies were pursued as far as the banks of the Black Sea, when all the princes swore fealty and bound themselves to pay tribute. On the return march the town Milidia, *i.e.* Melitene on the Euphrates, was taken and forced to pay tribute.

The next, the fourth campaign of the king was directed against the Aramaeans, of the North Mesopotamian steppe; he penetrated as far as the Euphrates, and conquered several places in the vicinity of Carchemish. Then followed an expedition to the east against [the Musri and] the then unknown race of the Qumani. In later years Tiglathpileser undertook campaigns in the west. An inscription at the source of the Supnat, the first easterly tributary of the Tigris, tells us that he traversed the country of Nairi (Armenia) three times, and that he subjugated all the country "from the great sea of the west country to the sea of Nairi." In particular we learn that he made a voyage in ships from Arvad (Aradus) on the Mediterranean Sea, that he hunted in Lebanon (he was a passionate hunter), and that the kings of Egypt sent him some rare sea fishes as a present. It is very probable that one of the mutilated inscriptions which the Assyrian kings had put up on the Dog River (the Nahr-el-Kelb, north of Beirut), quite close to the victory monuments of Ramses II, related to Tiglathpileser. He also made war against Marduk-nadin-akhe of Babylon, but with no success; at least we learn that the Babylonian king, in the year 1110 BCE, carried off images of gods from an Assyrian city. [According to Professor Rogers, Tiglathpileser marched to Babylon and was there acknowledged King of the Four Quarters of the World.]

However, Tiglathpileser in a second campaign was completely victorious in a battle of the Lower Zab, and took all the capitals of the northern half of Accad: Dur-Kurigalzu, the double town Sippar, Babylon, and Upi. The steppe district on the western bank of the Euphrates (the land of the Shuhi or Sukhi) was also subjugated by him. Thus did Tiglathpileser create a great kingdom, which included the whole district of the Euphrates and Tigris, as far as Babylon, as well as the mountainous country of western Armenia and eastern Asia Minor, as far as Pontis; and his supremacy was also recognized by northern Syria.... We hear that Asshur-bel-kala (about 1090 BCE), the son of Tiglathpileser, lived in the greatest peace with Marduk-shapik-zer-mati, the Babylonian king. When, after the latter's fall, Adad-apal-iddin, the son of Esagila-shaduni, was raised to the throne, Asshur-bel-kala married his daughter and brought her home to Assyria, with many presents....

c. 1050–884 BCE

Asshur-bel-kala was succeeded by his brother Shamshi-Adad (about 1080 BCE), of whom we know nothing further; and then follows a great gap in the line of kings. [Here may be inserted the names of Asshurnazirpal II about 1050 BCE, Erba-Adad, and Asshur-nadin-akhe.]

Of King Asshur-erbi it is only mentioned that under him the districts conquered by Tiglathpileser ... were taken by the Aramaean king. This was evidently the king of the country of Bit-Adini, whose chief dominion lay east of the Euphrates.... At the beginning of the ninth century BCE we again have more accurate information about Assyria, and so find that, beyond a part of the mountainous district east and southeast of Nineveh, the kings now have only the country on the upper Tigris (around Amida), Kummukh, and a great part of the cultivated land of Mesopotamia....

ASSYRIA

c. 1090–885 BCE

The eleventh and tenth centuries BCE confirmed the complete freedom of the local government of the countries of Western Asia. Whilst the kingdom of the Pharaohs was decaying from age, a new nation was rising in Syria and evolving an active intelligent life of its own.

The Phoenician merchants circulated the products of the civilization of Syria along all the coasts of the Mediterranean, and the dwellers on the Aegean Sea having already entered the circle of cultured races, competing with the Phoenicians in trade and the traverse of the sea, took possession of the coasts one after another and thereby developed a complete political and intellectual life. The fate of Western Asia was determined by the evolution of Syria's culture not taking a wide-reaching, powerful, political form, but rather hindering it. Since the days of the Kheta kingdom's glory, there has been no great power in Syria. So when a conquering, military state was now formed on the Tigris, under a fearless, warlike prince, it met with no sustained resistance.

The success of Assyria was due to her military organization. Little as we know of its particulars, there can be no doubt that the whole race regarded war and conquest as the real aims of existence, and the more successful they were, the more they ignored all other sides of life; whereas the little states of Syria made tillage, trade, and industry the chief occupations of their life, albeit every inhabitant was presumably bound, like the Israelites, to take up arms in case of need, in the defence of his country. The sole great military power was Egypt, but her warrior caste was composed of foreign mercenaries who exploited the country, although from a military point of view they evidently did not benefit it more than the generality of their class in similar cases.

The outcome of events was thus a foregone conclusion. The Assyrian campaigns of two centuries ended in the political and national fall of the races of Syria. The progress of events then led further to the annihilation of nationality in the whole of Western Asia. The kingdom of Tiglathpileser I fell, soon after his death, and there now ensues a little later a gap of more than a century in our information about Assyria. The very scanty notices commence about 950 BCE. Asshur-dan II, mentioned as "the maker of a canal," reigned at that time. [A recently discovered inscription of Adad-nirari II speaks of his grandfather Tiglathpileser. Therefore, a new Tiglathpileser, the second of his name, is now reckoned in the list of kings, and the approximate dates 950–930 BCE assigned to his reign. Nothing is known of him except that he is called "King of Kishshati and King of Asshur." Asshur-dan II's reign is now put down as beginning 930 BCE, and Adad-nirari II's at 911.] Asshur-dan's successor, Adad-nirari II, mentioned with the building at the "Gate of the Tigris" (890 BCE), conquers King Shamash-mudammik of Babylon in a battle on Mount Yalman, and made war against his successor, Nabu-shum-ishkun [who was also defeated and yielded certain cities]. In the peace made by an alliance, the boundary was fixed near the city of Tel-Bari, south of the Lower Zab.

The next king, Tukulti-Ninib II (890–885 BCE), fought in the northwest mountains, and at the source of Supnat, the first tributary of the Tigris, he had his statue (stele) erected near that of Tiglathpileser. In spite of repeated attacks, the mountainous districts on the east as far as the lake of Van, the chief part of the land of Qurkhi, retained essentially their independence. The warlike efforts of these rulers had been hitherto directed against the races of the mountains of Kasjar (Masius), the south of the Tigris, and close to Aramaean Mesopotamia, which, in spite of numerous campaigns, had never been subjugated. If Nisibis, Gozan, and the valley of the Khabur, and apparently also Kharran, belonged to the Assyrians under Asshurnazirpal, they either remained independent after the twelfth century BCE, or were subjugated by the kings of this period. In the east, the mountainous races of Khubushkia and Kirruri (on the Upper Zab, and as far as the lake of Urumiyeh) are tributary, and on the Lower Zab, we find under Asshurnazirpal, an Assyrian governor of Dagara, in the land of the Euphrates, whose fortified citadels were mostly situated on the banks of the river, or like Anat, on an island, paid tribute. Tukulti-Ninib's son, Asshurnazirpal III (885 to 860 BCE), entered on fresh conquests directly after his accession to the throne.

THE REIGN AND CRUELTY OF ASSHURNAZIRPAL

c. 885–880 BCE

Tiglathpileser's work of conquest was to be begun over again; Asshurnazirpal felt the full force of the mission, and he accomplished it with a cruelty worthy of the hero he took for pattern, and his successors applied themselves, as did he, to avenge, arms in hand, Asshur's temporary humiliation.

Scarcely was Asshurnazirpal seated on the throne, when he turned attention to his armies, – his war chariots and armed men were numerous and well equipped; they were ready to take the march. It was the land of Numme which received the first blow. Accustomed to prolonged and uninterrupted peace, the inhabitants had never even thought of measures for defence, and they fled to the mountains at the approach of the Assyrians, who made bloodless captures of the towns of Libe, Surra, Abuku, Arura, and Arubi, situated at the base of Mounts Rime, Aruni, and Etini. "These majestic peaks," relates Asshurnazirpal, "rise up like daggers' blades, and only the birds of the sky in their flight can reach their summits. The natives entrenched themselves among them as though in eagles' nests. None of the kings, my fathers, had ever penetrated so far. In three days I reached those heights; I brought terror in the midst of their hiding places, I shook their nests; two hundred defenders perished by the sword, and I seized their flock and a rich booty. Their corpses strewed the mountains like leaves from the trees, and those who escaped had to take refuge in caves." These proceedings terrified the peaceful inhabitants of the Kirruri district, who hastened from Simirra, Ulmania, Adanit, Khargai, and Kharasi, to throw themselves at the conqueror's feet and offered all that he was wont to seize – horses, oxen, sheep, and brazen vessels. They were given an Assyrian governor. Such was the fright throughout the whole of Nairi that while he still lingered

ASSYRIA

in Kirruri, Asshurnazirpal received ambassadors from the people of Gozan and Khubushkia who came from far to the east, bringing presents asking for the chains of slavery.

From Kirruri the Assyrian king went a little to the east into the district of Qurkhi, pillaging in turn at least a dozen towns and finally arrived at the borders of Urartu. The only serious resistance he encountered was under the walls of Nishtum, which paid dear for its courage. These beginnings were a forecast of the future, and Asshurnazirpal did not even wait for the following year to recommence. While still wearing the dignity of "limmu," on the 24th day of the month Abu (July–August), he set out to lay waste to the country now called the Bohtan district, between the Tigris and the western spurs of the Judi Mountains. Here were the districts of Nippur and Pazati, comprising more than twenty important towns, among which Atkun and Pilazi were burned. Asshurnazirpal then crossed the Tigris and invaded Kummukh to claim the annual tribute it had forgotten to furnish. [It is possible that he went for the purpose of quelling a rebellion.]

At the moment he was thinking of going on to the Moschi, more to the northwest, a messenger brought him a letter which contained the following news: "The city of Suru (Surieh of the present day), which is subject to Bit-Khalupe, is in revolt; the inhabitants have put Khamitai, their governor, to death, and have proclaimed Akhi-yababa, son of Lamaman, whom they have brought from Bit-Adini, as their king." Furious at this information, Asshurnazirpal invoked Asshur and Adad, counted his chariots and soldiers, and flew to the seat of trouble by descending the course of the Khabur. His progress was hampered by the arrival of many persons, their hands filled with presents and their mouths with protestations of fidelity. There were Shulman-khaman-ilani of Sadikkan, Ilu-Adad of Shuma, and a hundred others.

The city of Suru took fright, and the rebels came out to meet him, bringing the keys of the citadel. They kissed his feet, but Asshurnazirpal was inflexible. "I killed one out of every two of them," he says, and one-half of the remainder was reduced to slavery. Akhi-yababa, a prisoner, witnessed the pillage of his palace, he saw his wives, sons, and daughters in chains, and his tutelary gods, his chariot, his armour, and his treasure carried off. He saw all his ministers flayed alive as well as the leaders of the rebellion. A pyramid erected at the city gate was covered with their skins; some were walled up in the masonry, others were crucified and exposed on stakes along the side of the pyramid. One would hesitate to believe all this and would willingly take the Assyrian monarchs for boasters of their cruelty, if the bas-reliefs with which they decorated their palace walls, and which today ornament our museums, did not speak to our eyes or their accompanying inscriptions speak to our intelligence. We must tax our wits to imagine more refinement of torture or of methods of execution.

Before Asshurnazirpal returned to Nineveh, he made a military tour of the regions about the junction on the Khabur and Euphrates, which formed the country of Laqi. All the petty dynasties of this land brought their tribute. Then he advanced as far as Khindanu, on the Euphrates, the frontier of the Shuhi country. On returning to his capital the king was followed by an endless file of slaves, horses, oxen, sheep, chariots laden with stuffs of wool and linen, ingots of gold, bronze and iron, copper and leaden vessels, and wooden framework; the booty, he says, was as numberless as the stars of the sky. The soldiers had laid hold of every manner of object, and in the division a use was found for everything.

At Nineveh the king occupied himself with embellishing his palace while he waited for the spring. In one of the inner courts he erected a statue to himself of colossal size, and the history of his recent conquests was engraved on the palace gates. He was daily obliged to receive the homage of ambassadors who arrived from all parts to acknowledge his suzerainty, offer presents, and claim the sad honour of serving such a master, for they had learned by experience that it was too late for a city to offer its submission when the king was at its gates.

880–876 BCE

It happened that Asshurnazirpal was *en pleine fête* surrounded by his court when news came of a rebellion in the region situated around the sources of the Tigris. The leader of this insurrection was an Assyrian, Khula by name, whom in former days Shalmaneser had appointed governor of Darudamusa and Khalzilukha. The king set out at once, and, arriving at the sources of the Tigris, he sought out the steles which his predecessors, Tiglathpileser and Tukulti-Ninib, had erected, and by their side set up one for himself. On the way he stopped to levy tribute on the country of Izalla and took by assault the cities of Kinabu, Mariru, and Tela. After a bloody contest under the walls of the last place he put out the eyes and cut off the noses and ears of the prisoners whose lives he spared. Khula was flayed alive.

There stood in this region, within the land of Nirbu, a city which bore the name of Asshur and had probably been built by Tiglathpileser in order to control the surrounding country. Since this town had also taken part in the rebellion, Asshurnazirpal caused it to be razed to its foundations as well as the city of Tushka, upon whose ruins he built a pyramid surmounted by his statue and bearing an inscription which related the conquest of the land of Nairi. Here he received tribute of the kings of Nairi. The districts of Urumi and Bituni also brought their gifts. But scarcely had Asshurnazirpal turned his back when all the tribes of Nairi revolted, and he had to return and prosecute a regular man-hunt among the mountains.

The year had been very full, and it was easy to foresee that the disasters following the reign of Tiglathpileser would soon be repaired. In three campaigns Asshurnazirpal had carried the torch over a portion of the land of Nairi, to the south and east of Lake Van, to the sources of the Tigris, through the Khabur Valley, and down the Euphrates. But like the effect of a tempest which passes and devours everything, the Assyrian domination founded only in fear was fatally ephemeral and became shaky just as soon as the chastising arm was observed to withdraw.

876–854 BCE

Feeling secure in the direction of Nairi, which he had treated so harshly, Asshurnazirpal turned his attention to the fertile slopes along the left bank of the Tigris. He risked encountering the Babylonians, but these latter had no longer any fear for him, and the weakened, scattered Kassite (or Kossaean) tribes could scarcely be called formidable. Babitu, Dagara, Bara, Kakzi, and twenty other places underwent the fate reserved for cities taken by assault; one hundred and fifty towns were pillaged and burnt, and the whole land of Nishir was devastated. The rainy season suspended hostilities, and Asshurnazirpal returned to winter quarters at Nineveh, but as soon as the weather permitted on the first of Sivan (May) he returned to Zamua. The capital of Zamua was Zamri, and there King Amikha resided, in no condition to resist. He fled to the mountains where Asshurnazirpal dared not pursue him, and contented himself with laying hands on the riches of the palace. All the surrounding districts hastened to offer their submission with the exception of the city of Mizu, which was taken by assault.

The following year was consumed in military expeditions to the sources of the Tigris, in the lands of Kummukh, Qurkhi, and Kashiari, where certain cities like Mattiate and Irisia had neglected to pay tribute or manifested symptoms of rebellion. Asshurnazirpal experienced no serious or well-organized resistance except beneath the walls of Bit-Ura in the land of Dirra. "The city," he says, "crowns a height, is surrounded by a strong double enceinte and lifts itself like a great thumb above the mountain. With the help of Asshur my lord – I attacked it with my valorous soldiers, and besieged it for two days from the side of the rising sun. Arrows fell upon it like the hail of the god Adad. Finally, my warriors, whose zeal I had encouraged, fell upon the city like vultures. I took the citadel, I put eight hundred men to the sword, and I cut off their heads.

I made a mound with their corpses before the city gate; the prisoners were beheaded and I put seven hundred of them to the cross. The city was pillaged and destroyed; I transformed it into a heap of ruins." Passing thence into the land of Qurkhi, Asshurnazirpal committed the same atrocities: two hundred captives had their heads cut off, and two thousand others were reduced to slavery. One of the kinglets of the land who had succeeded in winning the king's good graces from the time of the first war, Ammibaal, by name, son of Zamani, had become odious to his people, because of his friendship for the tyrant, and he was put to death by his own officers. The king of Assyria hastened to avenge his faithful vassal. When the culprits saw the storm advancing, they tried to ward it off by offering all they possessed to the invader, and for once he remained satisfied.

He had under his authority all the regions between the source of the Supnat and the borders of the land of Shabitani on one side; between the land of Kirruri and that of Kilzani on the other, from the banks of the Zab to the city of Tel-Bari which is above Zaban from Tel-Sa-abtan to Tel-Sa-zabtan; besides this he annexed to his empire the cities of Kimiru and Kuratu, the land of Birut and of Kardunyash, and he imposed tribute upon the whole of Nairi.

What was to be done with so much wealth constantly accumulating in the storehouses of Nineveh, and for whom was this gold, these jewels, this bronze, these rich stuffs? To what use could he put these thousands of slaves who ran the risk of becoming so many idle mouths to feed? Asshurnazirpal had the idea of building a palace which would surpass the wildest dreams of his predecessors, and he fixed its location in the city of Calah, which was particularly *the* city of his dynasty.

ASSYRIA

British archaeologists, who have made a special study of the ruins of Calah, astonished at the treasures they found buried under the mound Nimrud, have attempted to reconstruct from their own imaginations and the recovered documents the general aspect of the city in the days of Asshurnazirpal, who has left his name and inscriptions in every corner of it. "In a strong and healthy position," says George Rawlinson, "on a low spur of the Jebel Maklub, protected on either side by a deep river, the new capital grew to greatness. Palace after palace rose on its lofty platforms, rich with carved woodwork, gilding, painting, sculpture, and enamel, each aiming to outshine its predecessors...."

From the pyramid of the temple of Ninib the Assyrian priests observed the motions of the heavens, calculated the return of eclipses, and questioned the future. In the temple searched by Layard traces were everywhere found of Asshurnazirpal and what he himself calls "the glory of his name." His portrait has been found repeated a dozen times on the bas-reliefs; he has all the features of a corrupt and cruel monarch. His low, retreating forehead lacks nobility; the eyes are unusually large; the cheekbones stand out prominently; the nostrils of the round, aquiline nose are too large; the clipped moustache, brushed and curled at the ends, reveals thick, sensual lips, while the chin and face are covered with that heavy false beard which falls upon the breast in symmetrical twists, and was worn by all the kings. The thick, short neck, the broad shoulders and thick-set body, gave the king a robust, vigorous aspect. His statue in the British Museum represents him standing. In one hand he holds a scythe, in the other a sceptre. On his breast is written, "Asshurnazirpal, great king, powerful king, king of legions, king of Assyria, son of Tukulti-Ninib (?), great king, powerful king, king of legions, king of Assyria, son of Adad-nirari, great king, powerful king, king of Assyria. He possesses lands from the shores of the Tigris as far as Labana [Lebanon]; he has subjected to his power the great sea, and all the lands from the rising to the setting of the sun."

Several years after this statue was erected Asshurnazirpal would not have fixed the Lebanon range as the western limit of his empire, for the fortunes of war still smiled upon him. The last portion of his reign is filled with two great expeditions in which he covered himself with glory. The definite submission of the middle and lower Euphrates region, including the land of Kardunyash, and the conquest of a part of Syria and Phoenicia. A revolt in the lands of Laqi and Shuhi, on the Middle Euphrates, was an excellent pretext for recommencing the war interrupted by the work of embellishing Calah. [He marched upon Suru, levying tribute at every step.] For a long time this little land of Shuhi had been warring with the Assyrians, and though unceasingly beaten and ransomed, it nevertheless managed to hold up its head, and had been able hitherto to maintain its independence. Its sovereigns appear to have had continual friendly relations with their neighbours the kings of Babylon, at least on the occasions when it was necessary to resist the men of the north.

This time the Shuhites again appealed to the Chaldeans, whom the inscription, through tradition, doubtless, still calls the Kassites or Kossaeans. [Suru was taken, and among the prisoners were the brother and the general of Nabu-apal-iddin, king of Babylon.]

Then terror seized the soul of the weak Nabu-apal-iddin, king of Babylon, and all Chaldea trembled. Unfortunate wars and intestine quarrels had put Babylon out of condition to fight against the all-pervading Assyrian superiority. Nevertheless Asshurnazirpal does not say that he entered Babylonia, which he even seems to have prudently respected. He contents himself with telling us that he erected his statue in the city of Suru, and spread terror throughout Chaldea and all the lands watered by the Euphrates.

The following year he was compelled to suppress a revolt of the mountaineers inhabiting the southern slopes of Mount Masius in the very heart of Mesopotamia. This was the state of Bit-Adini, whose principal cities were Kaprabi and Tel-Aban. Asshurnazirpal scattered an army of eight thousand horsemen, and brought back to Calah two thousand four hundred slaves to work at the embellishment of his capital.

In spite of the peace which ruled in the Tigris and Euphrates basins, whose resources were, moreover, completely exhausted, Asshurnazirpal now resolved to strike a great blow on their western side, which would be a field for rapine in which no Assyrian had ever yet set foot. The occasion seemed favourable, for on the west of the Euphrates the Hittites were in no condition to wage war; they had not yet recovered from the terrible blows dealt them by Tiglathpileser, and their resistance in any case would not be very great.

Asshurnazirpal went right ahead ... traversing the states of Bit-Bahian, Amila, and Bit-Adini as far as the Euphrates, which he crossed on floats in sight of Carchemish. Into the city he made a bloodless entry, receiving the homage and tribute of King Sangara. A Hittite prince, Lubarna, ruled in the valley of the River Apre (modern Afrin) [in a state called Patin] and possessed places of considerable importance such as Hazaz and Kunulua (the capital). Lubarna made preparations to oppose the march of the invader, but on seeing him approach fell on his knees and stripped himself of all he possessed for offerings. He was soon master of both slopes of the Lebanon, and he could see the great Phoenician Sea (Mediterranean). There, in astonishment, and grateful to the gods for all their blessings, he offered them a sacrifice of thanks on a wave-washed rock. "I received," he says, "the tribute of the kings of the land of the sea, the people of Tyre, Sidon, Byblus, Makhallat, Maiz, Kaiz, Akharri, and of Arvad, which is situated full on the sea; they brought me silver, gold, tin, iron, iron utensils, garments of wool and linen, 'pagut,' large and small, of sandal and ebony wood, skins of marine animals, and they kissed my feet."

Asshurnazirpal, protected by Ninib and Nergal, the gods of strength, embarked on a vessel which he captured in the harbour of Arvad and took a sea trip, during which he killed a dolphin. Several days later he hunted among the steep gorges of Lebanon, killed buffaloes and boars, capturing a number of them alive, which he sent to Assyria. He boasts of having killed one hundred and twenty lions himself, and claims that these animals succumbed to fright before his almightiness. He further enumerates troops of wild animals which he drove back to their lairs, – antelopes, deer, ibexes, gazelles, tigers, foxes, leopards; he also killed some eagles and vultures. Among these mountains this true son of Nimrod quite forgot himself until the king of Egypt, whom the fame of his deeds had reached, sent a congratulatory embassy asking for his friendship. When later the kings of Egypt and Assyria met on the shore of the

Mediterranean, it was by no means for mutual congratulation and the exchange of presents.

After this, Asshurnazirpal turned northward into the Amanus Mountains, where he cut down cedar, pine, and cypress trees for his great buildings in Calah. No one will ever know how much effort, nor the lives of how many slaves it cost, to transport those gigantic logs cut in the Amanus forests over the mountainous and trackless country to the banks of the Tigris.

Asshurnazirpal never revisited the shores of the Mediterranean, and like Moses he but caught a glimpse of the promised land which his successors were destined to conquer, and whose inexhaustible riches they so long exploited. What we know of the remainder of his reign is the story of unimportant expeditions, principally for the collection of tribute in the north of Mesopotamia and around the sources of the Tigris. The district of Khipani and its capital, Khuzirina, as well as the states of Assa, Qurkhi, and Adini, underwent new trials; the city of Amida, the modern Diarbekir, witnessed a pyramid of human skulls rising before its walls, and three thousand slaves – those whose eyes were not put out or who were not crucified – were sent to Nineveh, where they were employed in digging a great irrigation canal to make use of the waters of the Upper Zab, the borders of which were planted with trees torn from the forests of Syria.

The last eight years of his life seem to have been more peaceful than their predecessors, although we can scarcely suppose that he passed them in profound peace, which would be as hard to reconcile with his turbulent and sanguinary nature as with the terrible condition of the lands he had conquered,

SHALMANESER II AND HIS SUCCESSORS

Aside from the ruthlessness of his conquests, Asshurnazirpal was chiefly remarkable for rebuilding the city of Calah, constructing a canal, erecting himself a wonderful palace, whose ruins have been found at Nimrud, and the building or rebuilding of a great aqueduct. He, who had butchered and battled so liberally, died in 860 BCE in peace.

His son, Shalmaneser II (Shulman-asharid) (860–824 BCE) commenced warlike operations at once. After a campaign eastward (860 BCE) he entered upon a systematic conquest of the western countries. After several campaigns (859–856 BCE) Akhuni's district of Bit-Adini, on both sides of the Euphrates, was completely subjugated, incorporated with the kingdom, and peopled with Assyrian colonists, and Tel-Barship on the Euphrates was changed into an Assyrian residence city under the name of Kar-Shulman-asharid (City of Shalmaneser). Finally he succeeded in capturing the prince who had fled across the Euphrates into the mountains. Next followed the campaigns on the west of the Euphrates. In the year 859 BCE he twice defeated a coalition of North Syrian princes, the rulers of Carchemish, Patin, Sama'al, etc., joined by the kings of Que and Khilukha; then he subjugated the Amanus district and the district on the lower Orontes (the country of Patin). In the following year, the annual tribute of all the North Syrian states was definitely settled.

854–829 BCE

In the year 854 BCE Shalmaneser advanced farther south. Khalman made submission, but a strong coalition was formed against him in the district of Hamath by Hadad-ezer, or Ben-Hadad II, of Damascus, Irkhulina of Hamath, and Ahab of Israel. The adjacent smaller states of the princes, Matinu-Baal of Arvad (Aradus), Baasha of Ammon, etc., followed suit.

The Syrian states evidently recognized the full extent of the danger threatening them; Ahab of Israel probably made peace with Damascus so as to be able to withstand the Assyrians. Only the Phoenician cities were obdurate; whilst the Arabian prince, Gindibu, sent a thousand camel riders, and even the Egyptian king sent one thousand men. A battle took place at Qarqar in the vicinity of the Orontes. Shalmaneser boasts of a complete victory. [His inscription says: "Fourteen thousand of their warriors I slew with arms; like Adad I rained a deluge upon them, I strewed hither and yon their bodies, I filled the face of the ruins with their widespread soldiers; chariots, saddle-horses, and yoke-horses I took from them."]

But he attained no further successes, and his power was limited to northern Syria. In the years 850, 849, and 846 BCE, Shalmaneser renewed his attacks upon central Syria, the last time with one hundred and twenty thousand men, but without great success. Their tribute money was not much safeguard to the North Syrian princes, the places in the district of Carchemish and in the Amanus Mountains were again and again plundered and burned, and the inhabitants massacred. Only the king of Patin, who was farthest away, and therefore the most powerful of the vassals, seems to have been better treated.

The fifth campaign, in 842 BCE, was more successful, but in the meanwhile the revolutions in Damascus and Samaria overthrew the old dynasties, and Hazael and Jehu ascended the throne. In a battle at the foot of Mount Lebanon, Hazael was conquered and shut up in his capital; but Damascus was not taken. Shalmaneser laid waste to the Hauran, then repaired to the coast, where Tyre and Sidon, and also Jehu of Israel, paid him tribute. The tribute payment of the latter (gold, lead, vessels, etc.) is depicted on Shalmaneser's black obelisk. In the year 839 BCE the campaign was repeated without any far-reaching success; and Tyre, Sidon, and Byblus paid tribute. When the people of Patin slew their king, the Assyrian general, Asshur-daian (or Dan-Asshur), took fearful revenge for the death of the faithful vassal. But Shalmaneser extended his dominion in this district northward only. In the years 838 and 837 BCE, twenty-four kings of Tabal (in Cappadocia), as well as the king of Milid (Melitene), were compelled to pay tribute; and in 835 and 834 BCE, King Kati of Que, *i.e.* East Cilicia west of Mount Amanus, was vanquished, and the town Tarzi (*i.e.* in all probability Tarsus), was taken and given to his brother Kirri.

Shalmaneser II had the same success in the east and north of his kingdom. After the mountainous district on the Tigris had been conquered, the Assyrians came into direct contact with the powerful race of the Alarodians, whose territory extended on both sides of the Lake of Van, from the source of the Euphrates to the land of Garzan, or Gozan, on Lake

Urumiyeh. After making a fearful visitation to Khubushkia and its vicinity, Shalmaneser had already attacked their king, Arame, on the east in 860 BCE. In 857 BCE he invaded his district on the west, after crossing the Arsanias. In 845 BCE he penetrated as far as the source of the Euphrates, and in 833 BCE Asshur-daian, his commander-in-chief, repeated the same campaign. It seems that Arame and his successor, Siduri (or Sarduris), in the year 833 BCE, made, on the whole, a valiant defence.

Much greater success attended the campaigns against the southeasterly mountainous races of Urartu on the "sea of the land of the Nairi," *i.e.* the lake of Urumiyeh, and the districts of Manna, Parsua, Amada (Media), etc., at the south and east of the same as well as that against the land of Namri southeast of the Zab. In the years 844, 836, 830, and 829 BCE the campaigns in these districts were conducted sometimes by the king himself, and sometimes by his commander-in-chief.

The famous representations on Shalmaneser's black obelisk show how King Sua of Gozan and the Lord of Musri (*i.e.* the eastern mountainous district) sent him a collection of wonderful animals, double-humped camels, apes, a rhinoceros, an elephant, and a yak, besides gold, silver, bronze vessels, and horses.

Between the great campaigns there were a few smaller struggles; in 855 BCE in the Masius Mountains, in 853 BCE against the kings of Tel-Abnai, and in 847 against the town of Ishtarat and the country of Yati, districts south of the source of the Tigris; in 848 BCE against the unknown land of Paqarakhubuni, west of the Euphrates, and finally in 831 against the Qurkhi. The black obelisk records that the desert district of Sukhi, on the other side of the Euphrates, subjected by Asshurnazirpal, remained dependent, and Marduk-bel-usur of Sukhi brings to the king as tribute silver and gold, elephants' teeth, garments, and also stags and lions. In the years 852 and 851 BCE Shalmaneser advanced to Babylon. The king of Babylon, Nabu-apal-iddin, had just died, and his brother Marduk-bel-usate had taken up arms against Marduk-nadin-shum, the son of Nabu-apal-iddin. Shalmaneser went to the assistance of the rightful king, defeated the rebels in two expeditions, and presented rich gifts in the sacred cities of Babylon, Borsippa, and Kutha to the chief gods enthroned there. Then repairing farther southward into the land of Chaldea proper, he vanquished the kings of Bit-Adini and of Bit-Dakkuri, and exacted tribute from Mussallim-Marduk and Yakin, who was ruler of the sea country, which was subsequently called Bit-Yakin after him.

We see that the unity of the kingdoms of Sumer and Accad was now no more; but that south of Kardunyash, the district of Babylon, there arose a line of smaller states. Perhaps the South was always separated from Kardunyash after the Kossaean conquest.

829–783 BCE

In the last years of Shalmaneser's reign his son Asshur-danin-apli rebelled against him with a great portion of the kingdom, including Asshur, Arbela, the town of Imgur-Bel, founded by Asshurnazirpal, Amido, and Tel-Abnai, on the upper Tigris, Zaban on the Zab, etc. But another son, Shamshi-Adad IV, quelled the insurrection [and it took him four years of hard fighting to dissipate the opposition] and succeeded his father on the throne. The first campaigns of the new ruler were directed against the Nairi countries, the mountains on the north and east of the Tigris, and his general, Mushaqqil-Asshur, penetrated as far as the "Sea of the Sunset," which means as far as the Black Sea. Then the king attacked Babylonia; a line of frontier places was taken, and [in the battle of Dur-Papsukal, in northern Babylonia] King Marduk-balatsu-iqbi, who had been supported by the rulers of Chaldea, Elam, Namri, and the Aramaean races of eastern Babylonia, was slain.

This expedition was repeated in the years 813 and 812 BCE; and other wars the king mentioned, in shorter notices, cannot be more accurately localised. He made no attempt of any encroachment of Syria's rights.

806–774 BCE

The successes of [his son] Adad-nirari III (811–783 BCE) are of greater importance. In the North and South all the races hitherto subjugated, including the Medes, the people of Parsua, etc., were kept in subjection. Frequent mention is made of expeditions against Manna, Khubushkia, Namri, and Aa. The king says that his kingdom was extended as far as the coasts of the "great Sea of the Sunrise," *i.e.* the Caspian Sea. In 803 BCE mention was made of an expedition "to the sea coasts" (*i.e.* Babylonia, not Syria). As in Shalmaneser's time, all the kings of the land of Kaldi (Chaldea) paid tribute; in the chief cities of Babylonia the king offers sacrifice, gains rich booty, and fixes boundaries. Many expeditions were moreover made against the Aramaean race of Itu'a which dwelt in Babylonia, and these were repeated in subsequent reigns. "On the west of the Euphrates," says Adad-nirari, "I subjugated the land of Khatti, the whole land of Akharri, Phoenicia, Tyre, Sidon, the kingdom of Israel (Bit-Khumri), Edom and Philistia as far as the coasts of the West Sea, and imposed taxes and tribute upon them." He makes special mention of an expedition against Mari, King of Damascus, who was besieged in his capital and forced to capitulate, and pay 2300 talents of silver, 20 talents of gold, 300 talents of bronze, 5000 talents of iron, so that the loot of the Assyrian king was very considerable. These events cannot be accurately fixed, chronologically. The chronological lists mention campaigns in 806, 805, and 797, against Arpad, Khazaz, and Mansuate in northern Syria. The war against Damascus was included in one of them, for it led to the payment of tribute by the Phoenician cities and the southern states (Israel, Edom, and Philistia). [There exists an inscription of this reign referring to Sammuramat as "Lady of the Palace and its Mistress." There is some reason for conjecturing that this might have been the woman round whose name and undoubted prestige in so glorious a reign, clustered the legends of Semiramis. No previous Assyrian king ruled over so great a territory, or collected so much tribute as Adad-nirari III, or, as it is sometimes written, Ramman-nirari III. After him came a period of decline in which there are no royal inscriptions, and of which our knowledge comes from brief notes in the Eponym lists.]

774–745 BCE

The next king Shalmaneser III (782–773 BCE) also went to Syria and made war against Damascus, 773, the land of Khatarikka, 772, and the land of Lebanon.

His successor Asshur-dan III (772-754 BCE) also made war against Lebanon in the years 767 and 755, and against Arpad in the year 754. The subjugation of Hamath probably occurred in one of these expeditions. Battles are mentioned against Babylonia (in the district of the Aramaean race, Itu'a and the city of Gannanat) in 777, 771, 769, and 767 BCE, in which the city of Kalneh was presumably taken. But Shalmaneser III was chiefly concerned in the subjugation of the land of Urartu, the Alarodians. He is mentioned fewer than six times as taking the field against them (781–778, 776, 774 BCE); but his efforts met with no, or at least no enduring, success.

In all probability the formation of a great Armenian kingdom with the city of Van (Thuspa of the Greeks) as the central point dates from this period. Its founder was Sarduris, the son of Litipris, who was probably identical with the king Sarduris who was conquered in 833 BCE by Shalmaneser. In two inscriptions written in Assyrian, he calls himself "King of the land of Nairi." His successors (Ispuinish, Minuas, Argistis I, Sarduris II) then utilised the Assyrian writing for inscribing the language of their country. For in the same record they call their kingdom Biaina, whilst it is called Urartu by the Assyrians. The inscriptions of the rulers are rather numerous and written quite in the Assyrian style. They record the buildings of the kings in Van itself, where a citadel was built by Argistis, sacrifices and gifts to Khaldi and the numerous other deities of the Armenian Pantheon, campaigns and conquests.

When still co-regent with Ispuinish, his father, Minuas erected monuments in the two high passes south of Lake Urumiyeh which record his conquests, and other inscriptions also relate his successes against the land of Manna and its vicinity. These battles presumably occurred in the latter time of Adad-nirari III, and are the continuation of his campaigns in the eastern mountains. Minuas also fought against the land of Alzi, against the king of the city of Milid (Melitene), and against the Kheta. An inscription on a wall of rock on the Arsanias below an old castle (near Palu) records among others his successes in this direction. In the north he penetrated to and beyond the Araxes; one of his inscriptions is to be found on the right bank of the river opposite Armavir, and two others, written by his son Argistis, north of Eriwan. The latter seems to have been the most powerful ruler of Urartu. A long inscription on the rock of the citadel of Van records his successes in the land of Manna, which he seems to have subjugated, and also in the west, against Melitene, the land of Khatti (Kheta), etc.

Repeated victories over the Assyrians are mentioned, which were evidently won against Shalmaneser III and Asshurdan III, or their generals. Sarduris II, the son of Argistis, was also very successful in both districts. For it appears from his inscriptions, confirmed by later events, that Melitene, Kummukh, Gurgum, and other princedoms on the Amanus, became feudal states of the kingdom of Urartu, which included the whole Armenian plateau from the sources of the Euphrates and Araxes across Lake Urumiyeh. How Sarduris II succumbed to the Assyrian will be shown later.

The reign of Asshur-dan III seems to have been much more peaceful than the preceding ones, for the short chronicle of this period repeatedly records that the king remained "in the land," and therefore undertook no campaign.

The successes of Argistis were of great importance. Insurrections also broke out in the interior in the years

763 to 758, first in the city of Asshur, then in Arrapachitis (Arpakha), a city situated in the vicinity of the Upper Zab, east of Nineveh, and finally in Guzanu, in the Khabur country. After its subjugation, Asshur-dan, as already related, repaired twice more to Syria (755 and 754 BCE), but it was not possible with the increasing extension of the Armenian power in this direction to retain supremacy over the smaller states of Syria.

747-740 BCE

The next reign, that of Asshur-nirari II (754–745 BCE) was still less eventful. He took the field only in the years 749 and 748 BCE against the mountainous country of Namri, in the southeast [and in 754 BCE against Arpad]. Otherwise, he remained "in the land." In the last year of his reign the chronicle mentions an insurrection in Calah. The fact doubtless was that in the spring of the following year (746 BCE) the throne was ascended by a usurper who called himself after the first of the great Assyrian conquerors, Tiglathpileser.

The overthrown dynasty, which went back to Ishme-dagan and Shamshi-Adad and the ancient Bel-kap-kapu, had held the throne in uninterrupted succession for more than a thousand years.

TIGLATHPILESER III (745-727 BCE)

The eminent Dutch historian Tiele calls the new monarch Tiglathpileser II, but a recently discovered inscription of Adad-nirari II speaks of his grandfather, Tiglathpileser, and so the latter, of whom nothing is known beyond his name, is now denoted the second ruler of his name. Therefore the subject of the present chapter is here called Tiglathpileser III.

Tiglathpileser III mounted the throne of Assyria on the 13th Airu (about April) of the year 745 BCE, and resided, says Tiele, during the greater part of his reign at Calah and Nineveh, where he built palaces. He was without any doubt an Assyrian, and not a Chaldean, as has been supposed. Whether he was the rightful heir, or whether he was even of royal blood, remains undecided. His real name was Pulu (Pul, Poros), and there is reason to suppose that he was either a military commander or a younger son of the king, who took advantage of the confusion during the last years of the reign of Asshurnirari II to put the crown on his own head. He assumed the name of the great conqueror, Tiglathpileser.

He may have employed the first months of his reign in restoring quiet in the country and establishing himself securely on the throne. It is only in September of the year 745 (month Tasrit) that he marches into the field and turns his arms against Babylonia. Nabonassar (Nabu-nasir) had ruled at Babylon since 747, but nothing else is known of him, though he seems to have been the founder of a new method of reckoning time. Tiglathpileser's first campaign was not, however, directed against him, at least not immediately; his first object was to destroy the Aramaeans' and Chaldeans' ever-increasing power in that country. After he had won possession of the city of Sippar, which lay between the Tigris and the Euphrates, and perhaps even of Nippur also, and had conquered Dur-Kurigalzu, together with some other less important strongholds of Kardunyash, as far as the Ukni, he subdued the nomadic

Aramaeans east of the Tigris, reorganized the government of the conquered territory, dividing it into four provinces, over which Assyrian governors were placed, founded two cities [Kar-Asshur was one and probably Dur-Tukulti-apal-esharra the other] as administrative centres to preserve the allegiance of the new territory, and peopled the new settlements with the prisoners of war. The priesthood of Babylon, Borsippa, and Kutha brought gifts from the temples of their gods into the king's headquarters, and thus averted the danger which threatened their towns also. For the time Tiglathpileser contented himself with the successes gained. It was not at present his intention to subdue all Babylonia, or perhaps he was not yet strong enough to do so. Apparently all he desired was to secure the southern frontiers of Assyria against the invasions of the Aramaeans and Chaldeans, who were becoming more and more audacious, before he ventured farther afield.

The security of the eastern border was of scarcely less importance. In the year 744 he marched against the ever turbulent Namri which lay in this direction; here, too, he compelled all to bow to his victorious arms, even penetrated the western portion of the future Media, and exacted tribute from all the Median princes as far as the eastern mountains of Biknu. He did not proceed in person to further conquests, but entrusted the punishment of those Medians who dwelt farther east to his general, Asshur-daninani, who returned victorious, bringing with him rich booty, especially in horses. However, this country was not incorporated in the empire.

His hand was now free for the re-establishment of the weakened power of Assyria in the west. But one of his most powerful enemies who had, perhaps, already stirred up Namri to resistance, namely Sarduris II of Urartu, or Chaldia, sought to prevent this. When Tiglathpileser had reached Arpad in Syria, he found his flank, and when he would have marched still farther, his rear, threatened by a considerable army at whose head was Sarduris, and which besides the latter's troops consisted of those of the northern Hittite states of Melid, Gurgum, Kummukh, and Agusi. The defeat of the allies was complete. Sarduris had to abandon his camp and seek refuge in flight. About seventy-three thousand prisoners fell into the Assyrians' hands.

740–732 BCE

The three following years were not fortunate. When Tiglathpileser marched against Kummukh he does not appear to have left an adequate garrison behind him in Arpad, for in the year 742 BCE the town, and with it the key of the west country, was in the power of his enemies, and he found himself obliged to besiege it for three years. Not till the year 740 BCE did he take it, and thither came Kushtashpi of Kummukh, Rezin of Damascus, Hiram of Tyre, Uriakki of Que, Pisiris of Carchemish, and Tarkhulara of Gurgum, to offer him rich presents. One of the Hittite princes, Tutammu of Unqi, a district between the Orontes and the Afrin, refused his submission. His capital, Kinalia, was taken for the second time and the whole country placed under an Assyrian governor. In the year 739 BCE Tiglathpileser continued his conquest northeast of Arpad, devastated Kilkhi, a district belonging to Nairi, and conquered Ulluba, where he founded an Assyrian capital under the name of Asshuriqisha. But it was long before the land of the Khatti (Syria) was pacified. Between 740 and 738 no fewer than nineteen districts belonging to the Syrian kingdom of Hamath, and some other adjacent districts, broke away from Assyria, and from some mutilated parts of the inscriptions it is believed we may conclude that they asked for help from Azariah [Uzziah], the warlike king of Judah. At all events, the latter at that time ventured to defy the power of Assyria, and Tiglathpileser connected this hostile attitude with the rising of the people of Hamath. About 738 BCE Azariah was defeated and the country of Hamath added to Assyria. Then the king had recourse to his favourite means for the suppression of the sentiment of nationality – namely, the transplantation of prisoners of war in the most extensive fashion. Whilst all princes of any consideration and even an Arabian queen now offered the conqueror their submission and presents, he received the joyful tidings of important successes won by his generals on the other frontiers of the empire. The eastern Aramaeans had shaken off the Assyrian yoke and advanced to the Zab, but were driven back, though with some difficulty. At the same time the governor of Lullume was harassing the Babylonians, whilst the governor of Nairi held in check the populations on the northern frontier. Booty and prisoners were sent to the king in the land of the Khatti.

The three following years (737–735 BCE) he was occupied with expeditions in the east and northeast. Some districts of Media were then under the Babylonian rule, and now passed to that of the Assyrians. But the most important event of this year was the march to Turushpa, the capital of Urartu [Chaldia], the residence of Sarduris, on the lake of Van. No Assyrian conqueror had penetrated so far as this, nor did Tiglathpileser succeed in taking the town in which Sarduris had fortified himself after his first defeat; but the power of this dangerous rival was broken for a long time.

732–731 BCE

Tiglathpileser now determined to bring the west under his yoke, and did not rest until he had brought all the Hittite and Semitic countries to the coast of the Mediterranean and the frontiers of Egypt, except some Arabian districts, under his sway. This took him three years, from 734–732 BCE. The immediate inducement to this expedition was probably that Ahaz of Judah, threatened by Rezin of Damascus and Pekah of Israel, called in the aid of Assyria. Moreover, the last two had probably paid no tribute, and, generally speaking, Assyria needed little persuasion to fish in troubled waters. The first attack was directed against Rezin. Beaten in the open field, he was compelled to retreat to his capital. Here Tiglathpileser shut him in "like a bird in its cage"; he conquered all the towns round about, including the important city of Sam'ala, and marched on, after having destroyed, according to his wont, all crops around Damascus, and thus increased the difficulty of transporting the means of existence. He marched into Israel (Bit-Khumri), wasting whole districts, some of which he added to his empire, – for the present, however, leaving the capital undisturbed. The immediate goal was now the Philistine Gaza, whose king, Hanno (Khanunu), probably trusting in Damascus and Israel, had at first renounced his allegiance, but now on the approach of the Assyrian army fled to Egypt. The town was taken, and a rich booty fell into the hands of the victors. Askalon, whose prince Mitinti had made an attempt at rebellion, was punished – though probably not till later – and Rukipti, Mitinti's son, raised to the throne. Shamshi, "the queen of Arabia in the land of Sheba," also offered resistance, but was likewise utterly defeated and with difficulty escaped with bare life. Her country, which is certainly not to be confounded with the Sheba of the South, became an Assyrian province. Other Arab tribes submitted voluntarily, and amongst them the well-known Tema; and Tiglathpileser appointed the powerful tribe of the Idibi'il, as being nearest to Egypt, to be wardens of the marches at the gates of that still mighty empire. Now came the turn of Samaria, the only city of Israel which the conqueror had not yet reduced. He appears, indeed, to have visited it, but not to have besieged and taken it, yet he raised Hoshea, who had meantime slain Pekah, to the throne, or confirmed him in its possession. It was longer before Damascus fell. It continued to hold out for two years more. That it was then taken is probable.

Of all the kingdoms of the West there now remained only Tyre and Tabal, which latter lay much farther north. The king did not go in person against either of these towns, but he sent Rabshakeh, who subdued them and changed the government in Tabal, while on Tyre he imposed a tax of not less than one hundred and fifty talents. Whether this took place now or later, cannot be said with certainty.

731–726 BCE

Victorious over all rebellious subjects in his colossal empire, and dreaded by all his neighbours, Tiglathpileser now felt himself strong enough to make a direct attack on the Aramaeans and

Chaldeans of Babylonia, and to conquer the holy city itself. In the year 731 BCE he ventured and accomplished this act of daring. In Babylonia itself no one seems to have resisted him, and the population seem rather to have received him as a deliverer. He entered Sippar, Nippur, Babylon, Borsippa, Kutha, Kish, Dilbat, and Erech, each in their turn, and received the protection of the great gods, by offering them sacrifices. Then he fell on the Aramaic-Chaldean tribe of Pekud (Pekod), subdued it as far as the frontiers of Elam, continued his victorious march through the Chaldean states of Bit-Silani and Bit-Sha'alli, which soon succumbed to his arms. Nabu-ushabshi, the king of the former state, was impaled before the gate of his capital, Sarrabani, and the town levelled with the ground; Zakiru of Sha'alli was sent to Assyria in chains, and the capital, which still offered resistance, was starved into surrender. Bit-Amukkani, whose king, Ukinzer (Chinziros), who appears to have been at that time the leading chief of the Chaldeans, and consequently regarded as king of Babylon, was not so easily overcome. It is true that the whole country was ravaged and the king shut up in his capital of Sapia; that a sortie of the garrison miscarried; that in fear of the overwhelming strength of Assyria, Balasu of Bit-Dakkuri, Nadin of Larak (Bit-Shala), and even Marduk-bal-iddin [Merodoch-baladan] of Bit-Yakin on the seacoast, the man who was later to become so terrible an enemy to Assyria, came here to offer their costly gifts and their submission; but Sapia was not taken and Ukinzer not conquered, so that nominally he shared the rule over Babylon for yet another year. Still, from this time forward it was not without reason that Tiglathpileser styled himself king or overlord of Babylon, king of Sumer and Accad; he might boast that he ruled from the Persian Gulf to the Far East, over the coasts of the Mediterranean as far as Egypt, and that he had extended his kingdom farther than any of his predecessors. He reigned for three years more, for the most part in peace, as far as we know. Of his last two years it is reported that he clasped the hands of Bel; that is, that he received the highest religious consecration as king of Babylon. In the year 727 BCE Shalmaneser IV succeeded him on the throne. The latter only ruled for five years, and of his short reign little is known.

SHALMANESER IV

In the list of the Babylonian kings for these five years, there stands, not his name, but that of Ulule, who was neither, as has been believed hitherto, an independent prince nor a viceroy appointed by Shalmaneser, but none other than Shalmaneser himself, who also probably resided at Babylon. Perhaps his expedition against Phoenicia and Israel falls as early as the year of his accession. The occasion of the war against Tyre, whose king, Elulaeus, at that time stood at the head of the Phoenician towns, is said to have been an expedition undertaken by the latter against the Khittim of Cyprus. It is more probable that the Tyrian king, like Hoshea of Israel, had taken advantage of Tiglathpileser's death to renounce his allegiance to Assyria. Shalmaneser again subdued Hoshea and raised tribute from him. At the same time he sent into Phoenicia a part of his army, which devastated the whole country, and once more made it tributary. After this the whole empire seems to have quieted down, for the following year (726 BCE) was a year of peace. But the calm was not of long duration. Scarcely had the Assyrian troops marched away, when Hoshea turned to the Egyptian king, in the hope that with his aid he might free himself from the yoke of Assyria, and from thenceforward once more refused the tribute.

We have here probably a great conspiracy, in which Elulaeus was also concerned, for Shalmaneser now marched against both kings. He took Hoshea prisoner, evidently after a struggle, wasted the whole land of Israel, but at Samaria, whose population may very likely have incited the king to revolt, he encountered an obstinate resistance. Meantime the whole Phoenician mainland, either from fear or under pressure from the superior force of Assyria, hastened to desert from Elulaeus and to submit to Shalmaneser. The Tyrian king found himself under the necessity of retreating to his fortress on the island of Tyre, where he was at once besieged. It was only under Shalmaneser's successor that Samaria was taken after a three years' siege, and Tyre after one of five years. We cannot but experience a feeling of respect for these two cities, which ventured unaided – for the help from Egypt failed, as usual, to appear – to defy the gigantic power of Assyria....

FOUR GENERATIONS OF ASSYRIAN GREATNESS (722–626 BCE)

After the death of Shalmaneser IV, the throne of Assyria was taken by a man of doubtful antecedents, who became the founder of a very powerful dynasty. This king, like some previous usurpers, adopted a name famous in Assyrian history. He became known to the world as Sargon II, and Rogers says he was not of royal blood; Tiele, however, from whom we shall quote, thinks differently.

722–716 BCE

In the year 722 BCE Sargon became king in Asshur. He was an Assyrian of royal blood, who seems, however, to have belonged to another branch than that of the dynasty which had ruled before Tiglathpileser III, nor does he appear to have been closely related to the latter and his successor. He boasts that he restored to the ancient seat of government, the city of Asshur, her long usurped rights, and to Kharran, the object of his especial favour, her former liberties, which had also long been curtailed. Evidently, therefore, he appeared to a certain extent in the character of an innovator, or rather as the restorer of the ancient order.

Samaria fell shortly after his accession, and a part of its inhabitants were led away into banishment, to be replaced later on by others. Whether or not Sargon was present in person is not clear, but it is certain that he could not long devote his attention to the western portion of the empire. Scarcely was Shalmaneser IV dead before the Chaldeans revenged themselves for the humiliation they had suffered at the hands of Tiglathpileser. Marduk-baliddin [Merodach-baladan] of Bit-Yakin, at that time the most powerful amongst them, since through his timely submission to the Assyrians his country had been preserved from the miseries of war, had made himself master of the city of Babylon, and now ruled as king over the whole Babylonian country. Sargon marched south, perhaps in the hope of recovering what was lost. But in this he was unsuccessful. He did not venture to attack Babylon itself, but turned his arms against an Aramaean tribe, the Tu'mun, who had surrendered their chief to the Chaldean king. The tribe was subjugated and carried to Syria. Sargon now pressed on as far as the town of Dur-ilu in whose suburb he sustained with Babylon's ally, the Elamite king Khumbanigash, a hotly contested fight, from which he asserts that he came off victor. This campaign, however, yielded no further advantages. Elam retained its independence and Merodach-baladan possession of Babylon. An indirect result was that the South had learned to know Sargon as a military commander, and, for the future, good care was taken not to molest him.

The danger threatened from another quarter. Syria was up in arms. At the head of the rising was Hamath, where a man of mean origin, Ya-ubidi or Il-ubidi, had seized the government. Arpad, Simirra, Damascus, and Samaria followed his example. He found a support in Hanno (Khanunu) of Gaza, who had resumed his throne, and even in Shabak, the Ethiopian king of Egypt, whom Hoshea's unhappy fate does not seem to have frightened from endeavouring to measure his strength with the imperial might of Assyria. Even before the allies could unite their forces, Sargon, who probably received early intelligence of what was going on in the countries of the Mediterranean coast, encamped before Qarqar, where Ya-ubidi had fixed his headquarters, stormed and burnt the city, had the ringleader flayed alive and his principal adherents put to death, increased his host with three hundred warriors who fought in chariots, and six hundred horsemen from amongst the conquered, and then marched south against the allied armies of Hanno and Shabak. At Raphia on the Egyptian frontier was fought the decisive battle, which turned out a brilliant victory for the Assyrians. Hanno was taken and carried off to Assyria with nine thousand of his subjects, and Shabak owed his safety only to his precipitate flight in which he was accompanied only by his chief herdsman. Hezekiah seems to have thought it wise not to defy the victor; perhaps he even sent Sargon a present. Tyre also must have been pacified in this year (720 BCE).

Meantime the other enemies of the empire were not yet cowed. The whole north, northeast and northwest, longed impatiently to shake off the Assyrian yoke. In this they were supported by Mitatti of Zikirtu, Rusas of Urartu and Mita of Muskhe, who had secretly formed a league over which Sargon was to triumph only after a long and fierce struggle. In the year 719 Mitatti contrived to persuade some towns of the loyal Iranzu of Man to revolt, whilst Rusas brought several other towns under his sway. Sargon proceeded against them with so much energy that the instigators themselves held cautiously aloof, while they beheld their country laid waste and most of its inhabitants carried into the west, especially to Damascus. In the year 718 BCE unrest revealed itself in Tabal, where Kiakki, prince of Sinukhtu, refused to pay his tribute. But he, too, was soon led away captive to Assyria, together with seven thousand of his subjects, and Matti of Atun, a faithful vassal, was invested with Kiakki's province. In the year 717 BCE Sargon had to suppress a dangerous rising. Pisiris, the Hittite prince of Carchemish, which was one of the keys of the West, attempted, with the support of Mita of Muskhe, to make himself independent. But his city was taken, the majority of his subjects carried off, and an enormous booty stored in Asshurnazirpal's palace at Calah, which Sargon had restored for himself.

716–715 BCE

These disturbances were nothing compared with the war which now, in the year 716 BCE, broke out against Sargon and lasted several years. Rusas of Urartu had persuaded the chief men of the Assyrian provinces of Karalla and Man to secede, in which he was supported by Zikirtu and by the mountain region of Umildish, which was governed by a certain Bagdatti. It appears that the rebellion had spread all over the eastern frontier, and the princes of western Media also took arms. Sargon boldly attacked his enemies. He began with the country of Man, which lay nearest, soon got Bagdatti into his power, and had him flayed. The chief men of Man raised Ullusunu, the brother of Aza, whom Bagdatti had murdered, to the throne and compelled him to join Rusas's party, to which the princes of the Nairi states, Karalla and Allabra, whose names, Asshurli and Itti, denote them as Assyrian deserters, also went over. But scarcely had Sargon set out against them before Ullusunu and his nobles found themselves obliged to offer their submission. Sargon confirmed the former in his kingdom, and compelled his two allies with other petty chiefs to return to their allegiance. The territory of the city of Kisheshim was ruled by a governor, Bel-shar-usur, probably a Babylonian. Sargon gave it the name of Kar-Nergal and made it into an Assyrian province. A like fate befell the west Median town of Kharkhar, which had expelled its sovereign, Kibaba, and solicited support from Dalta of Ellipi; henceforth it was called Kar-Sharrukin [City of Sargon]. On this the governors of other Median towns made their submission.

715–711 BCE

But after these isolated successes it was still long before the eastern states were quieted. In the following year (715) Rusas wrested twenty-two towns from Ullusunu, and a certain Daiukku, who is called viceregent of Man, was involved in the affair. Khubushkia, a state of Nairi, and the neighbouring districts, became refractory, and the territory of Kar-Sharrukin, incorporated only the year before, again seceded. At the same time in the west Mita of Muskhe made an invasion into the Assyrian district of Que [in eastern Cilicia] with considerable success. Nevertheless, Sargon succeeded in maintaining the upper hand at all points. He reconquered Kar-Sharrukin, fortified it more strongly than before, and received the homage of the governors of twenty-two Median cities. His general in the west was not content with reconquering the towns taken by Mita, but even pressed southward as far as the Arabian Desert, and transferred the tribes subdued there to Samaria.

Secure of the west, Sargon now felt in a condition to strike at the real authors of all the trouble in the east. After Man and some Median districts had paid their tributes, the next thing was to proceed against Mitatti of Zikirtu. So complete was the overthrow of this prince that, after the burning of his capital, Parda, and the desolation of his country, he with his whole people sought another home. It was a harder task to subdue Rusas, the soul of the confederacy. But this, too, was accomplished by the warlike king. Rusas was defeated among his high hills. His whole royal house, amounting to some 250 persons, fell with his horsemen into the victor's hands, and he himself only escaped with much difficulty and hid in the mountains. Rusas still built hopes on one of his allies; if he would make a stand all was not yet lost. This was Urzana of Muzazir, a former vassal of Asshur, who had, however, joined Rusas as the chief of a kindred tribe. In his mountain country, protected by its natural strength and almost impenetrable, he believed himself entirely safe. But the dauntless spirit of the ancient Assyrian warriors was not extinct in Sargon. He piously commended himself to the protection of the gods, assembled a carefully selected body of troops, and ventured with them on the almost impossible enterprise. When Urzana understood that the valiant hero was actually approaching with his veterans, he fled, according to the praiseworthy custom of Asiatic despots, with all speed into the higher mountains, leaving his capital and his own family to the mercy of the enemy. Muzazir's fate was now soon decided; with a large number of prisoners, and an extraordinarily rich booty, including the two great gods of the country, Sargon returned to his own country. This was the death-blow for Rusas. The whole structure so laboriously prepared lay in ruins, and filled with despair he fell upon his sword.

When Sargon had thus secured his empire against the danger threatening from the half-savage barbarians of the north, he re-established order in the northwest and west. Next he turned, not against the chief author of the trouble, Mita of Muskhe himself, but against Tabal, which lay not far and somewhat to the south of Muskhe. Ambaris of Tabal, to whom previously, while his father Khulle was still alive, Sargon had amongst other tokens of favour given one of his daughters to wife, and whose kingdom he had increased by the grant of Cilicia, had been ungrateful enough to join with Rusas and Mita. In the year 713 BCE Sargon punished him as he had deserved, and made his country into an Assyrian province. The same thing happened to Khamman and Melid in the following year. Sargon peopled the country with foreign prisoners of war, and endeavoured by the erection of ten fortresses to secure it against Urartu and Muskhe. Continuing its southward march, the Assyrian army remained for a time in the region of the Amanus, and then, in the year 711 BCE, attacked Gurgum in the neighbourhood of Kummukh, which became an Assyrian province.

711–709 BCE

It is very doubtful whether Sargon took a personal share in these expeditions. It was during just these years that he was occupied with the construction of his new residence of Dur-Sharrukin. It is certain that the devastation of Ashdod, which concluded the campaign of 711, was effected not under the king's superintendence, but under that of the king, Akhimiti, whom Sargon had installed there, but who had been expelled, and Yaman, a man of mean origin, raised to the throne by the people. On the approach of the Assyrian army this hero fled to Egypt, but the king of Melukhkha (Egypt), fearing the vengeance of Assyria, sent him back loaded with iron bands. The population of Ashdod was also carried away and replaced by other tribes. Fortified by these triumphs, Sargon could now collect his forces in order to undertake a war which should set the crown to all his achievements. This was the conquest of Babylon, which had been for the last twelve years in the possession of the Chaldean king, Merodach-baladan.

Two years were required for this undertaking, in which Sargon proceeded with great caution. Merodach-baladan was ready for the attack. He had not neglected to make the necessary dispositions and to strengthen his fortresses. In one of them, Dur-Atkhara, which was probably the nearest to Assyria, and whose defensive works he had caused to be raised, he had concentrated the whole military power of the Aramaean tribe of Gambuli, and had sent to their assistance a portion of his own choicest troops, six hundred horsemen and four thousand foot. Sargon directed himself against this fortress, and whilst he was besieging it, it is probable that another division of his army won several successes in the east, where it had to keep the Elamite king, Shutur-nakhundi, occupied, and prevent him from joining hands with his ally. Dur-Atkhara fell; more than eighteen thousand prisoners and a great booty became the spoil of the conqueror, and the rest of the defenders hastily took to flight. The Assyrian king made the town his headquarters; he subsequently gave it the name of Dur-Nabu, and placed it under an Assyrian governor. The Khamarani tribe which dwelt on the banks of the Euphrates, in their terror at the approach of his army, had already taken refuge in the town of Sippar. At the news of the surrender of Dur-Atkhara, and the defeat of the Gambuli, the Aramaean tribes of Rubu, Khindaru, Yatburu, and Puqudu, who dwelt east of the Tigris, and relied on the protection of Babylon and Elam, withdrew behind the River Ukni. The Assyrians threw a bridge across the Umlias, a river to the north of Elam, and took several strongholds there, whereupon some chiefs of the Aramaeans did homage to the king at Dur-Atkhara. They were assigned to the new government of Gambuli. The remainder were attacked and defeated in the territory of the Ukni, so that of them also many submitted, and were made subject to Gambuli. Now the army of Assyria operating east of the Tigris attacked Elam from Yatburu, subdued all the surrounding country, the seven principalities of Yatburu, with which two fortresses conquered from Elam were incorporated, and a part of the Elamite territory itself. It compelled the forces of the land of Rash, which belonged to Elam, to retire to a fortress, and the Elamite king to seek refuge in the high mountains of his country. Secured against any surprise from this quarter, Sargon himself with the main body now crossed the Euphrates into the Chaldaic-Babylonian state of Bit-Dakkuri, whose capital, Dur-Ladinna, henceforth became his headquarters.

There was now no room for Merodach-baladan in Babylon. Threatened on three sides, and in danger of being cut off by Sargon from his own principality, he and his troops left the city during the night and directed their steps to the Elamite part of Yatburu, whence they might advance against the enemy in co-operation with Shutur-nakhundi. But, although he offered the latter the most costly presents, the Elamite had not yet forgotten the lesson he had received. He declined to expose himself to new defeats, and so, perhaps, lose both land and people. Merodach-baladan left Yatburu, having gained nothing, and collected his army in a stronghold of his own country, called Iqbi-Bel.

Meantime, at Dur-Ladinna, in Bit-Dakkuri, not only did Sargon receive the submission of the inhabitants and the neighbouring Bit-Amukkani, but the authorities of Babylon also came in solemn embassy, bringing an invitation to enter the holy city, with which he immediately complied. At the great festival of the lord of the gods in the month of Shabat (January) he was permitted "to clasp the hands" of that great Bel-Marduk and Nabu, the king of the universe.

But still the south of Babylonia was not yet subjugated, for there Merodach-baladan was still in arms. He collected all his forces in the immediate neighbourhood of his capital, and at the same time, for fear of treachery, led thither the population of the ancient cities of Ur, Larsa, Kishik, etc. Strong defences were set up and special canals dug, behind which he entrenched himself with his allies. But the great king did not shrink before all these obstacles. Scarcely was the campaign of the year 709 begun, before he marched south, distributed his troops along the enemy's whole line of defence, and inflicted on the latter so terrible a defeat that the trenches appeared as though full of blood, and the Suti, who had marched from Bit-Yakin to the rescue, did not venture an attack, but hurriedly retreated. Then Sargon fell on the auxiliaries and slaughtered them like sheep. Terror now seized on the Chaldeans' main army; Merodach-baladan left his camp with all speed and retreated to his city. But it, too, was soon taken after a short siege, and with this the power of Merodach-baladan was broken. It is uncertain whether he himself fell into his enemy's hands or saved himself by flight; but probably the latter was the case, for immediately after Sargon's death he is again in a position to take action, at least if the Merodach-baladan, who then revolted against

Sennacherib, is the same who was conquered by Sargon and his son. But for the time Babylonia was freed from the Aramaic-Chaldean domination, and breathed again. Sargon restored the ancient rights of the natives which the oppressors had curtailed in favour of the foreigners. To the towns of southern Babylonia he gave back their stolen gods; he everywhere showed himself extremely liberal to the temples and the ancient religion of the country. In all directions he appeared as deliverer, avenger of the insulted gods, restorer of the ancestral religion, protector of the priests and of all the natives of the country. His triumph did not signal the commencement of foreign rule, but, on the contrary, it was he who put an end to it.

709–708 BCE

Sargon's rejoicings over his victory were still further increased by the embassies and reports which he received one after the other. Uperi, the king of the island of Dilmun, in the Persian Sea, did homage to him while he was still at Bit-Yakin, and gave costly presents. When he had marched from southern Babylonia to consolidate his dominion in the conquered countries, still more welcome tidings reached him at Irma'i. Even his great enemy in the northwest, Mita of Muskhe, who had stood with Rusas at the head of the confederacy against Asshur, but who had been overcome by the governor of Que, now sent ambassadors to Sargon with presents and protestations of homage and devotion. When, finally, the king had again returned to Babylon, there came envoys from seven districts of Cyprus, "whose names had never been known to the kings, his fathers, since the rule of the god Sin," and who offered him valuable gifts and kissed his feet. Thus the empire of the mighty conqueror stretched from the island of Dilmun, in the Persian Gulf, to the Isle of Cyprus, in the Mediterranean.

Sargon returned to Calah in the beginning of 708, his fourteenth year as king of Assyria, and third as king of Babylon, after spending some time in the latter city. Whilst he was at Calah, resting on his laurels – he did not again, himself, take the field – and from thence prosecuting the construction of his new residence of Dur-Sharrukin, not far from Nineveh, his armies had still to conduct two wars, one in the year 708, the other, perhaps, in the same, but probably in the following year. Urartu had to a certain extent recovered from the blows it had suffered in the defeats and death of its king, Rusas; and the new king, Argistis, began to grow restless, and persuaded Prince Mutallu of Kummukh to a revolt against the Assyrian domination. Sargon sent a high official with a powerful army and full royal authority, who put Mutallu to flight, taking the capital of the province, and so restoring the Assyrian dominion. The rich booty was sent to Calah to the king, and the latter placed a very strong garrison at the disposal of the new viceroy, to prevent any further attempts at risings, and at the same time to constitute a defence against Argistis. But it was once more apparent that the Assyrian Empire, as a purely military power, rested on a tottering foundation, and could only be sustained by continued wars and victories....

708–705 BCE

Sargon, who, even in the early years of his reign, in the midst of his most terrible wars, had not neglected the reconstruction of palaces and temples at Nineveh and Calah, now devoted himself entirely to the realisation of a long cherished plan, whose execution he had begun long ago. A new suburb of Nineveh, called by his name, was to come into existence as a permanent memorial of his fame and piety, and at the same time serve as a summer residence. This was Dur-Sharrukin with its temples to various gods, with its palaces and gardens, whose walls and gates, like those of a sacred city, looked to the four quarters of the heavens and were named after the high gods, and whose inhabitants, selected from the prisoners of war of all the nations whom the king had conquered and placed under Assyrian magistrates, afforded a living testimony to his mighty deeds. On the 22nd Tasrit (September) 707, the gods were solemnly introduced into their temples, and on the 6th Airu (April) of the following year, the king took possession of the new residence. He was not permitted to enjoy it long. In the year 705 BCE he fell by an assassin's hand. [This is doubted by some authorities, who believe that he died a natural death.]

Sargon was, without doubt, one of the greatest princes who sat on the throne of Assyria and Babylon. He was no mere conqueror, who thought merely of increasing the size of his empire, but also a true king who occupied himself for its welfare. What chiefly strikes us in him is the comparative moderation by which he was distinguished from his predecessors and in particular from his son and successor. The horrors and devastations of war were the inevitable accompaniment of the forcible subjugation of the whole of western Asia, and some obstinate rebels were punished according to the barbarous custom of his age and race. But in general he contented himself with expelling the conquered prince or making him prisoner. He also remained faithful to the policy first pursued by Tiglathpileser III, namely that of furthering the unity of the empire by transplanting whole populations to other districts. But in his records it is only now and then that we encounter the refined cruelties perpetrated by the other Assyrian kings, and he never dwells on them with so much complacency as they display.

SENNACHERIB

705–681 BCE

Sargon II was succeeded by his son Sin-akhe-erba, the Sennacherib of the Bible, who reigned long and gloriously. The period now in question has a double interest. It is a time when Assyria is at the height of its power; and the interest that attaches to any strong empire is enhanced by the fact that the Assyrians of this period came in contact with the people of Israel. Sennacherib, in particular, bears a name familiar to all succeeding generations because of the repeated mention of this ruler in the Hebrew scriptures....

705–702 BCE

It was in the year 705 BCE that Sennacherib, who was not, perhaps, entirely guiltless of Sargon's death, mounted the throne and became the supreme king both in Babylon and Assyria. To Merodach-baladan, who may have been either the recognized king of the Sea Lands, or the son or namesake of the latter, the occasion now seemed favourable for recovering the throne lost to Sargon. Sennacherib and his army marched up in all haste, and though it appears that Merodach-baladan had all the Aramaean and Chaldean tribes on his side, and was moreover supported by Elamite auxiliaries, he suffered a defeat and so lost his kingdom. According to the Assyrian narrator, this defeat was so complete that the Chaldean was forced to take flight in the greatest haste, leaving behind him his whole baggage-train, as well as his family and court. He had reigned nine months. The land was heavily scourged, great and small towns were taken and laid waste, and the inhabitants dragged into exile. The same fate was meted out to all Arabians, Aramaeans, and Chaldeans who were living in the Babylonian towns.

When the campaign in Chaldea was at an end, the troops were sent against the Aramaean tribes, which dwelt on the banks of the Tigris and Euphrates. Here, too, there was devastation and plundering. A considerable booty, as was to be expected from these nomads, consisting chiefly of cattle, but also including camels, fell into the hands of the conquerors, and no less than two hundred thousand men and women were carried off to Assyria as slaves. It fared still worse with one small, heroic tribe, the Hirimmi, who offered an obstinate resistance to the Assyrians. When, finally, the latter succeeded in overcoming them, of all the rebels they left no prisoner of war alive, and hanged the corpses on poles upon the wall surrounding the town. Sennacherib annexed the whole territory to his realm, while he laid on it a very moderate tax for the benefit of the Assyrian god.

We may assume it as probably certain that the king did not personally take part in the campaign, but occupied himself the while with the adjustment of Babylonian state affairs. His policy may be distinctly followed. It was only toward the Chaldeans and their allies that he appeared in the character of an enemy. They alone were punished or carried off. The actual citizens of Babylon, Erech, Nippur, Kish, and Kharsag-kalama he left unmolested, and to propitiate them still further, he even gave them a king belonging to the ruling Babylonian house – namely, the young Bel-ibni, whose father held an important office, and who had himself been brought up from childhood at the Assyrian court. Of him Sennacherib might hope that he would be faithful to Assyria and at the same time not unfriendly to the Babylonians, and therefore he now bestowed on him the title of "King of Sumer and Accad."

The establishment of order in Babylon was turned to account by Sennacherib for the purpose of averting the danger with which his eastern frontier was threatened by the nomads who wandered there, and by the mountain people, and also for extending his empire in every direction. He now attacked the Kasshu and Yasubigallu, by which names we doubtless have to understand those barbarous Kossaeans, and their allies, whose successors, centuries later, according to Diodorus, still made the Mesopotamian frontier insecure, and who were related to those Kassites who had so long reigned over Babylon. Their surest protection was the inaccessible nature of the country. Steep mountain paths and thick forests made it difficult for an Assyrian army to advance, while for vehicles it was impossible.

The king himself led the march, and thus showed himself a worthy successor of the undaunted heroes who in earlier centuries had founded the Assyrian power. His chariot had frequently to be carried behind him, and then he mounted on horseback or performed the journey on foot at the head of his troops. Sennacherib succeeded in taking their three strongholds. The smaller places he laid in ashes and the nomads' tents were burnt. But for greater security he desired to bring the wild tribes under Assyrian rule, and to force them to settle in fixed abodes. He selected Bit-Kilamzakh as a centre, fortified it far more effectually than before, making it a formidable fortress to keep the inhabitants of the country in check, and peopled it with captives whom he had carried off in former warlike expeditions. He caused a tablet inscribed with the history of this campaign to be set up in the capital, in order that the terror of the Assyrian arms might be kept perpetually alive. As soon as he had subdued the Kasshu he marched against Ellipi. Sennacherib fell on the country like a tempest. The two royal seats Marubishti and Accudu, with all the smaller towns, were taken by him and given up to be plundered and burnt, whilst all crops were destroyed and even the cornfields delivered over to the fire. It was with a certain satisfaction that Sennacherib boasted of having transformed Ellipi into a desert, and led away the whole population with its goods and chattels. When these successes became known, a number of Median princes, dwelling at a more remote distance, hastened to offer their submission.

Meantime the king's attention was directed to events in the west. The elevation of the young and high-spirited Tirhaqa to the throne of Egypt, probably as husband of King Shabak's widow, and guardian of his son who was a minor, had aroused in some princes of the strips of land along the Mediterranean coast the hope that by an alliance with him they might shake off the Assyrian yoke. To these belonged Elulaeus (Luli) king of Tyre and Sidon, Zedekiah (Zidga) king of Askalon, and above all Hezekiah, the king of Judah. The latter took on himself the leadership, at least in the southwest.

Sennacherib's third campaign was directed against this coalition, and is probably to be assigned to the year 702 BCE. With its usual promptitude, the Assyrian army marched on Phoenicia, and thus attacked one of the allies before the rest had a chance to unite their forces. Elulaeus fled in haste to Cyprus, where Citium still belonged to him; and all his towns on the continent, within a short space of time, fell into the hands of the Assyrian. All the princes of the other petty Phoenician states came that they might offer their submission.

701 BCE

Sennacherib immediately starts along the seacoast for Askalon, southernmost of the revolted states, and soon overpowers it. Zedekiah, the king, suffers the usual fate; with the hereditary gods of his house, his wife, his sons, daughters, brothers, and his whole family he is dragged away to Assyria.

Now that the whole coast-line had submitted, Sennacherib turned to Ekron, which lay farther to the north, but more inland. But in Altaku [Eltekeh], which lay south of Ekron and belonged to it, he encountered some resistance, and was at the same time caught by an Egyptian army, which at last appeared to the rescue of the Philistine towns. According to the Assyrian account it was very numerous and was composed of the troops of the king of Musuri, and of the bowmen, chariots, and horses of the king of Melukhkha. Still, whatever these two names may mean here, it is certain that neither Tirhaqa himself nor any other Egyptian king was leading the army, but that it was merely commanded by Egyptian princes and two generals belonging to the horsemen. These did not show themselves a match for the powerful Assyrian conqueror. In spite of the number of their followers they suffered a total defeat, and it does not say much for their skill and courage that they all, princes and commanders, fell alive into the enemy's hands. In consequence of this, the relieving army appears to have retraced its march to Egypt, so that nothing now stood in the way of Sennacherib continuing his conquests in Philistia and Canaan. The ruling high priest and the princes who had stirred up the rebellion, he caused to be put to death and their corpses displayed on stakes on the town walls; such of the inhabitants as had made common cause with the rebels were led away captive; the innocent, on the contrary, went free.

Now at last came the turn of Hezekiah. The following is the main outline of what the Assyrians relate concerning the campaign against Judah. When it became apparent that even after the overthrow of his allies, Hezekiah was not inclined to give himself up readily to the mercy of his powerful enemy, the latter marched into his country. Forty strong towns besides the citadels and countless smaller places were beleaguered, taken by storm, razed to the ground or burned, and more than two hundred thousand prisoners, with a great number of horses, asses, and camels were carried away from them. Hezekiah himself, Sennacherib shut up in his capital, Jerusalem (Ursalimmu), like "a bird in its cage." But the town was in a strong position and provided with a good garrison. Hezekiah had not only assembled his faithful warriors, but had also enlisted a number of Arabian soldiers. When these, however, required pay, and in case of refusal threatened to withdraw, Hezekiah – the Assyrian says from dread of the glory of Asshur – paid the heavy tribute which Sennacherib demanded of him – namely, thirty talents of gold [about £9000 or $45,000] and three hundred talents of silver, besides precious stones, woods, and other articles, and also sent to Nineveh his daughters and the women of the palace, accompanied by male and female slaves together with an envoy, who was at the same time commissioned to proffer his master's homage.

From this narrative no one who did not know the official style of the Assyrian historical writers would guess that Jerusalem was not taken, and that Sennacherib, with the remainder of his army, was obliged to quit Judah with all possible speed. But it was not their business to report failures of this kind. Doubtless in this account of the course of Sennacherib's campaign, the main features are correct and also described in the right chronological order. It is certain that, after the overthrow of Phoenicia, the king found it advisable first to reduce the small Philistine states on the seacoast to obedience that he might then attack the Jewish king, who at last, when he had been deprived of everything save his capital, and when his own soldiers were deserting him, saw himself compelled to produce the war-tax demanded. The assertion that he sent it by an envoy to Nineveh cannot possibly be correct, and must have been invented for the purpose of rounding off the narrative without relating the true issue of the affair.

ASSYRIA

We possess two traditions concerning the close of the war which, though they may differ from one another in other respects, agree in this, that an extraordinary event unexpectedly compelled Sennacherib to return with some trepidation to Assyria. One is the biblical tradition; the other is the account of Herodotus.

The biblical account, as found in 2 Kings, we have already quoted. The account of Herodotus relates to a certain king Sethos, a priest of Vulcan (believed to represent Shabak of the XXVth Dynasty). This king, says Herodotus, treated the military of Egypt with extreme contempt, and as if he had no occasion for their services. Among other indignities he deprived them of their arurae, or fields of fifty feet square, which, by way of reward, his predecessors had given to each soldier; the result was that, when Sennacherib, king of Arabia and Assyria, attacked Egypt with a mighty army, the warriors whom he had thus treated refused to assist him. In this perplexity the priest retired to the shrine of his god, before which he lamented his danger and misfortunes; here he sank into a profound sleep, and his deity promised him, in a dream, that if he marched to meet the Assyrians, he should experience no injury, for that he would furnish him with assistance. The vision inspired him with confidence; he put himself at the head of his adherents and marched to Pelusium, the entrance of Egypt: not a soldier accompanied the party, which was entirely composed of tradesmen and artisans. On their arrival at Pelusium, so immense a number of mice infested by night the enemy's camp that their quivers and bows, together with what secured their shields to their arms, were gnawed in pieces. In the morning the Arabians, finding themselves without arms, fled in confusion, and lost great numbers of their men. There is now to be seen in the Temple of Vulcan a marble statue of this king, having a mouse in his hand, and with this inscription, "Whoever thou art, learn, from my fortune, to reverence the gods."

Taking together all the circumstances in which the somewhat contradictory reports are agreed, we may picture the course of events as follows: On the advance of the Assyrian king, Hezekiah collects his picked men, who are reinforced by foreign soldiers, in his capital, and resolves to defend it. Meantime the Assyrian army overruns the whole of Judah, takes one fortified town after another, and all the citadels and smaller places, and Sennacherib has penetrated as far as Libnah, a small town lying in the southwest of the Jewish territory. There he learns that Tirhaqa is approaching with an Egyptian army, to fight against him and liberate Judah. So long as the capital is not yet in his power, and Judah consequently not wholly subdued, he cannot go out against him without losing all the advantages gained. He will therefore try whether he cannot, by threatening Hezekiah, induce him to deliver up the town of his own accord; and he sends him messengers with letters peremptorily calling on him to submit. But with prophetic fire Isaiah pours out his wrath at the insults offered to Jehovah by this servant of Asshur, and vehemently urges steadfast resistance.

701–696 BCE

Sennacherib meantime continues his victorious march, and now that he is master of all Judah with the sole exception of the capital, he can detach a part of his army. If Hezekiah will not yield of his own free will he must be compelled to do so. A strong body of troops under the leadership of the Rabshakeh, or generalissimo, marched against the strong fortress and closely beset it on all sides. But it is the Rabshakeh who chiefly figures in the foreground of the affair. The Hebrews tell of his efforts to induce the people and the garrison of Jerusalem to desert their king. He sought to attain this end by means of scornful speeches on the helplessness of Judah.

Hezekiah, perhaps again spurred on by Isaiah, who still continues to trust in a miraculous deliverance, does not give way at once, but defends the city against a superior foe for some time, though it was the only town that remained to him and was as isolated and forsaken "as a cottage in a vineyard, as a lodge in a garden of cucumbers." But at last, when famine in the town has reached its highest pitch and signs of impatience and discontent manifest themselves among the garrison, he makes up his mind to submission, and sends a messenger to Lachish to inquire the terms of surrender. They are very hard. But there is no longer any choice, and he tenders the Assyrian conquerors the amount required at the hand of the envoy, who subsequently accompanied it to Nineveh. Whether the siege was thereupon immediately raised, or whether it was thought well to keep the town still under observation until the contest with Egypt was decided, we cannot say positively. But, as a great misfortune, either pestilence or some other natural phenomenon, actually did soon after smite the Assyrian army, and the whole of the conqueror's force, reduced to a miserable handful, quitted Judah and the West, the true believers among the Egyptians and Israelites saw in it a miraculous deliverance which the gods had sent them, and the latter at the same time regarded it as a fulfilment of the prophecies of Isaiah, which at first did not seem to be coming true.

Of course the event had not in reality the importance which the grateful Egyptians and Israelites attributed to it. Although it secured them relief, and Sennacherib's army was so weakened that he thought it advisable to beat a hasty retreat, yet his supremacy over Phoenicia and Canaan remained for a long time unshaken, and in the following year he was again in the field with a powerful army. Subsequently he appears again to have marched westward and to have made a particular fight against Arabia and Edom. But it does not appear that in this campaign he also made war against Phoenicia, Philistia, and Judah, as he certainly would not have failed to do had traces of insubordination showed themselves. The chastisement had been too severe, and the country was too greatly exhausted.

In the year 700 BCE Sennacherib's presence was again required in Babylonia. It was the third and last year of Bel-ibni's rule at Babylon. Sennacherib had him brought to Assyria, together with his whole family. He had proved unequal to the task which Sennacherib had assigned him.

After the victories, which intimidated even Elam, Sennacherib went to Babylon, and there in place of Bel-ibni, set up his own eldest son Asshur-nadin-shum on the throne as king of Sumer and Accad. His six years' reign began in the year 700 BCE, and now Sennacherib thought himself safe from the machinations of Chaldean pretenders.

For some years he had really had his hands free in the south. He employed the time in bringing into subjection some of the northwestern neighbours of his empire. This campaign, which the Assyrians reckon as the fifth, and which must have taken place somewhere between 699 and 696, ended with a war in

Cilicia. According to Berosus it was occasioned by a Greek invasion, and the Assyrian army obtained the victory only after suffering great loss. Abydenus even speaks of a sea-fight on the Cilician coast, in which the Greek fleet was worsted. Both historians agree in this, that Sennacherib immortalised his famous deeds by the erection of his statue or the setting up of bronze pillars with inscriptions, and that he built the town of Tarsus, which he called Tharsin, so that the Cydnus flowed through it as the Arazanes (Aralshtu) through Babylon. Strange as it may seem, the Assyrians themselves make no mention of the foundation of this important town, but Berosus is too credible a witness for his statement to be rejected.

Even before 694 Sennacherib had busied himself in the preparations of a great plan. Merodach-baladan had sought and found in Nagitu, on the coast of Elam, a refuge and place of security where he believed his deadly enemy could not reach him. After the latter's expedition against Bit-Yakin in the year 700 BCE, the remainder of the population of that territory had found it expedient to take ships with their gods, as their master had done, and cross to the region where the latter had taken up his abode. Sennacherib apparently feared that this new state would prove a source of danger to the province entrusted to his son; all the more since Merodach-baladan had now become a vassal of Elam, Asshur's ancient and hereditary enemy. The difficulty was great, particularly as Nagitu was not accessible from the land side, without passing through Elamite territory. He had among his captives shipbuilders from Khatti, and he set them to work at Nineveh on the Tigris and Tel-Barsip on the Euphrates. The ships were towed down the Euphrates and the Tigris [or they may have been transported overland by camels].

They were manned by Tyrian, Sidonian, and Ionic seamen, who were also prisoners of war. He, himself, had meantime marched to the Persian Gulf with his army, and had fixed his camp close to the ships. From the description of the voyage it is evident what a deep impression this very unusual expedition made on the Assyrians. Even before they set sail they made an unexpected acquaintance with the sea, which they believed four hours' distance away; they may perhaps have been aware that, even so far up as Bab-Salimeti, the river was subject to the ebb and flow; but a spring flood, which suddenly laid the camp under water, and even made its way into the royal tent, took them by surprise. They had to seek refuge on the ships and remain on them five days and nights, "as in a great birdcage," says Sennacherib. Whether this experience of life on shipboard was enough for the bold monarch, or whether he had no intention of taking part in the maritime expedition, it is certain that he did not leave the shore. The transports were taken to the mouth of the Euphrates; costly sacrifices to Ea, the sea god, among which were a golden ship and a golden fish, were thrown into the rivers to obtain his protection for the fleet, and then it set sail. It is not told how long the voyage lasted, but merely that the country whither they went lay at the mouth of the Eulaeus (Ulai), the chief river of Elam. There the great battle was fought, and of course the Assyrians came off the victors. They took possession of various Elamite towns, and carried off the Chaldeans and all the goods from Bit-Yakin, together with a number of Aramaeans and captured ships, to Bab-Salimeti, where the king awaited them. Of Merodachbaladan not a word is said. Therefore he did not fall into the hands of the Assyrians, and was not robbed of his sovereignty by the defeat. Thus far, at least, the victory was of no lasting significance for the Assyrians. It appears simply to have destroyed the prosperity of the Chaldean colony for some time, and to have deterred the indefatigable adversary from direct attacks. But this extraordinary and costly expedition shows how greatly he was dreaded and with what implacable hatred his house was pursued by that of Sargon.

696–692 BCE

While the Assyrian king was engaged in the seacoast war, Khallus, the King of Elam, instigated by the Babylonians who had left the town in good time with Merodach-baladan and had sought refuge with him, invaded Accad with his army, penetrated as far as Sippar, where he instituted a massacre, and brought Asshur-nadin-shum prisoner to Elam. On the Babylonian throne he set up a Babylonian, Suzub, son of Gakhul. It is a characteristic trait that the Assyrian account is silent as to the unhappy fate which overtook Sennacherib's oldest son. Suzub, on his accession to the throne, took the name of Negal-ushezib. He is the Regebelos of the Ptolemaic Canon, and must be carefully distinguished from the Chaldean Suzub who did not reign over Babylon till a later date (692 BCE) and under another name.

But the new king was lord over only part of the country. The whole South was still in the hands of the Assyrians and had to be conquered by him.

About June, 694 or 693 BCE, he succeeded in getting possession of Nippur, but his farther advance was checked by the tidings that the Assyrians had meantime marched as far as Erech. Sennacherib immediately despatched a large force against the king of Elam, whom he rightly regarded as the chief author of all the trouble. Erech fell and was sacked, and, laden with rich booty, including even the chief gods of the sacred city, the Assyrians marched forward. At Nippur, Nergal-ushezib awaited them, and in the battle which followed he remained victor. But his rule was of short duration. As to the end of his reign the Babylonian and Assyrian records are agreed. The former asserts that, after the Assyrians had carried away the gods and inhabitants of Erech, Nergal-ushezib was taken prisoner in the battle at Nippur and conducted to Assyria. According to the second, he was thrown from his horse in the battle, taken prisoner and brought in chains before Sennacherib, who then shut him up in prison at the gate of Nineveh. The two accounts seem to make the story complete.

After the misfortune that had overtaken their king, the Babylonians bestowed the crown on Suzub the Chaldean, who had also fled to Elam. He reigned independently for four years, under the name of Mushezib-Marduk. The Assyrians consequently content themselves with mentioning several advantages won by them over the Elamites, and also relating that they took Suzub prisoner on their march from Erech to Asshur. They themselves practically acknowledged that Babylon did not fall into their hands, when they inform us that, after Suzub's capture, the Babylonians closed their city gates against the Assyrians and offered an obstinate resistance.

So far as we may judge, the whole of this campaign of Sennacherib's was a political blunder, which does not speak well for his sagacity. There was in fact nothing to be feared from Merodach-baladan; the real peril, which threatened from Elam, escaped the Assyrian king. The maritime expedition undertaken at so much labour and expense, was more adventurous than glorious, and failed in its main object: the arch enemy, at whom it was aimed, retained his liberty and his kingdom. And meantime Babylon was left without protection, and Sennacherib's own son was bereft of throne and freedom. He had not even provided himself with sufficient forces to avenge the descent of the Elamites and reconquer the lost territory. The sole fruit of the campaign (exclusive of booty and prisoners) was the carrying away of a Babylonian king, whose place was at once taken by another prince, not less hostile. A poor compensation for the loss of the capital, the whole territory belonging to it and of his own son! Under Sennacherib's government it was continually apparent that only under compulsion had the Babylonians submitted to the yoke of the Assyrians, and that they preferred to unite with Elam rather than again obey a Sargonid.

692–689 BCE

In Elam, meantime, a rising took place against Khallus, possibly because he had been unsuccessful in his war against Assyria. [He was killed in the uprising.] Kudur-nankhundi became king in his stead. Sennacherib thought this a favourable opportunity to attack his old enemies, the Elamites. It was in 692, probably, that he took advantage of Elam's disordered condition to inflict a heavy punishment on that country. From Rasa to Bit-Burnaki he ravaged and plundered to his heart's content. He introduced Assyrian garrisons and placed the territory under the care of a governor. Besides this, he took thirty-five fortified towns. Such was the devastation "that the smoke of the flames covered the face of the wide heaven like a heavy storm," and so great was the terror he spread that Kudur-nankhundi left his residence at Madaktu in all haste, and fled to a town called Khaidala, which lay far up in the mountains. But nature saved him from the hands of the Assyrians. Sennacherib did indeed give orders to march to Madaktu, but he could not carry his intention into effect. It was winter, and in (Tebet) December an earthquake, coupled with storms of rain and snow, compelled him to retreat. The mountain streams were so swollen that no army could now cross them with safety. Only three months afterwards Kudur-nankhundi died "suddenly, before his time," and his own brother Umman-minanu mounted the throne. Scarcely had Umman-minanu assumed the sceptre of Elam than he allowed himself to be beguiled into an alliance with Babylon against Asshur. At Babylon now reigned Suzub II, the Chaldean, Mushezib-Marduk. After his flight from Sennacherib, in the year 700 or 699, he had returned to Babylon, where, after the misfortunes that overtook his namesake, he was made king, no doubt to the great chagrin of the Assyrians. When he sent gold and silver from the treasury of E-sagila, the great temple of Marduk and Zarpanit, to the Elamite king, he found the latter prepared to collect an army at once and march with it to Babylon for a joint attack upon Asshur. Sennacherib was astounded that the lesson he had imparted to Elam in the previous year had borne no better fruit. But the Chaldeans and Elamites had good ground to hope for success. The Assyrian's latest victories had not been rich in lasting results. He had not succeeded in conquering Babylon. He had been obliged to retreat hastily from Elam. He had not been able to defend Chaldea. Moreover, the kings of Babylon and Elam could now count on a number of allies. The number of the enemy impressed the Assyrians, who likened them to a swarm of locusts. "Like a violent gale which drives the rain-clouds across the firmament, so rose the cloud of dust at their approach." But calling on the gods, his heavenly protectors, Sennacherib ventures an attack.

It was a fierce battle; both sides fought with the greatest fury. Sennacherib, himself, was distinguished by his personal courage. With helm and mail, spear and bow, Asshur's sacred bow, which none but the kings of Assyria carried, he stands in his war chariot like an angry lion, and like a heavy storm from Adad, the god of tempests, he rushes on the enemy, covering the plain with corpses as with grass. His horses wallow in blood; blood and fragments of the slain cleave to the pole of his war chariot. A choice troop of Elamite nobles, equipped with golden daggers and bracelets, are slaughtered like sheep, and the Elamite commander and grand vizier, Khumbanundash, a man of great ability, also falls. Others are taken prisoners. Yet the kings of Elam and Babylon and the Chaldean chiefs got away, according to the Assyrian writer, who delights in depicting their sufferings in a very imaginative fashion, with a loss of tents and baggage and of one hundred and fifty thousand dead left on the battle-field. They were pursued for a distance of some miles, but their capture was not effected. There is something loathsome in the lively colours in which the scene is painted; the pitiless slaughter and horrible mutilation of the slain are described with bloodthirsty complacency. The writer of the Assyrian tablet knew well that his savage, revengeful master based his renown on such inhuman acts. And yet it was no victory for the Assyrians. They may have remained in possession of the field, but the murderous battle was so undecisive that the Elamites and Babylonians could claim the victory as well. The losses on both sides must have been so great that neither of the two parties ventured to continue the war. Both sides assumed the attitude of waiting for a more favourable opportunity. The prevalent idea that after the battle of Khalule Sennacherib immediately conquered Babylon is decidedly false and is contradicted by the true reading of both Assyrian and Babylonian records.

Not till the year 690 or 689 did Sennacherib find a favourable opportunity to risk another attack on Babylon. From Elam there was now nothing more to fear. The power of Umman-minanu was much weakened and he was soon to lose it altogether. The Assyrian king marched on Babylon with the impetuousity which distinguished all his warlike expeditions, and was at times disadvantageous to him; and on this occasion his effort was crowned with the desired success. Now he directed his arms against Mushezib-Marduk's town, not as his predecessors, including his own father, had done, as a rescuer bringing deliverance from a usurper and therefore striking at the latter and his dependents, and sparing the inhabitants: upon the town which had so long withstood him, so repeatedly and obstinately lifted its head against him, a fearful vengeance was to be taken. It was literally wiped out; nothing was spared; corpses lay piled up in the streets; all its treasures were pillaged and divided amongst the soldiers; the temples were desecrated, and the gods torn from their sanctuaries. Then the whole town was delivered up to the flames; the walls and ramparts, the temples and the ziggurat, (probably the two towers of Babylon and Borsippa), were thrown down and hurled into the Arakhtu or other canals, and the water from the river and the canals was turned on the ruins that they might be flooded. The very place where the sacred town had stood became unrecognisable and was changed into a marsh. Mushezib-Marduk escaped and sought refuge in Elam, but Umman-minanu, fearing Assyrian vengeance, surrendered his ally, and the latter and his family were brought prisoners to Nineveh.

Such a deed may well have spread fear and horror even in Assyria itself. Sennacherib had done what none had even ventured before. Towards the town which many an Assyrian king had treated with respect and which had never been sacked, he had behaved with a relentlessness which hitherto had only been exhibited to foreign rebels. He was now master of Babylon. For the remaining eight years of his life, he was called King of Babylon, even according to the Babylonian list of kings, although the Ptolemaic Canon mentions this period as an interim. King Ummanaldash [Khumba-Khaldashu] who (the 7th of Adar 690 or 689?) succeeded Umman-minanu on the throne of Elam, and who reigned eight years, left the Assyrian king in peaceful possession. There are sufficient grounds for the assumption that this supremacy over Babylon of a tyrant embittered by earlier reverses was a reign of terror.

For the last years of Sennacherib's reign authentic accounts are almost entirely wanting. An expedition to Arabia, against a certain King Hazael (Khazailu), in which the capital of Edom is stormed and the deity of the place falls into his hands, certainly belongs to this period of his reign.

695–681 BCE

Like most of the Assyrian princes, Sennacherib, in spite of his unsettled existence, was a great builder. But he bestowed the most care on the re-establishment and embellishment of his beloved Nineveh. In the earlier part of his reign he had also strengthened this town with an outer wall and an inner rampart (*duru* and *shalkhu*), and in the year 695 he had built a great palace by the northwest wall, after pulling down a small palace which stood there. The latter had fallen into decay, partly as a result of the overflowings of the canal on which it stood, partly from the heat of the sun. The canal was now diverted, and on its margin was built a new and loftier palace, in which ivory and costly woods were not spared. There the king had a park laid out and irrigated by the waters of the Khushur (Khosr) which were made to flow through it, and it was planted with trees from the Amanus Mountains. At the same time the town was extended and embellished.

Scarcely was this structure completed when Sennacherib caused another palace, which lay farther south of the same wall, to be pulled down. It had served former kings as armoury, magazine, and stables, and had now become not only too small but also decayed. Some fields were added to it and earth brought to raise them, and upon this now rose a palace, not of tiles, but of hewn stone after the fashion of the land of Khatti (Aram). For this also cedars from Amanus and great lion and animal colossi, which had been hewn out of stone in the town of Baladai and then cased in bronze, were employed, and cunning architects disposed them with great care and magnificence. The purpose of the building remained the same; horses and every sort of cattle found stabling, stuffs and weapons were laid up there, but it had now also to serve as a barrack for the national troops. The king's name is displayed on every wall.

Immediately after the completion of this building on the 20th day of Adar, 691, that is, in the same year in which the Battle of Khalule took place, Sennacherib began another and not less important work, which was only completed and inaugurated after the sack of Babylon. This was an undertaking intended to provide the city of Nineveh with good drinking water. A number of canals had to be dug, which served at the same time to fertilise some uncultivated strips of land. In the capital which was thus, as it were, born again, the old warrior now probably rested on his laurels for a few years longer.

In the latter period of his life, Sennacherib appears to have handed over a part of his royal functions to his son Esarhaddon (Asshur-akhe-iddin), if he did not actually make him co-ruler. The latter was not his eldest son, for his name, "Asshur grants brothers, or, a brother," shows the contrary, but he was perhaps, the second, and therefore direct heir to the throne after the death, or at least in the absence of, the king's eldest son, Asshur-nadin-shum, who had been carried off by the Elamites. Esarhaddon was certainly destined to the succession by his father, and was the latter's favourite. Sennacherib issued a decree by which the whole of his booty brought from the Babylonio-Chaldean district of Bit-Amukkani was assigned to him, and his name was at the same time changed to Asshur-etilli-ukinnibal (Asshur, the lord has lent a son) – a name which was more appropriate for one who now took the place of eldest son, but which Esarhaddon himself does not appear to have adopted. His brothers, whether younger or older, were not pleased at this. Two of them at least, Sharezer, whose full name was probably Nergal-shar-usur (or the Nergilus of Berosus), and Adarmalik, disputed the succession, taking advantage of the circumstance that Esarhaddon, at the head of the army, was absent in the northwest, most probably in a war with Armenia. Whilst Sennacherib was praying in a temple, they fell on him and slew him, and Nergal-shar-usur took possession of the throne, [but was at once superseded. Some histories deny his accession]. Thus died Sennacherib, on the 20th Tebet (about December) 681, by the hands of his own sons.

From the official sources, which are the only ones we possess, it is difficult to obtain an idea of the character of the Assyrian sovereign, but the records of Sennacherib's reign certainly make a far more unfavourable impression than those which Sargon left behind. Both were conquerors, but the one shows more respect for law and justice. Stern, at times to harshness, against uncompromising adversaries, Sargon yet gives place to mildness where mercy can be made to harmonise with the interests of the empire. Sennacherib, on the other hand, takes an obvious delight in scenes of blood and desolation, in inflicting punishments which only awaken disgust at their brutish cruelty. The destruction of Babylon, the burning and blotting out of a town venerable from its age and importance, and so sacred to the pious Assyrians, was indeed a blind vengeance which fixes an indelible blot on the name of the author of the crime. Not less courageous and warlike than his predecessors, he was rash and presumptuous rather than bold, and his plans were rather venturesome than well calculated. Impetuous in attack, he neglected the needful precautions, and attained the immediate goal, often only to lose more than he gained. Whether he was concerned in his father's murder cannot be determined; that he was, as his name indicates, a younger son, is no certain evidence of this, but it is a suspicious circumstance that he nowhere mentions his celebrated father's name. If he was guilty, Nemesis overtook him. As a king he was far inferior to Sargon. Nineveh alone had much to thank him for. Babylon, on the contrary, which had called in Sargon as her deliverer, sought to secure her independence of him, and preferred to his yoke the dearly bought protection of Elam. After he died, having reigned something like twenty-four years, it was a long time before the empire was as powerful and flourishing as at the commencement of his rule. In thinking of Sargon and Sennacherib we are involuntarily reminded of Cyrus and Cambyses, who differed from one another in the same way.

ESARHADDON AND ASSHURBANAPAL

681–668 BCE

Sennacherib, as we have seen, was murdered by his sons. It appears that this event did not occur at once after the return from the disastrous campaign against the Israelites, as might be inferred from the Hebrew record, but a good many years later. Esarhaddon, who succeeded his father, was obliged to win back the kingdom from the regicides before he could securely occupy the throne of Assyria. He seems to have had no great difficulty in this, however, and for many years he continued in undisputed sway, not merely sustaining but extending the influence that his father had wielded. The greatest glory of his reign was his successful invasion of Egypt. Opinions have differed considerably as to the character of Esarhaddon....

The opinion of Professor Maspero is perhaps worth quoting in some detail. He says:

"Esarhaddon is one of the finest and most attractive characters of Assyrian history. He was as active and resolute as Asshurnazirpal or Tiglathpileser, without being hard on his subjects or cruel to those he conquered, as they were. He delighted in being merciful as much as his predecessors had rejoiced in being merciless, and the accounts of his wars no longer make constant mention of captives being burnt alive, kings impaled on the gates of their cities, or whole populations being burnt out by fire. He took pleasure in restoring the ruins with which his father and grandfather had covered the land, and in the first year of his reign he gave orders for the rebuilding of Babylon, which was commenced on a grand scale.

"All the Chaldean prisoners were set free, and those who liked to work under the architects could do so for payment in oil, wine, honey, and other commodities of life; and when laying the foundation stones of different edifices, he himself wore the special dress of the masons. The temple of Bit-Zaggaton, the seat of Marduk, the protector of the town, issued from the ruins and the walls, and royal castles were raised beyond their former height. Beyond Babylon Esarhaddon consecrated thirty-six temples at Asshur and Agade; and they were lined with shining sheets of gold and silver.

"The palace which he built at Nineveh on the site of an old building surpassed all that had hitherto been seen. The quarries of alabaster in the mountains of Gordyene and the forests of Phoenicia furnished material for the halls; thirty-two Hittite kings on the Mediterranean coast sent great beams of pines, cedars, and cypresses. The roof was made of carved cedar wood, supported by columns of cypress encircled with gold and silver; stone lions and bulls stood at the doorways; the panels of the doors were made of ebony and cypress, encrusted with iron, silver, and ivory. The palace of Babylon was entirely destroyed, and the one commenced at Calah with Egyptian booty was never finished. The conquerors had been much impressed by the long avenues of sphinxes at the entrance of the Memphite temples, and in imitation of the idea Esarhaddon had sphinxes, lions, and bulls at the entrances of his buildings. The construction lasted three years (671–669), and it was only just far enough completed for the decoration to be started, when he fell seriously ill in 669." Two years later he died.

It will probably be felt by most readers of the records left by Esarhaddon himself – which are, of course, our sole authority in the matter, save for a few chance biblical references – [that] it can hardly be doubted that Esarhaddon was in many ways a much more admirable character than his father. The following excerpt from one of Esarhaddon's inscriptions, contained on a hexagonal prism of baked clay found near Nineveh, and now in the British Museum, will suggest something as to the precise interpretation one should place upon the words "attractive" and "merciful" as applied to an Assyrian conqueror:

"Esarhaddon, king of Sumer and Accad, (son of Sennacherib, king of) Assyria, (son of Sargon) king of Assyria, (who in the name of Asshur, Bel,) the Moon, the Sun, Nabu Marduk, Ishtar of Nineveh, and Ishtar of Arbela, the great gods his lords from the rising of the sun to the setting of the sun marched victorious without a rival.

"Conqueror of the city of Sidon, which is on the sea, sweeper away of all its villages; its citadel and residence I rooted up, and into the sea I flung them. Its place of justice I destroyed. Abd-milkot its king who away from my arms into the middle of the sea had fled; like a fish from out of the sea I caught him, and cut off his head. His treasure, his goods, gold and silver and precious stones, skins of elephants, teeth of elephants, dan wood, ku wood, cloths, dyed purple and yellow, of every description, and the regalia of his palace I carried off as my spoil. Men and women without number, oxen and sheep and mules, I swept them all off to Assyria. I assembled the kings of Syria and the seacoast, all of them. (The city of Sidon) I built anew, and I called it 'The City of Esarhaddon.' Men, captured by my arms, natives of the lands and seas of the East, within it I placed to dwell, and I set my own officers in authority over them.

"And Sanduarri king of Kundu and Sizu, an enemy and heretic, not honouring my majesty, who had abandoned the worship of the gods trusted to his rocky stronghold and Abd-milkot king of Sidon took for his ally. The names of the great gods side by side he wrote and to their power he trusted; but I trusted to Asshur, my lord. Like a bird from out of the mountains I took him, and I cut off his head. I wrought the judgment of Asshur my lord on the men who were criminals. The heads of Sanduarri and Abd-milkot by the side of those of their chiefs I hung up: and with captives young and old, male and female, to the gate of Nineveh I marched.

"Trampler on the heads of the men of Khilakki and Duhuka, who dwell in the mountains, which front the land of Tabal, who trusted to their mountains and from days of old never submitted to my yoke: twenty-one of their strong cities and smaller towns in their neighbourhood I attacked, captured, and carried off the spoil; I ruined, destroyed, and burnt them with fire. The rest of the men, who crimes and murders had not committed, I only placed the yoke of my empire heavily upon them."

It is notable that the successor of Esarhaddon, his son Asshurbanapal, seems to have placed the same favourable opinion upon the character of his father, as compared with his grandfather Sennacherib, that moderns are disposed to adjudge. This is suggested by the fact that Asshurbanapal in various inscriptions refers to "Esarhaddon, king of Assyria, the father, my begetter," and never to his grandfather, whom he probably would have mentioned, following custom, had he held him in any particular regard. Asshurbanapal himself was, at least in his earlier years, a warrior of no mean quality; but he was, it would appear, primarily a lover of the arts of peace. There is a marked difference in the tone of his inscriptions, as compared with those of his predecessors, even when describing his conquests. Many times they suggest one who loves the pleasures of life rather than one who gloats over the infliction of death. The following are the words in which he describes the expedition against Egypt and

Ethiopia, and against Tyre, as recorded on a cylinder now preserved in the British Museum:

"In my second expedition to Egypt and Ethiopia I directed the march. Tandamani [Tanut-Amen] of the progress of my expedition heard, and that I had crossed over the borders of Egypt. Memphis he abandoned, and to save his life he fled into Thebes. The kings, prefects, and governors, whom in Egypt I had set up, to my presence came, and kissed my feet. After Tandamani the road I took, I went to Thebes the strong city. The approach of my powerful army he saw, and Thebes he abandoned, and fled to Kipkip. That city (Thebes) the whole of it, in the service of Asshur and Ishtar, my hands took; silver, gold, precious stones, the furniture of his palace, all there was, garments of wool and linen, great horses, people male and female, two lofty obelisks covered with beautiful carving, two thousand five hundred talents (over ninety tons) their weight, standing before the gate of a temple, from their places I removed and brought to Assyria. The spoil great and unnumbered, I carried off from the midst of Thebes. Over Egypt and Ethiopia, my soldiers I caused to march, and I acquired glory. With a full hand peacefully I returned to Nineveh, the city of my dominion.

"In my third expedition against Baal, king of Tyre, dwelling in the midst of the sea, I went; who my royal will disregarded, and did not hear the words of my lips. Towers round him I raised, on sea and land his roads I took, their spirits I humbled and caused to melt away, to my yoke I made them submissive. The daughter proceeding from his body and the daughters of his brothers, for concubines he brought to my presence. Yahimelek his son, the glory of the country, of unsurpassed renown, at once he sent forward to make obeisance to me. His daughter and the daughters of his brothers with their great dowries I received. Favour I granted him, and the son proceeding from his body, I restored and gave him. Yakinlu, king of Arvad, dwelling in the midst of the sea, who to the kings my fathers was not submissive, submitted to my yoke. His daughter with many gifts, for a concubine to Nineveh he brought, and kissed my feet. Mukallu, king of Tabal, who against the kings my fathers made attacks, the daughter proceeding from his body, and her great dowry, for a concubine to Nineveh he brought, and kissed my feet. Over Mukallu great horses an annual tribute I fixed upon him. Sandasharme of Cilicia, who to the kings my fathers did not submit, and did not perform their pleasure, the daughter proceeding from his body, with many gifts, for a concubine to Nineveh he brought, and kissed my feet."...

ESARHADDON'S REIGN (681-668 BCE)

681 BCE

Sennacherib's murderers did not stand alone, but had a considerable following. Asshur-akhe-iddin (Asshur is brother), Esarhaddon, as the Hebrews call him, who had been already destined to the throne by his father, had therefore to conquer the crown assigned him at the point of the sword. Although it was (Tebet) December – Sennacherib, as we have seen, had fallen on the 20th of this month – and consequently the time favourable for warlike operations had gone by, yet he perceived that this was a case for prompt action. He lay with his army in the northwest, but without waiting a single day, without stopping to collect men, horses, chariots, or material, without even supplying himself with provisions, and in spite of snow and tempest, which might be feared at that season, he hurried straight to Nineveh; "like a bird of prey with outstretched wings." At Khanigalbat, a neighbourhood the position of which is unknown to us, but which must be sought in or near North Aramaea [probably near Melid], the army of the rebels intercepted him. But these were soon defeated and scattered. A great part very probably went over to Esarhaddon. The two chiefs of the rebellion, his brothers, sought safety in flight and were received in Urartu. That one of them, as Abydenus would have us believe, fell in the battle, is not very probable. Still it is certain that they never again attempted to get possession of the government. On the 2nd of Adar (February) the rising was extinguished, and five weeks later, on the 8th of Nisan, that is, the beginning of the year 681 BCE, Esarhaddon mounted the throne of his father.

When his brothers' rebellion was suppressed, Esarhaddon was indeed in safe possession of the Assyrian throne, but by no means in undisputed enjoyment of the sovereignty over the whole of his father's empire. He was continually obliged to engage in wars and to quell risings.

The son of that arch-enemy of the Assyrians, Merodach-baladan, who is generally called Nabu-ziru-kinish-lishir (Nabu, guide the true scion!), had naturally taken advantage of the confusion resulting from the murder of Sennacherib and the war of the succession, to repudiate his allegiance, and may perhaps have already thought of reconquering Babylon. From Esarhaddon's accession he had ceased to send the presents required from a vassal, and had also omitted to appoint an envoy to offer his homage to the new king, and thus to recognise his overlordship. He had evidently overestimated the difficulties with which the king had to contend, and had not anticipated that the latter would so soon repress the rebellion and be in a position to proceed against him with decisive energy. It is uncertain whether he himself risked the attack; it appears, however, that he had already penetrated as far as Ur. Esarhaddon, who was at Nineveh when he received the news of his defection, could certainly not now be spared there. But he ordered the governors of the province bordering on the maritime country to go out against the rebellious Chaldean at the head of an army which was despatched to them, and this proved sufficient. According to the Assyrian accounts Nabu-ziru-kinish-lishir did not await the attack, but fled to Elam. But this realm was no longer what it once had been. Ummanaldash II, who now reigned there, was not inclined to endanger the peace of his kingdom and involve himself in a war with Assyria for a stranger's sake; the fugitive was seized and put to death. Na'id-Marduk, who accompanied him on his expedition to Elam, feared a like fate. He chose the wiser course; he hastened to Assyria, made his submission, and in reward was invested with the sovereignty of his brother's kingdom, that is, of the whole seacoast. Henceforth he faithfully paid the annual tribute.

677–676 BCE

It was not so easy to put down another movement at another end of the empire. Very soon after Esarhaddon's accession, perhaps even before, certain kings of the west country planned an attempt to free themselves from the Assyrian yoke. These were the kings of Sidon and of two other cities whose position is uncertain, but is certainly to be sought east of Sidon, namely Kundu and Sizu. Over the two last ruled Sanduarri, whose name proclaims him as one of the Hittites or related to them, and over Sidon, Abd-milkot. They had to bind themselves by an oath to recover their independence with their united forces, and fought with great persistence. This is shown by the fact that they were not subdued till the fourth year of Esarhaddon, and also of the fearful vengeance of the Assyrians, so little in accordance with this king's customary procedure. In the year 677 Sidon succumbed to the besieging force. The city was plundered, wasted, and depopulated. Town and citadel were "thrown into the sea" and the place where they had stood made unrecognisable. The population was brought to Assyria, with all its goods and cattle and all the treasures of that rich commercial city.

But Esarhaddon did not, like his father, take pleasure in mere destruction. A new town rose in the place where the former had stood. He called it by his own name [Kar-Asshur-akhe-iddin], and allowed conquered mountain peoples and inhabitants of the coast of the Persian Gulf to settle there – the old means, devised by Tiglathpileser, for absorbing sentiments of nationality and independence into

ASSYRIA

the unity of the great empire. Abd-milkot had meantime fled, probably to Cyprus; for Esarhaddon says that he "took him out of the sea like a fish." He was overtaken, made prisoner, and put to death, and in the month Tasrit of the following year, 676, his severed head reached Assyria. It was some time before Sanduarri was conquered in his mountain country, but in the month Adar of the same year he suffered a like fate to that which had overtaken his ally. Then the barbarous triumph took place in Nineveh. All the captured subjects of the defeated kings, with the great and distinguished men at their head, were led through the broad streets of the capital, and two of the noblest carried the severed heads of the rulers round their necks. Revolt against the supreme king, which meant sin against Asshur, the god of the gods, when conducted with much obstinacy as was displayed by these two men, could not be severely enough punished.

If Esarhaddon intended by these severities to spread terror among the kings of the west country, he attained his object. Although according to the wont of the Assyrian annalists, the scribe places the narrative of the war in the king's own mouth, he took no personal part in it, but remained quietly at Nineveh. Thither now came the ambassadors of some twelve kings, whom the Assyrians called simply Khatti-kings and kings of the seacoast, and with them those of ten kings who ruled in Cyprus, to offer him their homage and presents.

When the ten Cypriote rulers, whose names have for the most part a Greek sound, joined in the homage of the Assyrian, Phoenician, and Canaanite kings, it is obvious that

Esarhaddon's army, when it pursued the flying king to Cyprus, had there re-established the Assyrian rule which had not been exercised since the time of Sargon.

All these princes had to bring him costly material for the building of his great palace at Nineveh. There is an inclination to credit Esarhaddon with a special preference for Babylon, and to assume that he had made that town his headquarters, at least towards the end of his life. Our knowledge of the building he erected is, however, not favourable to this view. He certainly governed directly and not merely by vassal-kings that part of his realm of which Babylon was the capital, and there are good grounds for the assumption that he actually cherished the intention of establishing himself at Babylon; but it is none the less certain that for him, as for his fathers, until the nomination of Asshurbanapal as vassal-king of Assyria, the centre of the dominion was Assyria, and the Assyrian capital was his chief home.

676–673 BCE

Although Esarhaddon now imitated his father in his care for the decoration of the Assyrian capital, he did not limit himself to this so exclusively as his predecessors. On the contrary he boasts of having built the temples of the town of Asshur and Accad, and of having adorned them with silver and gold. That he did not neglect Accad or Babylonia is shown by the work, which surpassed all other undertakings, completed in his reign and for which he gave orders in his early years, – the reconstruction of the ruined capital itself.

In Elam it was with disapproving eyes that men regarded this renovation of Babylon by an Assyrian king and with it the re-establishment of the Assyrian rule in that territory. The king of Elam, Ummanaldash II, therefore decided to attack Esarhaddon in this part of the country. In 675, the sixth year of Esarhaddon's reign, he invaded Babylon with an army, we know not on what pretext, and penetrated as far as Sippar. The misfortune was not, however, a lasting one. In that very year Ummanaldash died in his palace. Perhaps there is some connection between these Elamite disturbances and Esarhaddon's campaign against the (to us) unknown country of Ruriza which he conquered in Tebet of the year 673. This may be said with certainty of the measures which he took against the Gambuli. That warlike Aramaic-Chaldean race, which had once constituted the vanguard of Merodach-baladan's army, had then, at least, dwelt in a swampy tract of country where they lived "like fish in the midst of the rivers." At this time their king was Belbasha (En-basha?), the son of Bananu, and in his impracticable country he had been able to preserve his independence. It was not he and his Gambulians that Esarhaddon now feared, but rather that he might easily be won over to ally himself with his neighbour Elam. Belbasha is pressed to choose and Esarhaddon makes ready to convince him by the unanswerable argument of his arms. But the Aramaean does not wait for the struggle. Knowing well that he has now no help from Elam to look to, he decides of his own accord to attest his submission to Assyria and sends the required presents. Thus Esarhaddon gains his object. The submission is accepted, the country spared, the capital, Shapi-Bel, extraordinarily fortified, the command laid on the prince to furnish it with bowmen and to defend it as "the door which unlocks Elam." How well Esarhaddon had judged was to be shown later, when his heir had to punish the son and successor of Bel-basha for his intrigues with Elam.

673–672 BCE

These few facts, with the circumstance that, in the same year, 673, probably while the court was at Babylon, the queen died, are all that we know concerning the history of the southern realm under the reign of Esarhaddon.

More is known of the king's warlike expeditions, or at least those of his army, for it is not likely that he himself took part in them all. Some of them are of little importance to history, or were directed against tribes whose locality we can no longer determine. We pass them over in silence here. Attention may, however, be called to an expedition against Teushpa, the king of the Kimmirri or Cimmerians, or more accurately against the Umman-manda, who dwelt at a great distance, and who were afterwards to be the cause of so much trouble to Asshur and Babylon.

The Cimmerians are also referred to in other records as the enemies of Assyria in Esarhaddon's day. According to these they joined in a great coalition which was formed against Asshur; at its head stood Kashtariti of Kar-Kasshi, a Median prince, who evidently dwelt on the borders of Elam, and Mamitiarsu, governor of the Medes, and to which the Manneans also belonged. At the outset, at least, they were successful, took several towns now unknown to us (Khartam,

Kishassu, and five others), and so great was the fear which they thus spread through Assyria, that in order to propitiate the gods, the priest (*amelu khalti*) was commanded to perform sacred rites and celebrate festivals in their honour from 3rd Airu to the 15th Abu – that is, during one hundred days. The issue of the struggle is not given in the Assyrian records, but it appears that the Babylonian chronicle told of the invasion of Assyria by the Kimmirri and of their defeat.

Perhaps this gave Esarhaddon an opportunity to revenge himself on the Medes and to conduct a war against their country with great persistence. He penetrated farther into it than any of his forefathers – namely, to the land of Patusharra (Patiskhoria?) which lay deep in Median territory, in the neighbourhood of the Bikni Mountains, where so much crystal was found. There ruled Shitir-parna and Eparna, two powerful princes whose names appear to be Iranian. They were subdued by the Assyrians and carried to Assyria with a rich booty, consisting chiefly of cattle, horses, and chariots. This visitation had the result that other princes from farther Media, who had not hitherto acknowledged the Assyrian supremacy, came of their own accord and tendered their submission.

At the other extremity of his empire, Esarhaddon maintained his sovereignty in the same fashion. The means by which Assyria had made herself, and remained during many centuries, the mistress of western Asia, was the pursuit of a traditional policy whose principles the impulsive Sennacherib had forsaken in the most deplorable fashion, but which distinguished Esarhaddon, as well as his grandfather Sargon. By a judicious blending of gracious forgiveness on the one hand and severe punishment on the other, he managed not only to confirm Assyrian sovereignty in the northern regions of Arabia, but also to extend it. Faithful to the rule by which those who had submitted of their own accord must be at once taken in favour, and admitted as allies, he listened to the petition of King Hazael (Khazailu) of Kedar when the latter came to Nineveh and requested that the images of the gods which had been carried thither, might be given back. Esarhaddon had them restored, caused his name and his famous deeds to be inscribed on them, and gave them back to Hazael. But on this king's death he took care that the latter's son Ya'lu, whom he raised to be king in his father's stead, should be still more closely bound to Assyria and pay higher tribute....

672–671 BCE

The glory of Esarhaddon's reign is the conquest of Egypt.... A decisive contest with Egypt was sooner or later unavoidable, especially since Tirhaqa had just brought the divided kingdom into a certain unity and was evidently striving again to raise it to the position of a great power.

In the year 672 Egypt took the first step. As usual, the prize was the overlordship of the West. Tirhaqa managed to persuade Baal, the King of Tyre, to break with Assyria, and thus threatened to draw the whole of the Mediterranean coast into rebellion. Prompt measures were taken, and in Nisan of 671 a powerful Assyrian army marched westward. The immediate goal is Tyre. It is surrounded and the water-supply cut off. Without waiting for the town to fall, Esarhaddon now proceeds south and halts at Aphek, not far from Samaria, thence within fifteen days, with a certain caution and perhaps not without encountering resistance, he leads his army to Rapikhu [Raphia] on the Egyptian stream which forms the boundary between that country and Canaan. Unfortunately the text breaks off abruptly where the narrative of the actual struggle with Egypt begins. But we learn from other sources that the object was attained and Egypt conquered. On the 3rd, 16th, and 18th Tammuz (June) three battles were fought, in which the Assyrians remained victorious. Memphis was taken on the 12th of the month, and although Tirhaqa succeeded in fleeing to his own land of Ethiopia, his son and his brother's sons were taken prisoners.

671–668 BCE

Esarhaddon was now actually king over Egypt, and here again shows himself to be a prudent ruler. He was content with the title of dignity of "King of the Kings of Egypt" – that is, with the overlordship of the country. Had he incorporated it into Assyria, he would have weakened rather than strengthened his empire. His sole aim was to keep it disunited and consequently weak, and by the expulsion of the Ethiopian to put an end to the latter's dangerous intrigues in the west. Therefore he did not put in his own generals, courtiers, or governors, but sought to bind the provincial princes to him by granting them a certain measure of independence. The sole danger for him lay in a united Egypt under the warlike king on whose assistance the ever restless kings of Phoenicia, Philistia, and Canaan might reckon; and he therefore contented himself with obtaining from the provincial princes an oath of fidelity to Assyria. Only the supremacy of Asshur must be distinctly apparent, so the Egyptian name of the northern capital, Saïs, was altered to the Assyrian one of Kar-bel-matati (fortress of the lord of the lands), and that of Neku's son into Nabu-shezib-anni (Nabu preserve me!). After this Esarhaddon went back to Assyria, and on his homeward march he gave orders to carve his royal image and the account of his conquest of Egypt on the rocks by the Dog River (Nahr-el-Kelb) at Beirut, where, besides inscriptions and images of various Egyptian kings, some of his forefathers had caused theirs also to be cut.

The conquest of Egypt is the last great undertaking of Esarhaddon's reign, which was to last only two or three years longer. In the year 670 he was occupied with Assyrian affairs, all details of which are, however, wanting. But by the following year it had become manifest that conditions in Egypt were not permanently settled. It was evident that a new expedition to the valley of the Nile was imperative. Esarhaddon assembled his forces and proposed to head his troops himself, to assert upholding the Assyrian domination in Egypt. Yet first – perhaps because he already had a presentiment of his approaching end, or because he did not trust the aspect of internal affairs – he appointed his eldest son, Asshurbanapal, as co-ruler in Assyria; if we are not to assume, what is also possible, that this was done before the campaign of the year 671. The expedition came to nothing. On the 10th of the month Arakhsamnu (Marsheshwan, about October), of the year 668, in the twelfth year of his reign, the king died, either in Egypt or, as it is probable, before he reached it.

As the great king of a mighty empire Esarhaddon indeed stands very high; for although he was not more soft hearted, or, indeed, where insubordination had to be punished, less harsh than his predecessor, yet he did not act in obedience to ungoverned passion, but with deliberation, and this foresighted policy allowed him always to choose the golden mean between needless severity and dangerous indulgence. In a few years he strengthened the foundations of the Assyrian rule, and considerably extended it; he erected magnificent buildings, and made desolated Babylon rise again from her rubbish-heaps. By raising his son, Asshurbanapal, to the throne during his own lifetime, he made a struggle for the possession of the crown such as that with which his own reign had begun an impossibility, while by his wise and firm government he had laid the foundations for his son's long, and, at least in the beginning, brilliant and glorious reign. Sennacherib had little in common with his great father; Esarhaddon was worthy to be the grandson of Sargon.

ASSHURBANAPAL'S EARLY YEARS (668-652 BCE)

We have already seen that Esarhaddon made his son Asshurbanapal vassal-king of Assyria during his own lifetime. With festive display the young prince entered the royal palace which his grandfather Sennacherib had built, where his father Esarhaddon was born, and grown to manhood and had since held his court, and where he himself, as a friend of learning and science, now began to collect that extensive library which, after centuries had passed, was to make his deeds and the traditions of his nation known to the learning of the West. There in the presence of his father and his brothers, of the princes, captains, and great men of Assyria, he received the oath of fealty from the dependent kings and courtiers, calling on the name of the gods and binding themselves to obedience to his commands, and the maintenance of the ancient laws and institutions. It was an important step on the part of the old king. He did not indeed resign the government of Assyria. He remained king over this part of his kingdom as well as of the others, and the dignity to which he raised his son was only the petty or vassal-kingship, a filial government under his own still existing supremacy, whilst he was himself apart from this primarily king of Babylon, Sumer, and Accad, as well as king of the kings of the Egyptian countries. But for this very reason the appointment of the crown-prince as vassal-king of Assyria, in reality implied the transformation of that country, hitherto the centre of the empire, and whose capital had been the seat of the central government, into a kingdom occupying merely a secondary position, whilst Babylon became the seat of the chief rule and assumed the first place. It had become manifest that the true centre of the empire had shifted to Babylon, and that the latter now possessed more vital energy than Assyria.

668–664 BCE

Esarhaddon's death had opened up to the Ethiopian the prospect of a reconquest of his lost territory. It was to be expected that

Tirhaqa would take advantage of an opportunity so favourable to him, and soon, no doubt as early as the year 668, there came a messenger to Nineveh with the announcement that the king of Cush had marched into Egypt and not only overrun the whole south of the country, but had even made a triumphant entry into Memphis, the town which Esarhaddon had included in Assyria. The governors whom the last Assyrian king had set up had not indeed gone over to the enemy, but neither had they ventured to resist him. On his advance they had deserted their chief towns and retired with their armed forces to the desert. Asshurbanapal recognized the gravity of the event, for it endangered the peace of the coast districts along the Mediterranean. He did not himself take the field, but he immediately sent a considerable force into the west under the leadership of the Tartan and other captains. The latter proceeded to Egypt by those forced marches for which the Assyrian army was distinguished, and hastened to the assistance of the governors who were hard pressed by Tirhaqa. At Karbanit, or Karbana, a town which lay west of the Canopic branch of the Nile, near its mouth, the armies joined battle. The defeat of the Egyptians was so complete that Tirhaqa thought it advisable to evacuate Memphis without giving himself time to break up his camp. This and all the Ethiopians' armed river-boats fell into the hands of the Assyrians. Tirhaqa withdrew to Thebes and entrenched himself there.

Asshurbanapal, who had been informed of these successes of his army, decided to attack the enemy in Thebes. But as the Tartan's army had also greatly suffered, he ordered the Rabshakeh, who apparently commanded the garrisons of the

West, to collect a new army from the soldiers and auxiliaries under his command belonging to all governors and vassal-kings west of the Euphrates. Impressed by the defeat which Tirhaqa had sustained, the twenty-two kings of the seacoast, the plain, and the island of Cyprus hastened to obey this command, and not only to furnish soldiers, but also on demand of the supreme king to supply ships for the purpose of blockading the coast and prevent possible attempts at risings on the part of the maritime states on the banks of the Mediterranean, and perhaps also for sailing up the Nile. This army pushed on to join that of the Tartan and the troops of the loyal Egyptian vassals, and the united forces then marched against Thebes, which was reached a month and ten days later.

Meanwhile Tirhaqa had abandoned the town itself while it was still time, and had entrenched himself on the other bank of the river in the city of the tombs. Besides this, he had persuaded three of the principal vassal-kings to desert from the Assyrian and go over to his side. These were Sharludari, Prince of Pelusium (Si'nu), Pakruru, ruler of Pisept in Egyptian Arabia, and no less a person than Neku himself, the king whom Esarhaddon had placed at the head of all. They even seem to have taken the initiative, because they preferred to have a ruler of kindred race as overlord, rather than obey a foreigner. So they offered to conclude an alliance with the Ethiopian, by which his supremacy was recognized, and they undertook the defence of Lower Egypt. Had their design succeeded, the Assyrian army would also have had a hostile power in its rear and have seen its retreat cut off. But fortunately for the Assyrians the conspiracy was discovered. Their messengers were seized, the letters intercepted, and their cunning plans thus cunningly frustrated.

But first Asshurbanapal had followed the example of his father and pardoned Neku. After he had exacted from him an oath of fealty to Asshur, and laid him under heavier burdens than before, he again put upon him the royal purple and furnished him with the symbols of his office: golden rings on hands and feet, a carved sword in a golden sheath, horses, and chariots; and so he sent him back to Egypt, that he might rule it as chief of the other vassals in Asshur's name. He himself was again invested with Kar-bel-matati, – that is, Saïs, – and his son, Nabu-shezib-anni, received the principality of Athribis in Lower Egypt, to which also a significant Assyrian name, Limir-shakku-Asshur (let the governor of Asshur beware) was given. The other kings also renewed their alliance with Assyria. But Asshurbanapal did not omit to strengthen the garrisons, and to give those whom he had pardoned Assyrian officers intended to keep a watchful eye upon them.

For a time Egypt enjoyed peace under Neku's sway and Assyria's lordship. But after the death of Tirhaqa, Tamut-Amen, too, began to think of a reconquest of Egypt. He set out with his army, and like the former Ethiopian king, was hailed with delight in Elephantine and Thebes as a deliverer; then after he has fortified the southern capital, he continues his march to Memphis, where he first encounters resistance. But the rebels, as the king calls them – these were of course the Assyrian garrison with the troops of Neku who ruled over Memphis and Saïs – were so thoroughly beaten in a desperate sally, that they evacuated Memphis and retired to the strongholds of the Delta. Some princes headed by that Pa-Kerer (Pakruru) of Pisept, who had always borne the Assyrian yoke with reluctance, came to offer their submission, which was graciously accepted. This was the last time that an Assyrian army undertook a campaign against Egypt.

While Asshurbanapal had restored his supremacy in Egypt for a certain time, for the present at least, it was unshaken in the northern provinces of the West. The most important event mentioned by the Assyrian record of these days (evidently about 664) is the accession of Lydia. Asshurbanapal relates that the Lydian king, prompted by a dream which revealed to him the magnanimity of Asshur, sent his ambassadors to Nineveh to request the alliance and protection of the great ruler. For the deity had said to him that by the renown of this name he should overcome his enemies. He did in fact succeed in doing so. The Cimmerians were beaten by him. It may be assumed, though it is not stated, that Gyges received other help from the Assyrians besides the recognition as their ally. However that may be, he conquered, and, on the successful termination of the war, sent two Cimmerian rebels with a great present to Nineveh. There they were no little flattered at this homage, but also no little embarrassed to make themselves understood by the newcomers, or to understand them; for even at a court where, as the Assyrian writer says, the languages of East and West were met together, there was no one acquainted with the speech of these barbarians.

Probably for the same reason as Gyges, Mukallu of Tabal, his eastern neighbour, and Yakinlu of Arvad, with perhaps also Sandasharme, of Cilicia, placed themselves under the protecting wing of Assyria. Knowing the tastes of the great ruler of nations, each of them sent him a daughter for his harem, with a rich present, and it appears that this was the custom. Some even, that they might exhibit the more zeal, sent him, besides their own daughters, those of their brothers and other relatives.

In the east, too, Asshurbanapal manifested the still unbroken superiority of his arms. There, shortly after or at the same time as the Egyptian campaigns, he had already chastised a mountain people whose raids had greatly distressed the inhabitants of Yamudbal [E-mutbal], on the borders of Elam, so that the chiefs of the town of Dur-ilu had made complaints concerning them. He had sent a force which subdued the tribe, brought the chieftain Tandai alive to Assyria and carried off a great number of captives. The king had them taken to Egypt and in their place peopled the wasted country with prisoners of war from other regions.

664 BCE

Of far greater importance was the campaign against Man. The cause is not stated, but may well have been that the king of Man, Akhsheri, declared himself independent, or had shown an evident disposition to attack Assyria. If this were so, he had been over-hasty in his proceedings. However little of the warrior there may have been in Asshurbanapal's nature, the Assyrian army, in the early periods of his reign at least, was yet too fearless and its commanders too valiant for any man to be able to defy the powerful monarchy. Akhsheri attempted a night surprise of the troops sent against him, before they had even crossed his frontiers; but in this he was not successful. The Manneans were defeated in a bloody battle, and for a distance of six leagues round their dead covered the battle-field. Nothing retarded the victorious army from entering

Man, where it laid waste eight great towns whose position is unknown to us, as well as a crowd of small places, and so reached the domain of the capital, Izirtu. It was surrounded, together with the towns of Urbija and Armijate, and after the inhabitants, driven to the last extremity, had surrendered, they were led away and their whole territory conquered and laid waste.

But the object was attained. The frightful misery of the war which had visited that unhappy country had embittered the population against the man to whom they ascribed its guilt, namely, their old king, Akhsheri. In any case, he had shown his incapacity to defend his country. With all his brothers and his father and family, he was put to death, and so great was the nation's fury that they would not even concede him an honourable tomb, but threw the corpse on to the streets of his city. His son Ualli, himself already a middle-aged man, was raised to the throne, and he hastened to acknowledge Assyria's supreme authority. He sent his young son to Nineveh, to kiss the monarch's feet, and did not neglect to send his daughter also, to add to Asshurbanapal's crowd of women. His submission was of course accepted, but his annual tribute was raised by some thirty horses. Other attempts at rebellion in the northeast were soon suppressed.

c. 664–648 BCE

But whilst these disturbances in the northeast were suppressed without much difficulty, in the southeast signs soon appeared which gave warning of that great storm which in a few years was to be raised there and to threaten the empire with destruction. The throne of Elam was still occupied by Urtaki, who had always preserved a friendship with Esarhaddon, and had received from him repeated tokens of good will. Asshurbanapal had followed up this policy of his father and treated Urtaki as an ally, and when Elam was suffering from a severe famine after a prolonged drought he had not even refrained from extending a helping hand. He sent grain into the afflicted country, and not only permitted those of Urtaki's subjects who fled to his country to settle there, but also allowed them to return to their native land, unhindered, when the rains had again appeared and a sufficient harvest secured. If in this he was prompted by motives of policy it was at least an intelligent and peaceable one. In a proclamation to the Elamite tribe of the Rash, and the tribes of the Sea Lands, he could appeal with truth to these tokens of neighbourliness. But they did not prevent Urtaki from taking arms against him and invading Babylonia.

It seems that Asshurbanapal could scarcely believe the news which he received. Instead of hurrying to the spot to avert the danger, as had been the custom of his warlike father, he sent a messenger to inquire into the state of affairs and to report to him upon it. The latter returned with the tidings that the Elamites had poured themselves over Accad like a swarm of locusts, and had even set up a fortified camp in sight of the city of Babylon. He now hastily collected an army which drove the invaders from Accad, and even inflicted a defeat on them on the frontier. It is with a certain unction that the Assyrian scribe recounts the melancholy fate which soon after overtook all these enemies of his king. In the year which followed these events they all died: Bel-basha, as it seems, from a poisonous bite; Nabu-shum-eresh in a flood; Urtaki and his generals, in their despair, by their own hands in each other's presence. Whether the narrator learned this on good authority or had only heard it from rumour, can scarcely be determined; but that in reality they all died soon after is certain; for in the subsequent war with Elam, sons or successors are found in their places.

The crown of Elam fell to Teumman, brother of the two previous kings, who was "like a devil," says our Assyrian informant. That he was a tyrant who would shrink from no means of preserving his power, was also the conviction of the relatives of Ummanaldash and Urtaki, the last two kings of Elam. The one had left two sons, Kudurru and Paru, the other three, Ummanigash, Ummanappa, and Tammaritu. Well aware that their uncle was determined to remove them from his path, with all that belonged to them, in order to secure the succession to his own son, they abandoned their country with a great following, among which were included sixty members of the royal family and a bodyguard of bowmen, and sought shelter and protection with Asshurbanapal.

Naturally Teumman could not let this pass unnoticed. He therefore hastened to despatch two ambassadors to Nineveh, Umbadara, an Elamite, and a Chaldean, Nabu-dammik, and to demand through them the surrender of the fugitives. But Asshurbanapal, encouraged by favourable omens, dreams of his seers, and oracles of the gods; in other words, incited by his priesthood to whose guidance he always submitted in pious zeal, steadfastly refused to comply with Teumman's demand and assembled an army. In the month of Ulul it was ready to march. He did not himself take the field, for in fact his army, led by one of his generals, had merely to support the Elamite force of Ummanigash, his brothers and cousins. Ummanigash himself was generalissimo, if only in name. The Assyrian general was empowered to set Ummanigash on the throne of Elam in the name of the Assyrian supreme king, after the conquest of the country.

Teumman was also in the field with an army. But when he learned that the troops of his rival and of the Assyrians had already marched into the towns of Dur-ilu, which lay not far from the frontier of his country, and several times therefore had been the scene of a struggle between the two powers, he turned back, abandoning the western provinces of his kingdom, and entrenched himself in his capital, Shushan [Susa], which lay on the eastern bank of the River Ulai [modern Karun]. Meanwhile the allied Assyrians and Elamites entered the royal city of Mataktu, which lay to the west of that river, and there Ummanigash is crowned king. Teumman, indeed, makes one more effort; owing to the damage which the text had undergone it is not exactly shown of what kind, but from the context it is plain that he sent out an army in vain to hinder the advance of his enemies. The latter, once more encouraged by a dream, cross the river after Teumman's troops have suffered a defeat at Tul-Liz, and now attack Shushan itself. There the decisive battle takes place. It ends with the complete defeat of the Elamites: a great massacre begins, the river is filled with corpses, and innumerable women wander about the neighbourhood lamenting. Many distinguished and a large number of lesser prisoners fall into the hands of the Assyrians. All seek safety in flight. One of Teumman's sons, who had advised him against the war and had foretold the issue, rends his clothes in his despair. The eldest son, Tammaritu, follows his father in his flight to the forest, and when the king's chariot breaks down there, they are overtaken and both slain. The king's head is sent as a trophy to Assyria, where it was set up on the great gate of Nineveh, an eloquent witness to the nation of the might of Asshur and Ishtar. His son-in-law, Urtaki, himself begged an Assyrian to cut off his head and send it as good tidings to Asshurbanapal. Yet others of the great men of the kingdom come of their own accord and make their submission. The chief magistrates of the province of Khidali behead their own prince, Ishtarnandi, and one of them himself brings his master's severed head into the Assyrian camp. Tammaritu, the third brother of Ummanigash, entrusts the government of this principality to the Assyrian generals, and Ummanigash himself now makes his entry into Shushan, and is there crowned as a vassal of Assyria. As pledge of his loyalty he delivers a grandson of Marduk-bal-iddin, better known by the Hebrew appellation Merodach-baladan, probably the author of the whole resistance to the Assyrian king, to the latter's representatives.

But the war was not ended with the punishment of Elam. Dunanu, the son of Bel-basha, Prince of Gambul, was now to be taught what it was to side with the enemy. The army, on its return from Elam, breaks into his territory, conquers the capital Shapi-Bel, carries away from it all who have not fallen by the sword, lays the whole place waste, and flings the ruins into the waters of the stream which flows around it; whereupon a motley crew of human beings are raked together and brought there to re-people the desolate country.

It was a grim revenge that was taken on all enemies, even when they were already dead, on their corpses. At the triumphal entry of the army into Nineveh, Dunanu was compelled to carry the head of his ally, Teumman, round his neck. When Teumman's ambassadors, who had remained in Nineveh, saw this, one of them tore out his beard in his despair, and the other plunged a dagger into his own heart. Dunanu was placed on the rack in Arbela and died in tortures. All his brothers, including Samgunu, as well as Merodach-baladan's grandson and his brothers, were also put to death; the chiefs of the Gambuli were even flayed, after they had had their tongues torn out as blasphemers of the high gods, after which all corpses were cut in pieces, and were then sent all over the empire, in token of the overlordship of Assyria. With a refinement of cruelty Asshurbanapal even caused the corpse of his old opponent, the Tigenna Nabu-shum-eresh, which he had had brought to Assyria from Gambul for the purpose, to be disfigured in the great gate of Nineveh by the latter's own sons. Even before all this was brought to a conclusion, Sarduris III of Urartu, perhaps because he was already threatened by the Iranian enemies, who were soon to put an end to the Kingdom of Van, and was anxious to obtain the help of his powerful neighbour, despatched an ambassador to the latter. Asshurbanapal did not omit to make use of the occasion to bring Teumman's ambassadors before the newcomers, in order to inspire the former with a consciousness of his greatness, and to give the latter a warning example in case their sovereign also should prove unfaithful.

Thus the greatest danger that had hitherto threatened the empire seemed permanently averted, and if ever a pitiless revenge was qualified to deprive the conquered nations of the desire to fight for their independence, this must certainly have been the case after such a sanguinary judgment. But it was soon to be manifested that it had availed nothing. Assyria had only succeeded in making herself more detested than before, and had only stirred up princes and peoples alike to resist everything rather than any longer endure the yoke of the hangman of Asia.

THE BROTHERS' WAR (652–648 BCE)

About the year 652 BCE a formidable war broke out against Assyria. It had, perhaps, long been secretly preparing before Asshurbanapal had any suspicion of the danger which threatened him. He believed that his conciliatory policy had secured the permanent attachment of the Babylonians. He had invested his brother, Shamash-shum-ukin, with the royal dignity, raised him to be lord of all Sumer and Accad, and had placed an army of foot-soldiers, horses, and chariots at his disposal. Those of the inhabitants of towns, plains, and farms who had left the country during the period of anarchy, or had been carried off, he had permitted to return. As for the Babylonians who had settled in Assyria, he did not merely place them on a level with his own immediate subjects, but treated them with especial distinction, continued the privileges which Esarhaddon had granted them, and raised them to important offices, and they even moved about his royal court unmolested, clad in magnificent garments with golden ornaments. They still continued to protest their submission to the Assyrian domination, yet all the time they were conspiring with Shamash-shum-ukin against the king.

The first intimation of this conspiracy came to the king from Kudur, the governor of Erech. This faithful servant had received from Sin-tabni-usur, the governor of Ur, information to the effect that envoys from the king of Babylon had been there and that some of the people had already risen. Sin-tabni-usur had no mind to give ear to the proposals from Babylon, and had consequently requested reinforcements. Kudur sent him five hundred men, who, at his request, were afterwards increased by troops belonging to the governor of Arpakha and Amida. But it seems that Sin-tabni-usur was unable to maintain himself until these supports came up, and even before their arrival found himself constrained to go over to the party of the rebels.

Asshurbanapal was soon to learn with horror that the movement, the soul of which was his disloyal brother, had spread with great swiftness, and that Kudur's anxiety was not without foundation. Shamash-shum-ukin sent messengers in all directions, and they did not work in vain. All Accad and Chaldea, all the Aramaeans of Babylonia, all the inhabitants of the Sea Lands joined with him. His chief allies in this district were: Nabu-bel-shume, grandson of Merodach-baladan, that irreconcilable enemy of Assyria, who was now king of Chaldea; Mannuki-Babili, prince of Bit-Dakkuri; Ea-shum-basha, prince of Bit-Amukkani, and

Nadan of Puqudu. Ummanigash, king of Elam, who owed his throne to Asshurbanapal, was also gained over by Shamash-shum-ukin. Asshurbanapal had fancied that he might venture to impose on the Elamite, who owed him so much, conditions which the latter could certainly only fulfil with great difficulty. He had demanded the restoration of the goddess Nana of Erech, which had been in the possession of Elam for centuries, and whose worship had become so popular that the kings still sent their gifts to the goddess of Erech. Ummanigash could not comply with this demand without exciting universal discontent in his kingdom, and, doubtless, in consequence of this, was all the more inclined to listen to the proposals of the Babylonian prince. They were supported by a rich gift, for which the temple treasures of Bel-Marduk in Babylon, of Nabu in Borsippa, and of Nergal in Kutha had been plundered. Ummanigash immediately sent auxiliaries to Chaldea. The Guti nomads on the Assyrio-Babylonian frontier, the kings of the West, with Baal of Tyre at their head, and the king of Melukhkha, by whom Psamthek is here doubtless meant; these, too, Shamash-shum-ukin found prepared to join him in a rising against Assyria. The secession of Gyges, king of Lydia, who had previously concluded an alliance with the Egyptian king, probably also belongs to this time, and it is certain that various Egyptian sheikhs also sided with Babylon. Only the peoples of the northeast and north of the empire appear to have taken no part in the movement. They were held in check by the energetic governors of Amida and Arpakha, the last of whom even prevented the north of Elam from rising against the supreme king.

There was need of energy and wisdom to exorcise the storm, which was approaching from so many sides at once. Asshurbanapal, with whom religion occupied so prominent a place, of course turned first to his gods. But he did not neglect active measures. Yet it is not clear or probable that he himself took up arms. When Tammaritu came to him in the year 650, he was at Nineveh. But in the preceding years he had sent out various armies to attack the allies at different points. As soon as the news from Babylon reached him, he issued a proclamation to the Babylonians, in which he denounced his brother's treachery as ingratitude and exhorted those whom he had so favoured not to join Shamash-shum-ukin. It is true that these words found no echo amongst the nobility of Babylon, but they were not perhaps without influence on the temper of the nation. At any rate, the latter finally turned against their king. When Ummanigash's troops invaded Chaldea and Kardunyash, in the year 657, they encountered an Assyrian force. At the head of the Elamites was the son of Teumman, that Elamite king whom Asshurbanapal had put to death, and who had been chosen by Ummanigash as his general, because he had the death of his father to revenge on the Assyrians. With him came the governors of Billate and Khilmu, Zazaz and Paru, Attumetu, the captain of the bowmen, Neshu the Elamite commander, and a Babylonian division joined them. The account of the battle is too much damaged for us to form any conclusion about it. But it is evident that the Assyrians obtained some success, to which the severed head of Attumetu, which was sent to Asshurbanapal at Nineveh, bore witness.

It was not so easy to coerce the chief author of the war. Shamash-shum-ukin's first measure was to close all the gates of Babylon, Borsippa, and Sippar, to place garrisons in all places of any importance, and make himself master of all the towns in Babylonia. As a sign that he renounced his allegiance, he caused all the sacrifices to the highest gods, which Asshurbanapal had instituted, to be suspended, and appropriated all the gifts assigned to them, a measure which excited the indignation of the supreme king more than anything else.

This happened in the year 650, for it must have been in the April of that year that Bel-ibni was appointed governor of the lands on the coast. Chaldea and the surrounding territories were now also subdued. These had revolted in the previous year after Shamash-shum-ukin had raised the standard of rebellion in the year 652. On the 4th Nisan 651, Merodach-baladan's grandson, Nabu-bel-shume, had collected an army of Accadians, Chaldeans, and Kardunyashu (the men of the coast) in which he had included the Assyrians whom Asshurbanapal had sent him as auxiliaries or garrison. Between the 22nd Tammuz and 22nd Abu of the same year, Sin-tabni-usur, the governor, had joined them, and between 7th Abu and the 7th Ulul the Elamite auxiliaries had also marched up. But in the end the Assyrian army had defeated them all and compelled the Elamites to retreat. Nabu-bel-shume had followed them with his troops to Elam. The Assyrians, on whom he could not depend, he had previously sent under a reliable commander in the same direction, very probably under pretence of letting them march against Elam, and thus had delivered into the hands of Indabigash. Perhaps this defeat was the cause of Tammaritu's fall. It must have at least followed soon after. The south of Babylonia was certainly again brought under the Assyrian dominion towards the end of year 651.

Asshurbanapal could now turn his thoughts to attacking the arch-rebel in his own territory. It seems that the latter had again entered into relations with Elam, and either now went there in person or sent messengers. But on the 17th Arakhsamnu (Marsheshwan) 651, Asshurbanapal's warriors advanced against his brother. In the year 650 they stormed in fearful fashion through northern Babylonia, instituted a formidable massacre of Shamash-shum-ukin's subjects in town and country, made themselves masters of the canals, and finally surrounded Sippar, Babylon, and Borsippa, which the Babylonian king had fortified. The siege must have lasted a year or two, for it was not till 648 that the capital was taken.

And it would not have fallen then – so obstinately was it defended – had not the misery within the walls reached the acme. The famine was so dreadful that the besieged fed on the flesh of their own children, and famine was followed by plague. The gods themselves fought for the Assyrians, as the historian remarks. Then despair fell upon the people. In their fury they laid hold on Shamash-shum-ukin, and threw him, doubtless together with some of his satellites, into the fire. The town was then, of course, handed over to the enemy, and thus escaped the fate which Sennacherib had already inflicted on it. A strict trial was held. Those who had been concerned in the rebellion, such of them as had escaped the sword, hunger, and plague, who had saved themselves betimes during the rising and so could not be burnt with their master, were dragged from the hiding-place where they had concealed themselves into the light of day, and slain without grace or mercy, so that not one of them escaped. Those who had incited to rebellion and defamed Asshur had their tongues torn out of their mouths before they were sent to death. But the heaviest punishment overtook those who had already been punished as rebels by the king's grandfather, Sennacherib, and whose severed limbs were now thrown to the dogs and all kinds of beasts of prey. The corpses of those who had been destroyed by disease, hunger, and wretchedness, and which filled the streets of Babylon, Sippar, Kutha, and the surrounding country, were dragged away and piled up in heaps, and the insulted gods and angry goddesses were appeased by the care which was now bestowed upon their sanctuaries and altars. All fugitives were pardoned and granted life; they were permitted to settle in Babylon. Nor was the town plundered in any way. Asshurbanapal contented himself with the spoil from the palace of his rebellious brother, with his harem, household chariots, munitions of war, and the tokens of his royal dignity, and all this he had carried to Assyria with the captured warriors.

648 BCE

In the south of the country the ferment seems to have lasted longer. The Accadians, Chaldeans, Aramaeans, and inhabitants of the coast, who had formerly served Shamash-shum-ukin and then submitted to the Assyrian governor,

Bel-ibni, had now of their own accord once more risen against Asshurbanapal; but the Assyrian army, now the army of Babylon, marched into their territory, and soon brought the whole country back to the Assyrian dominion. Governors and princes appointed by the king reintroduced the Assyrian laws, and saw that the yearly tribute was henceforth paid regularly.

THE LAST WARS OF ASSHURBANAPAL (648-626 BCE)

As before related, Merodach-baladan's grandson, Nabu-bel-shume, had delivered those troops which Asshurbanapal had sent him for the defence of his country against the Elamites and insurgent Babylonians into Indabigash's hand. Even before Babylon was taken, the Assyrian king had sent an envoy to the latter to demand the release of these men. Indabigash had answered with proposals for peace. He does not seem to have dared to risk a struggle with Assyria, nor yet to have been prepared to comply with Asshurbanapal's request; the party of the Chaldeans and their friends was probably too powerful in Elam for this. After Babylon had fallen, the Assyrian sent a fresh messenger, supported by a numerous army, with a vigorous ultimatum to Elam. "If thou restorest not these men," so ran the message, "then will I come and destroy thy cities, carry away the people of Shushan, Madaktu, and Khidalu, thrust thee from thy royal throne, and put another in thy place. As formerly I destroyed Teumman, so will I destroy thee." But the envoy had not yet got so far as

Deri, when the war party killed Indabigash from a natural fear lest he should yield, and had made Ummanaldash, the son of Attumetu, king.

Of course the latter refused Asshurbanapal's request, and the war broke out afresh. Asshurbanapal now intended to establish Tammaritu for the second time in the government of Elam, a policy which again was destined not to be realised. A powerful army, led by this claimant, marched into the enemy's country, and several border-towns immediately submitted through fear, and came to offer their men and cattle. The first resistance was encountered at Bit-Imbi, once a royal city of Elam, "which shut in the front of Elam like a great bulwark," and had been conquered by Sennacherib and razed to the ground. But a later Elamite king had built a new Bit-Imbi opposite the old town and surrounded it with a strong wall and outworks. This town defended itself obstinately, but it was conquered, and those who would not submit were beheaded and their lips sent to Assyria as trophies of victory. The captain of the bowmen, Imbappi, who was a son-in-law of the Elamite king and had commanded in the city, fell alive into the enemy's hands, together with the harem, the sons of the former king Teumman, and the rest of the population, and was led away to Assyria.

This feat of arms appears to have been of great importance, for no sooner did it reach Ummanaldash's ears than he fled from Madaktu into the mountains. The same course was followed by another prince (Umbahabua?) who had reigned in Elam for a time, before Ummanaldash, but, in face of a rebellion, had retreated to Bubilu. He too left his dwelling, and hid himself in the low-lying districts on the seacoast. Elam was now open to the Assyrian army, which made use of the opportunity to march into Shushan and there again consecrate Tammaritu king. But the latter perceived that it was only as a shadow king that he had been set up. When the Assyrian troops who had accompanied him withdrew to their own country with the greater part of the population as prisoners and an enormous spoil, he was completely undeceived and sought to prevent this impoverishment of the land by force. But he was unsuccessful. In the eyes of the Assyrians this was base ingratitude; he was deposed and again carried off, and before the return march was finally entered upon, a regular drive was made over the whole of Elam, during which the chief towns were sacked. But no Assyrian garrison remained behind in the country, and there is no word of its permanent annexation. Immediately after the withdrawal of the Assyrian army, Ummanaldash II came out from his hiding-place and once more obtained possession of the government.

But Asshurbanapal was not satisfied with this *non possum*, and this time he sent Tammaritu himself as ambassador with another demand. The oracle he had asked from the goddess of Erech had enjoined on him to fetch back the image of the goddess Nana, which had been carried off to Elam centuries before. It will be remembered that this oracle had already served as an excuse to draw Ummanigash into a war. It was now again made use of. But Ummanaldash, no more than his predecessor, could comply with the demand without setting throne and life at stake. No other choice remained for him than to try the fortune of war.

The war proceeded as it had the first time, but was conducted with more energy and certainly lasted longer. Bit-Imbi was again taken, then the Rashi country and the city of Khamanu with its territory, a conquest which the Assyrians thought important enough to be perpetuated in a relief. Although all this was only frontier territory, Ummanaldash thought it advisable to leave Madaktu, the western capital of his country, and to retreat to Dur-Undasi, a town on the farther side of the Ulai, but west of the River Ididi, which formed a strong natural defence. Thus he abandoned a great part of his country, but even there he did not feel himself safe and crossed the Ididi that he might range his troops behind it in order of battle. The Assyrians pursued their triumphal march, took one town after the other, and at last came to Dur-Undasi. But here the army refused to go farther, and two days went by before they could make up their minds to cross the apparently dangerous river. However, in the nick of time, Ishtar of Arbela, the warlike goddess, whose priesthood doubtless accompanied the army with a portable sanctuary or ark, sent one of her seers a dream in which she promised her help, and this restored the army's courage. The crossing was a success, the army of Ummanaldash was beaten, and twelve Elamite provinces east of the Ididi with fourteen royal cities and a number of smaller places were abandoned to destruction.

Still there was no intention of taking possession of the country, and when Ummanaldash with the remnant of his army had gone farther into the mountains, and consequently there was no longer a dangerous enemy on the east side of the Ididi to hinder the operations on the west side, the Assyrians marched back into Shushan. There was the goddess for whose sake the whole expedition had been undertaken. On former occasions, when Shushan had been taken, the object of the war was to set the Elamite pretender on the throne, then the restoration could hardly be demanded. But now Asshur was in arms against Elam itself, and consideration need no longer be shown. The goddess was brought back to Erech to her sanctuary, E-khili-anha, "the house of power in the heavens," and the king caused new and permanent sanctuaries to be erected for her.

To all appearances and contrary to his practice, he had himself come to Shushan. At least, it is related that he clasped the hands of the goddess, that is, performed a religious ceremony in her sanctuary and that he also had the gratification of entering the palace of Shushan and seating himself on the throne of the hereditary enemy of Assyria. Elam was one of the oldest and most famous monarchies of Asia, and Shushan was the sacred city, the seat of the gods and the place of their oracles. In the treasure chamber of the royal citadel were heaped up all those valuables which the kings of Elam had collected "down to the kings of those days," and which had never yet been touched by a victorious enemy. No little of the treasure had been taken away by former Elamite kings from Sumer, Accad, and Kardunyash, and there was also a collection of valuables and jewels with royal insignia, which former kings of Accad, down to Shamash-shumukin, had presented to Elam in exchange for her help. All this, with all the glories of the royal palace, where a rich and splendour-loving court had resided, Asshurbanapal took with him to his own states. The very tombs of the kings were not spared by the conqueror:

they were destroyed and exposed to the light of day; even the corpses were carried off, so that the shades had to wander about homeless. In order to mortify the enemy as much as possible, the Assyrian soldiers were allowed to desecrate those sacred forests, whose precincts no unhallowed foot might ever tread, and then to burn them.

Whilst the Elamite war was still raging in the west, the Arabs had again arisen. Abiyate, whom Asshurbanapal had appointed in the place of Yauta-ben-Hazael as Assyrian vassal-king of Aribi, entered into negotiations with Natnu, prince of Nabathea, to whom Yauta had formerly fled, but who had at that time thought it safer to seek the friendship of Assyria. He now allowed himself to be persuaded to trouble the borders of the western provinces of Assyria, in conjunction with Abiyate. Lest the forces in this district should not be strong enough to face the joint attacks of the Arabs, a powerful army was despatched from Assyria to quell the rising. Arriving on the 25th Sivan at Khadata, which probably lay at the eastern extremity of this desert, the army pursued its way unchallenged to Laribda, a well-watered oasis, where the camp was fixed, and then marched on to Khurarina, not far from Yarki and Azalli, still in the same desert, where the first encounter took place. There the Isamme, the Bedouins, who worship the god Atarsamain and the Nabatheans, sought to stop the further progress of the Assyrian army, but were defeated. The victors, having provided themselves with water from Azalli, marched on to Kurasiti. There again stood Bedouins who worship Atarsamain, with Yauta-ben-Bir-Dadda and the men of Kedar, but they too gave way, and not only a rich booty, but Yauta's gods and women, with his mother, fell into the Assyrians' hands and were carried with them to Damascus. On the night of the 3rd Abu, after a rest of about forty days, the Assyrian army marched to the town of Khulkhuliti, south of Damascus, and in the mountain region of Khulkurina a battle was fought with the two sons of Te'ri, namely, the leaders of the rebellion, Abiyate and Aamu. Aamu was taken alive, chained hand and foot, and sent to Nineveh, where Asshurbanapal had him flayed. The remainder of the troops sought refuge in the hiding-places in the mountains; but when the Assyrians set guard in all the surrounding places and cut off their supplies of water, they found themselves under the necessity first of killing their camels and then of surrendering themselves. They, too, were taken to Assyria, and thus the country was as though "inundated with Arabs and camels." Yauta-ben-Bir-Dadda still kept the field with his troops; but when disease and famine had made terrible havoc among them, they came to the conclusion that they were no match for the might of the Assyrian gods, rose against their king, and drove him from them. He was seized by the enemy and sent to Assyria. There his son was killed before his eyes by Asshurbanapal's own hand, and he and his cousin bound with a dog-chain to Nerib-mashuakti-atuati, the eastern gate of Nineveh. The king counted it as a favour that he escaped with his life.

Even Ummanaldash was also destined to fall into the Assyrians' hands. His own subjects rose against him, perhaps at the instigation of a certain Ummanigash, a son of Ametirra, and he sought refuge in the mountains. The Assyrians made use of these disturbances to march into Elam, fan the fire of rebellion, and lead Ummanaldash in triumph to their own country. The ancient monarchy, which had so often threatened Assyria, was now entirely broken. For a time Elam still prolonged a melancholy existence. She was not annexed to the Assyrian Empire. But when, within a few years, the latter's power had disappeared, Elam fell an easy prey to the Persians, when Prince Sispis, or Teispes, of the race of the Achaemenidae, placed himself on the throne of Shushan.

Little dreaming that the hour of Asshur's downfall was so soon to strike, Asshurbanapal revelled in the joy of victory. In memory of all these triumphs, and in order to show his gratitude for the help of the gods, he built a new sanctuary for the great goddess of Nineveh, the spouse of Asshur, and when it was ready and he presented himself in it in order to consecrate it with ceremonial sacrifices, he had his royal chariot dragged to the gate of the temple by four captive kings, – Tammaritu, Pa'e, Ummanaldash, and Yauta. This barbarous triumph was his last, and the last also of the renowned Assyrian army.

THE DECLINE AND FALL OF ASSYRIA (626-609 BCE)

We have followed the fortunes of Assyria through several dynasties of clearest historical record. But, curiously enough, as we now proceed the landmarks disappear, and we enter a realm of myth, as if we were going backward instead of forward in time. Even while Asshurbanapal lives, the record becomes vague, and after him there is almost nothing securely known of its details. Even the names of his successors are somewhat in doubt. The only sure thing is the broad historical fact that the empire declined in power until it was completely overthrown by the Scythians and Babylonians about twenty years after the death of Asshurbanapal – the precise date of this closing scene being, like all other details of the epoch, more or less in doubt.

Our surprise at this cataclysmic overthrow is the greater in that we have just seen the Assyrian Empire at such a height of apparent power under Asshurbanapal. The palaces, libraries, and art treasures of that king as now known to us convey an irresistible impression of a powerful monarch. Yet it is held that the decline in Assyrian affairs had begun even during the life of Asshurbanapal....

In all probability, Asshurbanapal lived until 626, and during the whole of his reign he remained firmly established in possession of the Assyrian throne and also of the kingdom of Babylon. Elam had been rendered powerless, Babylon had been conquered, and the desert dwellers of the west were too much weakened and impoverished by the severe lesson taught them, as well as by hunger and disease, to be dangerous. Media was only in her youth, and Assyria was still strong enough to resist the first onrush of this new, conquering state. Besides her northeastern and northern neighbours, the states of Asia Minor and the inhabitants of the Mediterranean coast had enough to do to defend themselves against the barbarians who were pressing upon them from the north and east. Egypt was indeed independent, but could not seriously think of conquests in

Asia. The condition of the Assyrian Empire resembled the calm before the storm.

In his latter years the king doubtless devoted himself by preference to the works of peace. He had already erected many buildings, even during the period of his great wars. He had continued and completed the work on the temples of Assyria and Babylonia, which Esarhaddon had begun. Unfortunately the inscription which enumerates the principal structures belonging to the first half of his reign only occasionally mentions the places in which the temples he erected stood. In the later years of the king's reign the walls of Nineveh demanded his attention. They were loosened by annual rains and the violent showers of Adad, and had sunk. Asshurbanapal restored them and made them stronger than before. When he had seen his great campaigns crowned with victory, he at last undertook an important work in Nineveh, the town of Bel and Ishtar. Bit-Riduti, the great palace, which Sennacherib had built and established as a royal dwelling, had fallen to ruins. This king did nothing without the gods. It was now again a dream which made known to him their will that he should repair the damage to the palace. This was done. The forced labour of Assyrian subjects brought the stone in carts from the spoil of Elam; and the captive Arabian kings, decked out with appropriate marks of distinction, shared in the labour as workmen. When the palace was completed to the pinnacles and enlarged, it was surrounded with noble grounds; and when the victims were slaughtered at the consecration, the king made his entry carried in a gorgeous palanquin and with festive rejoicings.

Of all the objects assembled in this palace the king set the highest value on the library which he had founded and which has now for the most part been unearthed and brought to Europe. Asshurbanapal was, without any doubt, an admirer and patron of learning and a prince who loved art. He did not allow the libraries of Babylonia to be plundered, but he had the literary treasures which were buried there, including whole works on philosophical, mythological, and poetic subjects, copied in Assyrian characters and added to the historical records of his own predecessors. He even seems to have studied them diligently himself, and to have encouraged their perusal. The fruit of this study is shown in his own memorials. In fact these have some literary value, which cannot be said of the dry chronicles of former kings.... It cannot be denied that Asshurbanapal earned the gratitude of scholars by rendering so many treasures of the Babylonian libraries accessible to his compatriots, and also by founding libraries in other places; as, for example, in Babylon, and that he devoted more attention to these things than any of his predecessors.

626-609 BCE

The popular tradition of the downfall of the Assyrian Empire, which took shape in later years and came from the Persians to the Greeks, represents Sardanapalus (by whom none other than Asshurbanapal can be meant) as the type of a luxurious, effeminate, oriental despot, who forgets his kingly duties in the enjoyments of his harem, abandons his empire to the enemies rising against him on all sides, and finally, shut up in his capital, delivers himself in despair to the flames with his wives and all his treasures. We now know how little this picture agrees with the truth, but from what is historically credible we can gather how it arose. Asshurbanapal did indeed take pleasure in filling his women's palace with the daughters of all the princes subdued by him, and with those of their nearest relatives; and these princes knew well what was pleasing to the supreme king. It is true that this proceeded as much from love of display as from an inclination to voluptuousness; it is true that policy also had a share in it, because by this means his supremacy was confirmed and a pledge given for further submissiveness; it is true that the custom was a usual one with oriental monarchs; but a king who pursued it to such an extent must have been easily transformed into a voluptuary in the minds of his people.

There was also some reason for regarding him as weak and effeminate. The great Assyrian monarchs, at least during the years of their youth and vigorous manhood, had themselves frequently led their armies to victory. It was seldom, if ever, that Asshurbanapal joined in the fight. His official historians do, indeed, ascribe to him the honour of all the victories during his reign, but they have not succeeded in hiding the fact that his generals fought the battles. Yet he was by no means a weakling. That he was an eager hunter is testified by a number of hunting inscriptions, some of them accompanied by reliefs. In any case, a prince who could find pleasure in so manly a pastime was no effeminate voluptuary, little warlike though he may have shown himself to be.

The king's tragic end in the flames of his own palace, of which the legend speaks, may have been shifted on to him from his brother, Shamash-shum-ukin, or, still more probably, from the last Ninevite king. That he, the last great king of Assyria, should have been supposed to continue reigning until the end of the empire, while the insignificant kings who really followed him were forgotten, is natural enough. In short, Asshurbanapal was not a hero who strove to reap the laurels of the battle-field through difficulty and privations on distant campaigns. He preferred to linger in his luxurious palace, and to alternate the delights of the harem and the pursuit of learning with the royal lion-hunting. He was very pious, and did nothing without consulting the oracles of his gods or the dreams of his seers. If he thought the dignity of his empire, and with it the honour of his gods, insulted by an obstinate rebellion, he would avenge them as his predecessors had done by punishments of ingenious cruelty, inflicted both on individuals and on whole countries. The fearful suffering which the war on Asshur's enemies wrought in its train, the pestilence which filled the streets with corpses, the famine which drove parents to destroy their own children, filled him with transports of joy. His ruling idea was the unity and vastness of his empire. If he left the sword in its sheath, the love of pleasure did not make him neglect his duties as a ruler. He took care that his armies should always be ready to take the field, which would not have been possible without good organisation; and they triumphed over almost all his enemies, maintained his sway against a powerful coalition, crushed the formidable Elam so severely that she never recovered from the blows she had received, and, if not during his reign, at least shortly after it, repelled the advancing Medes. He regularly transmitted his orders to all the governors in his empire, and was by them kept carefully informed of anything of importance which happened in their provinces. No one of his victorious military leaders ever ventured to turn his arms against him. All, including the governors, recognized him and honoured him as their king. Such he was in the fullest sense of the word. In his palace at Nineveh, during two-and-forty years, he held the reigns of government with a strong hand. And this is all the more creditable to the influence of his personality, since the empire was internally weakened by his own political mistakes, in particular by the removal of the centre of government from Babylon, which Esarhaddon had made its seat, to Nineveh, and by other causes, so that it went to pieces a few years after his death....

ASSYRIA

NEW BABYLON

In this chapter, Henry Smith Williams tells the political history of the Neo-Babylonian empire from the defeat of the Assyrians until Persian supremacy under Cyrus the Great. What may be added is that the Neo-Babylonian kings also enacted many internal reforms, apart from the many conquests abroad. Nebuchadnezzar, especially, transformed many Babylonian cities through numerous building projects and changes of their administrative and social structures.

Some specific updates to Smith Williams' account of the Levant may be of interest. Cuneiform texts concerning Tyre, Babylonian Ṣūru, were published in 1926. They show avid investments that were managed by the main temples in Uruk, Sippar and Nippur. After the long siege of Tyre, costs of military equipment are mentioned more frequently. A good modern synopsis for the account of Tyre in Neo-Assyrian and Neo-Babylonian sources and their implications for our understanding of the city's history is C. van der Brugge & K. Kleber, 'The empire of trade and the empires of force: Tyre in the Neo-Assyrian and Neo-Babylonian periods,' in J.C. Moreno García (ed.), *Dynamics of Production in the Ancient Near East, 1300–500* BCE (Oxford & Philadelphia, Oxbow Books, 2016), pp. 187–222.

Only recently have the so-called Āl Yaḫūdu ('town of Judah') tablets been published in two volumes: L. Pearce & C. Wunsch, *Documents of Judean Exiles and West Semites in Babylonia in the Collection of David Sofer* (Bethesda, CDL Press, 2014), and C. Wunsch, *Judaeans by the Waters of Babylon: New Historical Evidence in Cuneiform Sources from Rural Babylonia Primarily from the Schøyen Collection* (Dresden, ISLET, 2022). They come from a few settlements where exiled Judeans made their living from agriculture. They give a small glimpse into the daily lives of the Judean deportees in Babylonia, which is mostly restricted to their settlements. They grew barley and dates, bought land, paid taxes, performed state labour, and some became rich by providing credit to the other Judeans. The origin in Judah of these people is practically only visible in their personal names, often consisting of an element referring to the Judean god YHWH.

THE BREAKDOWN OF THE EMPIRE

612–609 BCE

Immediately after Asshurbanapal's death, or perhaps even in the last year of his reign, Babylon broke away from the Assyrian rule, and this time the separation was permanent. The empire was much weakened by it. The north and northwest, Urartu and the states of Asia Minor, gradually fell into the power of the ever-advancing Medes. The Assyrian lordship over the countries on the coast of the Mediterranean Sea now existed in name only, so that King Josiah of Judah was able to effect his reform unhindered, and to act as master in the territory of the ancient kingdom of Israel, which for years had been an Assyrian province. And in the year 608 Neku II, king of Egypt, was able to think of extending his empire to the Euphrates, as in days long past, and to take arms against Assyria with the idea of wresting from her all her western provinces. The foundation of the new Babylonian Empire and the invasion of the Egyptians, who could no longer be repelled by the Assyrians, but were only to give way before the Babylonian arms, are described elsewhere. Here we only mention them as among the causes which brought about the fall of the Assyrian Empire. That empire no longer had any real existence, at least as a ruling power. Thrust back to its old frontiers, the ancient Assyrian state slowly languished and only awaited the death-blow.

That blow was to come from the Medes in alliance with the Babylonians, and was partly hastened, partly stayed, by the great migratory streams of the Cimmerians and Scythians.

Historians are now able to place the conquest of the city by the Manda in the reign of Sin-shar-ishkun. Without overlooking a certain Sin-shum-lishir, who is mentioned in several places as an Assyrian king, and must have ruled about this time, but whose personality has not yet been unwrapped from the historic gloom, it is safe to say that this Sin-shar-ishkun was Asshur-etil-ili's successor. From contract tablets found at Sippar and Erech we know that he occupied the Assyrian throne in 612 BCE, and that his dominion included a part of Babylonia as well. Later records would show him to be of much stronger character than the man he succeeded. In 610 or 609 he attempted to wrest more of the Babylonian provinces from Nabopolassar, and the harassed king took the fatal step of appealing to that people from the north, who for the most part had formed part of the great Indo-European migration into western Asia. Already these Scythian hordes, the Manda, had their eye on the rich Mesopotamian Valley, and therefore Nabopolassar's appeal did not fall upon unwilling ears.

Sin-shar-ishkun was indeed driven back, but when that happened the Manda were in the coveted land.... Like his father, Cyaxares perceived that it would not be possible for the Medes to extend and maintain their conquests westward so long as he had to dread the rivalry of the Assyrian Empire, so lately the mistress of those regions. Consequently he put into practice the lesson which his father had received from the Assyrians. The as yet untrained hordes of Medians were evidently no match for the better military organisation of the Assyrians and the military skill of the Assyrian generals. Cyaxares, therefore, began as became a warlike prince with the remodelling of his army, dividing his troops, after the pattern of the Assyrians, into the various arms – spearmen, bowmen, and horsemen – and fortifying his citadel, Ecbatana. Then he again ventured to attack Assyria, this time with better success. The Assyrian army was beaten in Nineveh at last, and was surrounded. But an unexpected event came to the assistance of the hard-pressed Ninevites – the Scythians invaded Media.

Their invasion compelled Cyaxares to evacuate Assyria, and for a time Nineveh breathed again. But only for a short time. Cyaxares succeeded in putting an end to the Scythian domination in his kingdom in the course of a few years.

609–401 BCE

About 609 the Median army under the command of Cyaxares appeared for the second time at the gates of Nineveh. According to Berosus, the Babylonian king, whose son Nebuchadrezzar had married the Median king's daughter, also took part in this siege. It is easy to understand how it was that Herodotus knew nothing of this, for the Persians were his authorities. But he is certainly right in assigning the chief rôle to the Medes, of whom Abydenus says nothing, for from this time forward they kept possession of Assyria itself; and he is also right in placing the taking of Nineveh during the period of Cyaxares' government, and not, like Berosus and the authors who follow him, in the time of Astyages, since the latter did not ascend the throne of Media before 584 BCE. It is sufficient that Nineveh fell, and Assyria passed to the power of the Medes, who at the same time acquired the dominion over the north and the countries of Asia Minor as far as the Halys. All other provinces of the fallen empire as far as the Mediterranean Sea, including probably that part of ancient Assyria whose capital was the city of Asshur, and also Kharran and Carchemish, fell to Babylonia.

We have no historical account of the details connected with the fall of Nineveh. The story of the last Assyrian king, Asshur-etil-ili, or, as some authorities call him, Saracus, which represents him in his despair burning himself with his palace and his treasures, is a popular tale which is not indeed impossible, but probably arose by confusion with Shamash-shum-ukin's end. Nineveh was so completely desolated that when Xenophon passed with the Ten Thousand in the year

401 BCE he took the ruins for the remains of Median towns destroyed by the Persians. Subsequently a fortress, Ninus, seems to have been built there by the Parthians. Calah also once more rose from its rubbish heaps after lying desolate for a long time. Arbela remained untouched, and it is therefore probable that it fell unresisting into the hands of the conquerors. But the Assyrian monarchy was gone forever.

606 BCE

The Assyrian monarchy was gone, but not the empire at whose head the kings of Asshur had stood. It has been matter of astonishment that so powerful an empire, to which through a series of centuries the whole of western Asia had been subdued, could have been so suddenly overturned by the fall of the capital. But this surprise proceeds from an incorrect conception of history. Events had long prepared the fall of Nineveh. The keen eye of Esarhaddon had already perceived that it would be safer to remove the centre of the empire to Babylon. His son Asshurbanapal, a less acute statesman than he, but a great king and a strong administrator, had once more attempted to secure the hegemony for Assyria. In this he had succeeded, being supported by favourable circumstances and the influence of his own personality. But when the sceptre fell from his strong hand, little more was needed to put an end to the Assyrian dominion, and that end was only a question of time. However, the empire survived for a few years longer, though not in its full vigour. The hegemony now passed again to Babylon; but not unimpaired, for, since Media had conquered Nineveh, the lion's share of Assyria itself fell to the Median kingdom, together with those northern and northwestern provinces which had been lost long before. But the Assyrian survived in the new Babylonian Empire, which continued its policy of conquest, and the Greeks, who not long afterwards called the Babylonians themselves Assyrians, were in this not so very far from the truth. But the days of the Semitic dominion were hastening to their end. Even the new monarchy under Babylon's hegemony could only be propped up by the force of Nebuchadrezzar's personality. His feeble successors were in no condition to prevent the spread of the Median power nor the rise of the Persian monarchy, which had grown to such proportions by the conquest of Elam, until the genius of Cyrus founded a dominion which soon embraced the four ancient empires – the Median, the Elamite, the Assyrio-Babylonian, and the Egyptian – and gave the sceptre of western Asia to the Aryans.

RENASCENCE AND FALL OF BABYLON

Nowhere is there a more striking illustration of national regeneration than is furnished by the story of the new Babylonian Empire. Freed from Assyrian thraldom, Babylon, the old, old city, came forward to take the place of the fallen Nineveh as the world-metropolis.

It has been customary to think and speak of the new Babylonian Empire as evidencing the rejuvenation of an old people. In one sense this view has full validity. But it must not be supposed that the new Babylonians who came to power when Nineveh fell were the *bona fide* descendants of the rulers of old Babylonia. New blood had made itself felt in the old race; indeed, without its influence it is highly improbable that the rejuvenation could have been effected. The outsiders who made their influence felt with such potency to restore and rejuvenate the old empire, are known as the Chaldeans. The precise origin of this people is in doubt. It is held to be established, however, that they were Semitic, and hence could claim cousinship with the Babylonians and Assyrians. They inhabited the Sea Lands to the south of Mesopotamia at an early date, and have been supposed to come originally from Arabia. They are heard of from time to time in Babylonian and Assyrian annals as a half-barbaric and often troublesome people, divided into various tribes or clans or petty principalities, bearing such unfamiliar names as Bit-Silani, Bit-Sa'alli, and Bit-Sala.

It is supposed by modern orientalists that the Chaldeans long had their eyes upon the fertile regions of the north, and even, from time to time, been presumptuous enough to cross swords with the Babylonians and Assyrians in the hope of dethroning them. Certain it is that the rulers of the north had at various times waged war against their less civilised cousins of the Sea Lands. Yet the evidence does not seem to be very clear as to the precise share which the Chaldeans took in the new movement inaugurated in Babylon with the death of the last really powerful Assyrian king, Asshurbanapal. The name of the new ruler who now came to power in Babylon was Nabopolassar; but it cannot be asserted with confidence that he was of Chaldean origin. It is held, however, that the influences that dominated the kingdom under his reign were clearly Chaldean; though considering the vagueness that surrounds the entire subject, it must be admitted that this assertion is much easier to make than to prove. Still, all that we know about the degeneration of old nations elsewhere, and the extreme difficulty of resuscitating a senescent people, except by a mixture of races, tends to confirm the theory that a race relatively new to civilization was chiefly instrumental in working the miracle of Babylonian regeneration.

In any event, the people who for something less than a century made Babylon a great centre of world-influence were known to their contemporaries and to succeeding generations as Chaldeans rather than as Babylonians. Just to what extent the old Babylonian people shared in the new work, can perhaps never be known; but the question is relatively unimportant, because in any event it was a people of the same old Semitic stock that carried on the historic story.

The most brilliant period of the new Babylonian Empire came soon after the fall of Nineveh, in the reign of the world-famous king, Nebuchadrezzar, the monarch who built the marvellous wall about the city and the fabulous hanging gardens; the conqueror who overthrew the Phoenicians and carried the Israelites into captivity....

CONTEMPORARY CHRONOLOGY

615–538 BCE

The epoch of the new Babylonian Empire covers a period of time from about 615 to 538 BCE, approximately three-quarters of a century. We have already, at the beginning

NEW BABYLON

of this book, outlined the position of contemporary civilizations during the entire sweep of Assyrian and new Babylonian history; but it may be well briefly to recapitulate the position of other nations during the epoch of new Babylonian domination, that a clearer picture of the time may be before the eyes as we view the details of Babylonian history.

While reading of the achievements of Nebuchadrezzar and his successors, then, it will be well to recall that:

Egypt under the XXVIth Dynasty enjoys a brief period of rejuvenescence as a world-power; curiously linked in time with the new awakening of her old-time rival, Babylonia;

In *India*, at about this period, Buddha lives and founds the religion that is to bear his name;

Greece and *Rome* are in a relative youth, not yet reckoning time from a fixed era, and only beginning to make secure records on which future generations may build. Their civilization does not compare in importance with that of Babylon, which is the recognized centre of culture, looking upon these "new" nations in the west as utter barbarians;

Phoenicia is far past the zenith of its power; Samaria has fallen; Jerusalem is to become subject to Babylon itself;

In *Asia Minor*, Sardis, the capital of Lydia, is waxing in power.

But the coming nation of the epoch is *Persia*, which turns the tables on its fellow, Manda, hitherto the stronger of the half-civilised pair of nations, and which finally, under Cyrus, captures Babylon itself, and assumes undisputed sovereignty over the whole of southwestern Asia.

THE ANCIENT NEAR EAST

NABOPOLASSAR AND NEBUCHADREZZAR

626–562 BCE

Nabopolassar (Nabu-apal-usur, *i.e.* "Nabu protect the heir"), according to the Ptolemaic canon, reigned from 625 BCE (the date of his accession thus being 626) until 605 BCE, in which year he died, shortly before the victory won by his son Nebuchadrezzar over the Egyptians at Carchemish, having been in ill health before Nebuchadrezzar started for Syria. We have seen how immediately upon his accession to the throne of the Pharaohs, Neku II profited by the impotence of the Assyrian kingdom, which was enfeebled to the last degree by long years of Scythian incursions, to penetrate into the Hamath district.

[He encountered the army of Judah at Meggido – the same historical locality where, a thousand years before, Tehutimes III had vanquished the combined forces of Syria and Phoenicia. The king of Jerusalem was slain on the field, and his army, retreating in terror to the capital, made his young son, Jehoahaz, king, ignoring the claims of Eliakim, the eldest, probably because he was in favour of submitting to Neku. Pharaoh now proceeded, unmolested, to Riblah in Cœle-Syria, where he made his headquarters, and confident in his mastery over Judah, ordered Jehoahaz to appear before him. When the new king arrived he was thrown into chains and Eliakim put in his place under the name of Jehoiakim.]

Neku's ambition was next directed to the conquest of the whole of northern Syria; a project which he actually accomplished to a great extent during the years 608 to 606, whilst the Babylonians, with their Median allies, were besieging Nineveh. He must certainly have advanced as far as Carchemish, since that was the spot where the Egyptian and Babylonian forces met in 605 BCE. The fate of Syria was sealed thereby; it became a province of Babylonia even as it had once been a province of Assyria, and Judah became a vassal kingdom to Babylonia.

602–587 BCE

Thus Nabopolassar, who died in 605 BCE, while his son was on the march for Syria, only just missed the satisfaction of seeing the new kingdom of Babylonia which he had founded enter upon the heritage of the Assyrian Empire, out of which the western province could least of all be spared. He did not see it: instead the news of his father's death reached the young Nebuchadrezzar (Nabu-kudur-usur, *i.e.* "Nabu protect the crown") shortly after the victory of the Egyptians, which decided the fate of Syria for the time being; and leaving his generals to follow up the victory, he had to return to Babylon in hot haste to assume the royal dignity that awaited him. There he received the crown at the hands of the great nobles without encountering any obstacles, and for the long period of his glorious reign, which lasted forty-two years (604–562 BCE) he guided the destinies of his country, extended and strengthened its borders, and thus made Babylonia a great power, and Babylon one of the most splendid and illustrious cities of ancient times. If we further take into consideration that it was he who likewise conquered Syria for Babylonia, we cannot but acknowledge his claim to be counted the first ruler who entered upon the full possession of Assyria and consolidated it.

Amid all the many and sometimes detailed inscriptions of Nebuchadrezzar which have been found in the ruins of Babylon and other cities, not one contains any account of his campaigns; but from a passage in the preamble of the great inscription of the kingdom, we see that in spite of his preference for building and other peaceful labours he was a mighty warrior. It runs: "Under his mighty protection (*i.e.* that of the god Marduk) I have passed through far countries, distant mountains, from the upper sea even to the lower sea (*i.e.* probably from the Gulf of Issus to the mouth of the Nile) far-reaching ways, closed paths where my step was stayed and my foot could not stand, a road of hardships, a way of thirst; the disobedient I subdued and took the adversaries captive, the land I guided aright, the people I caused to be seized; I carried away the bad and the good among them, silver and gold and precious stones, copper, palm wood and cedar wood, whatsoever was costly, in gorgeous abundance; the products of the mountains and that which the sea yielded, brought I as a gift of great weight, as a rich tribute into my city of Babylon before his (the god's) face." And although the different campaigns of which we know are distributed over almost the whole of his long reign, we find mention of only one short war against Aahmes of Egypt in the thirty-seventh year of it.

With regard to these wars, most of them aimed at completing the work begun at the battle of Carchemish, and more particularly at preventing further interference on the part of Egypt, and at banishing her influence completely from Babylonian territory, which had now been extended to her very

NEW BABYLON

frontier. It was probably in the third year after Nebuchadrezzar's battle (therefore in 602 BCE) that Syria was completely incorporated into the Babylonian kingdom, leaving him free to think of displaying his power in the eyes of Jehoiakim, whom Neku had set up as king in Jerusalem, by advancing against him with an army. The desired result promptly followed, and from 601 to 599 Jehoiakim became tributary to the king of the Chaldeans. In the fourth year, 598, the king of Judah withheld the tribute, probably at the instigation of Egypt. When the Babylonians invaded Judah (probably at the beginning of 587) Jehoiakim was just dead; his son Jehoiachin (known also as Jeconiah) was besieged at Jerusalem and, seeing further resistance useless, surrendered to Nebuchadrezzar. He was carried away captive to Babylon with his family and nearly all the princes, warriors, masons, and smiths; but, once there, their lot was no hard one, for they were permitted to settle without molestation and to exercise their own religion…. Jerusalem was not destroyed, but Jehoiachin's kinsman, Mattaniah (another son of Josiah), was set over the few inhabitants that remained there as a vassal of Babylonia, under the new name of Zedekiah (595-587). The newly installed sovereign was a weak man, who by his own good will would have been a loyal vassal; but ultimately in spite of the warnings of the prophet Jeremiah, who fully realised the true state of affairs, he threw in his lot with the war party, who relied on the help of Egypt, and rebelled against Babylonia

In 589 Psamthek II (Neku's successor) himself was succeeded by the young and warlike Uah-ab-Ra (the Hophra of the Bible and the Apries of the Greeks), who sent a fleet to the assistance of the Phoenicians in an attempt they made to revolt. Thereupon Nebuchadrezzar marched his troops into Syria and set up his headquarters at Riblah, the old headquarters of Neku, so as to operate from thence against Zedekiah, Tyre, and Pharaoh. How Jerusalem was besieged (589–587) and destroyed, how in the meantime Uah-ab-Ra's army was vanquished, and how Tyre was then invested (the siege lasting thirteen years) and forced to pay tribute, if no more – all these events are likewise known to us only from other sources than cuneiform inscriptions, and the detailed description of them, at least in so far as they relate to the downfall of the kingdom of Judah, and thus form a part of (not the opening era of) Jewish history, lies ready to every reader's hand in the books of the Bible of which we have given a brief outline.

As for Tyre (after the siege), she remained under the rule of her own kings, though as a vassal to Babylonia. All the worse was the fate which, in 587, overtook Judah, whose hopes had been so cruelly deceived, for not only was the city utterly destroyed (see the moving laments in the so-called Book of Lamentations), and the king, blinded and fettered, carried away into captivity after seeing his sons slain before his face; but with the exception of the poor, the day labourers absolutely necessary for the cultivation of the soil and vineyards, all who had escaped the previous deportation were carried away by the Babylonian king to the "waters of Babylon" (Psalm 137).

587–568 BCE

[While his soldiers were keeping their long and weary station under the walls of Tyre, Nebuchadrezzar turned his attention to another important matter. Because the people of Judah and

Tyre had looked to Egypt for assistance, they had given the Babylonian king much trouble. Egypt, therefore, must suffer for this; so that she would not feel inclined to repeat her action of sending an army to Zedekiah's aid. A new Egyptian campaign was planned.]

A fragment at the beginning of which a prayer ("Thou destroyest my enemies and makest my heart to rejoice") was set down, assigns the above-mentioned campaign in Egypt to the year 568 (*i.e.* the thirty-seventh year of the reign). The passage which refers to it, – "Year 37 of Nebuchadrezzar, king of (Babylonia to the land of) Misir, (*i.e.* Egypt) to give a battle, he marched and (his troops A-ma)-a-su, the king of Misir assembled and …" leaves no doubt that Aahmes or Amasu is the king here meant, for only the year before, in 569, Aahmes had revolted against Uah-ab-Ra and forced him to recognise him (Aahmes) as co-regent. He soon afterward became sole ruler in Egypt; and, as such, he died in the year 528, shortly before the conquest of Egypt by the Persians. Nebuchadrezzar meanwhile contented himself with humbling the pride of Egypt, and refrained from conquering the country, which even had it been successfully done would but have raised difficulties for the Babylonian kingdom to cope with. His chief aim, to keep Syria and Palestine clear of Egyptian influence, was attained by the campaign.

Of Nebuchadrezzar's other military expeditions, the one mentioned (Jeremiah xlix. 28–33) against the Bedouins of Kedar and the Arab tribes, which had settled to the east of Palestine, leads us again to the borders of the Occident. The town of Teredon, at the mouth of the Euphrates, was founded at this time as a bulwark against the Bedouins, and by reason of its situation became, like Gerrha, on the Persian Gulf, and Thapsacus, Tiphsah, on the middle Euphrates, a mercantile station of some importance. Not until the time of the New Kingdom of Babylonia did a flourishing trade develop along the Euphrates, with Armenia and the east coast of Arabia for its extreme poles; and from the reign of Nebuchadrezzar dates the part played by Babylon, his capital, as the greatest emporium of the ancient world, and the proverbial meaning which the name of Babylon has retained down to our times, to signify the worst aspects (luxury and license) of a capital city....

THE FOLLOWERS OF NEBUCHADREZZAR

560–555 BCE

We know from the Ptolemaic Canon ... that after Nebuchadrezzar's death (562) Illoarudamos (probably a clerical error for Illoarudakos, *i.e.* Amil-Marduk), the biblical Evil-Merodach, ascended the throne and died in the second year of his reign (560). Berosus calls him a son of Nebuchadrezzar, and describes his short reign as unjust and licentious, this being the reason why he was murdered by Neriglissor (Nergal-shar-usur), his sister's husband, and thus son-in-law to Nebuchadrezzar....

From the reign of Amil-Marduk we have no inscription, but we are in better case as regards his successor, Nergal-shar-usur (the Nergal-sharezer of the Bible; Berosus, Neriglissor, Ptolemaic Canon, Neriga-solasar). He reigned from 559–556, for there are two inscriptions on cylinders and a brief inscription on brick which we may assign to this reign. The subject appears to be some restoration in the shrine of E-zida at Babylon. Where the inscription again becomes legible, the king gives an account of the construction of a canal, the waters of which had gone away and withdrawn, and of palace building....

THE REIGN OF NABONIDUS (556–538 BCE)

On the death of Neriglissor in 556, he was succeeded, according to Berosus, by his son Labassarachos or Labarosoarchodos (in inscriptions Labashi-Marduk), but it appears that a Babylonian of high rank, Nabu-naidu ("Nabu is glorious"), the son of Nabu-balatsu-iqbi ("Nabu hath foretold his life"), was immediately proclaimed king by an opposition party, and although Labashi-Marduk made head against Nabu-naidu (or Nabonidus, as he is usually known) for nine months, the latter dates the beginning of his reign from the death of Neriglissor. According to Berosus, Labashi-Marduk was a child, and fell victim to a conspiracy, having already betrayed tokens of a bad disposition.

According to the Ptolemaic canon, Nabonidus reigned seventeen years, which agrees with the circumstance that the latest of the numerous contract tablets belonging to his reign up to this time discovered are dated the 5th of Ulul (the middle of August) in his seventeenth year. He concerned himself chiefly with the restoration of old temples elsewhere than in Babylon, as those at Ur, Larsa, Sippar, and even at Kharran in Mesopotamia, that is, the oldest sanctuaries in the country; while in Babylon, where he certainly resided, if only at intervals, he seems to have done nothing except to proceed with the building of the walls on the river bank. Nabonidus was actuated not merely by religious motives, but by an interest in history and archaeology, which grew to be an absolute mania with him.

His inscriptions give us minute information as to how he dug and hunted for the foundation cylinders of these primitive temples, nor does he fail to deal many a sly hit at his predecessors (Nebuchadrezzar, for example), who had not always conscientiously done this, and had consequently many a time built something that was not in the original plan. When, after long search, Nabonidus found these cylinders, often buried deep down in the ground, he reproduced the tenor of them exactly, frequently giving the precise number of years between his own reign and that of the ancient Babylonian king in question, and so providing us with the most valuable data for determining the earliest periods of Babylonian history. In this way we have learned the date of Naram-Sim, the ancient king of Agade, of Shagarakti-Buriash [sometimes read Shagarakti-Shuriash], and lastly, as it would appear, of Khammurabi, together with many other data of historical importance. For this reason the reign of Nabonidus is to us among the most important in Babylonian history, but his passion for archaeology – which seems to have made him forget the world entirely, and, in particular, overlook the danger with which the victories of Cyrus menaced Babylonia – was of less service to himself, and ultimately cost him his throne and liberty.

NEW BABYLON

555–538 BCE

After the deliverance of Kharran, Nabonidus summoned his troops from the frontier of Egypt and onward to the Gulf of Issus and the Persian Gulf, to the work of building, or the collection of building material; these were not military enterprises in the strict sense of the term (and this is characteristic), but merely expeditions for peaceful ends, which were all the easier for Nabonidus to achieve, because, since the reign of Nebuchadrezzar the Babylonians had held undisputed possession of the "Occident" right up to the Egyptian frontier. The only exception to this rule seems to be the account of the beginning of the first year (or the beginning of his reign) given in the chronicle, where, among other things, it is said, "the king summoned his warriors." But this expedition was, in all likelihood, only the less laborious gleaning left to Nabonidus after the conquest of the Medes by Cyrus.

The next event narrated in the chronicle is the final defeat of the Medes by Cyrus, which cannot, therefore, have taken place later than the sixth year of the reign of Nabonidus, that is, 550 BCE, and may have been earlier....

Of greater importance, historically, is the account of the ninth year (547 BCE)....

We know from Herodotus that an expedition of Cyrus against King Croesus of Lydia took place at this very time, and ended with the siege and reduction of Sardis and the fall of the kingdom of Lydia, after an indecisive battle had been fought in Cappadocia, near Pteria (Boghaz-köi), a place since made famous by the discovery of a Hittite bas-relief.

Nabonidus had joined the alliance between Lydia, Sparta and Aahmes of Egypt, on which Croesus relied when he began the war against Cyrus; probably he thought he could make an easy conquest of Media and Elam after the defeat he expected Cyrus to suffer in Asia Minor. The Babylonians do not seem to have taken any active part in the struggle after Cyrus' speedy victory over the Lydians, but nevertheless with that victory the fate of Babylonia was practically sealed. For it was obvious that Cyrus, who had not only ruled over the whole of Media, since the taking of Ecbatana, but was also undisputed master of Armenia right up to the western coast of Asia Minor, and thus had really become emperor (or great king) would take the first opportunity of seizing upon Babylonia and its wealthy Syrian provinces. Moreover, from this time forth he had the best of reasons for regarding Nabonidus as a disloyal neighbour who deserved condign punishment....

538 BCE

Thus we see that Babylon itself received King Cyrus with open arms, and that, even as the Kossaeans had usurped and long maintained the mastery of Accad, so now the Persians superseded the native dynasty. The event was therefore no new thing, and, as a matter of fact, Babylonian history proceeds upon the old lines under Cyrus and his successors, so that it is hard to see why most narratives should break off at this point. The national literature and mode of writing continued to flourish, but the history of Babylonia and Assyria, of which the short-lived prosperity of the New

Babylonian Kingdom was the last chapter, concluded with the entry of Cyrus into Babylon; the subsequent history of Babylonia is of local interest only, and has no further significance for the world.

THE ANCIENT NEAR EAST

THE PERSIAN EMPIRE

In this chapter, George Rawlinson focuses on the founding of the Persian Empire and its first ruler Cyrus. Rawlinson knows the Greek sources well, although Xenophon's *Education of Cyrus* is rather a biographical work of fiction than of history. Unfortunately, the important contemporary Babylonian texts, the 'Chronicle of Nabonidus' and the 'Cyrus Cylinder' were discovered only in the late nineteenth century.

Talking about the early state of the Median and Persian kingdoms, it is quite clear now that these were rather loosely organized coalitions of towns and tribes. Belonging to the tribe of Pasargadae, Cyrus's first achievement was to unite the Persian and defeated Median tribes under one rule. Elam was probably an early, important addition.

Regarding the fall of Babylon, one must be critical about what consequences this nominal loss of sovereignty really meant for the religious and social systems in place. Contrary to Rawlinson, Babylonian temples continued to thrive during Achaemenid rule. It was only under Xerxes that major changes occurred as reprisals after failed rebellions. Due to this cultural continuity, not least thanks to Persian cultural syncretism and tolerance, the period from the Neo-Babylonian Empire until the rule of Xerxes is now called the 'long sixth century' (c. 620–484 BCE) in Mesopotamian history.

Although quite tame here, we may point out how Rawlinson's was a time when the racial stereotype of the lazy and decadent 'Oriental' readily served to depict Cyrus's greatness as an atypical case.

THE BEGINNINGS OF THE EMPIRE

The Persians would thus appear not to have completed their migrations till near the close of the Assyrian period, and it is probable that they did not settle into an organized monarchy much before the fall of Nineveh. At any rate we hear of no Persian ruler of note or name in the Assyrian records, and the reign of petty chiefs would seem therefore to have continued at least to the time of Asshur-bani-pal, up to which date we have ample records. The establishment, however, about the year 660 BCE, or a little later, of a powerful monarchy in the kindred and neighboring Media, could not fail to attract attention, and might well provoke imitation in Persia; and the native tradition appears to have been that about this time. Persian royalty began in the person of a certain Achaemenes (Hakhamanish), from whom all their later monarchs, with one possible exception, were proud to trace their descent.

The name Achaemenes cannot fail to arouse some suspicion. The Greek genealogies render us so familiar with heroes eponymi – imaginary personages, who owe their origin to the mere fact of the existence of certain tribe or race names, to account for which they were invented – that whenever, even in the history of other nations, we happen upon a name professedly personal, which stands evidently in close connection with a tribal designation, we are apt at once to suspect it of being fictitious. But in the East tribal and even ethnic names were certainly sometimes derived from actual persons; and it may be questioned whether the Persians, or the Iranic stock generally, had the notion of inventing personal eponyms. The name Achaemenes, therefore, in spite of its connection with the royal clan name of Achaemenidae, may stand as perhaps that of a real Persian king, and, if so, as probably that of the first king, the original founder of the monarchy, who united the scattered tribes in one, and thus raised Persia into a power of considerable importance.

The immediate successor of Achaemenes appears to have been his son, Teispes. Of him and of the next three monarchs, the information that we possess is exceedingly scanty. The very names of one or two in the series are uncertain. One tradition assigns either to the second or the fourth king of the list the establishment of friendly relations with a certain Pharnaces, King of Cappadocia, by an intermarriage between a Persian princess, Atossa, and the Cappadocian monarch. The existence of communication at this time between petty countries politically unconnected, and placed at such a distance from one another as Cappadocia and Persia, is certainly what we should not have expected; but our knowledge of the general condition of Western Asia at the period is too slight to justify us in a positive rejection of the story, which indicates, if it be true, that even during this time of comparative obscurity, the Persian monarchs were widely known, and that their alliance was thought a matter of importance.

PERSIAN POLITICS

The political condition of Persia under these early monarchs is a more interesting question than either the names of the kings or the foreign alliances which they attracted. According to Herodotus, that condition was one of absolute and unqualified subjection to the sway of the Medes, who conquered Persia and imposed their yoke upon the people before the year 634 BCE. The native records, however, and the accounts which Xenophon preferred, represent Persia as being at this time a separate and powerful state, either wholly independent of Media, or, at any rate, held in light bonds of little more than nominal dependence. On the whole, it appears most probable that the true condition of the country was that which this last phrase expresses. It maybe doubted whether there had ever been a conquest; but the weaker and less developed of the two kindred states owned the suzerainty of the stronger, and though quite unshackled in her internal administration, and perhaps not very much interfered with in her relations towards foreign countries, was, formally, a sort of Median fief, standing nearly in the position in which Egypt now stands to Turkey. The position was irksome to the sovereigns rather than unpleasant to the people. It detracted from the dignity of the Persian monarchs, and injured their self-respect; it probably caused them occasional inconvenience, since from time to time they would have to pay their court to their suzerain; and it seems towards the close of the Median period to have involved an obligation which must have been felt, if not as degrading, at any rate as very disagreeable. The monarch appears to have been required to send his eldest son as a sort of hostage to the Court of his superior, where he was held in a species of honorable captivity, not being allowed to quit the Court and return home without leave, but being otherwise well treated. The fidelity of the father was probably supposed to be in this way secured while it might be hoped that the son would be conciliated, and made an attached and willing dependent.

CAMBYSES AND CYRUS THE GREAT

When **Persian history first** fairly opens upon us in the pages of Xenophon and of Nicolaus Damascenus, this is the condition of things which we find existing. Cambyses, the father of Cyrus the Great – called Atradates by the Syrian writer – is ruler of Persia, and resides in his native country, while his son Cyrus is permanently, or at any rate usually, resident at the Median Court, where he is in high favor with the reigning monarch, Astyages. According to Xenophon, who has here the support of Herodotus, he is Astyages' grandson, his father, Cambyses, being married to Mandane, that monarch's daughter. According to Nicolaus, who in this agrees with Ctesias, he is no way related to Astyages, who retains him at his court because he is personally attached to him. In the narrative of the latter writer, which has already been preferred in these volumes, the young prince, while at the Court, conceives the idea of freeing his own country by a revolt, and enters into secret communication with his father for the furtherance of his object. His father somewhat reluctantly assents, and preparations are made, which lead to the escape of Cyrus and the commencement of a war of independence. The details of the struggle, as they are related by Nicolaus, have been already given. After repeated defeats, the Persians finally make a stand at Pasargadae, their capital, where in two great battles they destroy the power of Astyages, who himself remains a prisoner in the hands of his adversary.

In the course of the struggle the father of Cyrus had fallen, and its close, therefore, presented Cyrus himself before the eyes of the Western Asiatics as the undisputed lord of the great Arian Empire which had established itself on the ruins of the Semitic. Transfers of sovereignty are easily made in the East, where independence is little valued, and each new conqueror is hailed with acclamations from millions. It mattered nothing to the bulk of Astyages' subjects whether they were ruled from Ecbatana or Pasargadae, by Median or Persian masters. Fate had settled that a single lord was to bear sway over the tribes and nations dwelling between the Persian Gulf and the Euxine; and the arbitrament of the sword had now decided that this single lord should be Cyrus. We may readily believe the statement of Nicolaus that the nations previously subject to the Medes vied with each other in the celerity and zeal with which they made their submission to the Persian conqueror. Cyrus succeeded at once to the full inheritance of which he had dispossessed Astyages, and was recognized as king by all the tribes between the Halys and the desert of Khorassan.

He was at this time, if we may trust Dino, exactly forty years of age, and was thus at that happy period in life when the bodily powers have not yet begun to decay, while the mental are just reaching their perfection. Though we may not be able to trust implicitly the details of the war of independence which have come down to us, yet there can be no doubt that he had displayed in its course very remarkable courage and conduct. He had intended, probably, no more than to free his country from the Median yoke; by the force of circumstances he had been led on to the destruction of the Median power, and to the establishment of a Persian empire in its stead. With empire had come an enormous accession of wealth. The accumulated stores of ages, the riches of the Ninevite kings – the "gold," the "silver," and the "pleasant furniture" of those mighty potentates, of which there was "none end" – together with all the additions made to these stores by the Median monarchs, had fallen into his hands, and from comparative poverty he had come per saltum into the position of one of the wealthiest – if not of the very wealthiest – of princes. An ordinary Oriental would have been content with such a result, and have declined to tempt fortune any more. But Cyrus was no ordinary Oriental. Confident in his own powers, active, not to say restless, and of an ambition that nothing could satiate, he viewed, the position which he had won simply as a means of advancing himself to higher eminence. According to Ctesias, he was scarcely seated upon the throne, when he led an expedition to the far north-east against the renowned Bactrians and Sacans; and at any rate, whether this be true or no – and most probably it is an anticipation of later occurrences – it is certain that, instead of folding his hands, Cyrus proceeded with scarcely a pause on a long career of conquest, devoting his whole life to the carrying out of his plans of aggression, and leaving a portion of his schemes, which were too extensive for one life to realize, as a legacy to his successor. The quarter to which he really first turned his attention seems to have been the north-west. There, in the somewhat narrow but most fertile tract between the River Halys and the Egean Sea, was a state which seemed likely to give him trouble – a state which had successfully resisted all the efforts of the Medes to reduce it, and which recently, under a warlike prince, had shown a remarkable power of expansion. An instinct of danger warned the scarce firmly-settled monarch to fix his eye at once upon Lydia; in the wealthy and successful Croesus, the Lydian king, he saw one whom dynastic interests might naturally lead to espouse the quarrel of the conquered Mede, and whose power and personal qualities rendered him a really formidable rival.

LYDIA

The **Lydian monarch**, on his side, did not scruple to challenge a contest. The long strife which his father had waged with the great Cyaxares had terminated in a close alliance, cemented by a marriage, which made Croesus and Astyages brothers. The friendship of the great power of Western Asia, secured by this union, had set Lydia free to pursue a policy of self-aggrandizement in her own immediate, neighborhood. Rapidly, one after another, the kingdoms of

Asia Minor had been reduced; and, excepting the mountain districts of Lycia and Cilicia, all Asia within the Halys now owned the sway of the Lydian king. Contented with his successes, and satisfied that the tie of relationship secured him from attack on the part of the only power which he had need to fear, Croesus had for some years given himself up to the enjoyment of his gains and to an ostentatious display of his magnificence. It was a rude shock to the indolent and self-complacent dreams of a sanguine optimism, which looked that "tomorrow should be as today, only much more abundant," when tidings came that revolution had raised its head in the far south-east, and that an energetic prince, in the full vigor of life, and untrammelled by dynastic ties, had thrust the aged Astyages from his throne, and girt his own brows with the imperial diadem. Croesus, according to the story, was still in deep grief on account of the untimely death of his eldest son, when the intelligence reached him. Instantly rousing himself from his despair, he set about his preparations for the struggle, which his sagacity saw to be inevitable. After consultation of the oracles of Greece, he allied himself with the Grecian community, which appeared to him on the whole to be the most powerful. At the same time he sent ambassadors to Babylon and Memphis, to the courts of Labynetus and Amasis, with proposals for an alliance offensive and defensive between the three secondary powers of the Eastern world against that leading power whose superior strength and resources were felt to constitute a common danger. His representations were effectual. The kings of Babylon and Egypt, alive to their own peril, accepted his proposals; and a joint league was formed between the three monarchs and the republic of Sparta for the purpose of resisting the presumed aggressive spirit of the Medo-Persians.

THE GREAT ADVANCEMENT

Cyrus, meanwhile, was not idle. Suspecting that a weak point in his adversary's harness would be the disaffection of some of his more recently conquered subjects, he sent emissaries into Asia Minor to sound the dispositions of the natives. These emissaries particularly addressed themselves to the Asiatic Greeks, who, coming of a freedom-loving stock, and having been only very lately subdued, would it was thought, be likely to catch at an opportunity of shaking off the yoke of their conqueror. But, reasonable as such hopes must have seemed, they were in this instance doomed to disappointment. The Ionians, instead of hailing Cyrus as a liberator, received his overtures with suspicion. They probably thought that they were sure not to gain, and that they might possibly lose, by a change of masters. The yoke of Croesus had not, perhaps, been very oppressive; at any rate it seemed to them preferable to "bear the ills they had," rather than "fly to others" which might turn out less tolerable.

Disappointed in this quarter, the Persian prince directed his efforts to the concentration of a large army, and its rapid advance into a position where it would be excellently placed both for defence and attack. The frontier province of Cappadocia, which was only separated from the dominions of the Lydian monarch by a stream of moderate size, the Halys, was a most defensible country, extremely fertile and productive, abounding in natural fastnesses, and inhabited by a brave and warlike population. Into this district Cyrus pushed forward his army with all speed, taking, as it would seem, not the short route through Diarbekr, Malatiyah, and Gurun, along which the "Royal Road" afterwards ran, but the more circuitous one by Erzerum, which brought him into Northern Cappadocia, or Pontus, as it was called by the Romans. Here, in a district named Pteria, which cannot have been very far from the coast, he found his adversary, who had crossed the Halys, and taken several Cappadocian towns, among which was the chief city of the Pterians. Perceiving that his troops considerably outnumbered those of Crocesus, he lost no time in giving him battle. The action was fought in the Pterian country, and was stoutly contested, terminating at nightfall without any decisive advantage to either party. The next day neither side made any movement; and Crocesus, concluding from his enemy's inaction that, though he had not been able to conquer him, he had nothing to fear from his desire of vengeance or his spirit of enterprise, determined on a retreat. He laid the blame of his failure, we are told, on the insufficient number of his troops, and purposed to call for the contingents of his allies, and renew the war with largely augmented forces in the ensuing spring.

Cyrus, on his part, allowed the Lydians to retire unmolested, thus confirming his adversary in the mistaken estimate which he had formed of Persian courage and daring. Anticipating the course which Croesus would adopt under the circumstances, he kept his army well in hand, and, as soon as the Lydians were clean gone, he crossed the Halys, and marched straight upon Sardis. Croesus, deeming himself safe from molestation, had no sooner reached his capital than he had dismissed the bulk of his troops to their homes for the winter, merely giving them orders to return in the spring, when he hoped to have received auxiliaries from Sparta, Babylon, and Egypt. Left thus almost without defence, he suddenly heard that his audacious foe had followed on his steps, had ventured into the heart of his dominions, and was but a short distance from the capital. In this crisis he showed a spirit well worthy of admiration. Putting himself at the head of such an army of native Lydians as he could collect at a few hours' notice, he met the advancing foe in the rich plain a little to the east of Sardis, and gave him battle immediately. It is possible that even under these disadvantageous circumstances he might in fair fight have been victorious, for the Lydian cavalry were at this time excellent, and decidedly superior to the Persian. But Cyrus, aware of their merits, had recourse to stratagem, and by forming his camels in front, so frightened the Lydian horses that they fled from the field. The riders dismounted and fought on foot, but their gallantry was unavailing. After a prolonged and bloody combat the Lydian army was defeated, and forced to take refuge behind the walls of the capital.

Croesus now in hot haste sent off fresh messengers to his allies, begging them to come at once to his assistance. He had still a good hope of maintaining himself till their arrival, for his city was defended by walls, and was regarded by the natives as impregnable. An attempt to storm the defences failed; and the siege must have been turned into a blockade but for an accidental discovery. A Persian soldier had approached to reconnoitre the citadel on the side where it was strongest by nature, and therefore guarded with least care, when he observed one of the garrison descend the rock after his helmet, which had fallen from his head, pick it up, and return with it. Being an expert climber, he attempted the track thus pointed out to him, and succeeded in reaching the summit. Several of his comrades followed in his steps; the citadel was surprised, and the town taken and plundered.

Thus fell the greatest city of Asia Minor after a siege of fourteen days. The Lydian monarch, it is said, narrowly escaped with his life from the confusion of the sack; but, being fortunately recognized in time, was made prisoner, and brought before Cyrus. Cyrus at first treated him with some harshness, but soon relented, and, with that clemency which was a common characteristic of the earlier Persian kings, assigned him a territory for his maintenance, and gave him an honorable position at Court, where he passed at least thirty years, in high favor, first with Cyrus, and then with Cambyses. Lydia itself was absorbed at once into the Persian Empire, together with most of its dependencies, which submitted as soon as the fall of Sardis was known. There still, however, remained a certain amount of subjugation to be effected. The Greeks of the coast, who had offended the Great King by their refusal of his overtures, were not to be allowed to pass quietly into the condition of tributaries; and there were certain native races in the south-western corner of Asia Minor which declined to submit without a struggle to the new conqueror. But these matters were not regarded by Cyrus as of sufficient importance to require his own personal superintendence. Having remained at Sardis for a few weeks, during which time he received an insulting message from Sparta, whereto he made a menacing reply, and having arranged for the government of the newly-conquered province and the transmission of its treasures to Ecbatana, he quitted Lydia for the interior, taking Croesus with him, and proceeded towards the Median capital. He was bent on prosecuting without delay his schemes of conquest in other quarters – schemes of a grandeur and a comprehensiveness unknown to any previous monarch.

Scarcely, however, was he departed when Sardis became the scene of an insurrection. Pactyas, a Lydian, who had been entrusted with the duty of conveying the treasures of Croesus and his more wealthy subjects to Ecbatana, revolted against Tabalus, the Persian commandant of the town, and being joined by the native population and numerous mercenaries, principally Greeks, whom he hired with the treasure that was in his hands, made himself master of Sardis, and besieged Tabalus in the citadel. The news reached Cyrus while he was upon his march; but, estimating the degree of its importance aright, he did not suffer it to interfere with his plans. He judged it enough to send a general with a strong body of troops to put down the revolt, and continued his own journey eastward. Mazares, a Mede, was the officer selected for the service. On arriving before Sardis, he found that Pactyas had relinquished his enterprise and fled to the coast, and that the revolt was consequently at an end. It only remained to exact vengeance. The rebellious Lydians were disarmed. Pactyas was pursued with unrelenting hostility, and demanded, in succession, of the Cymaeans, the Mytilenseans, and the Chians, of whom the last-mentioned surrendered him. The Greek cities which had furnished Pactyas with auxiliaries were then attacked, and the inhabitants of the first which fell, Priene, were one and all sold as slaves.

THE PERSIAN EMPIRE

Mazares soon afterwards died, and was succeeded by Hapagus, another Mede, who adopted a somewhat milder policy towards the unfortunate Greeks. Besieging their cities one by one, and taking them by means of banks or mounds piled up against the walls, he, in some instances, connived at the inhabitants escaping in their ships, while, in others, he allowed them to take up the ordinary position of Persian subjects, liable to tribute and military service, but not otherwise molested. So little irksome were such terms to the Ionians of this period that even those who dwelt in the islands off the coast, with the single exception of the Samians – though they ran no risk of subjugation, since the Persians did not possess a fleet – accepted voluntarily the same position, and enrolled themselves among the subjects of Cyrus.

One Greek continental town alone suffered nothing during this time of trouble. When Cyrus refused the offers of submission, which reached him from the Ionian and Aeolian Greeks after his capture of Sardis, he made an exception in favor of Miletus, the most important of all the Grecian cities in Asia. Prudence, it is probable, rather than clemency, dictated this course, since to detach from the Grecian cause the most powerful and influential of the states was the readiest way of weakening the resistance they would be able to make. Miletus singly had defied the arms of four successive Lydian kings, and had only succumbed at last to the efforts of the fifth, Croesus. If her submission had been now rejected, and she had been obliged to take counsel of her despair, the struggle between the Greek cities and the Persian generals might have assumed a different character.

THALES AND HARPAGUS

Still **more different** might have been the result, if the cities generally had had the wisdom to follow a piece of advice which the great philosopher and statesman of the time, Thales, the Milesian, is said to have given them. Thales suggested that the Ionians should form themselves into a confederation, to be governed by a congress which should meet at Teos, the several cities retaining their own laws and internal independence, but being united for military purposes into a single community. Judged by the light which later events, the great Ionian revolt especially, throw upon it, this advice is seen to have been of the greatest importance. It is difficult to say what check, or even reverse, the arms of Persia might not have at this time sustained, if the spirit of Thales had animated his Asiatic countrymen generally; if the loose Ionic amphictyony, which in reality left each state in the hour of danger to its own resources, had been superseded by a true federal union, and the combined efforts of the thirteen Ionian communities had been directed to a steady resistance of Persian aggression and a determined maintenance of their own independence. Mazares and Harpagus would almost certainly have been baffled, and the Great King himself would probably have been called off from his eastern conquests to undertake in person a task which after all he might have failed to accomplish.

The fall of the last Ionian town left Harpagus free to turn his attention to the tribes of the south-west which had not yet made their submission – the Carians, the Dorian Greeks, the Caunians, and the people of Lycia. Impressing the services of the newly-conquered Ionians and Aeolians, he marched first against Caria, which offered but a feeble resistance. The Dorians of the continent, Myndians, Halicarnassians, and Cnidians submitted still more tamely, without any struggle at all; but the Caunians and Lycians showed a different spirit. These tribes, which were ethnically allied, and of a very peculiar type, had never yet, it would seem, been subdued by any conqueror. Prizing highly the liberty they had enjoyed so long, they defended themselves with desperation. When they were defeated in the field they shut themselves up within the walls of their chief cities, Caunus and Xanthus, where, finding resistance impossible, they set fire to the two places with their own hands, burned their wives, children, slaves, and valuables, and then sallying forth, sword in hand, fell on the besiegers' lines, and fought till they were all slain.

CONQUEST IN THE FAR EAST

Meanwhile Cyrus was pursuing a career of conquest in the Far East. It was now, according to Herodotus, who is, beyond all question, a better authority than Ctesias for the reign of Cyrus, that the reduction of the Bactrians and the Sacans, the chief nations of what is called by moderns Central Asia, took place. Bactria was a country which enjoyed the reputation of having been great and glorious at a very early date. In one of the most ancient portions of the Zendavesta it was celebrated as "Bahhdi eredhwo-drafsha," or "Bactria" with the lofty banner; and traditions not wholly to be despised made it the native country of Zoroaster. There is good reason to believe that, up to the date of Cyrus, it had maintained its independence, or at any rate that it had been untouched by the great monarchies which for above seven hundred years had borne sway in the western parts of Asia. Its people were of the Iranic stock, and retained in their remote and somewhat savage country the simple and primitive habits of the race. Though their arms were of indifferent character, they were among the best soldiers to be found in the East, and always showed themselves a formidable enemy. According to Ctesias, when Cyrus invaded them, they fought a pitched battle with his army, in which the victory was with neither party. They were not, he said, reduced by force of arms at all, but submitted voluntarily when they found that Cyrus had married a Median princess. Herodotus, on the contrary, seems to include the Bactrians among the nations which Cyrus subdued, and probability is strongly in favor of this view of the matter. So warlike a nation is not likely to have submitted unless to force; nor is there any ground to believe that a Median marriage, had Cyrus contracted one, would have made him any the more acceptable to the Bactrians.

On the conquest of Bactria followed, we may be tolerably sure, an attack upon the Sacae. This people, who must certainly have bordered on the Bactrians, dwelt probably either on the Pamir Steppe, or on the high plain of Chinese Tartary, east of the Bolar range – the modern districts of Kashgar and Yarkand. They were reckoned excellent soldiers. They fought with the bow, the dagger, and the battle-axe, and were equally formidable on horseback and on foot. In race they were probably Tatars or Turanians, and their descendants or their congeners are to be seen in the modern inhabitants of these regions. According to Ctesias, their women took the field in almost equal numbers with their men; and the mixed army which resisted Cyrus amounted, including both sexes, to half a million. The king who commanded them was a certain Amorges, who was married to a wife called Sparethra. In an engagement with the Persians he fell into the enemy's hands, whereupon Sparethra put herself at the head of the Sacan forces, defeated Cyrus, and took so many prisoners of importance that the Persian monarch was glad to release Amorges in exchange for them. The Sacae, however, notwithstanding this success, were reduced, and became subjects and tributaries of Persia.

Among other countries subdued by Cyrus in this neighborhood, probably about the same period, may be named Hyrcania, Parthia, Chorasmia, Sogdiana, Aria (or Herat), Drangiana, Arachosia, Sattagydia, and Gandaria. The brief epitome which we possess of Ctesias omits to make any mention of these minor conquests, while Herodotus sums them all up in a single line; but there is reason to believe that the Cnidian historian gave a methodized account of their accomplishment, of which scattered notices have come down to us in various writers. Arrian relates that there was a city called Cyropolis, situated on the Jaxartes, a place of great strength defended by very lofty walls, which had been founded by the Great Cyrus. This city belonged to Sogdiana. Pliny states that Capisa, the chief city of Capisene, which lay not far from the upper Indus, was destroyed by Cyrus. This place is probably Kafshan, a little to the north of Kabul. Several authors tell us that the Ariaspae, a people of Drangiana, assisted Cyrus with provisions when he was warring in their neighborhood, and received from him in return a new name, which the Greeks rendered by "Euergetse" – "Benefactors." The Ariaspae must have dwelt near the Hamoon, or Lake of Seistan. We have thus traces of the conqueror's presence in the extreme north on the Jaxartes, in the extreme east in Afghanistan, and towards the south as far as Seistan and the Helmend; nor can there be any reasonable doubt that he overran and reduced to subjection the whole of that vast tract which lies between the Caspian on the west, the Indus valley and the desert of Tartary towards the east, the Jaxartes or Sir Deria on the north, and towards the south the Great Deserts of Seistan and Khorassan.

More uncertainty attaches to the reduction of the tract lying south of these deserts. Tradition said that Cyrus had once penetrated into Gedrosia on an expedition against the Indians, and had lost his entire army in the waterless and trackless desert; but there is no evidence at all that he reduced the country. It appears to have been a portion of the empire in the reign of Darius Hystaspis, but whether that monarch, or Cambyses, or the great founder of the Persian power conquered it, cannot at present be determined.

The conquest of the vast tract lying between the Caspian and the Indus, inhabited (as it was) by a numerous, valiant, and freedom-loving population, may well have occupied Cyrus for thirteen or fourteen years. Alexander the Great spent in the reduction of this region, after the inhabitants had in a great measure lost their warlike qualities, as much as five years, or half the time occupied by his whole series of conquests. Cyrus could not have ventured on prosecuting his enterprises, as did the Macedonian prince, continuously and without interruption, marching straight from one country to another without once revisiting his capital. He must from time to time have returned to Ecbatana or Pasargadae; and it is on the whole most probable that, like the Assyrian monarchs, he marched out from home on a fresh expedition almost every year. Thus it need cause us no surprise that fourteen years were consumed in the subjugation of the tribes and nations beyond the Iranic desert to the north and the north-east, and that it was not till 539 BCE, when he was nearly sixty years of age, that the Persian monarch felt himself free to turn his attention to the great kingdom of the south.

THE FINAL FALL OF BABYLON

The expedition of Cyrus against Babylon has been described already. Its success added to the empire the rich and valuable provinces of Babylonia, Susiana, Syria, and Palestine, thus augmenting its size by about 240,000 or 250,000 square miles. Far more important, however, than this geographical increase was the removal of the last formidable rival – the complete destruction of a power which represented to the Asiatics the old Semitic civilization, which with reason claimed to be the heir and the successor of Assyria, and had a history stretching back for a space of nearly two thousand years. So long as Babylon, "the glory of kingdoms," "the praise of the whole earth," retained her independence, with her vast buildings, her prestige of antiquity, her wealth, her learning, her ancient and grand religious system, she could scarcely fail to be in the eyes of her neighbors the first power in the world, if not in mere strength, yet in honor, dignity, and reputation. Haughty and contemptuous herself to the very last, she naturally imposed on men's minds, alike by her past history and her present pretensions; nor was it possible for the Persian monarch to feel that he stood before his subjects as indisputably the foremost man upon the earth until he had humbled in the dust the pride and arrogance of Babylon. But, with the fall of the Great City, the whole fabric of Semitic greatness was shattered. Babylon became "an astonishment and a hissing" – all her prestige vanished – and Persia stepped manifestly into the place, which Assyria had occupied for so many centuries, of absolute and unrivalled mistress of Western Asia.

The fall of Babylon was also the fall of an ancient, widely spread, and deeply venerated religious system. Not of course, that the religion suddenly disappeared or ceased to have votaries, but that, from a dominant system, supported by all the resources of the state, and enforced by the civil power over a wide extent of territory, it became simply one of many tolerated beliefs, exposed to frequent rebuffs and insults, and at all times overshadowed by a new and rival system – the comparatively pure creed of Zoroastrianism, The conquest of Babylon by Persia was, practically, if not a death-blow, at least a severe wound, to that sensuous idol-worship which had for more than twenty centuries been the almost universal religion in the countries between the Mediterranean and the Zagros mountain range. The religion never recovered itself – was never reinstated. It survived, a longer or a shorter time, in places. To a slight extent it corrupted Zoroastrianism; but, on the whole, from the date of the fall of Babylon it declined. "Bel bowed down;

THE PERSIAN EMPIRE

Nebo stooped;" "Merodach was broken in pieces." Judgment was done upon the Babylonian graven images; and the system, of which they formed a necessary part, having once fallen from its proud pre-eminence, gradually decayed and vanished.

Parallel with the decline of the old Semitic idolatry was the advance of its direct antithesis, pure spiritual monotheism. The same blow which laid the Babylonian religion in the dust struck off the fetters from Judaism. Purified and refined by the precious discipline of adversity, the Jewish system, which Cyrus, feeling towards it a natural sympathy, protected, upheld, and replaced in its proper locality, advanced from this time in influence and importance, leavening little by little the foul mass of superstition and impurity which came in contact with it. Proselytism grew more common. The Jews spread themselves wider. The return from, the captivity, which Cyrus authorized almost immediately after the capture of Babylon, is the starting point from which we may trace a gradual enlightenment of the heathen world by the dissemination of Jewish beliefs and practices – such dissemination being greatly helped by the high estimation in which the Jewish system was held by the civil authority, both while the empire of the Persians lasted, and when power passed to the Macedonians.

On the fall of Babylon its dependencies seem to have submitted to the conqueror, with a single exception. Phoenicia, which had never acquiesced contentedly either in Assyrian or in Babylonian rule, saw, apparently, in the fresh convulsion that was now shaking the East, an opportunity for recovering autonomy. It was nearly half a century since her last struggle to free herself had terminated unsuccessfully. A new generation had grown up since that time – a generation which had seen nothing of war, and imperfectly appreciated its perils. Perhaps some reliance was placed on the countenance and support of Egypt, which, it must have been felt, would view with satisfaction any obstacle to the advance of a power wherewith she was sure, sooner or later, to come into collision. At any rate, it was resolved to make the venture. Phoenicia, on the destruction of her distant suzerain, quietly resumed her freedom; abstained from making any act of submission to the conqueror; while, however, at the same time, she established friendly relations for commercial purposes with one of the conqueror's vassals, the prince who had been sent into Palestine to re-establish the Jews at Jerusalem.

It might have been expected that Cyrus, after his conquest of Babylon, would have immediately proceeded towards the south-west. The reduction of Egypt had, according to Herodotus, been embraced in the designs which he formed fifteen years earlier. The non-submission of Phoenicia must have been regarded as an act of defiance which deserved signal chastisement. It has been suspected that the restoration of the Jews was prompted, at least in part, by political motives, and that Cyrus, when he re-established them in their country, looked to finding them of use to him in the attack which he was meditating upon Egypt. At any rate it is evident that their presence would have facilitated his march through Palestine, and given him a *point d'appui*, which could not but have been of value. These considerations make it probable that an Egyptian expedition would have been determined on, had not circumstances occurred to prevent it.

What the exact circumstances were, it is impossible to determine. According to Herodotus, a sudden desire seized Cyrus to attack the Massagetae, who bordered his empire to the north-east. He led his troops across the Araxes (Jaxartes?), defeated the Massagetae by stratagem in a great battle, but was afterwards himself defeated and slain, his body falling into the enemy's hands, who treated it with gross indignity. According to Ctesias, the people against whom he made his expedition were the Derbices, a nation bordering upon India. Assisted by Indian allies, who lent them a number of elephants, this people engaged Cyrus, and defeated him in a battle, wherein he received a mortal wound. Reinforced, however, by a body of Sacae, the Persians renewed the struggle, and gained a complete victory, which was followed by the submission of the nation. Cyrus, however, died of his wound on the third day after the first battle.

THE LEGACY OF CYRUS THE GREAT

This conflict of testimony clouds with uncertainty the entire closing scene of the life of Cyrus. All that we can lay down as tolerably well established is, that instead of carrying out his designs against Egypt, he engaged in hostilities with one of the nations on his north-eastern frontier, that he conducted the war with less than his usual success, and in the course of it received a wound of which he died (529 BCE), after he had reigned nine-and-twenty years. That his body did not fall into the enemy's hands appears, however, to be certain from the fact that it was conveyed into Persia Proper, and buried at Pasargadae.

It may be suspected that this expedition, which proved so disastrous to the Persian monarch, was not the mere wanton act which it appears to be in the pages of our authorities. The nations of the north-east were at all times turbulent and irritable, with difficulty held in check by the civilized power that bore rule in the south and west. The expedition of Cyrus, whether directed against the Massagetae or the Derbices, was probably intended to strike terror into the barbarians of these regions, and was analogous to those invasions which were undertaken under the wisest of the Roman emperors, across the Rhine and Danube, against Germans, Goths, and Sarmatae. The object of such inroads was not to conquer, but to alarm – it was hoped by an imposing display of organized military force to deter the undisciplined hordes of the prolific North from venturing across the frontier and carrying desolation through large tracts of the Empire. Defensive warfare has often an aggressive look. It may have been solely with the object of protecting his own territories from attack that Cyrus made his last expedition across the Jaxertes, or towards the upper Indus.

The character of Cyrus, as represented to us by the Greeks, is the most favorable that we possess of any early Oriental monarch. Active, energetic, brave, fertile in stratagems, he has all the qualities required to form a successful military chief. He conciliates his people by friendly and familiar treatment, but declines to spoil them by yielding to their inclinations when they are adverse to their true interests. He has a ready humor, which shows itself in smart sayings and repartees, that take occasionally the favorite Oriental turn of parable or apologue. He is mild in his treatment of the prisoners that fall into his hands, and ready to forgive even the heinous crime of rebellion. He has none of the pride of the ordinary eastern despot, but converses on terms of equality with those about him. We cannot be surprised that the Persians, contrasting him with their later monarchs, held his memory in the highest veneration, and were even led by their affection for his person to make his type of countenance their standard of physical beauty.

The genius of Cyrus was essentially that of a conqueror, not of an administrator. There is no trace of his having adopted anything like a uniform system for the government of the provinces which he subdued. In Lydia he set up a Persian governor, but assigned certain important functions to a native; in Babylon he gave the entire direction of affairs into the hands of a Mede, to whom he allowed the title and style of king; in Judaea he appointed a native, but made him merely "governor" or "deputy;" in Sacia he maintained as tributary king the monarch who had resisted his arms. Policy may have dictated the course pursued in each instance, which may have been suited to the condition of the several provinces; but the variety allowed was fatal to consolidation, and the monarchy, as Cyrus left it, had as little cohesion as any of those by which it was preceded.

Though originally a rude mountain-chief, Cyrus, after he succeeded to empire, showed himself quite able to appreciate the dignity and value of art. In his constructions at Pasargadae he combined massiveness with elegance, and manifested a taste at once simple and refined. He ornamented his buildings with reliefs of an ideal character. It is probably to him that we owe the conception of the light tapering stone shaft, which is the glory of Persian architecture. If the more massive of the

Persepolitan buildings are to be ascribed to him, we must regard him as having fixed the whole plan and arrangement which was afterwards followed in all Persian palatial edifices.

In his domestic affairs Cyrus appears to have shown the same moderation and simplicity which we observe in his general conduct. He married, as it would seem, one wife only, Cassandane, the daughter of Pharnaspes, who was a member of the royal family. By her he had issue two sons and at least three daughters. The sons were Cambyses and Smerdis; the daughters Atossa, Artystone, and one whose name is unknown to us. Cassandane died before her husband, and was deeply mourned by him. Shortly before his own death he took the precaution formally to settle the succession. Leaving the general inheritance of his vast dominions to his elder son, Cambyses, he declared it to be his will that the younger should be entrusted with the actual government of several large and important provinces. He thought by this plan to secure the well-being of both the youths, never suspecting that he was in reality consigning both to untimely ends, and even preparing the way for an extraordinary revolution.

THE PERSIAN EMPIRE

PHOENICIA

In this chapter, George Rawlinson tells the history of the loosely defined area of Phoenicia until the Achaemenid period.

As becomes clear also in Rawlinson's introduction, the Phoenicians themselves never needed a collective term for the different people from Sidon, the people from Tyre and those of many other varied places. The term 'Phoenicia' was coined in ancient Greece, probably already in Mycenaean Crete. For modern historiographical purposes, the common thread to follow is the Phoenician language which does not entail ethnic or political unity.

Rawlinson recognizes that the beginning of Phoenician history should not be restricted to the first millennium BCE, however it was only after his time that the correspondence of the Amarna period added much crucial information about the Phoenician city-states of the later second millennium BCE.

From these sources, significant continuity between the earlier and later periods can be understood. Phoenician cities have always been important places of trade. Of course, it is in the first millennium that Phoenician renown for trade, foremost that of Tyre, spread throughout the entire ancient Near East.

PHOENICIA, BEFORE THE ESTABLISHMENT OF THE HEGEMONY OF TYRE

When the **Phoenician** immigrants, in scattered bands, and at longer or shorter intervals, arrived upon the Syrian coast, and finding it empty occupied it, or wrested it from its earlier possessors, there was a decided absence from among them of any single governing or controlling authority; a marked tendency to assert and maintain separate rule and jurisdiction. Sidon, the Arkite, the Arvadite, the Zemarite, are separately enumerated in the Book of Genesis; and the Hebrews have not even any one name under which to comprise the commercial people settled upon their coast line, until we come to Gospel times, when the Greeks have brought the term "Syro-Phoenician" into use. Elsewhere we hear of "them of Sidon," "them of Tyre," "the Giblites," "the men of Arvad," "the Arkites," "the Sinites," "the Zemarites," "the inhabitants of Accho, of Achzib, and Aphek," but never of the whole maritime population north of Philistia under any single ethnic appellation. And the reason seems to be, that the Phoenicians, even more than the Greeks, affected a city autonomy. Each little band of immigrants, as soon as it had pushed its way into the sheltered tract between the mountains and the sea, settled itself upon some attractive spot, constructed habitations, and having surrounded its habitations with walls, claimed to be – and found none to dispute the claim – a distinct political entity. The conformation of the land, so broken up into isolated regions by strong spurs from Lebanon and Bargylus, lent additional support to the separatist spirit, and the absence in the early times of any pressure of danger from without permitted its free indulgence without entailing any serious penalty. It is difficult to say at what time the first settlements took place; but during the period of Egyptian supremacy over Western Asia, under the eighteenth and nineteenth dynasties (c. 1600–1350 BCE), we seem to find the Phoenicians in possession of the coast tract, and their cities severally in the enjoyment of independence and upon a quasi-equality. Tyre, Sidon, Gebal, Aradus, Simyra, Sarepta, Berytus, and perhaps Arka, appear in the inscriptions of Thothmes III, and in the "Travels of a Mohar," without an indication of the pre-eminence, much less the supremacy, of any one of them. The towns pursued their courses independently one of another, submitting to the Egyptians when hard pressed, but always ready to reassert themselves, and never joining, so far as appears, in any league or confederation, by which their separate autonomy might have been endangered. During this period no city springs to any remarkable height of greatness or prosperity; material progress is, no doubt, being made by the nation; but it is not very marked, and it does not excite any particular attention.

But with the decline of the Egyptian power, which sets in after the death of the second Rameses, a change takes place. External pressure being removed, ambitions begin to develop themselves. In the north Aradus (Arvad), in the south Sidon, proceed to exercise a sort of hegemony over several neighbouring states. Sidon becomes known as "Great Zidon." Not content with her maritime ascendancy, which was already pushing her into special notice, she aspired to a land dominion, and threw out offshoots from the main seat of her power as far as Laish, on the head-waters of the Jordan. It was her support, probably, which enabled the inhabitants of such comparatively weak cities as Accho and Achzib and Aphek to resist the invasion of the Hebrews, and maintain themselves, despite all attempts made to reduce them. At the same time she gradually extended her influence over the coast towns in her neighbourhood, as Sarepta, Heldun, perhaps Berytus, Ecdippa, and Accho. The period which succeeds that of Egyptian preponderance in Western Asia may be distinguished as that of Sidonian ascendancy, or of such ascendancy slightly modified by an Aradian hegemony in the north over the settlements intervening between Mount Casius and the northern roots of Lebanon. During this period Sidon came to the front, alike in arts, in arms, and in navigation. Her vessels were found by the earliest Greek navigators in all parts of the Mediterranean into which they themselves ventured, and were known to push themselves into regions where no Greek dared to follow them. Under her fostering care Phoenician colonisation had spread over the whole of the Western Mediterranean, over the Aegean, and into the Propontis. She had engaged in war with the powerful nation of the Philistines, and, though worsted in the encounter, had obtained a reputation for audacity. By her wonderful progress in the arts, her citizens had acquired the epithet of poludaidaloi, and had come to be recognized generally as the foremost artificers of the world in almost every branch of industry. Sidonian metal-work was particularly in repute. When Achilles at the funeral of Patroclus desired to offer as a prize to the fastest runner the most beautiful bowl that was to be found in all the world, he naturally chose one which had been deftly made by highly-skilled Sidonians, and which Phoenician sailors had conveyed in one of their hollow barks across the cloud-shadowed sea. When Menelaus proposed to present Telemachus, the son of his old comrade Odysseus, with what was at once the most beautiful and the most valuable of all his possessions, he selected a silver bowl with a golden rim, which in former days he had himself received as a present from Phaedimus, the Sidonian king. The sailors who stole Eumaeus from Ortygia, and carried him across the sea to Ithica, obtained their prize by coming to his father's palace, and bringing with them, among other wares,

> . . . *a necklace of fine gold to sell,*
> *With bright electron linked right wondrously and well.*

Sidon's pre-eminence in the manufacture, the dyeing, and the embroidery of textile fabrics was at the same time equally unquestionable. Hecuba, being advised to offer to Athêné, on behalf of her favourite son, the best and loveliest of all the royal robes which her well-stored dress-chamber could furnish:

> *She to her fragrant wardrobe bent her way,*
> *Where her rich veils in beauteous order lay;*
> *Webs by Sidonian virgins finely wrought,*
> *From Sidon's woofs by youthful Paris brought,*
> *When o'er the boundless main the adulterer led*
> *Fair Helen from her home and nuptial bed;*
> *From these she chose the fullest, fairest far,*
> *With broidery bright, and blazing as a star.*

Already, it would seem, the precious shell-fish, on which Phoenicia's commerce so largely rested in later times, had been discovered; and it was the dazzling hue of the robe which constituted its especial value. Sidon was ultimately eclipsed by Tyre in the productions of the loom; and the unrivalled dye has come down to us, and will go down to all future ages, as "*Tyrian* purple;" but we may well believe that in this, as in most other matters on which prosperity and success depended, Tyre did but follow in the steps of her elder sister Sidon, perfecting possibly the manufacture which had been Sidon's discovery in the early ages. According to Scylax of Cadyanda, Dor was a Sidonian colony. Geographically it belonged rather to Philistia than to Phoenicia; but its possession of large stores of the purple fish caused its sudden seizure and rapid fortification at a very remote date, probably by the Phoenicians of Sidon. It is quite possible that this aggression may have provoked that terrible war to which reference has already been made, between the Philistines under the hegemony of Ascalon and the first of the Phoenician cities. Ascalon attacked the Sidonians by land, blockaded the offending town, and after a time compelled a surrender; but the defenders had a ready retreat by sea, and, when they could no longer hold out against their assailants, took ship, and removed themselves to Tyre, which at the time was probably a dependency

In navigation also and colonisation Sidon took the lead. According to some, she was the actual founder of Aradus, which was said to have owed its origin to a body of Sidonian exiles, who there settled themselves. Not much reliance, however, can be placed on this tradition, which first appears in a writer of the Augustan age. With more confidence we may ascribe to Sidon the foundation of Citium in Cyprus, the colonisation of the islands in the Aegean, and of those Phoenician settlements in North Africa which were anterior to the founding of Carthage. It has even been supposed that the Sidonians were the first to make a settlement at Carthage itself, and that the Tyrian occupation under Dido was a recolonisation of an already occupied site. Anyhow, Sidon was the first to explore the central Mediterranean, and establish commercial relations with the barbarous tribes of the mid-African coast, Cabyles, Berbers, Shuloukhs, Tauriks, and others. She is thought to claim on a coin to be the mother-city of Melita, or Malta, as well as of Citium and Berytus; and, if this claim be allowed, we can scarcely doubt that she was also the first to plant colonies in Sicily. Further than this, it would seem, Sidonian enterprise did not penetrate. It was left for Tyre to discover the wealth of Southern Spain, to penetrate beyond the Straits of Gibraltar, and to affront the perils of the open ocean.

But, within the sphere indicated, Sidonian rovers traversed all parts of the Great Sea, penetrated into every gulf, became familiar sights to the inhabitants of every shore. From timid sailing along the coast by day, chiefly in the summer season, when winds whispered gently, and atmospheric signs indicated that fair weather had set in, they progressed by degrees to long voyages, continued both by night and day, from promontory to promontory, or from island to island, sometimes even across a long stretch of open sea, altogether out of sight of land, and carried on at every season of the year except some few of special danger. To

Sidon is especially ascribed the introduction of the practice of sailing by night, which shortened the duration of voyages by almost one-half, and doubled the number of trips that a vessel could accomplish in the course of a year. For night sailing the arts of astronomy and computation had to be studied; the aspect of the heavens at different seasons had to be known; and among the shifting constellations some fixed point had to be found by which it would be safe to steer. The last star in the tail of the Little Bear – the polar star of our own navigation books – was fixed upon by the Phoenicians, probably by the Sidonians, for this purpose, and was practically employed as the best index of the true north from a remote period. The rate of a ship's speed was, somehow or other, estimated; and though it was long before charts were made, or the set of currents taken into account, yet voyages were for the most part accomplished with very tolerable accuracy and safety. An ample commerce grew up under Sidonian auspices. After the vernal equinox was over a fleet of white-winged ships sped forth from the many harbours of the Syrian coast, well laden with a variety of wares – Phoenician, Assyrian, Egyptian – and made for the coasts and islands of the Levant, the Aegean, the Propontis, the Adriatic, the mid-Mediterranean, where they exchanged the cargoes which they had brought with them for the best products of the lands whereto they had come. Generally, a few weeks, or at most a month or two, would complete the transfer the of commodities, and the ships which left Sidon in April or May would return about June or July, unload, and make themselves ready for a second voyage. But sometimes, it appears, the return cargo was not so readily procured, and vessels had to remain in the foreign port, or roadstead, for the space of a whole year.

The behaviour of the traders must, on the whole, have been such as won the respect of the nations and tribes wherewith they traded. Otherwise, the markets would soon have been closed against them, and, in lieu of the peaceful commerce which the Phoenicians always affected, would have sprung up along the shores of the Mediterranean a general feeling of distrust and suspicion, which would have led on to hostile encounters, surprises, massacres, and then reprisals. The entire history of Phoenician commerce shows that such a condition of things never existed. The traders and their customers were bound together by the bonds of self-interest, and, except in rare instances, dealt by each other fairly and honestly. Still, there were occasions when, under the stress of temptation, fair-dealing was lost sight of, and immediate prospect of gain was allowed to lead to the commission of acts destructive of all feeling of security, subversive of commercial morals, and calculated to effect a rupture of commercial relations, which it may often have taken a long term of years to re-establish. Herodotus tells us that, at a date considerably anterior to the Trojan War, when the ascendancy over the other Phoenician cities must certainly have belonged to Sidon, an affair of this kind took place on the coast of Argolis, which was long felt by the Greeks as an injury and an outrage. A Phoenician vessel made the coast near Argos, and the crew, having effected a landing, proceeded to expose their merchandise for sale along the shore, and to traffic with the natives, who were very willing to make purchases, and in the course of five or six days bought up almost the entire cargo. At length, just as the traders were thinking of re-embarking and sailing away, there came down to the shore from the capital a number of Argive ladies, including among them a princess, Io, the daughter of Inachus, the Argive king. Hereupon, the trafficking and the bargaining recommenced; goods were produced suited to the taste of the new customers; and each strove to obtain what she desired most at the least cost. But suddenly, as they were all intent upon their purchases, and were crowding round the stern of the ship, the Phoenicians, with a general shout, rushed upon them. Many – the greater part, we are told – made their escape; but the princess, and a certain number of her companions, were seized and carried on board. The traders quickly put to sea, and hoisting their sails, hurried away to Egypt.

Another instance of kidnapping, accomplished by art rather than by force, is related to us by Homer. Eumaeus, the swineherd of Ulysses, was the son of a king, dwelling towards the west, in an island off the Sicilian coast. A Phoenician woman, herself kidnapped from Sidon by piratical Taphians, had the task of nursing and tending him assigned to her, and discharged it faithfully until a great temptation befell her. A Sidonian merchant-ship visited the island, laden with rich store of precious wares, and proceeded to open a trade with the inhabitants, in the course of which one of the sailors seduced the Phoenician nurse, and suggested that when the vessel left, she should allow herself to be carried off in it. The woman, whose parents were still alive at Sidon, came into the scheme, and being apprised of the date of the ship's departure, stole away from the palace unobserved, taking with her three golden goblets, and also her master's child, the boy of whom she had charge. It was evening, and all having been prepared beforehand, the nurse and child were hastily smuggled on board, the sails were hoisted, and the ship was soon under weigh. The wretched woman died ere the voyage was over, but the boy survived, and was carried by the traders to Ithaca, and there sold for a good sum to Laërtes.

It is not suggested that these narratives, in the form in which they have come down to us, are historically true. There may never have been an "Io, daughter of Inachus," or an "Eumaeus, son of Ctesius Ormenides," or an island, "Syria called by name, over against Ortygia," or even a Ulysses or a Laërtes. But the tales could never have grown up, have been invented, or have gained acceptance, unless the practice of kidnapping, on which they are based, had been known to be one in which the Phoenicians of the time indulged, at any rate occasionally. We must allow this blot on the Sidonian escutcheon, and can only plead, in extenuation of their offence, first, the imperfect morality of the age, and secondly, the fact that such deviations from the line of fair-dealing and honesty on the part of the Sidonian traders must have been of rare occurrence, or the flourishing and lucrative trade, which was the basis of all the glory and prosperity of the people, could not possibly have been established. Successful commerce must rest upon the foundation of mutual confidence; and mutual confidence is impossible unless the rules of fair dealing are observed on both sides, if not invariably, yet, at any rate, so generally that the infraction of them is not contemplated on either side as anything but the remotest contingency.

PHOENICIA

Of the internal government of Sidon during this period no details have come down to us. Undoubtedly, like all the Phoenician cities in the early times, she had her own kings; and we may presume, from the almost universal practice in ancient times, and especially in the East, that the monarchy was hereditary. The main duties of the king were to lead out the people to battle in time of war, and to administer justice in time of peace. The kings were in part supported, in part held in check, by a powerful aristocracy – an aristocracy which, we may conjecture, had wealth, rather than birth, as its basis. It does not appear that any political authority was possessed by the priesthood, nor that the priesthood was a caste, as in India, and (according to some writers) in Egypt. The priestly office was certainly not attached by any general custom to the person of the kings, though kings might be priests, and were so occasionally.

We do not distinctly hear of Sidon has having been engaged in any war during the period of her ascendancy, excepting that with the Philistines. Still as "the Zidonians" are mentioned among the nations which "oppressed Israel" in the time of the Judges, we must conclude that differences arose between them and their southern neighbours in some portion of this period, and that, war having broken out between them, the advantage rested with Sidon. The record of "Judges" is incomplete, and does not enable us even to fix the date of the Sidonian "oppression." We can only say that it was anterior to the judgeship of Jephthah, and was followed, like the other "oppressions," by a "deliverance."

The war with the Philistines brought the period of Sidonian ascendancy to an end, and introduces us to the second period of Phoenician history, or that of the hegemony of Tyre. The supposed date of the change is 1252 BCE.

PHOENICIA UNDER THE HEGEMONY OF TYRE (1252-877 BCE)

Tyre was noted as a "strong city" as early as the time of Joshua, and was probably inferior only to Sidon, or to Sidon and Aradus, during the period of Sidonian ascendancy. It is mentioned in the "Travels of a Mohar" (about 1350 BCE) as "a port, richer in fish than in sands." The tradition was, that it acquired its predominance and pre-eminence from the accession of the Sidonian population, which fled thither by sea, when no longer able to resist the forces of Ascalon. We do not find it, however, attaining to any great distinction or notoriety, until more than a century later, when it distinguishes itself by the colonisation of Gades (about 1130 BCE), beyond the Pillars of Hercules, on the shores of the Atlantic. We may perhaps deduce from this fact, that the concentration of energy caused by the removal to Tyre of the best elements in the population of Sidon gave a stimulus to enterprise, and caused longer voyages to be undertaken, and greater dangers to be affronted by the daring seamen of the Syrian coast than had ever been ventured on before. The Tyrian seamen were, perhaps, of a tougher fibre than the Sidonian, and the change of hegemony is certainly accompanied by a greater display of energy, a more adventurous spirit, a wider colonisation, and a more wonderful commercial success, than characterise the preceding period of Sidonian leadership and influence.

The settlements planted by Tyre in the first burst of her colonising energy seem to have been, besides Gades, Thasos, Abdera, and Pronectus towards the north, Malaca, Sexti, Carteia, Belon, and a second Abdera in Spain, together with Caralis in Sardinia, Tingis and Lixus on the West African coast, and in North Africa Hadrumetum and the lesser Leptis. Her aim was to throw the meshes of her commerce wider than Sidon had ever done, and so to sweep into her net a more abundant booty. It was Tyre which especially affected "long voyages," and induced her colonists of Gades to explore the shores outside the Pillars of Hercules, northwards as far as Cornwall and the Scilly Isles, southwards to the Fortunate Islands, and north-eastwards into the Baltic. It is, no doubt, uncertain at what date these explorations were effected, and some of them may belong to the *later* hegemony of Tyre, c. 600 BCE; but the forward movement of the twelfth century seems to have been distinctly Tyrian, and to have been one of the results of the new position in which she was placed by the sudden collapse of her elder sister, Sidon.

According to some, Tyre, during the early period of her supremacy, was under the government of *shôphetim*, or "judges;" but the general usage of the Phoenician cities makes against this supposition. Philo in his "Origines of Phoenicia" speaks constantly of kings, but never of judges. We hear of a king, Abd-Baal, at Berytus about 1300 BCE. Sidonian kings are mentioned in connection with the myth of Europa. The cities founded by the Phoenicians in Cyprus are always under monarchical rule. Tyre itself, when its history first presents itself to us in any detail, is governed by a king. All that can be urged on the other side is, that we know of no Tyrian king by name until about 1050 BCE; and that, if there had been earlier kings, it might have been expected that some record of them would have come down to us. But to argue thus is to ignore the extreme scantiness and casual character of the notices which have reached us bearing upon the early Phoenician history. No writer has left us any continuous history of Phoenicia, even in the barest outline. Native monumental annals are entirely wanting. We depend for the early times upon the accident of Jewish monarchs having come into contact occasionally with Phoenician ones, and on Jewish writers having noted the occasions in Jewish histories. Scripture and Josephus alone furnish our materials for the period now under consideration, and the materials are scanty, fragmentary, and sadly wanting in completeness.

A Phoenician Prince

It is towards the middle of the eleventh century BCE that these materials become available. About the time when David was acclaimed as king by the tribe of Judah at Hebron, a Phoenician prince mounted the throne of Tyre, by name Abibalus, or Abi-Baal. We do not know the length of his reign; but, while the son of Jesse was still in the full vigour of life, Abi-Baal was succeeded on the Tyrian throne by his son, Hiram or Hirôm, a prince of great energy, of varied tastes, and of an unusually broad and liberal turn of mind. Hiram, casting his eye over the condition of the states and kingdoms which were his neighbours, seems to have discerned in Judah and David a power and a ruler whose friendship it was desirable to cultivate with a view to the establishment of very close relations. Accordingly, it was not long after the Jewish monarch's capture of the Jebusite stronghold on Mount Zion that the Tyrian prince sent messengers to him to Jerusalem, with a present of "timber of cedars," and a number of carpenters, and stone-hewers, well skilled in the art of building. David accepted their services, and a goodly palace soon arose on some part of the Eastern hill, of which cedar from Lebanon was the chief material, and of which Hiram's workmen were the constructors. At a later date David set himself to collect abundant and choice materials for the magnificent Temple which Solomon his son was divinely commissioned to build on Mount Moriah to Jehovah; and here again "the Zidonians and they of Tyre," or the subjects of Hiram, "brought much cedar wood to David." The friendship continued firm to the close of David's reign; and when Solomon succeeded his father as king of Israel and lord of the whole tract between the middle Euphrates and Egypt, the bonds were drawn yet closer, and an alliance concluded which placed the two powers on terms of the very greatest intimacy. Hiram had no sooner heard of Solomon's accession than he sent an embassy to congratulate him; and Solomon took advantage of the opening which presented itself to announce his intention of building the Temple which his father had designed, and to request Hiram's aid in the completion of the work. Copies of letters which passed between the two monarchs were preserved both in the Tyrian and the Jewish archives, and the Tyrian versions are said to have been still extant in the public record office of the city in the first century of the Christian era. These documents ran as follows:

"Solomon to King Hiram [sends greeting]: Know that my father David was desirous of building a temple to God, but was prevented by his wars and his continual expeditions; for he did not rest from subduing his adversaries, until he had made every one of them tributary to him. And now I for my part return thanks to God for the present time of peace, and having rest thereby I purpose to build the house; for God declared to my father that it should be built by me. Wherefore I beseech thee to send some of thy servants with my servants to Mount Lebanon, to cut wood there, for none among us can skill to hew timber like unto the Sidonians. And I will pay the wood-cutters their hire at whatsoever rate thou shalt determine."

"King Hiram to King Solomon [sends greeting]: – Needs must I praise God, that hath given thee to sit upon thy father's throne, seeing that thou art a wise man, and possessed of every virtue. And I, rejoicing at these things, will do all that thou hast desired of me. I will by my servants cut thee in abundance timber of cedar and timber of cypress, and will bring them down to the sea, and command my servants to construct of them a float, or raft, and navigate it to whatever point of thy coast thou mayest wish, and there discharge them; after which thy servants can carry them to Jerusalem. But be it thy care to provide me in return with a supply of food, whereof we are in want as inhabiting an island."

The result was an arrangement by which the Tyrian monarch furnished his brother king with timber of various kinds, chiefly cedar, cut in Lebanon, and also with a certain number of trained artificers, workers in metal, carpenters, and masons, while the Israelite monarch on his part made a return in corn, wine, and oil, supplying Tyre, while the contract lasted, with 20,000 cors of wheat, the same quantity of barley, 20,000 baths of wine, and the same number of oil, annually. Phoenicia always needed to import supplies of food for its abundant population, and having an inexhaustible store of timber in Lebanon, was glad to find a market for it so near. Thus the arrangement suited both parties. The hillsides of Galilee and the broad and fertile plains of Esdraelon and Sharon produced a superabundance of wheat and barley, whereof the inhabitants had to dispose in some quarter or other, and the highlands of Sumeria and Judaea bore oil and wine far beyond the wants of those who cultivated them. What Phoenicia lacked in these respects from the scantiness of its cultivable soil, Palestine was able and eager to supply; while to Phoenicia it was a boon to obtain, not only a market for her timber, but also employment for her surplus population, which under ordinary circumstances was always requiring to be carried off to distant lands, from the difficulty of supporting itself at home.

A still greater advantage was it to the rude Judaeans to get the assistance of their civilised and artistic neighbours in the design and execution, both of the Temple itself and of all those accessories, which in ancient times a sacred edifice on a large scale was regarded as requiring. The Phoenicians, and especially the Tyrians, had long possessed, both in their home and foreign settlements, temples of some pretension, and Hiram had recently been engaged in beautifying and adorning, perhaps in rebuilding, some of these venerable edifices at Tyre. A Phoenician architectural style had thus been formed, and Hiram's architects and artificers would be familiar with constructive principles and ornamental details, as well as with industrial processes, which are very unlikely to have been known at the time to the Hebrews. The wood for the Jewish Temple was roughly cut, and the stones quarried, by Israelite workmen; but all the delicate work, whether in the one material or the other, was performed by the servants of Hiram. Stone-cutters from Gebal (Byblus) shaped and smoothed the "great stones, costly stones" employed in the substructions of the "house;" Tyrian carpenters planed and polished the cedar planks used for the walls, and covered them with representations of cherubs and palms and gourds and opening flowers. The metallurgists of Sidon probably supplied the cherubic figures in the inner sanctuary, as well as the castings for the doors, and the bulk of the sacred vessels. The vail which separated between the "Holy Place" and the Holy of Holies – a marvellous fabric of blue, and purple, and crimson, and white, with cherubim wrought thereon – owed its beauty probably to Tyrian dyers and Tyrian workers in embroidery. The master-workman lent by the Tyrian monarch to superintend the entire work – an extraordinary and almost universal genius – "skilful to work in gold and in silver, in brass, in iron, in stone, and in timber; in purple, in blue, in fine linen, and in crimson; also to grave any manner of graving" – who bore the same name with the king, was the son of an Israelite mother, but boasted a Tyrian father, and was doubtless born and bred up at Tyre. Under his special direction were cast in the valley of the Jordan, between Succoth and Zarthan, those wonderful pillars, known as Jachin and Boaz, which have already been described, and which seem to have had their counterparts in the sacred edifices both of Phoenicia and Cyprus. To him also is specially ascribed the "molten sea," standing on twelve oxen, which was perhaps the most artistic of all the objects placed within the Temple circuit, as are also the lavers upon wheels, which, if less striking as works of art, were even more curious.

The partnership established between the two kingdoms in connection with the building and furnishing of the Jewish Temple, which lasted for seven years, was further continued for thirteen more in connection with the construction of Solomon's palace. This palace, like an Assyrian one, consisted of several distinct edifices. "The chief was a long hall which, like the Temple, was encased in cedar; whence probably its name, 'The House of the Forest of Lebanon.' In front of it ran a pillared portico. Between this portico and the palace itself was a cedar porch, sometimes called the Tower of David. In this tower, apparently hung over the walls outside, were a thousand golden shields, which gave to the whole place the name of the Armoury. With a splendour that outshone any like fortress, the tower with these golden targets glittered far off in the sunshine like the tall neck, as it was thought, of a beautiful bride, decked out, after the manner of the East, with strings of golden coins. This porch was the gem and centre of the whole empire; and was so much thought of that a smaller likeness to it was erected in another part of the precinct for the queen. Within the porch itself was to be seen the king in state. On a throne of ivory, brought from Africa or India, the throne of many an Arabian legend, the kings of Judah were solemnly seated on the day of their accession. From its lofty seat, and under that high gateway, Solomon and his successors after him delivered their solemn judgments. That 'porch' or 'gate of justice' still kept alive the likeness of the old patriarchal custom of sitting in judgment at the gate; exactly as the 'Gate of Justice' still recalls it to us at Granada, and the Sublime Porte – 'the Lofty Gate' – at Constantinople. He sate on the back of a golden bull, its head turned over its shoulder, probably the ox or bull of Ephraim; under his feet, on each side of the steps, were six golden lions, probably the lions of Judah. This was 'the seat of Judgment.' This was 'the throne of the House of David.'"

Tyre

We have dwelt the longer upon these matters because it is from the lengthy and elaborate descriptions which the Hebrew writers give of these Phoenician constructions at Jerusalem that we must form our conceptions, not only of the state of Phoenician art in Hiram's time, but also of the works wherewith he adorned his own capital. He came to the throne at the age of nineteen, on the decease of his father, and immediately set to work to improve, enlarge, and beautify the city, which in his time claimed the headship of, at any rate, all Southern Phoenicia. He found Tyre a city built on two islands, separated the one from the other by a narrow channel, and so cramped for room that the inhabitants had no open square, or public place, on which they could meet, and were closely packed in overcrowded dwellings. The primary necessity was to increase the area of the place; and this Hiram effected, first, by filling up the channel between the two islands with stone and rubbish, and so gaining a space for new buildings, and then by constructing huge moles or embankments towards the east, and towards the south, where the sea was shallowest, and thus turning what had been water into land. In this way he so enlarged the town that he was able to lay out a "wide space" (Eurychôrus) as a public square, which, like the Piazza di San Marco at Venice, became the great resort of the inhabitants for business and pleasure. Having thus provided for utility and convenience, he next proceeded to embellishment and ornamentation. The old temples did not seem to him worthy of the renovated capital; he therefore pulled them down and built new ones in their place. In the most central part of the city he erected a fane for the worship of Melkarth and Ashtoreth, probably retaining the old site, but constructing an entirely new building – the building which Herodotus visited, and in which Alexander insisted on sacrificing. Towards the south-west, on what had been a separate islet, he raised a temple to Baal, and adorned it with a lofty pillar of gold, or at any rate plated with gold. Whether he built himself a new palace is not related; but as the royal residence of later times was situated on the southern shore, which was one of Hiram's additions to his capital, it is perhaps most probable that the construction of this new palace was due to him. The chief material which he used in his buildings was, as in Jerusalem, cedar. The substructions alone were of stone. They were probably not on so grand a scale as those of the Jewish Temple, since the wealth of Hiram, sovereign of a petty kingdom, must have fallen very far short of Solomon's, ruler of an extensive empire.

Hiram and Solomon

At the close of the twenty years during which Hiram had assisted Solomon in his buildings, the Israelite monarch deemed it right to make his Tyrian brother some additional compensation beyond the corn, and wine, and oil with which, according to his contract, he had annually supplied him. Accordingly, he voluntarily ceded to him a district of Galilee containing twenty cities, a portion of the old inheritance of Asher, conveniently near to Accho, of which Hiram was probably lord, and not very remote from Tyre. The tract appears to have been that where the modern Kabûl now stands, which is a rocky and bare highland, – part of the outlying roots of Lebanon – overlooking the rich plain of Akka or Accho, and presenting a striking contrast to its fertility. Hiram, on the completion of the cession, "came out from Tyre to see the cities which Solomon had given him," and was disappointed with the gift. "What cities are these," he said, "which thou hast given me, my brother? And he called them the land of Cabul" – "rubbish" or "offscourings" – to mark his disappointment.

But this passing grievance was not allowed in any way to overshadow, or interfere with, the friendly alliance and "entente cordiale" (to use a modern phrase) which existed between the two nations. Solomon, according to one authority, paid a visit to Tyre, and gratified his host by worshipping in a Sidonian temple. According to another, Hiram gave him in marriage, as a secondary wife, one of his own daughters – a marriage perhaps alluded to by the writer of Kings when he tells us that "King Solomon loved many strange women together with the daughter of Pharaoh, women of the Moabites, Ammonites,

PHOENICIA

Edomites, *Zidonians*, and Hittites." The closest commercial relations were established between the two countries, and the hope of them was probably one of the strongest reasons which attracted both parties to the alliance. The Tyrians, on their part, possessed abundant ships; their sailors had full "knowledge of the sea," and the trade of the Mediterranean was almost wholly in their hands. Solomon, on his side, being master of the port of Ezion-Geber on the Red Sea, had access to the lucrative traffic with Eastern Africa, Arabia, and perhaps India, which had hitherto been confined to the Egyptians and the Arabs. He had also, by his land power, a command of the trade routes along the Coele-Syrian valley, by Aleppo, and by Tadmor, which enabled him effectually either to help or to hinder the Phoenician land traffic. Thus either side had something to gain from the other, and a close commercial union might be safely counted on to work for the mutual advantage of both. Such a union, therefore, took place. Hiram admitted Solomon to a participation in his western traffic; and the two kings maintained a conjoint "navy of Tarshish," which, trading with Spain and the West coast of Africa, brought to Phoenicia and Palestine "once in three years" many precious and rare commodities, the chief of them being "gold, and silver, ivory, and apes, and peacocks." Spain would yield the gold and the silver, for the Tagus brought down gold, and the Spanish silver-mines were the richest in the world. Africa would furnish in abundance the ivory and the apes; for elephants were numerous in Mauritania, and on the west coast, in ancient times; and the gorilla and the Barbary ape are well-known African products. Africa may also have produced the "peacocks," if *tukkiyim* are really "peacocks," though they are not found there at the

351

present day. Or the *tukkiyim* may have been guinea-fowl – a bird of the same class with the peacock.

In return, Solomon opened to Hiram the route to the East by way of the Red Sea. Solomon, doubtless by the assistance of shipwrights furnished to him from Tyre, "made a navy of ships at Ezion-Geber, which is beside Eloth, on the shore of the Red Sea, in the land of Edom," and the sailors of the two nations conjointly manned the ships, and performed the voyage to Ophir, whence they brought gold, and "great plenty of almug-trees," and precious stones. The position of Ophir has been much disputed, but the balance of argument is in favour of the theory which places it in Arabia, on the south-eastern coast, a little outside the Straits of Bab-el-Mandeb. It is possible that the fleet did not confine itself to trade with Ophir, but, once launched on the Indian Ocean, proceeded along the Atlantic coast to the Persian Gulf and the peninsula of Hindustan. Or Ophir may have been an Arab emporium for the Indian trade, and the merchants of Syria may have found there the Indian commodities, and the Indian woods, which they seem to have brought back with them to their own country. A most lucrative traffic was certainly established by the united efforts of the two kings; and if the lion's share of the profit fell to Solomon and the Hebrews, still the Phoenicians and Hiram must have participated to some considerable extent in the gains made, or the arrangement would not have continued.

It is thought that Hiram was engaged in one war of some importance. Menander tells us, according to the present text of Josephus, that the "Tityi" revolted from him, and refused any longer to pay him tribute, whereupon he made an expedition against them, and succeeded in compelling them to submit to his authority. As the "Tityi" are an unknown people, conjecture has been busy in suggesting other names, and critics are now of the opinion that the original word used by Menander was not "Tityi," but "Itykaei." The "Itykaei" are the people of Utica: and, if this emendation be accepted, we must regard Hiram as having had to crush a most important and dangerous rebellion. Utica, previously to the foundation of Carthage, was by far the most important of all the mid-African colonies, and her successful revolt would probably have meant to Tyre the loss of the greater portion, if not the whole, of those valuable settlements. A rival to her power would have sprung up in the West, which would have crippled her commerce in that quarter, and checked her colonising energy. She would have suffered thus early more than she did four hundred years later by the great development of the power of Carthage; would have lost a large portion of her prestige; and have entered on the period of her decline when she had but lately obtained a commanding position. Hiram's energy diverted these evils: he did not choose that his kingdom should be dismembered, if he could anyhow help it; and, offering a firm and strenuous opposition to the revolt, he succeeded in crushing it, and maintaining the unity of the empire.

The Reign of Hiram

The brilliant reign of Hiram, which covered the space of forty-three years, was not followed, like that of Solomon, by any immediate troubles, either foreign or domestic. He had given his people, either at home or abroad, constant employment; he had consulted their convenience in the enlargement of his capital; he had enriched them, and gratified their love of adventure, by his commercial enterprises; he had maintained their prestige by rivetting their yoke upon a subject state; he had probably pleased them by the temples and other public buildings with which he had adorned and beautified their city. Accordingly, he went down to the grave in peace; and not only so, but left his dynasty firmly established in power. His son, Baal-azar or Baleazar, who was thirty-six years of age, succeeded him, and held the throne for seven years, when he died a natural death. Abd-Ashtoreth (Abdastartus), the fourth monarch of the house, then ascended the throne, at the age of twenty, and reigned for nine years before any troubles broke out. Then, however, a time of disturbance supervened. Four of his foster-brothers conspired against Abd-Ashtoreth, and murdered him. The eldest of them seized the throne, and maintained himself upon it for twelve years, when Astartus, perhaps a son of Baal-azar, became king, and restored the line of Hiram. He, too, like his predecessor, reigned twelve years, when his brother, Aserymus, succeeded him. Aserymus, after ruling for nine years, was murdered by another brother, Pheles, who, in his turn, succumbed to a conspiracy headed by the High Priest, Eth-baal, or Ithobal. Thus, while the period immediately following the death of Hiram was one of tranquillity, that which supervened on the death of Abd-Astartus, Hiram's grandson, was disturbed and unsettled. Three monarchs met with violent deaths within the space of thirty-four years, and the reigning house was, at least, thrice changed during the same interval.

At length with Ithobal a more tranquil time was reached. Ithobal, or Eth-baal, was not only king, but also High Priest of

Ashtoreth, and thus united the highest sacerdotal with the highest civil authority. He was a man of decision and energy, a worthy successor of Hiram, gifted like him with wide-reaching views, and ambitious of distinction. One of his first acts was to ally himself with Ahab, King of Israel, by giving him his daughter, Jezebel, in marriage, thus strengthening his land dominion, and renewing the old relations of friendship with the Hebrew people. Another act of vigour assigned to him is the foundation of Botrys, on the Syrian coast, north of Gebal, perhaps a defensive movement against Assyria. Still more enterprising was his renewal of the African colonisation by his foundation of Aüza in Numidia, which became a city of some importance. Ithobal's reign lasted, we are told, thirty-two years. He was sixty-eight years of age at his death, and was succeeded by his son, who is called Badezor, probably a corruption of Balezor, or Baal-azar – the name given by Hiram to his son and successor. Of Badezor we know nothing, except that he reigned six years, and was succeeded by his son Matgen, perhaps Mattan, a youth of twenty-three.

With Matgen, or Mattan, whichever be the true form of the name, the internal history of Tyre becomes interesting. It appears that two parties already existed in the state, one aristocratic, and the other popular. Mattan, fearing the ascendancy of the popular party, married his daughter, Elisa, whom he intended for his successor, to her uncle and his own brother, Sicharbas, who was High Priest of Melkarth, and therefore possessed of considerable authority in his own person. Having effected this marriage, and nominated Elisa to succeed him, Mattan died at the early age of thirty-two, after a reign of only nine years. Besides his daughter, he had left behind him a son, Pygmalion, who, at his decease, was but eight or nine years old. This child the democratic party contrived to get under their influence, proclaimed him king, young as he was, and placed him upon the throne. Elisa and her husband retired into private life, and lived in peace for seven years, but Pygmalion, being then grown to manhood, was not content to leave them any longer unmolested. He murdered Sicharbas, and endeavoured to seize his riches. But the ex-queen contrived to frustrate his design, and having possessed herself of a fleet of ships, and taken on board the greater number of the nobles, sailed away, with her husband's wealth untouched, to Cyprus first, and then to Africa. Here, by agreement with the inhabitants, a site was obtained, and the famous settlement founded, which became known to the Greeks as "Karchêdon," and to the Romans as "Carthago," or Carthage. Josephus places this event in the hundred and forty-fourth year after the building of the Temple of Solomon, or about 860 BCE. This date, however, is far from certain.

The Reign of Ithobal

It appears to have been in the reign of Ithobal that the first contact took place between Phoenicia and Assyria. About 885 BCE, a powerful and warlike monarch, by name Asshur-nazir-pal, mounted the throne of Nineveh, and shortly engaged in a series of wars towards the south, the east, the north, and the north-west. In the last-named direction he crossed the Euphrates at Carchemish (Jerablus), and, having overrun the country between that river and the Orontes, he proceeded to pass this latter stream also, and to carry his arms into the rich tract which lay between the Orontes and the Mediterranean. "It was a tract," says M. Maspero, "opulent and thickly populated, at once full of industries and commercial; the metals, both precious and ordinary, gold, silver, copper, tin (?), iron, were abundant; traffic with Phoenicia supplied it with the purple dye, and with linen stuffs, with ebony and with sandal-wood. Asshur-nazir-pal's attack seems to have surprised the chief of the Hittites in a time of profound peace. Sangar, King of Carchemish, allowed the passage of the Euphrates to take place without disputing it, and opened to the Assyrians the gates of his capital. Lubarna, king of Kunulua, alarmed at the power of the enemy, and dreading the issue of a battle, came to terms with him, consenting to make over to him twenty talents of gold, a talent of silver, two hundred talents of tin, a hundred of iron, 2,000 oxen, 10,000 sheep, a thousand garments of wool or linen, together with furniture, arms, and slaves beyond all count. The country of Lukhuti resisted, and suffered the natural consequences – all the cities were sacked, and the prisoners crucified. After this exploit, Asshur-nazir-pal occupied both the slopes of Mount Lebanon, and then descended to the shores of the Mediterranean. Phoenicia did not await his arrival to do him homage: the kings of Tyre, Sidon, Gebal, and Arvad, 'which is in the midst of the sea,' sent him presents. The Assyrians employed their time in cutting down cedar trees in Lebanon and Amanus, together with pines and cypresses, which they transported to Nineveh to be used in the construction of a temple to Ishtar."

The period of the Assyrian subjection, which commenced with this attack on the part of Asshur-nazir-pal, will be the subject of the next section. It only remains here briefly to recapitulate the salient points of Phoenician history under Tyre's first supremacy. In the first place, it was a time of increased daring and enterprise, in which colonies were planted upon the shores of the Atlantic Ocean, and trade extended to the remote south, the more remote north, and the still more remote north-east, to the Fortunate Islands, the Cassiterides, and probably the Baltic. Secondly, it was a time when the colonies on the North African coast were reinforced, strengthened, and increased in number; when the Phoenician yoke was rivetted on that vast projection into the Mediterranean which divides that sea into two halves, and goes far to give the power possessing it entire command of the Mediterranean waters. Thirdly, it was a time of extended commerce with the East, perhaps the only time when Phoenician merchant vessels were free to share in the trade of the Red Sea, to adventure themselves in the Indian Ocean, and to explore the distant coasts of Eastern Africa, Southern Arabia, Beloochistan, India and Ceylon. Fourthly, it was a time of artistic vigour and development, when Tyre herself assumed that aspect of splendour and magnificence which thenceforth characterised her until her destruction by Alexander, and when she so abounded in aesthetic energy and genius that she could afford to take the direction of an art movement in a neighbouring country, and to plant her ideas on that conspicuous hill which for more than a thousand years drew the eyes of men almost more than any other city of the East, and was only destroyed because she was felt by Rome to be a rival that she could not venture to spare. Finally, it was a time when internal dissensions, long existing, came to a head, and the state lost, through a sudden desertion, a considerable portion of its strength, which was transferred to a distant continent, and there steadily, if not rapidly, developed itself into a power, not antagonistic indeed, but still, by the necessity of its position, a rival power – a new commercial star, before which all other stars, whatever their brightness had been, paled and waned – a new factor in the polity of nations, whereof account had of necessity to be taken; a new trade-centre, which could not but supersede to a great extent all former trade-centres, and which, however unwillingly, as it rose, and advanced, and prospered, tended to dim, obscure, and eclipse the glories of its mother-city.

PHOENICIA DURING THE PERIOD OF ITS SUBJECTION TO ASSYRIA (877-635 BCE)

The first contact of Phoenicia with Assyria took place, as above observed, in the reign of Asshur-nazir-pal, about the year 877 BCE. The principal cities, on the approach of the great conquering monarch, with his multitudinous array of chariots, his clouds of horse, and his innumerable host of foot soldiers, made haste to submit themselves, sought to propitiate the invader by rich gifts, and accepted what they hoped might prove a nominal subjection. Arvad, which, as the most northern, was the most directly threatened, Gebal, Sidon, and even the comparatively remote Tyre, sent their several embassies, made their offerings, and became, in name at any rate, Assyrian dependencies. But the real subjection of this country was not effected at this time, nor without a struggle. Asshur-nazir-pal's yoke lay lightly upon his vassals, and during the remainder of his long reign – from 877 BCE to 860 BCE – he seems to have desisted from military expeditions, and to have exerted no pressure on the countries situated west of the

Euphrates. It was not until the reign of his son and successor, Shalmaneser II, that the real conquest of Syria and Phoenicia was taken in hand, and pressed to a successful issue by a long series of hard-fought campaigns and bloody battles. From his sixth to his twenty-first year Shalmaneser carried on an almost continuous war in Syria, where his adversaries were the monarchs of Damascus and Hamath, and "the twelve kings beside the sea, above and below," one of whom is expressly declared to have been "Mattan-Baal of Arvad." It was not until the year 839 BCE that this struggle was terminated by the submission of the monarchs engaged in it to their great adversary, and the firm establishment of a system of "tribute and taxes." The Phoenician towns agreed to pay annually to the Assyrian monarch a certain fixed sum in the precious metals, and further to make him presents from time to time of the best products of their country. Among these are mentioned "skins of buffaloes, horns of buffaloes, clothing of wool and linen, violet wool, purple wool, strong wood, wood for weapons, skins of sheep, fleeces of shining purple, and birds of heaven."

The relations of Phoenicia towards the Assyrian monarchy continued to be absolutely peaceful for above a century. The cities retained their native monarchs, their laws and institutions, their religion, and their entire internal administration. So long as they paid the fixed tribute, they appear not to have been interfered with in any way. It would seem that their trade prospered. Assyria had under her control the greater portion of those commercial routes across the continent of Asia, which it was of the highest importance to Phoenicia to have open and free from peril. Her caravans could traverse them with increased security, now that they were safeguarded by a power whereof she was a dependency. She may even have obtained through Assyria access to regions which had been previously closed to her, as Media, and perhaps Persia. At any rate Tyre seems to have been as flourishing in the later times of the Assyrian dominion as at almost any other period. Isaiah, in denouncing woe upon her, towards the close of the dominion, shows us what she had been under it:

> *Be silent (he says), ye inhabitants of the island,*
> *Which the merchants of Zidon, that pass*
> *over the sea, have replenished.*
> *The corn of the Nile, on the broad waters,*
> *The harvest of the River, has been her revenue:*
> *She has been the mart of nations . . .*
> *She was a joyful city,*
> *Her antiquity was of ancient days . . .*
> *She was a city that dispensed crowns;*
> *Her merchants were princes,*
> *And her traffickers the honourable of the earth.*

The Second Assyrian Empire

A change in the friendly feelings of the Phoenician cities towards Assyria first began after the rise of the Second or Lower Assyrian Empire, which was founded, about 745 BCE, by Tiglath-pileser II. Tiglath-pileser, after a time of quiescence and decay, raised up Assyria to be once more a great conquering power, and energetically applied himself to the consolidation and unification of the empire. It was the Assyrian system, as it was the Roman, to absorb nations by slow degrees – to begin by offering protection and asking in return a moderate tribute; then to draw the bonds more close, to make fresh demands and enforce them; finally, to pick a quarrel, effect a conquest, and absorb the country, leaving it no vestige of independence. Tiglath-pileser began this process of absorption in Northern Syria about the year 740 BCE. He rearranged the population in the various towns, taking from some and giving to others, adding also in most cases an Assyrian element, appointing Assyrian governors, and requiring of the inhabitants "the performance of service like the Assyrians." Among the places thus treated between the years 740 BCE and 738 BCE, we find the Phoenician cities of Zimirra, or Simyra, and Arqa, or Arka. Zimirra was in the plain between the sea and Mount Bargylus, not very far from the island of Aradus, whereof it was a dependency. Arqa was further to the south, beyond the Eleutherus, and belonged properly to Tripolis, if Tripolis had as yet been founded, or else to Botrys. Both of them were readily accessible from the Orontes valley along the course of the Eleutherus, and, being weak, could offer no resistance. Tiglath-pileser carried out his plans, rearranged the populations, and placed the cities under Assyrian governors responsible to himself. There was no immediate outbreak; but the injury rankled. Within twenty years Zimirra joined a revolt, to which Hamath, Arpad, Damascus, and Samaria were likewise parties, and made a desperate attempt to shake off the Assyrian yoke. The attempt failed, the revolt was crushed, and Zimirra is heard of no more in history.

But this was not the worst. The harsh treatment of Simyra and Arka, without complaint made or offence given, after a full century of patient and quiet submission, aroused a feeling of alarm and indignation among the Phoenician cities generally, which could not fail to see in what had befallen their sisters a foreshadowing of the fate that they had to expect one day themselves. Beginning with the weakest cities, Assyria would naturally go on to absorb those which were stronger, and Tyre herself, the "anointed cherub," could look for no greater favour than, like Ulysses in the cave of Polyphemus, to be devoured last. Luliya, or Elulaeus, the king of Tyre at the time, endeavoured to escape this calamity by gathering to himself a strength which would enable him to defy attack. He contrived to establish his dominion over almost the whole of Southern Phoenicia – over Sidon, Accho, Ecdippa, Sarepta, Hosah, Bitsette, Mahalliba, etc. – and at the same time over the distant Cyprus, where the Cittaeans, or people of Citium, held command of the island. After a time the Cittaeans revolted from him, probably stirred up by the Assyrians. But Elulaeus, without delay, led an expedition into Cyprus, and speedily put down the rebellion. Hereupon the Assyrian king of the time, Shalmaneser IV, the successor and probably the son of Tiglath-pileser II, led a great expedition into the west about 727 BCE, and "overran all Syria and Phoenicia." But he was unable to make any considerable impression. Tyre and Aradus were safe upon their islands; Sidon and the other cities upon the mainland, were protected by strong and lofty walls. After a single campaign, the Great King found it necessary to offer terms of peace, which proved acceptable, and the belligerents parted towards the close of the year, without any serious loss or gain on either side.

Unease Among Phoenician Cities

It seemed necessary to adopt some different course of action. Shalmaneser had discovered during his abortive campaign that there were discords and jealousies among the various Phoenician cities; that none of them submitted without repugnance to the authority of Tyre, and that Sidon especially had an ancient ground of quarrel with her more powerful sister, and always cherished the hope of recovering her original supremacy. He had seen also that the greater number of the Phoenician towns, if he chose to press upon them with the full force of his immense military organisation, lay at his mercy. He had only to invest each city on the land side, to occupy its territory, to burn its villas, to destroy its irrigation works, to cut down its fruit trees, to interfere with its water-supply, and in the last instance to press upon it, to batter down its walls, to enter its streets, slaughter its population, or drive it to take refuge in its ships, and he could become absolute master of the whole Phoenician mainland. Only Tyre and Aradus could escape him. But might not they also be brought into subjection by the naval forces which their sister cities, once occupied, might be compelled to furnish, and to man, or, at any rate, to assist in manning? Might not the whole of Phoenicia be in this way absorbed into the empire? The prospect was pleasing, and Shalmaneser set to work to convert the vision into a reality. By his emissaries he stirred up the spirit of disaffection among the Tyrian subject towns, and succeeded in separating from

Tyre, and drawing over to his own side, not only Sidon and Acre and their dependencies, but even the city of Palae-Tyrus itself, or the great town which had grown up opposite the island Tyre upon the mainland. The island Tyre seems to have been left without support or ally, to fight her own battle singly. Shalmaneser called upon his new friends to furnish him with a fleet, and they readily responded to the call, placing their ships at his disposal to the number of sixty, and supplying him further with eight hundred skilled oarsmen, not a sufficient number to dispense with Assyrian aid, but enough to furnish a nucleus of able seamen for each vessel. The attack was then made. The Assyro-Phoenician fleet sailed in a body from some port on the continent, and made a demonstration against the Island City, which they may perhaps have expected to frighten into a surrender. But the Tyrians were in no way alarmed. They knew, probably, that their own countrymen would not fight with very much zeal for their foreign masters, and they despised, undoubtedly, the mixed crews, half skilled seamen, half tiros and bunglers, which had been brought against them. Accordingly they thought it sufficient to put to sea with just a dozen ships – one to each five of the enemy, and making a sudden attack with these upon the adverse fleet, they defeated it, dispersed it, and took five hundred prisoners. Shalmaneser saw that he had again miscalculated; and, despairing of any immediate success, drew off his ships and his troops, and retired to his own country. He left behind him, however, on the mainland opposite the island Tyre, a certain number of his soldiers, with orders to prevent the Tyrians from obtaining, according to their ordinary practice, supplies of water from the continent. Some were stationed at the mouth of the river

Leontes (the Litany), a little to the north of Tyre, a perennial stream bringing down a large quantity of water from Coele-Syria and Lebanon; others held possession of the aqueducts on the south, built to convey the precious fluid across the plain from the copious springs of Ras el Ain to the nearest point of the coast opposite the city. The continental water supply was thus effectually cut off; but the Tyrians were resolute, and made no overtures to the enemy. For five years, we are told, they were content to drink such water only as could be obtained in their own island from wells sunk in the soil, which must have been brackish, unwholesome, and disagreeable. At the end of that time a revolution occurred at Nineveh. Shalmaneser lost his throne (722 BCE), and a new dynasty succeeding, amid troubles of various kinds, attention was drawn away from Tyre to other quarters; and Elulaeus was left in undisturbed possession of his island city for nearly a quarter of a century.

It appears that, during this interval, Elulaeus rebuilt the power which Shalmaneser had shattered and brought low, repossessing himself of Cyprus, or, at any rate, of some portion of it, and re-establishing his authority over all those cities of the mainland which had previously acknowledged subjection to him. These included Sidon, Bit-sette, Sarepta, Mahalliba, Hosah, Achzib or Ecdippa, and Accho (Acre). There is some ground for thinking that he transferred his own residence to Sidon, perhaps for the purpose of keeping closer watch upon the town which he most suspected of disaffection. The policy of Sargon seems to have been to leave Phoenicia alone, and content himself with drawing the tribute which the cities were quite willing to pay in return for Assyrian protection. His reign lasted from 722 BCE to 705

BCE, and it was not until Sennacherib, his son and successor, had been seated for four years upon the throne that a reversal of this policy took place, and war *à outrance* was declared against the Phoenician king, who had ventured to brave, and had succeeded in baffling, Assyria more than twenty years previously. Sennacherib entertained grand designs of conquest in this quarter, and could not allow the example of an unpunished and triumphant rebellion to be flaunted in the eyes of a dozen other subject states, tempting them to throw off their allegiance. He therefore, as soon as affairs in Babylonia ceased to occupy him, marched the full force of the empire towards the west, and proclaimed his intention of crushing the Phoenician revolt, and punishing the audacious rebel who had so long defied the might of Assyria. The army which he set in motion must have numbered more than 200,000 men; its chariots were numerous, its siege-train ample and well provided. Such terror did it inspire among those against whom it was directed that Elulaeus was afraid even to await attack, and, while Sennacherib was still on his march, took ship and removed himself to the distant island of Cyprus, where alone he could feel safe from pursuit and capture. But, though deserted by their sovereign, his towns seem to have declined to submit themselves. No great battle was fought; but severally they took arms and defended their walls. Sennacherib tells us that he took one after another – "by the might of the soldiers of Asshur his lord" – Great Sidon, Lesser Sidon, Bit-sette, Zarephath or Sarepta, Mahalliba, Hosah, Achzib or Ecdippa, and Accho – "strong cities, fortresses, walled and enclosed, Luliya's castles." He does not claim, however, to have taken Tyre, and we may conclude that the Island City escaped him. But he made himself master of the entire tract upon the continent which had constituted Luliya's kingdom, and secured its obedience by placing over it a new king, in whom he had confidence, a certain Tubaal (Tob-Baal), probably a Phoenician. At the same time he rearranged the yearly tribute which the cities had to pay to Assyria, probably augmenting it, as a punishment for the long rebellion.

The Reign of Sennacherib

We hear nothing more of Phoenicia during the reign of Sennacherib, except that, shortly after his conquest of the tract about Sidon, he received tribute, not only from the king whom he had just set over that town, but also from Uru-melek, king of Gebal (Byblus), and Abd-ilihit, king of Arvad. The three towns represent, probably, the whole of Phoenicia, Aradus at this time exercising dominion over the northern tract, or that extending from Mount Casius to the Eleutherus, Gebal or Byblus over the central tract from the Eleutherus to the Tamyras, and Sidon, in the temporary eclipse of Tyre, ruling the southern tract from the Tamyrus to Mount Carmel. It appears further, that at some date between this tribute-giving (701 BCE) and the death of Sennacherib (681 BCE) Tubaal must have been succeeded in the government of Sidon by Abdi-Milkut, or Abd-Melkarth, but whether this change was caused by a revolt, or took place in the ordinary course, Tubaal dying and being succeeded by his son, is wholly uncertain.

All that we know is that Esarhaddon, on his accession, found Abd-Melkarth in revolt against his authority. He had formed an alliance with a certain Sanduarri, king of Kundi and Sizu, a prince of the Lebanon, and had set up as independent monarch, probably during the time of the civil way which was waged between Esarhaddon and two of his brothers who disputed his succession after they had murdered his father. As soon as this struggle was over, and the Assyrian monarch found himself free to take his own course, he proceeded at once (680 BCE) against these two rebels. Both of them tried to escape him. Abd-Melkarth, quitting his capital, fled away by sea, steering probably either for Aradus or for Cyprus. Sanduarri took refuge in his mountain fastnesses. But Esarhaddon was not to be baffled. He caused both chiefs to be pursued and taken. "Abd-Melkarth," he says, "who from the face of my solders into the middle of the sea had fled, like a fish from out of the sea, I caught, and cut off his head . . . Sanduarri, who took Abd-Melkarth for his ally, and to his difficult mountains trusted, like a bird from the midst of the mountains, I caught and cut off his head." Sidon was very severely punished. Esarhaddon boasts that he swept away all its subject cities, uprooted its citadel and palace, and cast the materials into the sea, at the same time destroying all its habitations. The town was plundered, the treasures of the palace carried off, and the greater portion of the population deported to Assyria. The blank was filled up with "natives of the lands and seas of the East" – prisoners taken in Esarhaddon's war with Babylon and Elam, who, like the Phoenicians themselves at a remote time, exchanged a residence on the shores of the Persian Gulf for one on the distant Mediterranean. An Assyrian general was placed as governor over the city, and its name changed from Sidon to "Ir-Esarhaddon."

It seems to have been in the course of the same year that Esarhaddon held one of those courts, or *durbars*, in Syria, which all subject monarchs were expected to attend, and whereat it was the custom that they should pay homage to their suzerain. Hither flocked almost all the neighbouring monarchs – Manasseh, king of Judah, Qavus-gabri, king of Ammon, Zilli-bel, king of Gaza, Mitinti of Askelon, Ikasamsu of Ekron, Ahimelek of Ashdod, together with twelve kings of the Cyprians, and three Phoenician monarchs, Baal, king of Tyre, Milki-asaph, king of Gebal, and Mattan-baal, king of Arvad. Tribute was paid, home rendered, and after a short sojourn at the court, the subject-monarchs were dismissed. The foremost position in Esarhaddon's list is occupied by "Baal, king of Tyre;" and this monarch appears to have been received into exceptional favour. He had perhaps been selected by Esarhaddon to rule Southern Phoenicia on the execution of Abd-Melkarth. At any rate, he enjoyed for some time the absolute confidence and high esteem of his suzerain. If we may venture to interpret a mutilated inscription, he furnished Esarhaddon with a fleet, and manned it with his own sailors. Certainly, he received from Esarhaddon a considerable extension of his dominions. Not only was his authority over Accho recognized and affirmed, but the coast tract south of Carmel, as far as Dor, the important city Gebal, and the entire region of Lebanon, were placed under his sovereignty. The date assigned to these events is between 680 BCE and 673 BCE. It was in this latter year that the Assyrian monarch resolved on an invasion of Egypt. For fifty years the two countries had been watching each other, counteracting each other's policy, lending support to each other's enemies, coming into occasional collision the one with the other, not, however, as principals, but as partakers in other persons' quarrels. Now, at length there was to be an end of subterfuge and pretences. Esarhaddon, about 673 BCE, resolved to attempt the conquest of Egypt. He "set his face to go to the country of Magan and Milukha." He let his intention be generally known. No doubt he called on his subject allies for contingents of men, if not for supplies of money. To Tyre he must naturally have looked for no niggard or grudging support. What then must have been his disgust and rage at finding that, at the critical moment, Tyre had gone over to the enemy? Notwithstanding the favours heaped on him by his suzerain, "Baal, king of Tyre, to Tirhakah, king of Ethiopia, his country entrusted, and the yoke of Asshur threw off and made defiance." Esarhaddon was too strongly bent on his Egyptian expedition to be diverted from it by this defection; but in the year 672 BCE, as he marched through Syria and Palestine on his way to attack Tirhakah, he sent a detachment against Tyre, with orders to his officers to repeat the tactics of Shalmaneser, by occupying points of the coast opposite to the island Tyre, and "cutting off the supplies of food and water." Baal was by this means greatly distressed, and it would seem that within a year or two he made his submission, surrendering either to Esarhaddon or to his son Asshur-bani-pal, in about the year of the latter's accession (668 BCE). It is surprising to find that he was not deposed from his throne; but as the circumstances seem to have been such as made it imperative on the Assyrian king to condone minor offences in order to accomplish a great enterprise – the restoration of the Assyrian dominion over the

Nile valley. Esarhaddon had effected the conquest of Egypt in about the year 670 BCE, and had divided the country into twenty petty principalities; but within a year his yoke had been thrown off, his petty princes expelled, and Tirhakah reinstated as sole monarch over the "Two Regions." It was the determination of Asshur-bani-pal, on becoming king, to strain every nerve and devote his utmost energy to the re-conquest of the ancient kingdom, so lightly won and so lightly lost by his father. Baal's perfidy was thus forgiven or overlooked. A great expedition was prepared. The kings of Phoenicia, Palestine, and Cyprus were bidden once more to assemble, to bring their tribute, and pay homage to their suzerain as he passed on his way at the head of his forces towards the land of the Pharaohs. Baal came, and again holds the post of honour; with him were the king of Judah – doubtless Manasseh, but the name is lost – the kings of Edom, Moab, Gaza, Askelon, Ekron, Gebal, Arvad, Paphos, Soli, Curium, Tamassus, Ammochosta, Lidini, and Aphrodisias, with probably those also of Ammon, Ashdod, Idalium, Citium, and Salamis. Each in turn prostrated himself at the foot of the Great Monarch, paid homage, and made profession of fidelity. Asshur-bani-pal then proceeded on his way, and the kings returned to their several governments.

The Attack of Baal

It is about four years after this, 664 BCE, that we find Baal attacked and punished by the Assyrian monarch. The subjugation of Egypt had been in the meantime, though not without difficulty, completed. Asshur-bani-pal's power extended from the range of Niphates to the First Cataract.

Whether during the course of the four years' struggle, by which the reconquest of Egypt was effected, the Tyrian prince had given fresh offence to his suzerain, or whether it was the old offence, condoned for a time but never forgiven, that was now avenged, is not made clear by the Assyrian Inscriptions. Asshur-bani-pal simply tells us that, in his third expedition, he proceeded against Baal, king of Tyre, dwelling in the midst of the sea, who his royal will disregarded, and did not listen to the words of his lips. "Towers round him," he says, "I raised, and over his people I strengthened the watch; on sea and land his forts I took; his going out I stopped. Water and sea-water, to preserve their lives, their mouths drank. By a strong blockade, which removed not, I besieged them; their works I checked and opposed; to my yoke I made them submissive. The daughter proceeding from his body, and the daughters of his brothers, for concubines he brought to my presence. Yahi-milki, his son, the glory of the country, of unsurpassed renown, at once he sent forward, to make obeisance to me. His daughter, and the daughters of his brothers, with their great dowries, I received. Favour I granted him, and the son proceeding from his body, I restored, and gave him back." Thus Baal once more escaped the fate he must have expected. Asshur-bani-pal, who was far from being of a clement disposition, suffered himself to be appeased by the submission made, restored Baal to his favour, and allowed him to retain possession of his sovereignty.

Another Phoenician monarch also was, about the same time, threatened and pardoned. This was Yakinlu, the king of Arvad, probably the son and successor of Mattan-Baal, the contemporary of Esarhaddon. He is accused of having been wanting in submission to Asshur-bani-pal's fathers; but we may regard it as probable that his real offence was some failure in his duties towards Asshur-bani-pal himself. Either he had openly rebelled, and declared himself independent, or he had neglected to pay his tribute, or he had given recent offence in some other way. The Phoenician island kings were always more neglectful of their duties than others, since it was more difficult to punish them. Assyria did not even now possess any regular fleet, and could only punish a recalcitrant king of Arvad or Tyre by impressing into her service the ships of some of the Phoenician coast-towns, as Sidon, or Gebal, or Accho. These towns were not very zealous in such a service, and probably did not maintain strong navies, having little use for them. Thus Yakinlu may have expected that his neglect, whatever it was, would be overlooked. But Asshur-bani-pal was jealous of his rights, and careful not to allow any of them to lapse by disuse. He let his displeasure be known at the court of Yakinlu, and very shortly received an embassy of submission. Like Baal, Yakinlu sent a daughter to take her place among the great king's secondary wives, and with her he sent a large sum of money, in the disguise of a dowry. The tokens of subjection were accepted, and Yakinlu was allowed to continue king of Arvad. When, not long afterwards, he died, and his ten sons sought the court of Nineveh to prefer their claims to the succession, they were received with favour. Azi-Baal, the eldest, was appointed to the vacant kingdom, while his nine brothers were presented by Asshur-bani-pal with "costly clothing, and rings."

Two other revolts of two other Phoenician towns belong to a somewhat later period. On his return from an expedition against Arabia, about 645 BCE, Asshur-bani-pal found that Hosah, a small place in the vicinity of Tyre, and Accho, famous as Acre in later times, had risen in revolt against their Assyrian governors, refused their tribute, and asserted independence. He at once besieged, and soon captured, Hosah. The leaders of the rebellion he put to death; the plunder of the town, including the images of its gods, and the bulk of its population, he carried off into Assyria. The people of Accho, he says, he "quieted." It is a common practice of conquerors "to make a solitude and call it peace." Asshur-bani-pal appears to have punished Accho, first by a wholesale massacre, and then by the deportation of all its remaining inhabitants.

It is evident from this continual series of revolts and rebellions that, however mild had been the sway of Assyria over her Phoenician subjects in the earlier times, it had by degrees become a hateful and a grinding tyranny. Commercial states, bent upon the accumulation of wealth, do not without grave cause take up arms and affront the perils of war, much less do so when their common sense must tell them that success is almost absolutely hopeless, and that failure will bring about their destruction. The Assyrians were a hard race. Such tenderness as they ever showed to any subject people was, we may be sure, in every case dictated by policy. While their power was unsettled, while they feared revolts, and were uncertain as to their consequences, their attitude towards their dependents was conciliating. When they became fully conscious of the immense preponderance of power which they wielded, and of the inability of the petty states of Asia to combine against them in any firm league, they grew careless and confident, reckless of giving offence, ruder in their behaviour, more grasping in their exactions, more domineering, more oppressive. Prudence should perhaps have counselled the Phoenician cities to submit, to be yielding and pliant, to cultivate the arts of the parasite and the flatterer; but the people had still a rough honesty about them. It was against the grain to flatter or submit themselves; constant voyages over wild seas in fragile vessels kept up their manhood; constant encounters with pirates, cannibals, and the rudest possible savages made them brave and daring; exposure to storm, and cold, and heat braced their frames; the nautical life developed and intensified in them a love of freedom. The Phoenician of Assyrian times was not to be coaxed into accepting patiently the lot of a slave. Suffer as he might by his revolts, they won him a certain respect; it is likely that they warded off many an indignity, many an outrage. The Assyrians knew that his endurance could not be reckoned on beyond a certain point, and they knew that in his death-throes he was dangerous. The Phoenicians probably suffered considerably less than the other subject nations under Assyrian rule; and the maritime population, which was the salt of the people, suffered least of all, since it was scarcely ever brought into contact with its nominal rulers.

PHOENICIA DURING ITS STRUGGLES WITH BABYLON AND EGYPT (ABOUT 635-527 BCE)

It is impossible to fix the year in which Phoenicia became independent of Assyria. The last trace of Assyrian interference, in the way of compulsion, with any of the towns belongs to 645 BCE, when she severely punished Hosah and Accho. The latest sign of her continued domination is found in 636 BCE, when the Assyrian governor of a Phoenician town, Zimirra, appears in the list of eponyms. It must have been very soon after this that the empire became involved in those troubles and difficulties which led on to its dissolution. According to Herodotus, Cyaxares, king of Media, laid siege to Nineveh in 633 BCE, or very soon afterwards. His attack did not at once succeed; but it was almost immediately followed by the irruption into South-western Asia of Scythic hordes from beyond the Caucasus, which overran country after country, destroying and ravaging at their pleasure. The reality of this invasion is now generally admitted. "It was the earliest recorded," says a modern historian, "of those movements of the northern populations, hid behind the long mountain barrier, which, under the name of Himalaya, Caucasus, Taurus, Haemus, and the Alps, has been reared by nature between the civilised and uncivilised races of the old world. Suddenly, above this boundary, appeared those strange, uncouth, fur-clad forms, hardly to be distinguished from their horses and their waggons, fierce as their own wolves or bears, sweeping towards the southern regions, which seemed to them their natural prey. The successive invasions of Parthians, Turks, Mongols in Asia, of Gauls, Goths, Vandals, Huns in Europe, have, it is well said, 'illustrated the law, and made us familiar with its operations. But there was a time in history before it had come into force, and when its very existence must have been unsuspected. Even since it began to operate, it has so often undergone prolonged suspension that the wisest may be excused if they cease to bear it in mind, and are as much startled when a fresh illustration of it occurs, as if the like had never happened before.' No wonder that now, when the veil was for the first time rent asunder, all the ancient monarchies of the South – Assyria, Babylon, Media, Egypt, even Greece and Asia Minor – stood aghast at the spectacle of these savage hordes rushing down on the seats of luxury and power." Assyria seems to have suffered from the attack almost as much as any other country. The hordes probably swarmed down from Media through the Zagros passes into the most fruitful portion of the empire – the flat country between the mountains and the Tigris. Many of the old cities, rich with the accumulated stores of ages, were besieged, and perhaps taken, and their palaces wantonly burnt by the barbarous invaders. The tide then swept on. Wandering from district to district, plundering everywhere, settling nowhere, the clouds of horse passed over Mesopotamia, the force of the invasion becoming weaker as it spread itself, until in Syria it reached its term through the policy of the Egyptian king, Psamatik I. That monarch bribed the nomads to advance no further, and from this time their power began to wane. Their numbers must have been greatly thinned in the long course of battles, sieges, and skirmishes wherein they were engaged year after year; they suffered also through their excesses; and perhaps through intestine dissensions. At last they recognized that their power was broken. Many bands probably returned across the Caucasus into the Steppe country. Others submitted and took service under the native rulers of Asia. Great numbers were slain, and, except in a province of Armenia, which thenceforward became known as Sacasêné, and perhaps in one Syrian town, which acquired the name of Scythopolis, the invaders left no permanent trace of their brief but terrible inroad.

The shock of the Scythian irruption cannot but have greatly injured and weakened Assyria. The whole country had been ravaged and depopulated; the provinces had been plundered, many of the towns had been taken and sacked, the palaces of the old kings had been burnt, and all the riches that had not been hid away had been lost. Assyria, when the Scythian wave had passed, was but the shadow of her former self. Her *prestige* was gone, her armed force must have been greatly diminished, her hold upon the provinces, especially the more distant ones, greatly weakened. Phoenicia is likely to have detached herself from Assyria at latest during the time that the Scyths were dominant, which was probably from about 630 BCE to 610 BCE. When Assyrian protection was withdrawn from Syria, as it must have been during this period, and when every state and town had to look solely to itself for deliverance from a barbarous and cruel enemy, the fiction of a nominal dependence on a distant power could scarcely be maintained. Without any actual revolt, the Phoenician cities became their own masters, and the speedy fall of Assyria before the combined attack of the Medes and Babylonians, after the Scythians had withdrawn, prevented for some time any interference with their recovered independence.

A Double Danger

A double danger, however, impended. On the one side Egypt, on the other Babylon, might be confidently expected to lay claim to the debatable land which nature had placed between the seats of the great Asiatic and the great African power, and which in the past had almost always been possessed by the one or the other of them. Egypt was the nearer of the two, and probably seemed the most to be feared. She had recently fallen under the power of an enterprising native monarch, who had already, before the fall of Assyria, shown that he entertained ambitious designs against the Palestinian towns, having begun attacks upon Ashdod soon after he ascended the throne. Babylon was, comparatively speaking, remote and had troublesome neighbours, who might be expected to prevent her from undertaking distant expeditions. It was clearly the true policy for Phoenicia to temporise, to enter into no engagements with either Babylon or Egypt, to strengthen her defences, to bide her time, and, so far as possible, to consolidate herself. Something like a desire for consolidation would seem to have come over the people; and Tyre, the leading city in all but the earliest times, appears to have been recognized as the centre towards which other states must gravitate, and to have risen to the occasion. If there ever was such a thing as a confederation of all the Phoenician cities, it would seem to have been at this period. Sidon forgot her ancient rivalry, and consented to furnish the Tyrian fleet with mariners. Arvad gave not only rowers to man the ships, but also men-at-arms to help in guarding the walls. The "ancients of Gebal" lent their aid in the Tyrian dockyards. The minor cities cannot have ventured to hold aloof. Tyre, as the time approached for the contest which was to decide whether Egypt or Babylon should be the great power of the East, appears to have reached the height of her strength, wealth, and prosperity. It is now that Ezekial says of her – "O Tyrus, thy heart is lifted up, and thou hast said, I am a God, I sit in the seat of God in the midst of the seas – Behold, thou art wiser than Daniel, there is no secret that they can hide from thee: from thy wisdom and with thine understanding hast thou gotten thee riches, and hast gotten gold and silver into thy treasures: by thy great wisdom and by thy traffick thou hast increased thy riches, and thy heart is lifted up because of thy riches"; and again, "O thou that are situated at the entry of the sea, which art the merchant of the peoples unto many isles, thus saith the Lord God, Thou, O Tyre, hast said, I am perfect in beauty. Thy borders are in the heart of the sea; thy builders have perfected thy beauty. They have made all thy planks of fir-trees from Senir; they have taken from Lebanon cedars to make masts for thee; of the oaks of Bashan have they made thine oars; they have made thy benches of ivory, inlaid in boxwood, from the isles of Kittim . . . The ships of Tarshish were thy caravans for thy merchandise; and thou wast replenished, and made very glorious in the heart of the sea."

The Attack of Egypt

The first to strike of the two great antagonists was Egypt. Psamatik I, who was advanced in years at the time of Assyria's downfall, died about 610 BCE, and was succeeded by a son still in the full vigour of life, the brave and enterprising Neco. Neco, in 608 BCE, having made all due preparations, led a great expedition into Palestine, with the object of bringing under his dominion the entire tract between the River of Egypt (Wady el Arish) and the Middle Euphrates. Already possessed of Ashdod and perhaps also of Gaza and Askelon, he held the keys of Syria, and could have no difficulty in penetrating along the coast route, through the rich plain of Sharon, to the first of the mountain barriers which are interposed between the Nile and the Mesopotamian region. His famous fleet would support him along the shore, at any rate as far Carmel; and Dor and Accho would probably be seized, and made into depôts for his stores and provisions. The powerful Egyptian monarch marching northward with his numerous and well-disciplined army, partly composed of native troops, partly of mercenaries from Asia Minor, Greeks and Carians, probably did not look to meet with any opposition, till, somewhere in Northern Syria, he should encounter the forces of Babylonia, which would of course be moved westward to meet him. What then must have been his surprise when he found the ridge connecting Carmel with the highland of Samaria occupied by a strong body of troops, and his further progress barred by a foe who had appeared to him too insignificant to be taken into account? Josiah, the Jewish monarch of the time, grandson of Manasseh and great-grandson of Hezekiah, who, in the unsettled state of Western Asia, had united under his dominion the entire country of the twelve tribes, had quitted Jerusalem, and thrown himself across the would-be conqueror's path in the strong and well-known position of Megiddo. Here, in remote times, had the great Thothmes met and defeated the whole force of Syria and Mesopotamia under the king of Kadesh; here had Deborah and Barak, the son of Abinoam, utterly destroyed the mighty army of Jabin, king of Canaan, under Sisera. Here now the gallant, if rash, Judaean king elected to take his stand, moved either by a sense of duty, because he regarded himself as a Babylonian feudatory, or simply determined to defend the Holy Land against any heathen army that, without permission, trespassed on it. In vain did Neco seek to induce Josiah to retire and leave the way open, by assuring him that he had no hostile intentions against Judaea, but was marching on Carchemish by the Euphrates, there to contend with the Babylonians. The Jewish king persisted in his rash enterprise, and Neco was forced to brush him from his path. His seasoned and disciplined troops easily overcame the hasty levies of Josiah; and Josiah himself fell in the battle.

We have no details with respect to the remainder of the expedition. Neco, no doubt, pressed forward through Galilee and Coele-Syria towards the Euphrates. Whether he had to fight any further battles we are not informed. It is certain that he occupied Carchemish, and made it his headquarters, but whether it submitted to him, or was besieged and taken, is unknown. All Syria, Phoenicia, and Palestine were overrun, and became temporarily Egyptian possessions. But Phoenicia does not appear to have been subdued by force. Tyrian prosperity continued, and the terms on which Phoenicia stood towards Egypt during the remainder of Neco's reign were friendly. Phoenicians at Neco's request accomplished the circumnavigation of Africa; and we may suspect that it was Neco who granted to Tyre the extraordinary favour of settling a colony in the Egyptian capital, Memphis. Probably Phoenicia accepted at the hands of Neco the same sort of position which she had at first occupied under Assyria, a position, as already explained, satisfactory to both parties.

The Forces of Babylon

But the glory and prosperity which Egypt had thus acquired were very short-lived. Within three years Babylonia asserted herself. In 605 BCE, the crown prince, Nebuchadnezzar, acting on behalf of his father, Nabopolassar, who was aged and infirm, led the forces of Babylon against the audacious Pharaoh, who had dared to affront the "King of kings," "the Lord of Sumir and Accad," had taken him off his guard, and deprived him of some of his fairest provinces. Babylonia, under Nabopolassar and Nebuchadnezzar, was no unworthy successor of the mighty power which for seven hundred years had held the supremacy of Western Asia. Her citizens were as brave; her armies as well disciplined; her rulers as bold, as sagacious, and as unsparing. Habakkuk's description of a Babylonian army belongs to about this date, and is probably drawn from the life – "Lo, I raise up the Chaldaeans, that bitter and hasty nation, which shall march through the breadth of the land, to possess the dwelling-places that are not theirs. They are terrible and dreadful; from them shall proceed judgment and captivity; their horses are swifter than leopards, and are more fierce than the evening wolves; and their horsemen shall spread themselves, and their horsemen shall come from far; they shall fly as the eagle that hasteth to eat. They shall come all for violence; their faces shall sup as the east wind, and they shall gather the captivity as the sand. And they shall scoff at kings, and princes shall be a scorn unto them; they shall derive every stronghold; for they shall heap dust, and take it." Early in the year 605 BCE the host of Nebuchadnezzar appeared on the right bank of the Euphrates, moving steadily along its reaches, and day by day approaching nearer and nearer to the great fortress in and behind which lay the army of Neco, well ordered with shield and buckler, its horses harnessed, and its horsemen armed with spears that had been just furbished, and protected by helmets and brigandines. One of the "decisive battles of the world" was impending. If Egypt conquered, Oriental civilization would take the heavy immovable Egyptian type; change, advance, progress would be hindered; sacerdotalism in religion, conventionalism in art, pure unmitigated despotism in government would generally prevail; all the throbbing life of Asia would receive a sudden and violent check; Semitism would be thrust back; Aryanism, just pushing itself to the front, would shrink away; the monotonous Egyptian tone of thought and life would spread, like a lava stream, over the manifold and varied forms of Asiatic culture; crushing them out, concealing them, making them as though they had never been. The victory of Babylon, on the other hand, would mean room for Semitism to develop itself, and for Aryanism to follow in its wake, fresh stirs of population and of thought in Asia; further advances in the arts; variety, freshness, growth; the continuance of the varied lines of Oriental study and investigation until such time as would enable Grecian intellect to take hold of them, sift them, and assimilate whatever in them was true, valuable, and capable of expansion.

We have no historical account of the great battle of Carchemish. Jeremiah, however, beholds it in vision. He sees the Egyptians "dismayed and turned away back – their mighty ones are beaten down, and are fled apace, and look not back, since fear is round about them." He sees the "swift flee away," and the "mighty men" attempting to "escape;" but they "stumble and fall toward the north by the river Euphrates." "For this is the day of the Lord God of hosts, a day of vengeance, that He may avenge Him of His adversaries; and the sword devours, and it is satiate and made drunk with their blood, for the Lord God of hosts hath a sacrifice in the north country by the river Euphrates." The "valiant men" are "swept away" – "many fall – yea, one falls upon another, and they say, Arise and let us go again to our own people, and to the land of our nativity from the oppressing sword." Nor do the mercenaries escape. "Her hired men are in the midst of her, like fatted bullocks; for they also are turned back, and are fled away together; they did not stand because the day of their calamity was come upon them, and the time of their visitation." The defeat was, beyond a doubt, complete, overwhelming. The shock of it was felt all over the Delta, at Memphis, and even at distant Thebes. The hasty flight of the entire Egyptian host left the whole country open to the invading army. "Like a whirlwind, like a torrent, it swept on. The terrified inhabitants retired into the fortified cities," where for the time they were safe. Nebuchadnezzar did not stop to commence any siege. He pursued Neco up to the very frontier of Egypt, and would have continued his victorious career into the Nile valley, had not important intelligence arrested his steps. His aged father had died at Babylon while he was engaged in his conquests, and his immediate return to the capital was necessary, if he would avoid a disputed succession. Thus matters in Syria had to be left in a confused and unsettled state, until such time as the Great King could revisit the scene of his conquests, and place them upon some definite and satisfactory footing.

Bonds with Egypt

On the whole, the campaign had, apparently, the effect of drawing closer the links which united Phoenicia with Egypt. Babylon had shown herself a fierce and formidable enemy, but had disgusted men more than she had terrified them. It was clear enough that she would be a hard mistress, a second and crueller Assyria. There was thus, on Nebuchadnezzar's departure, a general gravitation of the Syrian and Palestinian states towards Egypt, since they saw in her the only possible protector against Babylon, and dreaded her less than they did the "bitter and hasty nation." Neco, no doubt, encouraged the movement which tended at once to strengthen himself and weaken his antagonist; and the result was that, in the course of a few years, both Judaea and Phoenicia revolted from Nebuchadnezzar, and declared themselves independent. Phoenicia was still under the hegemony of Tyre, and Tyre had at its head an enterprising prince, a second Ithobal, who had developed its resources to the uttermost, and was warmly supported by the other cities. His revolt appears to have taken place in the year 598

BCE, the seventh year of Nebuchadnezzar. Nebuchadnezzar at once marched against him in person. The sieges of Tyre, Sidon, and Jerusalem were formed. Jerusalem submitted almost immediately. Sidon was taken after losing half her defenders by pestilence; but Tyre continued to resist for the long space of thirteen years. The continental city was probably taken first. Against this Nebuchadnezzar could freely employ his whole force – his "horses, his chariots, his companies, and his much people" – he could bring moveable forts close up to the walls, and cast up banks against them, and batter them with his engines, or undermine them with spade and mattock. When a breach was effected, he could pour his horse into the streets, and ride down all opposition. It is the capture of the continental city which Ezekiel describes when he says: "Thus saith the Lord God: Behold, I will bring upon Tyrus Nebuchadnezzar, king of Babylon, a king of kings, from the north, with horses and with chariots, and with horsemen, and companies, and much people. He shall slay with the sword thy daughters in the field; and he shall make a fort against thee, and cast a mount against thee, and lift up the buckler against thee. And he shall set engines of war against thy walls, and with his axes he shall break down thy towers. By reason of the abundance of his horses, their dust shall cover thee; thy walls shall shake at the noise of the horseman, and of the wheels and of the chariots, when he shall enter into thy gates, as men enter into a city wherein is made a breach. With the hoofs of his horses shall he tread down all thy streets: he shall slay thy people by the sword, and thy strong garrisons shall go down to the ground. And they shall make a spoil of thy riches, and make a prey of thy merchandise; and they shall break down thy walls, and destroy thy pleasant houses: and they shall lay thy stones and thy timber and thy dust in the midst of the water." But the island city did not escape. When continental Phoenicia was reduced, it was easy to impress a fleet from maritime towns; to man it, in part with Phoenicians, in part with Babylonians, no mean sailors, and then to establish a blockade of the isle. Tyre may more than once have crippled and dispersed the blockading squadron; but by a moderate expenditure fresh fleets could be supplied, while Tyre, cut off from Lebanon, would find it difficult to increase or renew her navy. There has been much question whether the island city was ultimately captured by Nebuchadnezzar or no; but even writers who take the negative view admit that it must have submitted and owned the suzerainty of its assailant. The date of the submission was 585 BCE.

The Fall of Tyre

Thus Tyre, in 585 BCE, "fell from her high estate." Ezekiel's prophecies were fulfilled. Ithobal II, the "prince of Tyrus" of those prophecies, whose "head had been lifted up," and who had said in his heart, "I am a God, I sit in the seat of God, in the midst of the waters," who deemed himself "wiser than Daniel," and thought that no secret was hid from him, was "brought down to the pit," "cast to the ground," "brought to ashes upon the earth in the sight of all them that beheld him." Tyre herself was "broken in the midst of the seas." A blight fell upon her. For many years, Sidon, rather than Tyre, became once more the leading city of Phoenicia, was regarded as pre-eminent in naval skill, and is placed before Tyre when the two are mentioned together. Internal convulsion, moreover, followed upon external decline. Within ten years of the death of Ithobal, the monarchy came to an end by a revolution, which substituted for Kings Suffetes or Shophetim, "judges," officers of an inferior status, whose tenure of office was not very assured. Ecnibal, the son of Baslach, the first judge, held the position for no more than two months; Chelbes, the son of Abdaeus, who followed him, ruled for ten months; Abbarus, a high priest, probably of Melkarth, for three months. Then, apparently to weaken the office, it was shared between two, as at Carthage, and Mytgon (perhaps Mattan), together with Ger-ashtoreth, the son of Abd-elim, judged Tyre for six years. But the partisans of monarchy were now recovering strength; and the reign of a king, Balator, was intruded at some point in the course of the six years' judgeship. Judges were then abolished by a popular movement, and kings of the old stock restored. The Tyrians sent to Babylon for a certain Merbal, who must have been either a refugee or a hostage at the court of Neriglissar. He was allowed to return to Tyre, and, being confirmed in the sovereignty, reigned four years. His brother, Eirom, or Hiram, succeeded him, and was still upon the throne when the Empire of Babylon came to an end by the victory of Cyrus over Nabonidus (538 BCE).

Phoenicia under the Babylonian rule was exceptionally weak. She had to submit to attacks from Egypt under Apries, which fell probably in the reign of Baal over Tyre, about 565 BCE. She had also to submit to the loss of Cyprus under Amasis, probably about 540 BCE, or a little earlier, when the power of Babylon was rapidly declining. She had been, from first to last, an unwilling tributary of the Great Empire on the Lower Euphrates, and was perhaps not sorry to see that empire go down before the rising power of Persia. Under the circumstances she would view any chance as likely to advance her interests, and times of disturbance and unsettlement gave her the best chance of obtaining a temporary independence. From 538 BCE to 528 BCE or 527 she seems to have enjoyed one of these rare intervals of autonomy. Egypt, content with having annexed Cyprus, did not trouble her; Persia, engaged in wars in the Far East, made as yet no claim to her allegiance. In peace and tranquillity she pursued her commercial career, covered the seas with her merchant vessels, and the land-routes of trade with her caravans, repaired the damages inflicted by Nebuchadnezzar on her cities; maintained, if she did not even increase, her naval strength, and waited patiently to see what course events would take now that Babylon was destroyed, and a new and hitherto unknown power was about to assume the first position among the nations of the earth.

ANCIENT KINGS & LEADERS

Ancient cultures often traded with and influenced each other, while others grew independently. This section provides the key leaders from a number of regions, to offer comparative insights into developments across the ancient world.

ANCIENT NEAR EAST LEADER LIST

This list concentrates on leaders with at least some proven legitimate claim. Dates are based on archaeological evidence as far as possible but are approximate. Where dates of rule overlap, rulers either ruled jointly or ruled in opposition to one another. There may also be differences in name spellings between different sources.

SUMER

The Sumerian list that follows is based on the *Sumerian King List* or *Chronicle of the One Monarchy*. The lists were often originally carved into clay tablets and several versions have been found, mainly in southern Mesopotamia. Some of these are incomplete and others contradict one another. Nevertheless, the lists remain an invaluable source of information.

After the kingship descended from heaven, the kingship was in Eridug.

Alulim	28,800 years (8 *sars**)
Alalngar	36,000 years (10 *sars*)

Then Eridug fell and the kingship was taken to Bad-tibira.

En-men-lu-ana	43,200 years (12 *sars*)
En-mel-gal-ana	28,800 years (8 *sars*)
Dumuzid the Shepherd (or Tammuz)	36,000 years (10 *sars*)

Then Bad-tibira fell and the kingship was taken to Larag.

En-sipad-zid-ana	28,800 years (8 *sars*)

Then Larag fell and the kingship was taken to Zimbir.

En-men-dur-ana	21,000 years (5 *sars* and 5 *ners*)

Then Zimbir fell and the kingship was taken to Shuruppag.

Ubara-Tutu	18,600 years (5 *sars* and 1 *ner**)

Then the flood swept over.

*A *sar* is a numerical unit of 3,600; a *ner* is a numerical unit of 600.

FIRST DYNASTY OF KISH

After the flood had swept over, and the kingship had descended from heaven, the kingship was in Kish.

Jushur	1,200 years	Kullassina-bel	960 years

THE ANCIENT NEAR EAST

Nangishlisma	1,200 years	Enme-nuna)	1,200 years
En-tarah-ana	420 years	Zamug (son of	
Babum	300 years	Barsal-nuna)	140 years
Puannum	840 years	Tizqar (son of Zamug)	
Kalibum	960 years	305 years	
Kalumum	840 years	Ilku	900 years
Zuqaqip	900 years	Iltasadum	1,200 years
Atab (or A-ba)	600 years	Enmebaragesi	900 years
Mashda (son of Atab)		(earliest proven ruler	
Arwium (son of Mashda)	720 years	based on archaeological sources; Early Dynastic	
Etana the Shepherd	1,500 years	Period, 2900–2350 BCE)	
Balih (son of Etana)	400 years	Aga of Kish (son of	
En-me-nuna	660 years	Enmebaragesi)	625 years
Melem-Kish (son of Enme-nuna)	900 years	(Early Dynastic Period, 2900–2350 BCE)	
Barsal-nuna (son of			

Then Kish was defeated and the kingship was taken to E-anna.

FIRST RULERS OF URUK

Mesh-ki-ang-gasher (son of Utu)	324 years (Late Uruk Period, 4000–3100 BCE)
Enmerkar (son of Mesh-ki-ang-gasher)	420 years (Late Uruk Period, 4000–3100 BCE)
Lugal-banda the shepherd	1200 years (Late Uruk Period, 4000–3100 BCE)

Dumuzid the fisherman	100 years (Jemdet Nasr Period, 3100–2900 BCE)
Gilgamesh	126 years (Early Dynastic Period, 2900–2350 BCE)
Ur-Nungal (son of Gilgamesh)	30 years
Udul-kalama (son of Ur-Nungal)	15 years
La-ba'shum	9 years
En-nun-tarah-ana	8 years
Mesh-he	36 years
Melem-ana	6 years
Lugal-kitun	36 years

Then Unug was defeated and the kingship was taken to Urim (Ur).

FIRST DYNASTY OF UR

Mesh-Ane-pada	80 years
Mesh-ki-ang-Nuna (son of Mesh-Ane-pada)	36 years
Elulu	25 years
Balulu	36 years

Then Urim was defeated and the kingship was taken to Awan.

DYNASTY OF AWAN

Three kings of Awan	356 years

Then Awan was defeated and the kingship was taken to Kish.

SECOND DYNASTY OF KISH

Susuda the fuller	201 years
Dadasig	81 years
Mamagal the boatman	360 years
Kalbum (son of Mamagal)	195 years
Tuge	360 years
Men-nuna (son of Tuge)	180 years
Enbi-Ishtar	290 years
Lugalngu	360 years

Then Kish was defeated and the kingship was taken to Hamazi.

DYNASTY OF HAMAZI

Hadanish	360 years

Then Hamazi was defeated and the kingship was taken to Unug (Uruk).

SECOND DYNASTY OF URUK

En-shag-kush-ana	60 years (c. 25th century BCE)
Lugal-kinishe-dudu	120 years
Argandea	7 years

Then Unug was defeated and the kingship was taken to Urim (Ur).

SECOND DYNASTY OF UR

Nanni	120 years
Mesh-ki-ang-Nanna II (son of Nanni)	48 years

Then Urim was defeated and the kingship was taken to Adab.

DYNASTY OF ADAB

Lugal-Ane-mundu　　　　　　　　90 years (c. 25th century BCE)

Then Adab was defeated and the kingship was taken to Mari.

DYNASTY OF MARI

Anbu	30 years	Zizi of Mari, the fuller	20 years
Anba (son of Anbu)	17 years	Limer the 'gudug' priest	30 years
Bazi the leatherworker	30 years	Sharrum-iter	9 years

Then Mari was defeated and the kingship was taken to Kish.

THIRD DYNASTY OF KISH

Kug-Bau (Kubaba)　　　　　　　　100 years (c. 25th century BCE)

Then Kish was defeated and the kingship was taken to Akshak.

DYNASTY OF AKSHAK

Unzi	30 years	Ishu-Il	24 years
Undalulu	6 years	Shu-Suen (son of	
Urur	6 years	Ishu-Il)	7 years
Puzur-Nirah	20 years		

Then Akshak was defeated and the kingship was taken to Kish.

FOURTH DYNASTY OF KISH

Puzur-Suen (son of Kug-bau)	25 years (c. 2350 BCE)
Ur-Zababa (son of Puzur-Suen)	400 years (c. 2300 BCE)
Zimudar	30 years
Usi-watar (son of Zimudar)	7 years
Eshtar-muti	11 years
Ishme-Shamash	11 years
Shu-ilishu	15 years
Nanniya the jeweller	7 years

Then Kish was defeated and the kingship was taken to Unug (Uruk).

THIRD DYNASTY OF URUK

Lugal-zage-si	25 years (c. 2296–2271 BCE)

Then Unug was defeated and the kingship was taken to Agade (Akkad).

DYNASTY OF AKKAD

Sargon of Akkad	56 years (c. 2270–2215 BCE)
Rimush of Akkad (son of Sargon)	9 years (c. 2214–2206 BCE)
Manishtushu (son of Sargon)	15 years (c. 2205–2191 BCE)
Naram-Sin of Akkad (son of Manishtushu)	56 years (c. 2190–2154 BCE)
Shar-kali-sharri (son of Naram-Sin)	24 years (c. 2153–2129 BCE)

Then who was king? Who was not the king?

Irgigi, Nanum, Imi and Ilulu	3 years (four rivals who fought to be king during a three-year period; c. 2128–2125 BCE)
Dudu of Akkad	21 years (c. 2125–2104 BCE)
Shu-Durul (son of Duu)	15 years (c. 2104–2083 BCE)

Then Agade was defeated and the kingship was taken to Unug (Uruk).

FOURTH DYNASTY OF URUK

Ur ningin	7 years (c. 2091?–2061? BCE)
Ur-gigir (son of Ur-ningin)	6 years
Kuda	6 years
Puzur-ili	5 years
Ur-Utu (or Lugal-melem; son of Ur-gigir)	6 years

Unug was defeated and the kingship was taken to the army of Gutium.

GUTIAN RULE

Inkišuš	6 years (c. 2147–2050 BCE)
Sarlagab (or Zarlagab)	6 years
Shulme (or Yarlagash)	6 years
Elulmeš (or Silulumeš or Silulu)	6 years
Inimabakeš (or Duga)	5 years
Igešauš (or Ilu-An)	6 years
Yarlagab	3 years
Ibate of Gutium	3 years
Yarla (or Yarlangab)	3 years
Kurum	1 year
Apilkin	3 years
La-erabum	2 years
Irarum	2 years
Ibranum	1 year
Hablum	2 years
Puzur-Suen (son of Hablum)	7 years
Yarlaganda	7 years
Si'um (or Si-u)	7 years
Tirigan	40 days

Then the army of Gutium was defeated and the kingship taken to Unug (Uruk).

FIFTH DYNASTY OF URUK

Utu-hengal	427 years / 26 years / 7 years (conflicting dates; c. 2055–2048 BCE)

THIRD DYNASTY OF UR

Ur-Namma (or Ur-Nammu)	18 years (c. 2047–2030 BCE)
Shulgi (son of Ur-Namma)	48 years (c. 2029–1982 BCE)
Amar-Suena (son of Shulgi)	9 years (c. 1981–1973 BCE)
Shu-Suen (son of Amar-Suena)	9 years (c. 1972–1964 BCE)
Ibbi-Suen (son of Shu-Suen)	24 years (c. 1963–1940 BCE)

Then Urim was defeated. The very foundation of Sumer was torn out. The kingship was taken to Isin.

DYNASTY OF ISIN

Ishbi-Erra	33 years (c. 1953–1920 BCE)
Shu-Ilishu (son of Ishbi-Erra)	20 years
Iddin-Dagan (son of Shu-Ilishu)	20 years
Ishme-Dagan (son of Iddin-Dagan)	20 years
Lipit-Eshtar (son of Ishme-Dagan or Iddin Dagan)	11 years
Ur-Ninurta (son of Ishkur)	28 years
Bur-Suen (son of Ur-Ninurta)	21 years
Lipit-Enlil (son of Bur-Suen)	5 years
Erra-imitti	8 years
Enlil-bani	24 years
Zambiya	3 years
Iter-pisha	4 years
Ur-du-kuga	4 years
Suen-magir	11 years
Damiq-ilishu (son of Suen-magir)	23 years

BABYLON

FIRST DYNASTY OF BABYLON (AMORITE, *C.* 1894–1595 BCE)

Sumu-abum	1894–1881 BCE
Sumulael	1880–1845 BCE
Sabium	1844–1831 BCE
Apil-Sin	1830–1813 BCE
Sin-muballit	1812–1793 BCE
Hammurapi	1792–1750 BCE
Samsu-iluna	1749–1712 BCE
Abi-eshuh	1711–1684 BCE
Ammi-ditana	1683–1647 BCE
Ammi-saduqa	1646–1626 BCE
Samsu-ditana	1625–1595 BCE

KASSITE DYNASTY (*C.* 1729–1155 BCE)

Gandash	1729–1704 BCE
Agum I	1703–1682 BCE
Kashtiliashu I	1681–1660 BCE
Abi-Rattash?	
Kashtiliash II?	
Urzigurumash	
Harba-Shipak?	
Shipta'ulzi?	
Burna-Buriash I	
Ulamburiash?	

ANCIENT KINGS & LEADERS

Kashtiliash III?
Agum III?
Kara-indash
Kadashman-Harbe I
Kurigalzu I
Kadashman-Enlil I — 1374–1360 BCE
Burna-Buriash II — 1359–1333 BCE
Kara-hardash — 1333 BCE
Nazi-Bugash — 1333 BCE
Kurigalzu II — 1332–1308 BCE
Nazi-Maruttash — 1307–1282 BCE
Kadashman-Turgu — 1281–1264 BCE
Kadashman-Enlil II — 1263–1255 BCE
Kudur-Enlil — 1254–1246 BCE
Shagarakti-Shuriash — 1245–1233 BCE
Kashtiliashu IV — 1232–1225 BCE
Tukulti-Ninurta I of Assyria — 1225 BCE
Enlin-nadin-shumi — 1224 BCE
Kadashman-Harbe II — 1223 BCE
Adad-shuma-iddina — 1222–1217 BCE
Adad-shuma-usur — 1216–1187 BCE
Meli-Shipak — 1186–1172 BCE
Merodach-Baladan I — 1171–1159 BCE
Zababa-shuma-iddina — 1158 BCE
Enlil-nadin-ahi — 1157–1155 BCE

DYNASTY OF ISIN (C.1157–1026 BCE)

Marduk-kabit-ahheshu — 1157–1140 BCE

Itti-Marduk-balatu	1139–1132 BCE
Ninurta-nadin-shumi	1131–1126 BCE
Nebuchadrezzar I	1125–1104 BCE
Enlil-nadin-apli	1103–1100 BCE
Marduk-nadin-ahhe	1099–1082 BCE
Marduk-shapik-zeri	1081–1069 BCE
Adad-apla-iddina	1068–1047 BCE
Marduk-ahhe-eriba	1046 BCE
Marduk-zer-X?	1045–1034 BCE
Nabu-shumu-libur	1033–1026 BCE

SECOND DYNASTY OF THE SEALAND (C. 1025–1005 BCE)

Simbar-Shipak	1025–1008 BCE
Ea-mukin-zeri	1008 BCE
Kashshu-nadin-ahhe	1007–1005 BCE

DYNASTY OF BAZI (C. 1004–985 BCE)

Eulmash-shakin-shumi	1004–988 BCE
Ninurta-kudurri-usur I	987–985 BCE
Shirikti-Shuqamuna	985 BCE

DYNASTY OF ELAM (C. 984–979 BCE)

Mar-biti-apla-usur	984–979 BCE

ANCIENT KINGS & LEADERS

PERIOD OF MIXED DYNASTIES (C. 978–732 BCE)

Nabu-mukin-apli	978–943 BCE
Ninurta-kudurri-usur II	943 BCE
Mar-biti-ahhe-iddina	942–? BCE
Shamash-mudammiq	
Nabu-shuma-ukin I	
Nabu-apla-iddina	(33+ years)
Marduk-zakir-shumi I	(27+ years)
Marduk-balassu-iqbi	?–813 BCE
Baha-aha-iddina	812–? BCE
(interregnum)	
Ninruta-apl-X?	
Marduk-apla-usur	
Eriba-Marduk	(9+ years)
Nabu-shuma-ishkun	?–748 BCE (13+ years)
Nabonassar	747–734 BCE
Nabu-nadin-zeri	733–732 BCE
Nabu-shuma-ukin	732 BCE

NINTH DYNASTY OF BABYLON (C. 731–626 BCE)

Nabu-mukin-zeri	731 729 BCE
Tiglath-Pileser III of Assyria	728–727 BCE
Shalmaneser V of Assyria	726–722 BCE
Merodach-Baladan II	721–710 BCE
Sargon II of Assyria	709–705 BCE
Sennacherib of Assyria (first reign)	704–703 BCE
Marduk-zakir-shumi II	703 BCE

Merodach-Baladan II	703 BCE
Bel-ibni	702–700 BCE
Ashur-nadin-shumi	699–694 BCE
Nergal-ushezib	693 BCE
Mushezib-Marduk	692–689 BCE
Sennecherib of Assyria (second reign)	688–681 BCE
Esarhaddon of Assyria	680–669 BCE
Ashurbanipal of Assyria	668 BCE
Shamash-shuma-ukin	667–648 BCE
Kandalanu	647–627 BCE
(*interregnum*)	626 BCE

NEO-BABYLONIAN DYNASTY (C. 625–539 BCE)

Nabopolassar	625–605 BCE
Nebuchadrezzar II	604–562 BCE
Amel-Marduk	561–560 BCE
Neriglissar	559–556 BCE
Labashi-Marduk	556 BCE
Nabonius (co-ruler)	555–539 BCE
Belshazzar (co-ruler/regent)	555–539 BCE

ASSYRIA

PUZUR-ASHUR DYNASTY (2025–1809 BCE)

Puzur-Ashur I

Shalim-ahum
Ilu-shuma
Erishum I   1974–1935 BCE
Ikunum   1934–1921 BCE
Sargon I   1920–1881 BCE
Puzur-Ashur II   1880–1873 BCE
Naram-Sin   1872–1829 or 1819 BCE
Erishum II   1828 or 1818–1809 BCE

SHAMSHI-ADAD DYNASTY (1808–1736 BCE)

Shamshi-Adad I   1808–1776 BCE
Ishme-Dagan I   1775–1765 BCE
Mut-Ashkur
Rimush
Asinum

NON-DYNASTIC USURPERS (1735–1701 BCE)

Puzur-Sin
Ashur-dugul
Ashur-apla-idi
Nasir-Sin
Sin-namir
Ipqi-Ishtar
Adad-salulu
Adasi

ADASIDE DYNASTY (1700–722 BCE)

Belu-bani	1700–1689 BCE
Libaya	1688–1672 BCE
Sharma-Adad I	1671–1660 BCE
Iptar-Sin	1659–1648 BCE
Bazaya	1647–1620 BCE
Lullaya	1619–1614 BCE
Shu-Ninua	1613–1600 BCE
Sharma-Adad II	1599–1597 BCE
Erishum III	1596–1584 BCE
Shamshi-Adad II	1583–1578 BCE
Ishme-Dagan II	1577–1562 BCE
Sharmshi-Adad III	1561–1546 BCE
Ashur-nirari I	1545–1520 BCE
Puzur-Ashur III	1519–1496 BCE
Enlil-nasir I	1495–1483 BCE
Nur-ili	1482–1471 BCE
Ashur-shaduni	1471 BCE
Ashur-rabi I	1470–1451 BCE
Ashur-nadin-ahhe I	1450–1431 BCE
Enlil-nasir II	1430–1425 BCE
Ashur-nirari II	1424–1418 BCE
Ashur-bel-nisheshu	1417–1409 BCE
Ashur-ra'im-nisheshu	1408–1401 BCE
Ashur-nadin-ahhe II	1400–1391 BCE
Eriba-Adid I	1390–1364 BCE

MIDDLE ASSYRIAN EMPIRE (1363–912 BCE)

Ashur-uballit I	1363–1328 BCE
Enlil-nirari	1327–1318 BCE
Arik-den-ili	1317–1306 BCE
Adad-nirari I	1305–1274 BCE
Shalmaneser I	1273–1244 BCE
Tukulti-Ninurta I	1243–1207 BCE
Ashur-nadin-apli	1206–1203 BCE
Ashur-nirari III	1202–1197 BCE
Enlil-kudurri-usur	1196–1192 BCE
Ninurta-apil-Ekur	1191–1179 BCE
Ashur-dan I	1178–1133 BCE
Ninurta-tukulti-Ashur	1132 BCE
Mutakkil-Nusku	1132 BCE
Ashur-resh-ishi I	1132–1115 BCE
Tiglath-Pileser I	1114–1076 BCE
Ashared-apil-Ekur	1075–1074 BCE
Ashur-bel-kala	1073–1056 BCE
Eriba-Adad II	1055–1054 BCE
Shamshi-Adad IV	1053–1050 BCE
Ashurnasirpal I	1049–1031 BCE
Shalmaneser II	1030–1019 BCE
Ashur-nirari IV	1018–1013 BCE
Ashur-rabi II	1012–972 BCE
Ashur-resh-ishi	971–967 BCE
Tiglath-Pileser II	966–935 BCE
Ashur-dan II	934–912 BCE

NEO-ASSYRIAN EMPIRE (911–609 BCE)

Adad-nirari II	911–891 BCE
Tukulti-Ninurta II	890–884 BCE
Ashurnasirpal II	883–859 BCE
Shalmaneser III	858–824 BCE
Shamshi-Adad V	823–811 BCE
Adad-nirari III	810–783 BCE
Shalmaneser IV	782–773 BCE
Ashur-dan III	772–755 BCE
Ashur-nirari V	754–745 BCE
Tiglath-Pileser III	744–727 BCE
Shalmaneser V	726–722 BCE

SARGONID DYNASTY (722–609 BCE)

Sargon II	721–705 BCE
Sennacherib	704–681 BCE
Esarhaddon	680–669 BCE
Ashurbanipal	668–627 BCE
Ashur-etil-ilani	626–623 BCE
Sin-shumu-lishir	623 BCE
Sin-shar-ishkun	622–612 BCE
Ashur-uballit II	611–609 BCE

(fall of Assyrian Empire 609 BCE)

PERSIA

ACHAEMENID DYNASTY (559–330 BCE)

Cyrus the Great	559–530 BCE
Cambyses	529–522 BCE
Smerdis	522 BCE
Darius I the Great	521–486 BCE
Xerxes I	485–465 BCE
Ataxerxes I (Longimanus)	464–424 BCE
Xerxes II	424 BCE
Sogdianus	424 BCE
Darius II (Nothus)	423–405 BCE
Ataxerxes II (Mnemon)	404–359 BCE
Ataxerxes III (Ochus)	358–338 BCE
Arses	337–336 BCE
Darius III (Codomannus)	335–330 BCE

(The Persian Empire ended when Alexander the Great invaded in 330 BCE)

PHOENICIA

ANCIENT TYRIAN LEADERS (MYTHOLOGICAL), (2050–1450 BCE)

Agenor (son of Posiedon or Belus)	c.2050–1450 BCE
Phoenix (son of Agenor, gave his name to Phoenicia)	?

LATE BRONZE AGE (1350–1335 BCE)

Abi-Milku	c.1350–1335 BCE

KINGS OF TYRE AND SIDON (990–785 BCE)

Abibaal	c.993–981 BCE
Hiram I	980–947 BCE
Baal-Eser I	946–930 BCE
Abdastartus	929–921 BCE
Astartus	920–901 BCE
Deleastartus	900–889 BCE
Astarymus	888–880 BCE
Phelles	879 BCE
Ithobaal I	878–847 BCE
Baal-Eser II	846–841 BCE
Mattan I	840–832 BCE
Pygmalion (Dido's brother, who formed Carthage in 814 BCE)	831–785 BCE

UNDER ASSYRIAN CONTROL (C. 750–660 BCE)

Ithobaal II	750–739 BCE
Hiram II	739–730 BCE
Mattan II	730–729 BCE
Elulaios	729–694 BCE
Abd Melqart	694–680 BCE
Baal I	680–660 BCE

AFTER ASSYRIAN CONTROL (C. 592–573 BCE)

Ithobaal III   591–573 BCE

(Overthrow of monarchy in favour of oligarchic government)

RESTORATION OF MONARCHY (551–532 BCE)

Hiram III   551–532 BCE

UNDER PERSIAN CONTROL (539–411 BCE)

Mattan IV   c.490–480 BCE
Boulomenus   c.450 BCE
Abdemon   c.420–411 BCE

UNDER CYPRIOT CONTROL (SALAMIS, 411–374 BCE)

Evagoras of Salamis   411–374 BCE

UNDER PERSIAN CONTROL (374–332 BCE)

Eugoras   c.340s
Azemilcus   c.340–332 BCE

(The Phoenician Empire ended when Alexander the Great invaded in 332 BCE)

COLLECTOR'S EDITIONS

FLAME TREE

A wide range of new and classic fiction, including short story anthologies, *Collectable Classics*, *Gothic Fantasy* collections and *Epic Tales* of mythology.

•

Available at all good bookstores, and online at
flametreepublishing.com

FLAME TREE PUBLISHING